THE

Martin Hocke st
Academy of Dram
the Norwegian Merchant Navy, taught English,
translated and became senior language consultant to several major companies in Europe. He
has also worked for film and radio, and has spent
much time in remote places, writing stories. His
first novel, about owls, *The Ancient Solitary
Reign*, is currently enjoying international
acclaim. It has now found its way on to the
Italian schools' curriculum and is being serial-
ized, along with *The Lost Domain*, on Aus-
tralian radio.

Also by Martin Hocke

THE ANCIENT SOLITARY REIGN

SCIENCE
FICTION
FANTASY

MARTIN HOCKE

THE LOST DOMAIN

HarperCollins*Publishers*

HarperCollins Science Fiction & Fantasy
An Imprint of HarperCollins*Publishers*
77–85 Fulham Palace Road,
Hammersmith, London W6 8JB

This paperback edition 1994
3 5 7 9 8 6 4 2

First published in Great Britain by
HarperCollins*Publishers* 1993

ISBN 0 586 21688 X

Set in Linotron Sabon by
Rowland Phototypesetting Ltd
Bury St Edmunds, Suffolk

Printed in Great Britain by
HarperCollinsManufacturing Glasgow

For Malcolm Hopson

and with many thanks to Pauline Hocke
and Jenny Picton, without whose help, etc.

To every thing there is a season, and a time to
every purpose under the heaven:

Ecclesiastes, Chapter III, Verse 1

But leave the Wise to wrangle, and with me
The quarrel of the Universe let be:
And, in some corner of the Hubbub coucht,
Make Game of that which makes as much of Thee.

The Rubáiyát of Omar Khayyám, Verse 45
Done into English by Edward Fitzgerald, 1859

Though much is taken, much abides; and though
We are not now that strength which in old days
Moved earth and heaven; that which we are, we are;
One equal temper of heroic hearts,
Made weak by time and fate, but strong in will
To strive, to seek, to find, and not to yield.

Alfred Lord Tennyson, 1809–1892
Ulysses

Part One

... a time to embrace, and a time to refrain from embracing;

> *Ecclesiastes*, Chapter III, Verse 5

Ah Love! could thou and I with Fate conspire
To grasp this sorry Scheme of Things entire,
Would not we shatter it to bits – and then
Re-mould it nearer to the Heart's Desire!

> *The Rubáiyát of Omar Khayyám*, Verse 73
> Done into English by Edward Fitzgerald, 1859

'Tis better to have loved and lost
Than never to have loved at all.

> Alfred Lord Tennyson, 1809–1892
> *In Memoriam*

CHAPTER
1

I am old now and the one most able to tell the story. I shall tell it to the wind and the trees, for none of my own kind will listen.

There are other versions of the truth, of course. But like everything else, the truth is relative. It depends so much on your point of view – on the place where you are standing, or flying at the time. The Barn Owls have produced two epic versions of the historical events I am about to describe. Bardic's version has now been discredited, even by his own kind. Pompous and flamboyant Bardic, who would tell any version of the facts to gain his own advancement or favour. Quaver's version stands. His epic ballad holds now as a minor work of art and an accurate chronicle of events, as seen from the white owls' point of view.

Mine is different. Less lyrical, perhaps, but none the less authentic. I am aware of things he could not have known, and even had he known them, and known them to be true, he would never have allowed these things I shall relate to mar or blur his own pristine vision – his own complex process of rendering history into art.

The Barn Owls are one thing, but we Tawnies are a proud and ancient race, older than most other living creatures, but also a species forced to fight for survival in an ever-changing world. Survival can be a bloody business, and so, as well as love, my story tells of revenge, violence and war. But these are not the aspects of which my fellow Tawnies would altogether disapprove. The reason they would not listen is because I have learned to doubt the ancient wisdom of our days and ways. During my long lifetime I have begun to wonder whether we are really masters of the sky at night, and whether we have the right to drive other creatures from the woodland we have owned and known and where we have thrived for so many thousand springs.

Late in my third age I have begun to ask myself whether instead we might not strive to co-exist with other species, not only here in our ancestral woods, but also in the fields and meadows where the few remaining Barn Owls live, and even in no man's land with the little upstart owls – yes, even with the squatters, with the unwanted immigrants, call them what you will! But this is, of course, subversive talk, and for even hinting at this philosophy I have long been ostracized and branded a heretic.

The fact is we have always hated upstarts. First we learned to hate the Barn Owls and then – much later – we loathed and despised the little immigrants. We have always considered ourselves superior to all other forms of life, and for this reason none of my class or race would listen to a story which tells not only of our own glory, but also of friendships forged with other species – forged in times of peace and weathered by the storms of war. If these so-called heresies were overheard my life might be at risk. For example, Rowan, son of Birch, might kill me, using my supposed treachery as an excuse to occupy what is left of my ancestral territory. He thinks his own too small and has long awaited the opportunity to be rid of me and thus extend his own domain.

So at twilight and at dawn I shall whisper my story to

the trees instead, beginning from the time when I first met and fell in love with May Blossom. Before this fatal moment, there is little of consequence to tell, save that I was well and high born in rich, rolling woodland which my father and his ancestors had owned for centuries. He was leader of the Tawny Owl community in the entire county that stretched further than any owl could fly in a single night, and it was this distance that almost brought about my early downfall and would have done, had not May Blossom saved my life.

My father had sent me with a message to the farthest edge of his estates, and on the outward journey I followed his advice, stopping well before dawn in a large copse where May Blossom and her mother lived. I had some discourse with these two females, but I was tired and it was soon time to sleep. I remember little of what passed between us now, but it may be that in my subconscious the seeds of love were born – born in that brief exchange of courtesies before the rising sun limits our powers of flight and forces us to rest or sleep.

As soon as twilight had deepened into dark, I flew the short distance to the outer limits of my father's territory, hoping to deliver my message quickly and then return before sunrise to the place where I had slept and rested on the day before. However, as ill luck would have it, the recipient of my message was out hunting when I arrived. I waited patiently at first in the branches of his oak – and then less patiently as the night wore on and dawn approached. On the previous night I had eaten only one large vole and now I dared not hunt for fear of missing Beech on his return.

At last he came. I gave him my message and departed at once, although the night around me was dying and I could already sense the coming light.

Halfway to May Blossom's copse, I located a young rabbit where the meadow below me bordered on a stream.

By right this rabbit belonged to the Barn Owl incumbent, but being young, headstrong and hungry, I dived, caught the thing and ate it all at one go. It was only the third young rabbit I had ever eaten and this was the plumpest and tastiest of all. A young rabbit is, however, a heavy meal for one Tawny Owl, and afterwards I was so full that I could scarcely fly. I should, of course, have limped my way slowly to the spinney which lay beyond the stream, found a suitable tree and spent the day there to rest, digest my rabbit and to get some much-needed sleep.

Instead I made the near-fatal mistake of flying beyond the spinney and heading on across the fields and meadows towards the large copse where May Blossom and her mother lived. In the meantime the first red streaks of dawn were smearing the night sky, and I knew that soon my powers of flight would begin to fail, slowing me down much more than the succulent rabbit I now carried in my stomach.

No one has ever understood why we Tawnies become inebriated by the daylight, whilst lower forms of owl can fly just as well at dawn or dusk, and some, like the little immigrants, can hunt or travel even by the brightest light of day. This was one of the first things that made me doubt the ultimate supremacy of our species, but for many springs I pushed the question from my mind, supposing that every kind of creature – even Tawnies – must be tarnished by some fatal flaw.

As the sun rose high I found myself within two meadows' length of my destination for the day. It was then that I saw him coming. Huge, he was, with great widespread wings which seemed to glimmer in the first rays of dawn. Even in the darkness a buzzard is a frightening sight, but their numbers have long been in decline, and since they never fly by night, we hardly ever see them. You might think this strange, since our territories overlap, but since they kill by day and we kill by night, there has historically been very little conflict between our species. The rule however is that if they see a lone Tawny flying in the daylight, they will attack. They will fight to kill, fearing that if we took to hunting in the day, there would be no food left for them. I was brought up to consider this quite fair, since we would do the same if they threatened our woodlands between sunset and the dawn.

The huge eagle-like creature circled in the sky above me, preparing for the attack. I could have tried to make the woodland before he got to me, but tradition has it that we must fight. Never give in, never, never, never. This is part of the Tawny philosophy. Some you win and some you lose, but on your own territory – or territory you have claimed – never surrender, ever!

Wheeling to face the fast-approaching buzzard, I cursed the rising sun and the rabbit in my belly, both of which would slow me down. I must confess I was afraid, even before I saw the second bird approaching, presumably my aggressor's mate. In our glorious history Tawnies have been known to kill a buzzard in one-to-one conflict, but against two of them I knew I had no chance. Now there was no time to turn and try for help and safety in the woods, so I decided instead to die with honour, a concept that had been instilled into me from birth, but one which I have later come to challenge.

I won the first clash, ripping flesh and feathers from the place where the creature's wing is attached to its body. Howling with rage and pain, he wheeled and attacked again. Though I struck first myself and inflicted a second wound, he tore what seemed like a huge chunk from my chest. I have often thought how strange it is that in combat one does not feel the pain. Later, yes, but at the time one is merely conscious of the wound. Suffering, or death, come upon one later.

At the third engagement, and even as my strength began to wane, I ripped the creature's eye out. I did it with my right talons, one of which I was later so tragically to lose. Though not a fatal blow, it put the male buzzard out of action and I knew that it would kill him in the end.

I turned to face the female who had now closed the gap between us and who flew at me with a scream of rage. I damaged her belly in the first encounter, but in the process she slashed my head and ripped a small part of my wing away.

Facing her for the third time, I realized that the end was near. She was strong, furious and yearning for revenge. It was only then that I sensed the fast-approaching presence of another Tawny: a female Tawny flying faster than I could ever do, even without a rabbit in my stomach. As the buzzard and I clashed for the third time, May Blossom rose above my opponent and then fell on her from behind. Striking with both claws simultaneously, with one blow she practically severed the creature's head. As I fluttered in the sky, with my fast-fading strength, I saw the female buzzard attempt to turn and fight, almost as a reflex – as a chicken will do even after he is technically dead. Then the fatal wound took its full effect, the giant creature fluttered once, spun in the air, and then plummeted to the ground. I turned to locate the male and saw that he had landed in the meadow, not far from the place where his mate was now crashing to her death. For a moment or two I was sorry for her, and especially for him. His, I knew, would be a long and painful death.

'Come, Yoller!' May Blossom said. 'You must fly back to the woods, where you can recover in safety. If you land on the ground, wounded as you are, you will be killed by a kestrel, a sparrow hawk, a stoat or some other daytime creature.'

I nodded, gathered my fast-fading strength for the short flight, and then slowly set off in May Blossom's wake. It was a short distance, but one I shall never forget.

She had saved my life. She led, I followed. Little did I know then that this was to be the case for so much of my natural life.

CHAPTER

2

It was during my long period of convalescence with May Blossom and her mother that I first realized the degree of hardship suffered by Tawnies less fortunate than myself. I say degree of hardship, because as you – the wind and the trees – both know, hardship, like wealth, is relative. May Blossom and her mother were not poor. They did not live like the wretched little immigrants, or even like the lowest class of Tawny. Though modest, their territory was not in no man's land. It was quite a decent-sized copse, just big enough for two. If they were careful and contented themselves with the more plebeian forms of food – like vole or shrew – then there was just enough to eat. For a special treat, say a mole even, not to mention a rabbit, they had to hunt in the Barn Owl country which surrounded them. Being two females, they were loth to create conflict with their neighbours – even though these neighbours were thought to be an inferior species. So special treats were rare.

The other difference between my own background and theirs might be described as aesthetic. It was here with them, as I slowly got well again, that I first learned to appreciate the mighty oaks we had at home. The splendour of the beech trees, the silver colour of the birch, the red berries of the holly glowing bright against the winter snow – all these would have dwarfed and outdone a thousand times in splendour the hazel, dogwood, elder and willows which made up most of the vegetation in May Blossom's cramped little spinney. There were a few decent maples, some hawthorn with its white blossom, and one wild cherry tree, but there was nothing to compare with the birch, spruce and pine which mixed in such abundance with the native maple, ash and oak in the dense and broad expanse of my father's ancestral home. But in spite of the cramped circumstances, and the lack of true style or beauty, it was during this period of convalescence that I first fell in love with May Blossom and proposed to her. I fell in love with her because she endowed the small, box-like home with beauty and intelligence, making the lower trees, sometimes little more than shrubland, seem cosy and welcoming. With her radiance she made the claustrophobic little copse seem as attractive as the splendour and abundance of the mighty woodland to which I would soon return.

Yes, this was when I first proposed to her, and to my sorrow and surprise, she said no.

'But why not?' I asked, shocked into a mixture of pain and amazement. 'My father will give us a part of his territory at least three times the size of this tiny residence. You will live among tall, antique and stately trees and the forest floor below you will be carpeted by bluebells, early purple orchis and wood anemone.'

May Blossom did not reply at once, but looked at me with those clear, bright eyes – eyes which shone with determination and intelligence.

'You have saved my life, and I love you,' I continued, hoping that if I insisted she would change her mind. I was strong, young and arrogant at the time and – had heard it said – the most eligible male owl in the entire neighbourhood.

Still looking at me, May Blossom shook her head. 'We are both too young to mate,' she said. 'Before settling down, I want to travel, and most of all, I want to learn.'

I was shocked by this, and the idea of her travelling made me jealous – an emotion I had never experienced before. 'Where on earth do you want to go?' I asked. 'Everyone knows that this is the best place in the world to live. And I am offering you a home in the most beautiful and the richest part of it.'

'How do you know?' she asked, still looking at me, but now with her head inclined slightly to one side.

'How do I know what?'

'That this is the best place in the world.'

'Well, of course it is!' I said.

'I see, so where else have you lived?'

'Nowhere else, of course!'

'Then how can you tell this is the best?'

'Because everybody says so,' I replied, beginning to feel rather flustered. 'Abroad – anywhere beyond these territories – is quite awful, everyone knows that, and Tawnies do not travel well, you must be aware of that yourself.'

'Hearsay! Hearsay and tradition,' said May Blossom, with a little smile on what I considered at the time to be the most beautiful face in all of my father's territories. 'We don't know that what our parents and our elders tell us is all true. You may believe it, if you wish, but I need to make certain for myself. And to do that I must travel. Travel far and learn.'

'Learn what? What is there that you can't learn here, at home?'

'I want to know what is happening in the world around us.'

'What sort of thing?'

'Well, first of all, I want to know if it is true that man is cutting down more trees. I want to know if it is true that cities, towns and roads are spreading everywhere. I want to know how fast the little immigrants are multiplying and above all I want to know why the Barn Owl population is declining.'

'Why on earth do you want to know all that? Surely it's good news for us that the Barn Owls are declining. It's a bad thing that the Little Owls are spreading, but if the squatters proliferate too much we can either kill them or drive them out, or back to the place whence they once came. As for the woodland, men cutting down more trees is worrying, I admit. But according to our ancestors they've been doing it for centuries. That's how the Barn Owls thrived and prospered in the first place . . . '

'I know,' interrupted May Blossom. She was still smiling, but I detected a hint of impatience in her voice. 'I know that much history. The Barn Owls prospered because for centuries man has cut down woodland and forest to make the farms and farmland on which the white owls live. But now their numbers are diminishing. Why?'

'Who cares?' I said, feeling hurt and rather peeved by the outcome of my proposal. I had hoped for, no, expected a requited love, not history and intellect instead.

'We have to care!' said May Blossom, firmly. 'We have to care, because if man continues to cut down trees to make more farmland, more cities and more roads, we shall no longer have enough traditional territory on which to live. So we, too, shall have to live on farm and meadowland.'

'You mean have a war with the Barn Owls and then take over their territory?'

'One day it might be necessary. But what would be the use if our numbers began to diminish, too, like theirs?'

'Where did you get all this information about man building more roads and cities?' I asked, now resenting this lovely female for knowing so much more than I did. 'Who told you about the Barn Owls and the little immigrants?'

May Blossom hesitated before replying. Then she gave

me a tight, protective little smile, as if she knew that her answer would provoke a sudden and violent counter-attack.

'A media bird told me,' she said, lifting her face and keeping the slight smile intact as a kind of challenge.

'A media bird? You must be mad! How can you believe anything told to you by an owl with no ears – an owl who travels constantly and nests upon the ground?'

'They are nomads,' replied May Blossom, facing my onslaught very firmly. 'They travel. They know what goes on in the world. We don't. We Tawnies are too insular.'

'They invent things to get a living!' I protested. 'They fly into other owls' territories and then tell these stories in exchange for the food they steal!'

'They are not always accurate,' conceded May Blossom. 'I admit that in order to stay on and eat well, they may exaggerate from time to time. But I warn you, we ignore them at our peril. The secret is to listen and then to make up your own mind how much is true and how much is invented. But I agree with you, sooner or later one must go and find out for oneself.'

'Go where?' I asked, with the uncomfortable feeling that May Blossom had succeeded in turning my own words against me.

'To a city,' replied May Blossom. 'To the biggest city I can find.'

'You really are mad!' I cried, now beside myself with despair and frustration. 'No Tawny Owl in his right mind would live in a village, let alone a town or city.'

'Some do!' replied May Blossom, maintaining that infuriating, almost supercilious calm – a semi-patronizing air of superiority which was to be of such use to her in later life.

'Some do, of course they do!' I countered. 'But these are Tawnies with no land – outcasts, or criminals long since driven from their ancestral homes.'

'You believe that because your father told you so,' said May Blossom, in tones that were quiet but very firm. 'I happen to know, on the other hand, that some go to the city – and stay there – out of choice!'

'I don't believe it! How could anybody bear to live that close to man. I couldn't survive it for more than a single night!'

'Ah, but you could!' May Blossom said. 'And what's more, some time you might have to.'

'Barn Owls can't!' I said, triumphantly, at last having found an issue on which I was at least her equal. 'Barn Owls can't survive in a town or a city, yet here they live on farmland, much closer to man than we do.'

'How do you know this?' May Blossom enquired. The tone of her question was polite, but sceptical, as if my statement was based once more merely on folklore and hearsay.

'Because a Barn Owl told me so!' I said.

'You have spoken to a Barn Owl?'

'Of course,' I replied, and then exaggerated by adding: 'As a matter of fact, quite frequently!'

'Who is this bird?' May Blossom asked, challenging my claim with that polite but icy calm which in later years was to be of so much help in furthering her career.

'Beak Poke,' I said. 'He is a very old, decrepit owl whose job is to study the habits of all other birds who fly the skies at night.'

'He is the Owl Owl on their local council,' said May Blossom, nodding calmly and then smiling at me in a manner that was almost supercilious in one so lovely and so young.

'You know him?' I asked, deflated now that she had yet again taken the advantage from me.

'Not personally. But I have heard of him, of course!'

'Well, he says Barn Owls can't survive in towns or cities. He says the immigrants can, and we could if we wanted.

But they can't. Without farmland, pasture and open spaces, they can't survive.'

'What do you think of him?' May Blossom asked, raising her eyebrows slightly.

'Oh, he's all right, but as I said before, he's very old. He doesn't take care of himself properly. He has no mate and doesn't seem to bother much about what, if or when he eats. My personal opinion is that he hasn't long to live.'

'Frequent him while you can,' May Blossom said. 'You can learn much from a bird of his experience and intellect.'

'He's an interesting old soul,' I said, guardedly. 'But however old and wise, he's only a Barn Owl after all.'

'However inferior they may be, Barn Owls are better than we are at certain things,' May Blossom said. 'I don't like to admit it, but it's true. And if we are to defeat them in the future, we must emulate their strong points, not just despise them for the things they cannot do as well as us.'

'What strong points?' I asked.

'Frequent old Beak Poke, or other clever Barn Owls, and you will find out,' May Blossom said. 'Now you are well and must fly home again. I, too, shall leave as this twilight deepens and start my long journey to the city.'

'Don't go!' I pleaded, caring nothing now about Barn Owls, immigrants or man and his threat to our woodland habitat. 'Come with me instead. Come with me and you can study as much as you want to in my father's territories. I will not stand in your way. We can mate first and then have chicks later, when you are ready.'

'My mind is made up,' May Blossom said. 'Tonight I fly south, and that is final.'

'What does your mother think about all this?' I asked, clutching at some way of preventing her departure. 'Is she happy to be left here, all alone?'

'She would be alone if I came with you,' replied May Blossom, thwarting my emotion with her calm logic – a thing that in the future she was frequently to do.

'Well, I'd like to talk to her anyway,' I said, still hoping against hope to enlist the aid of middle-aged Iris to persuade her daughter not to undertake this suicidal mission to the city.

'Of course you may speak to her, if you wish, but it won't make any difference,' May Blossom said. 'My mind is made up, and I fly tonight, as soon as the setting sun has sunk below the distant crest of your ancestral woods.'

'Will you wait for me?' I asked, despairing now that her rare use of poetic language had somehow convinced me, finally, that she was not for turning.

'It is premature to speak of promises,' she said, looking at me with eyes that were now softened by a trace of tenderness. 'I shall not mate, either on the long journey or during my sojourn in the city. My purpose holds to go there, get knowledge and then return to these territories. But I shall be gone for a long time, and during my absence you may be tempted. If this happens – and if you are sure you have found the right owl – obey your instincts and mate with her. But be careful! You are a strong, handsome young bird and when your father dies you will probably become leader of the Tawny Owl community in these territories. Do not take this responsibility too lightly. To do the job well, you will need the right partner, so take care!'

Having said this she smiled and then flew off, without giving me a chance to reply. I sat on the branch of the solitary oak – the only real tree in her humble copse – and waited for her mother to arrive. She did so not long afterwards, while I was still struggling to comprehend and encompass the magnitude of the task May Blossom had imposed upon herself.

'You look worried,' Iris said, when she had perched beside me on the branch.

'I am,' I answered, and then, after giving her a brief, worried smile, I gazed out far to the west through the sparse trees of the copse, to where the sun was slowly falling in a red ball of fire behind the tall hills of my native woodland. In a few brief moments the red ball of flame would sink into extinction beyond the forest highland, signalling the departure of May Blossom on her long and dangerous quest.

'It's no good worrying,' said Iris, with a little sigh. 'May Blossom is headstrong, always has been. She's had her own way ever since she was a fledgling. Ever since her father died.'

'But it's so dangerous,' I said. 'And the city is so far away. I've asked her to mate with me. Is there nothing you can do to make her change her mind?'

'I have already tried,' said Iris, sadly. 'But once May Blossom has made up her mind, there's nothing any one of us can do. She's determined to travel and get knowledge. I can only hope and pray to the God Bird that I live to see the sunrise of her safe return.'

I nodded absently as I watched the sun sink still further behind the distant hills. 'Well, I will try to wait for her,' I said. 'But it won't be easy. With the coming of each spring, it won't be easy not to mate.'

'May Blossom has told me that you must not hesitate,' her mother said, looking at me with worn but kindly eyes. 'For my part, I have told her she is missing the best and biggest life-chance she may ever get. What more can I say, or do?'

'Nothing!' I replied, watching the last of the flaming ball drop into oblivion beyond the distant hills. Now it was moonlight, now reigned the night. 'Tonight I shall fly home,' I said. 'But I shall never forget your kindness, your care and your hospitality. Most of all I shall never forget that May Blossom risked her life for mine. If you need help, call and I will come.'

Iris gave me another sad, brave smile and nodded, close to tears, as I took off and flew west and homewards. Owls, even Tawny Owls, have hearts, in spite of all the bold exterior, the casual talk and the natural phlegm. Mine was breaking as I flew. It was torn and rent asunder as at least a half of it flew south, following the beautiful and intrepid May Blossom on her relentless quest for knowledge. Flying across Barn Owl country towards my own distant hills, I wept, for the first time since my first days as a fledgling. I wept for a love that I somehow sensed, whatever happened, would never be the same again.

As dawn rose I reached the last stage of my homeward journey and rose higher in the red-streaked sky to complete the flight back into the woodland of my ancestral domain.

Above a spinney in the foothills – before the real woodland began – I came across an early-morning sparrow hawk poaching in our night-time territory just a few moments before dawn. Though these little hawks are fierce opponents, and though I was still not well enough to fight, I dropped on the thing as it scavenged low above the ground.

The vicious little killer turned on me as I swiftly homed in and hit it from the still-dark sky. Before I tore its throat out with my strong talons, it clawed me in the chest and opened up the wound I had been nursing since my battle with the buzzards. I gasped in pain as the dying creature fluttered its short distance to death upon the ground. Feeling the warm blood trickle down from my chest to my nether belly, I flew slowly on to the heart of my homeland across the thickening forest that I loved so well.

As I completed the last stage of my journey, I was sorry for the dying sparrow hawk I had left behind. Now, with the tolerance and weakness that have come upon me with the passing years – now I would have flown on high above the poacher and left it to scavenge in the spinney and the woodland foothills throughout the coming day. But at that time I was young and bold, teeming with frustration and above all carrying that deadly mixture of a wounded ego and a broken heart. Often, in later life, I have wondered how a young male's ego could be tamed or in some way channelled into compassion to avoid so much of the senseless suffering and bloodshed that seem to repeat themselves in every generation. But that night – apart from a passing regret for the sparrow hawk who had died because he began hunting early, only a few moments before dawn – my heart and mind were occupied by May Blossom's departure and my own bloodstained return home.

Selfish, and occupied with our own small concerns, we do not see the changes in the wider world around us until it is too late. But it was ever thus, and now, approaching my third age, I still see little chance of any change.

CHAPTER
3

Bleeding, and snatched from death by May Blossom, I returned like the prodigal son and was thus welcomed by my parents, who were overjoyed to see me.

I had not realized how much they cared. I had always taken it for granted that they loved me and I, of course, loved them, bestowing the correct degree of filial affection and respect.

As I have already mentioned, any outward expression of emotion is considered bad form by any true, self-respecting Tawny. But for a while, in their delight at seeing me and in their grave concern about my wound, some of these false barriers fell, and so – in this new mood of intimacy – I told my parents about May Blossom.

To my great relief – and considerable surprise – my father was not half as disapproving as I had imagined. 'I think I remember her vaguely,' he said. 'She seemed a clever, handsome, bright-eyed bird. Of course, I recall her mother Iris very well, and her father, poor old Forest, who was murdered by a buzzard. By two buzzards, as a matter of fact.'

'Could it have been the same two?' I asked, for of course my parents and the whole district already knew about the battle May Blossom and I had won above the meadowland such a short distance from the daytime safety of the nearby spinney.

'Probably,' my father said. 'Forest was killed only two springs ago. Anyway, the district is well rid of them, and I am very proud of you, my son. Also, you should not allow the killing of the sparrow hawk to prey upon your conscience. We are well rid of him, as well, and it will serve as a warning to other daytime raptors. The territory is theirs by day and ours by night. It was ever thus. Lore and tradition must be respected, in the natural way. They kill by day, we kill by night. They must not be allowed to encroach upon our rights.'

'But it was only a few seconds before dawn,' I said. 'I could have pretended not to notice him and flown on by.'

'You did your duty,' my mother said, anxiously staring at my chest to check that the blood was now oozing more slowly from the re-opened wound.

'On the subject of land rights and encroachment,' my father added, 'rumour has it that a squatter has taken up residence on Beak Poke's land. This is too close for comfort. Once you let these wretches in, you will never be rid of them.'

'A Little Owl?' I asked.

'Vermin!' my father said. 'This one is said to be a female, and she has been reported as poaching in the copse where you killed the sparrow hawk at sunrise.'

'But the copse is strictly classified as no man's land,' I said. 'That's why the sparrow hawk is on my conscience. These creatures must feed somewhere, and I understand that these immigrants can also hunt by day, not only at night, as we do. So where lies the threat to us?'

'The thin end of the wedge!' my mother said, the harsh tone in her voice contrasting strangely with the tender concern in her eyes as she continued to observe the fast-abating drips of blood from my chest. 'If we let these poachers in, they will multiply. If this immigrant Beak Poke harbours is a female, she will breed. And breed fast, like a sparrow or a rabbit. Soon the copse will be swarming with them. They won't have enough to eat, so as sure as tomorrow's dawn, they'll spread into our woodland territory by day, taking vole, mole and shrew from the forest floor and contaminating the place with their multiplying presence. Soon no self-respecting Tawny will want to live with such daytime neighbours. The woodland we have inhabited for many thousand years will be devalued.'

'She's right!' my father said.

'So what do you want me to do?' I asked, my heart still flying with May Blossom, but at the same time sinking at the thought of more carnage. 'Do you want me to fly back there tonight and kill the wretched thing?'

'No!' my father said emphatically. 'You are hurt and must first recover from your wound. In any case, if I wanted a mere execution, I would send a lesser owl, like Birch. Though young, he is already good at that kind of thing. All you need to do is to speak to the decrepit Beak Poke. Tell him to expel the little immigrant from his land. That way she will no longer have access to the copse, or to the lower regions of our territory.'

'I will try,' I said, nodding as the pain in my chest began to ebb now, rather than flow fiercely as it had done on the last stretch home after my encounter with the sparrow hawk. 'But you know how Beak Poke is, and you know the brief he has been given?' I added, determined to capitalize on what little knowledge I had of the old white bird who lived on the flat Barn Owl territory, beyond the edge of our woodland domain. 'You know that he is Owl Owl on their local council. You know that his job is to study and to monitor the behaviour of all other birds who fly by night?'

'Of course I know!' my father said. 'We have been monitoring his behaviour since he first came here twelve or thirteen springs ago. At first we thought he might be a spy, but for a long time now we have been satisfied that he is genuine – merely a scientist obsessed by his own research. From time to time he has younger Barn Owls living with him to study what they call owlology. Of course, he is a bad influence on the district, but not a direct threat to our security.'

'What do you mean by a bad influence?' I asked, wondering how such an astute but dilapidated old bird as Beak Poke could ever have been seen as any kind of menace.

'Because he encourages squatters,' my father said. 'I want you to tell him that we disapprove of this, and if he persists in harbouring little immigrants, I may have him killed.'

'I'll try to explain it to him,' I said. 'But to tell you the truth, I don't think he will listen. By now I imagine he's too old to care whether he gets killed or whether he is merely permitted to work on until the time soon comes for him to die a natural death.'

'Be that as it may,' my father said, in the rather old-fashioned way he had of speaking, 'the fact remains that if you don't go and do it peacefully, I'll send Birch instead.'

'And if Beak Poke doesn't accept your conditions, Birch will kill him?'

'We are not barbarians here,' my father said. 'But if that desiccated old Barn Owl harbours immigrants on land adjacent to our own, then kill him we must. To preserve our heritage. This is why I am asking you to mediate. Because you know him. If your attempt fails, we shall send in Birch, who does not suffer from your scruples and will eliminate them both.'

'Both Beak Poke and the little squatter?'

'If this white bird refuses to co-operate, there will be no alternative,' my mother said. She spoke these words without compassion, but rather with an undisguised contempt. Because I knew she loved me, I could not understand why she was unable to extend that love, or at least charity, to other creatures of the night. It struck me that the ancient Beak Poke and the Little Owl who squatted on his land must both at some time have had mothers. Would these same mothers have been as pitiless as mine?

I did not understand it then, I do not understand it now, and it is partly due to this lack of comprehension that those of my own kind have now branded me as a heretic and threatened me with death. Would my mother have approved of this, I wonder?

She would not have approved of my so-called heresies, of this I am certain. But would she have condoned the eviction of her only and now ageing son from the ancestral domain where he was born and which she once loved so much?

Eviction or death, these are the alternatives that face me now, as I tell my story to the wind and the trees. Now I must make the same choice as my parents then imposed on Beak Poke and his little squatter. How would my mother have reacted, if she could have seen the roles reversed? It is too late to know, for she is now long dead.

Anyway, two nights later, when my wound had ceased to bleed, unwillingly I went. I flew down from the heart of our thickly wooded homeland to the copse that bordered on the meagre fields and meadows which comprised Beak Poke's territory – a territory I suspect which most other Barn Owls of his status would have considered as something less than a desirable domain.

Having reached the copse, I flew into my favourite willow, perched in one of the upper branches, and looked down through the darkness at the sluggish waters of the lowland stream, comparing the brackish, almost stagnant trickle with the wild water which burst from the rock source where I was born and where I am perching now. Here the stream gushes from the rocks and surges down the hill, slowly faltering in the foothills as it loses its native force and slows down to meander and dribble across the uninspiring plain.

Yes, as I perch here now, high in my native woods, toward the pain-racked end of my long days, I see the same stream gushing from its hillside source and remember well how I tried to brief myself that long-vanished night for confrontation with the white, wise old bird who lived, moved and had his being on the insipid patch of flatland below the willow and beyond the stream. Recalling my previous, casual encounters with Beak Poke, I came then to the conclusion that he really lived inside his head. He was an owl who lived inside his own mind and therefore the beauty or external status of his domain were of no consequence to him. As I perched high up in the willow, plucking up courage to confront him, it struck me that he could exist as well in no man's land. Only what went on inside his mind and inside others' heads was of concern to him.

This is why I perched in the willow for a while and peered down at the brackish stream below me in search of inspiration. Physically, of course, I was not afraid of him. I could have killed old Beak Poke with one single blow. But I was afraid of his mind – of his ancient but not yet addled brain. Yet at the same time I realized that my parents were quite right. Owls who lived here on the plain, in close proximity to humans, must perforce be inferior to us. And if they began to harbour little immigrants on their dull, lowland territory, where would the conflict ever end?

But I digress! My thoughts were not only with Beak Poke and the coming confrontation, but also with the female that I loved. How could I have doubts about the simple mission with which I had been entrusted when she had flown to the monstrous, far-off city to get knowledge?

With May Blossom in mind, I took off from my perch in the willow, flew across the stream, out of the copse and into the open country in search of the old white owl, determined to tell him that unless he got rid of his little squatter he would be condemned to death.

But – as it happens in bad dreams – I saw the little squatter first. Flying across flat Barn Owl country in the direction of the abandoned farmhouse where Beak Poke lived, I saw her flit across the hedge between the meadow and the man-made road below me. Wheeling above I watched as she flew into the shelter of a hollow tree. For some moments I hovered in the midnight air, wondering what my father would have done. Perhaps he would have dropped down from the dark sky and killed the creature without warning.

Urged on to kill by duty to my class and to my ancient race – to my kith, kind and stock – and yet held back by understandable reluctance to bloody my talons on yet another form of life, I veered in the sky and headed across the flat, neglected meadow towards the dilapidated building in which the ancient Barn Owl spent the last nights of his lifetime on research into comparative owl history and behaviour.

On powerful young wings, I crossed the meadow quickly and hooted to announce my coming. There was no answer from within so I dropped down from the sky, landed on the roof and hooted once again, but yet again no answer came.

As I knew then, Barn Owls cannot hoot properly, as we do, but merely screech or hiss in the most unmelodious way, though I have since learned that they themselves find this ghastly sound quite harmonious and attractive.

I perched for a while on the roof, hooted once more and, when no reply came, concluded that Beak Poke was out hunting somewhere above the dull field and meadowland in which he lived. I took off from the roof and flew back towards the copse on the edge of the forest, intending to wait in the willow above the stream until the old bird should make his presence in some way manifest. But crossing the narrow asphalt road, close to the gate and the hollow tree, I saw him homing in from the west far below the midnight crescent of the moon. He must have heard my powerful hoot and responded by flying towards me on his worn and desiccated wings, too ashamed – as I thought then – to call out to me with that awful Barn Owl screech or hiss.

Higher than he in the night sky, I hovered above the five-barred gate beside the road and watched him come, flapping towards me in the dotage of his old and crippled flight. As I dropped down from the sky to meet him a flood of white light lit up the road below.

This blinding flash emanated from one of the metal creatures man has made, bred or taken into captivity to transport him at high speed, not only in the ghastly city to which May Blossom had gone in search of knowledge, but also here in the depths of the countryside, where their noise, fumes and appalling smells molest our ancient and sacred reign.

High in the sky I watched as the aged Beak Poke flew across the road in front of the speeding vehicle and the blinding light. Low down, on his weak and desiccated wings, he paused halfway across the narrow strip of tarmac, dazzled by the bright white light projected by the eyes of the metal creature that tore towards him.

It was all over in seconds, and there was nothing I could do. The man-made or man-bred vehicle hit him at full speed, as he hovered there only two or three owl-lengths above the road.

Though high up in the sky, I too was partly dazzled by the blaze of bright white light, and only when the destructive thing had passed and vanished into the night was I able to discern Beak Poke's broken body lying in the middle of the narrow strip of road. Deeply shocked, I began to fly downward, though even at that safe distance I gathered that he must be on the verge of death, for he was muttering some gibberish that sounded like a prayer.

Before I had time to descend to within swooping distance of the road, a shadow flitted from the hollow tree below me as the little immigrant emerged from her squatter's hiding place and flew to the middle of the asphalt track to perch beside Beak Poke's shattered body.

Not knowing what to do, I hovered as she spread out one of her ragged, rounded little wings and held it over Beak Poke's broken head and neck as if trying to provide some comfort, or perhaps in an attempt to use some alien magic to bring him back from death.

The little alien must have sensed my presence – known that I was there – hovering high above her in the sky. In spite of this her purpose of compassion held and I sensed that she did not flinch at the prospect of a sudden death, a death similar to the one which both of us had just witnessed.

For a time I watched and hovered, wondering whether to swoop down and kill the little creature. If I did, my parents would be pleased with me, I knew, but after long hesitation I realized that I could not bring myself to do it. I could not bring myself to kill a creature – alien or not – when she was attempting to comfort *in extremis* one who had just been struck by sudden death.

So I turned in the sky, flew back to the willow in the copse and perched on my favourite branch, high above the slow meandering of the brackish stream. Here I stayed for quite some time, wondering as the night wore on what I must say to my parents about the mission I had been unable to complete.

Little did I realize then that my failure to execute the little alien was to have a profound effect, not only on my own life and on the lives of my fellow Tawnies, but also on the future of the Barn Owls and on the destiny of the ever-growing immigrant community. Most of all my reluctance to kill was to affect the future of the life-long friend I was destined to meet for the first time in this same copse and this same willow tree on the following night.

Though young, strong and arrogant, I was loth to kill. Had I done so then, as my parents would have wished, the recent history of we creatures who fly the sky at night might have taken an entirely different course. I am not saying whether it would have been for the better or for the worse. But different, yes! Different it would have been. But it is too late now to speculate, and in what way different, now only the wind and the trees will ever know.

CHAPTER
4

Flying home just before the first pale light of dawn, I caught a kestrel poaching on the lower reaches of our land. Reluctantly, I killed it, but kestrels are vicious little creatures and this one ripped my healing chest in his bold but vain attempt at self-defence. Since I had not dined that night, I ate the thing, though again, with great reluctance. It was the first and last time I ever ate another bird of prey, though we Tawnies are brought up to believe that consuming another raptor will give us greater strength and courage. I suppose I did it then to prove something to myself and to my parents.

Certainly arriving home with fresh blood oozing from my chest – and with the news that I had sustained this wound in the course of killing and then devouring a day-time raptor – provided an extenuating circumstance for not having properly fulfilled my mission.

'You should have killed the squatter!' my mother said, when I finally arrived home.

'But I was brought up to respect the dead. Brought up by you!' I said.

'You were brought up to respect our dead. Not the death of an ancient, decrepit Barn Owl, much less the life of an alien – an unwanted immigrant, whose species threaten our ancient solitary reign.'

'Father, what do you think?' I asked, determined to discover whether my sparing of the alien had been born of cowardice, of compassion – or of both.

'You must go again!' my father said. 'You must return the night after tomorrow and kill the thing. Otherwise I shall send Birch to do it. As I've told you before, he likes that kind of thing.'

'But wouldn't it be better to wait a night or two and see if Beak Poke's pupil appears,' I said, clutching desperately at straws.

'What pupil?' my father asked.

'A new one. The last time I spoke to Beak Poke he told me he was expecting this student who had been allocated to him for the study of owlology.'

'I thought he was too old for that kind of thing,' my father said. 'I thought he had retired from teaching.'

'Apparently he did, for a while, but as the result of a special request, he was persuaded to take it up again.'

'Well, he can't, because he's dead,' my mother said in that flat, pragmatic drawl that showed her class and breeding. 'Beak Poke is dead and so this young Barn Owl will have to go somewhere else to study, leaving the land to become infested by the friends and relations of that little squatter.'

'Quite right!' my father said. 'All the more reason to kill the creature now.'

'But it is still Barn Owl territory!' I protested. 'Are we allowed to kill things on their land, without first asking for permission?'

'A Tawny Owl can kill anything he likes,' my mother said. 'And asking other creatures for permission is not the way to get things done.'

'But Yoller has a point,' my father surprisingly conceded. 'According to the treaty we made with them after the last war between us – four hundred winters since – we have to inform them before killing any creature that lives, moves or has its being on their land. And under the same reciprocal agreement, they are not allowed to touch even a mouse or a shrew on ours.'

My mother gave my father a glacial stare – that glacial, disapproving stare which had terrified me since I was a fledgling. It was such a cold look that I had always thought it would freeze most living creatures even at the distance of a meadow.

'Very well, then,' my mother said eventually. 'Give this young bird a chance. Go there tomorrow night and see if he has arrived and, if so, whether he intends to stay or not. If he decides to stay, tell him to get rid of the little immigrant. If he decides to go elsewhere, you must kill the thing yourself.'

I thought about this very quickly and decided to accept. At least it gave me some breathing space. And if the young Barn Owl didn't put in an appearance, or else decided to leave straight away, when the time came to kill the little immigrant I could still refuse and let Birch do it. As my father had pointed out, Birch loved that kind of thing, as does his son Rowan, who is waiting to kill me now.

So two nights later I flew back to Beak Poke's territory in search of the new incumbent. I found him sooner than I expected. He was quartering the floor of the copse, close to the slow-running stream. Descending from above I must have taken him by surprise, for he turned upward and hissed at me as though he thought I was about to attack him. He was a big, strong young bird, and courageous, I could tell. If attacked, he was obviously ready to sell his life as dearly as he could.

In order to set his mind at rest, I hooted as melodiously as I was able.

'To tell the truth you gave me quite a shock,' he said, as we met and hovered opposite each other at eye level.

'Your shadow felt so big that for a moment or two I thought you were the monster owl come back to claim his own.'

'Good heavens, no!' I said. 'The monster owl is at least three times as big as I am, and if I'd been him you'd have been dead and torn to pieces at least ten times over before you realized what was happening. In any case, it's at least nine hundred winters since a monster owl was seen in any of these territories. The general theory is that they are quite extinct.'

'Not according to our information,' the young Barn Owl said. 'Apparently many of them are still living, but in other countries, far across the salty waters. Though we know that one was seen only two thousand meadows north of here less than fifty springs ago.'

Something about the way the young Barn Owl said this struck me as arrogant and annoying. My father had always told me that our Tawny Owl intelligence network was superior to those used by any other form of living creature.

'If you ask me, that's all an old crow's tale,' I said. 'Probably just a story that your parents tell you to frighten you and get you to behave. You know the sort of thing – Behave yourself, little chap, or the monster owl will gouge your eyes out – and all that sort of rubbish.'

'Shall we perch somewhere for a moment?' the young Barn Owl asked, and from the respectful tone of voice he used I could tell that he'd got my message.

'Right ho, then,' I said, relenting a little. 'I don't mind if I do, though I can't stay long because I haven't had my dinner yet. I just thought I'd pop over this way and see whether you'd arrived and how you were settling in.'

'You knew I was coming?' he asked, as I led him to the willow and we settled side by side on my favourite branch above the slow-running stream.

'Of course I knew. By the way, my name is Yoller. What's yours?'

'Hunter. But how did you know that I was coming?'

'Old Beak Poke told me just the other night. Incidentally, I hope you're finding enough food to eat. I'm afraid the poor old boy got rather feeble towards the end. He let the place run down pretty badly, sad to say.'

'Towards the end?'

'Yes, towards the end the poor old fellow was almost geriatric, I'm afraid. Poor old bird, I bet he didn't know what hit him.'

'What did hit him?' Hunter asked.

'Oh, you know, one of those things men tear about in on the roads. I suppose the poor old chap was dazzled and just flapped straight into it instead of veering to one side. I must say I'm surprised you hadn't heard.'

'I didn't even know that he was dead,' said Hunter, who looked and sounded very shocked. 'When exactly did it happen?'

'Two nights ago.'

'Did you see it happen?'

'I didn't see the actual impact. The thing with lights on had just begun to move again when I arrived and saw old Beak Poke lying in the road. I flew down to him at once, but there was nothing I could do.'

Of course, I was lying, but I thought then for a good purpose. I did not tell Hunter that the female immigrant attempted to comfort the ancient Beak Poke as he lay dying because I did not want him to feel any sympathy for the unwanted little creature. This tampering with the truth I thought at the time was the lesser of two evils. If Hunter evicted the immigrant I would not have to kill it, or worse, I wouldn't have to abdicate, lose face and leave the task to the bloodthirsty Birch.

'Did he say anything before he died?' asked Hunter.

'Not much, actually,' I answered. 'At any rate it wasn't very clear. He was babbling something incoherent – some sort of gibberish that might have been a hymn or prayer.

I suppose the pain and shock had addled his poor old brain and on the point of death he had no idea of what he was saying.'

The young Barn Owl seemed very moved by this partly false account of what had happened. He turned away from me to hide his emotion, but I could tell that he was very upset indeed — more upset than I had been, though at least I had known the old bird and apparently he hadn't. But then it struck me that he was still a young bird and probably for the first time in his life a long, long way from home.

'I say, are you all right?' I asked him. 'You haven't caught some kind of rheum or fever, have you? Your chest is going up and down as though you couldn't breathe!'

'Oh, it's nothing to worry about,' he said. 'I was just thinking how awful it must have been. For him, of course, but also pretty harrowing for you.'

'Oh, it wasn't very jolly,' I replied. I wouldn't have said it now, of course. But this was the way we talked before the war. 'But when you come to think of it, he didn't suffer for very long. His was a fairly quick, clean death, and I suppose that's as much as any of us can hope for when the final moment comes.'

'Well, there goes my further education, anyway,' said Hunter, with a sigh and a little shrug. 'They won't be able to find me an alternative seat of learning until the next council meeting — and even then there may not be any other places going till next spring.'

'I'd look on the bright side, if I were you,' I said. 'There is at least one consolation. With Beak Poke still alive, there'd hardly have been enough food to go around, especially not with that little immigrant on the scrounge.'

'Immigrant?'

'I'm afraid so! You've got a blasted little alien squatting on your land. I saw her on the night that Beak Poke died.

At least, I think it was a female. From that distance I couldn't really tell.'

'You mean a Little Owl?' Hunter asked.

'I mean a blasted immigrant, old boy!' I said, very sharply. 'Another bloody scavenger from overseas. Think what you like, but if you don't scare that one off your land, or kill it, you'll get damn all to eat.'

'Why didn't Beak Poke scare her off?' asked Hunter, who was now looking so perplexed that secretly I had begun to feel quite sorry for him. However, I had my mission to accomplish – the alien had to be got rid of and, as my father always used to say, I supposed then that the end must justify the means.

'Oh, you know Beak Poke! He was old and feeble and in any case he liked conversing with the wretched little things. You know, finding out where they came from, how they lived and all that sort of thing. Owlology! As if we didn't know enough already without all that blasted empirical research, or whatever it was he used to call it.'

I could see my words had made a strong impression on this young bird called Hunter because he opened his bill to say something, found no words and so closed it once again. More than perplexed, he now looked totally bewildered.

'Oh well, I must be going now,' I said, spreading my wings for take-off. 'Best of luck in your new territory, and do remember to get rid of that damned little immigrant!'

'Will you be around this way the same time tomorrow night?' asked Hunter.

'I might be,' I replied, and nodded to him, flapped my wings and sped away, convinced that I had now carried out my mission. Little did I know how wrong I was, and little did I know then why Hunter had been so moved by the fact that Beak Poke had attempted to mumble that hymn or prayer, even in the very throes of death.

Much later Hunter taught me the words of their creed

and I have to say they made a deep impression on me. As I remember them they run like this:

> Hoard and covet not
> But be brave and free.
> Quest always after knowledge
> And slowly learn to know
> What science cannot see.
> Seek and strive for learning,
> Be temperate and wise
> For skill and wisdom only
> Will help us to survive.

But the fact is that we Tawnies do hoard and covet, as Rowan, son of Birch, now covets what is left of my ancestral domain. Approaching my third age I have come to believe that our Tawny Owl society is based on tradition, chauvinism, fear and greed. Perhaps the Barn Owls will never be able to live up to their ideals — the ideals of skill and wisdom, the idea of seeing where learning has no light. The fact remains that they have these ideals and we do not. I have long been aware of this and I began to acquire this kind of knowledge even before Hunter taught me the Barn Owl credo. That was to happen later. Much later. The first thing to sow the seeds of doubt in my mind was the little alien's song. Seeds of doubt which slowly grew into what my own kind now describe as heresy. But a brief time was still to pass before I heard that song, and in the meantime — in the first flush and arrogance of youth — I was more than happy to belong to the finest breed of bird that has ever flown the sky at night. Not only did I believe then that I belonged to the finest race of bird, but also to the finest class. And this question of class and responsibility was something that my parents drew to my attention yet again when I arrived home soon before sunrise on that now long-distant night.

CHAPTER
5

'We must set an example,' my mother said. 'It is a question of *noblesse oblige.*'

'What does that mean?' I asked.

'It is an expression that has been in our family for many generations,' explained my father, as all three of us perched high up in my parents' favourite ancestral oak, which rises high beside the gushing stream – the oak in which I perch now, so many years later, and from whose dense and sturdy branches I tell my story to the wind and trees.

'But what exactly does it mean?' I asked again.

'It is an expression brought to our ancestors by a media bird two or three hundred winters since. One of those short-eared owls had somehow flown across the salty waters and discovered that the owls there – though similar to us – speak with a different tongue. There are also apparently concepts in their language which there is no exact way of translating into ours.'

'You still haven't told me what it means,' I said.

'Of course I have,' my mother said. 'I told you, it means that we must set an example. We high-born Tawnies must observe the correct form and show the lower class of bird how things are done. That is why you must go to the Lost Domain.'

'But it's dangerous!' I protested.

'Precisely! That is why one of us must be present when this search is done. If we left this dangerous mission to the lower classes, they would lose respect for us.'

'That is the meaning of *noblesse oblige*,' my father said, nodding in agreement. 'To lead by example and show that if necessary you will be the first to die.'

As you, the wind and the trees, will realize, this definition did not please me over-much, so I decided to challenge it, or rather to challenge the concept which lay behind it.

'When I was younger you forbade me and all other Tawnies to fly anywhere near the Lost Domain. You told us that the forest, lake and parkland were patrolled by men with firesticks who would kill us on sight if we attempted to go hunting there. Now you tell me I have to conduct this dangerous reconnaissance of the place with Ferocity, Stoop and Ripper. Stoop is retarded and to be quite frank I can't stand either Ferocity or Ripper. In my opinion they are both barbarians. So if I must perform this task, I'd rather go alone. But before I go I think it only fair to tell me the purpose of the mission. After all, when one risks one's life, one likes to know the reason why.'

'There you are wrong!' my father said, severely. 'That is not good thinking. A good military leader never asks the reason why. He merely carries out his mission. At the moment, that is what you are. A military leader, entrusted with dangerous reconnaissance work. One day, when I am dead, you may become the leader of this whole district. Then, and only then, you must not only ask the reason why, you must know the reason at its source and its beginning. In other words, you must have worked it out yourself. So I will ask you now – as a test of your future qualities of leadership – what reasons do you think we have for sending you on such a dangerous mission?'

I looked at my father and my mother and thought for a few moments before replying. One of the things that flitted through my mind was whether, in the future, if I ever had a son, I would ask him to do such a dangerous thing myself.

'I suppose you're thinking of recolonizing the Lost Domain,' I said eventually. 'I suppose you think that now, because man has for so long been cutting down our woodland territories, we must reclaim as many of them as we can.'

'Right!' my father said, exchanging a glance with my mother, a glance which showed that both of them were pleased with me and with my analysis.

'But what about the firesticks,' I persisted. 'I don't see the point of recolonizing the Lost Domain if the Tawnies who have to go there have to live in constant fear of man.'

'According to our intelligence service, the men have gone away,' my father said. 'Our information is that they left some time ago and that the Lost Domain is now practically deserted and rapidly reverting to the wild.'

'But why would they go away?' I asked. 'They took it from us four hundred winters since, built that huge edifice and also created the lake and parkland. Or so I have been told. After taking all that trouble, why on earth would they want to abandon the place now?'

'Nobody knows, for sure,' my father admitted. 'Some say there are different breeds and races of men, just as there are different types of owl. Those who sustain this theory say that at this moment in time these different species of men have organized a war, and that the men from the Lost Domain have gone away to fight.'

'Do you believe this theory?' I asked.

'It's a possibility,' my father said. 'If they can kill a Tawny Owl with one of those firesticks, they could certainly kill another man. And our intelligence service has it that in the city fire is falling from the sky and some of the buildings there are burning.'

My heart lurched when I heard this news, for of course I thought at once of May Blossom. My mother must have read my mind because I saw her eyes glint in the first light of dawn as she leaned forward on her perch to make her point.

'You see how essential this survey is!' she said. 'As it is, there is insufficient woodland for all the Tawnies in the district. You have seen the cramped copses and miserable little spinneys in which some of the less fortunate birds are forced to live. And if the city really is burning our cousins living there – those who have survived the holocaust – will want to return and settle in their native territory. Your distant cousin May Blossom may of course be one of these. So if the men with firesticks have indeed gone away, or else been killed, it's absolutely necessary that we should reclaim the woodland in the Lost Domain at once.'

'Otherwise the immigrants will move in and breed there like rabbits,' my father interjected. 'In fact, our information is that a few of them are squatting there already. If the men have gone away, one of your tasks will be to direct Ferocity, Stoop and Ripper to get rid of them.'

'How get rid of them?' I asked.

'By warning them to go and then, if they refuse, by killing them,' my mother said.

'But I thought the Lost Domain was classified as no man's land,' I said. 'I thought it had been set aside as such four hundred winters since.'

'Then we shall reclassify it,' said my mother, coldly. 'The forest of the Lost Domain belonged to us for centuries before man usurped it. Now we intend to take it back again. If we can't reclaim it, we higher-born birds will be obliged to give up a part of our ancestral territories to those less fortunate than ourselves. Do you really want to give away your birthright and live surrounded by the lower classes, like Ferocity and Ripper? Do you really want to live all cramped up like the wretched little squatters in no man's land?'

My mother was a very difficult and formidable owl to argue with. Not only was her use of logic generally impeccable, but on top of that she always used your own emotions – played on your weaknesses to make her point or get her way. She had done this to me many times before and was to do it many times again.

'And on the subject of Ferocity and Ripper, there's something else I have to say,' put in my father, before I had a chance to reply. 'However fierce they are in their own territory, in the Lost Domain they will be afraid of the firesticks. Any sensible owl would be afraid. So, as leader of this expedition, it is up to you to encourage them.'

'You may consider them to be uncouth barbarians,' my mother added. 'But I want you to remember this. They are birds who will kill and die for us and for this territory. Thugs they may be, but in time of war they are essential.'

'I did not know there was a war on at the moment,' I said, and then tried not to flinch under the glacial stare with which she responded to my attempt at irony.

'The sun is up and it is time we slept,' my father said, putting a peremptory end to what might have been an argument. 'At twilight I will give you your instructions on how to reach your trysting place with Ferocity and Ripper in the Lost Domain, and I will also confirm exactly when you are to meet them there. But tonight, I want you to make certain that this Barn Owl incumbent has got rid of his little squatter. For all we know, since his tutor is dead, he may have decided to leave and already gone home again.'

'I'll deal with that!' I said, secretly quite pleased at the prospect of meeting the young Barn Owl once again. Flying home at dawn, it had occurred to me that by conversing we could get some knowledge of each other's separate cultures. This sort of exchange is generally frowned on by all

49

classes of Tawny Owl, but one day I hoped I would have May Blossom to contend with, on her return from the city, provided, of course, that she had not already been burnt to a cinder by man-made fire falling from the sky. If she did come back, and if we mated, I did not wish to appear merely as a landed aristocrat who felt that most kinds of learning were a waste of time. Like most young owls who are in love, I wanted to impress her. I remembered that she'd raised her lovely eyebrows in great surprise – and, I suspect, approval – when I'd mentioned the meetings that I'd had with poor old Beak Poke.

But I digress, and none of this was then germane to the current issue. The fact of the matter was that I had to fly this dangerous mission and if possible see Hunter first. If I couldn't find him – or if he had gone away – I could put off the irksome matter of the little immigrant until after my expedition to the Lost Domain.

So that evening, shortly after twilight, I took off from the safety of our ancestral home, flew down to the copse, and at once found Hunter sitting high in the willow above the brackish stream.

'Hello there!' I said. 'How are you settling in?'

'Not too badly,' Hunter replied, as I perched on the branch opposite to his.

'Are you getting enough to eat?'

'Oh, it could be worse,' he said.

'What about your little squatter? Have you seen her yet?'

'Yes. I saw her last night. She was hunting near the place where Beak Poke died.'

'You confronted her, I hope?'

'Of course!' Hunter replied, in a firm, confident tone which set my mind at rest and caused me to believe that he would brook no further trespass by the wretched little creature.

'What happened when you confronted her?' I asked. 'I

suppose she told you that Beak Poke had granted her squatter's rights?'

'She did,' admitted Hunter, with a little nod of his fine, white head.

'And?'

'I told her that since Beak Poke was dead, there was no way I could get confirmation of her claim. She argued a lot, of course, and in some ways she sounded quite convincing, but I met her again just before twilight and told her that as the new landlord my decision must be final.'

'Where do you think she's gone?' I asked.

'Maybe to the Lost Domain? You know the place, of course.'

'You mean the great house, the parkland and the forest which lie beyond Beak Poke's territory, between the village and Ferocity and Ripper's wood?'

'That's the place I mean. I understand that the forest was Tawny territory once.'

'Of course it was. It belonged to my ancestors until the men built that edifice some four hundred winters past. As a matter of fact, we're thinking of taking the place back again.'

'What about the firesticks?'

'We're not sure. But we know that for some time past the men with firesticks have stayed away. In fact, our Tawny intelligence service tells us that in the recent past men's behaviour patterns have been the subject of very drastic change. If our survey shows that the men have gone away for good, then we shall probably recolonize the place. As you are doubtless aware, we have been losing woodland territories for many thousand winters now, and therefore we are keen to reclaim and resettle any traditional forest we can find.'

'I see,' said Hunter, and for some reason I could not at once fathom, he sounded rather sad. I reassured him at once that no Barn Owl territory would be touched and that even in the Lost Domain our only claim was to the forest, not to the parkland or lake, which would still be classified as no man's land.

'Have you any idea when this resettlement might happen?' he asked, still looking sad and worried. 'You see, I've only just got rid of my little squatter and if she's gone there — which is possible — then I'd much rather that she stayed.'

'I take your point,' I said, understanding the dilemma he would be faced with if the wretched little creature were to escape from the cruel talons of Ferocity or Ripper and then return to throw herself on Hunter's mercy. 'However, I can't be too optimistic, I'm afraid. All the arrangements have been made and the survey starts tomorrow night. They'll be reconnoitring the Lost Domain, and leaving Stoop at home to guard their own territory. Ferocity and Ripper will kill anything they find there, that's for sure! I mean, although they are my own kind — and perhaps I shouldn't say so — they really are the most frightful, atavistic thugs, those three. Positively barbaric, you might say. For them, killing things is more than mere necessity or sport. For them mindless, indiscriminate slaughter has become more like a religion or a way of life. And the funny thing is that Ferocity, the female, is the worst. A huge, bad-tempered, bony bird she is, and what a warrior! She's killed three kestrels that I know of and they say she once took on a peregrine, though she couldn't kill the thing, of course. Ripper, her mate, is almost as vicious, only lazier, you might say. A trifle less dedicated to carnage than Ferocity. After all, slaughtering other birds of prey is a risky and exhausting sort of business.'

'What about the third one?' Hunter asked.

'Oh, poor old Stoop is rather simple-minded,' I replied. 'He's Ferocity's younger brother, you know, and they say she used him as a sort of sparring partner when they were fledglings. She taught him how to fight extremely well. He's as tough and able as the other two, but he isn't awfully bright. They say it comes from Ferocity using his head for target practice when he was a chick.'

'Would they kill another owl?' asked Hunter, understandably concerned for his own safety. Or so I thought then.

'That depends,' I said. 'On their own territory they'll kill anything that moves, except a Short Eared Owl or a Barn Owl with a transit permit like yourself. But they'd tear a Little Owl to pieces, you can bet your life on that.'

'But why?' asked Hunter. 'After all, the immigrants are owls, like us. An inferior species, I admit, but only one rung below us. Hardly a lower form of bird life like the rook or crow!'

'In theory you are right,' I said. 'But there are Tawnies I know who would argue that almost any other form of bird life is preferable to those blasted little immigrants. They've only just arrived, they're tough, they're clever and they breed like sex-mad rabbits. What's more, they don't have any land, so what you get are squatters, overcrowding and a dire shortage in the food supply. That's why we chase them off our land.'

'Chasing off your land is one thing,' said Hunter. 'In the interests of survival, I entirely agree with that. But killing another owl is quite another thing. It's totally against our Barn Owl credo and I have to tell you that I strongly disapprove!'

Though I secretly agreed with Hunter's sentiments, I was riled and angered by what I then considered to be the high-flown arrogance of his bearing and his tone. There was no way I was going to allow a Barn Owl to put a Tawny down, so I gathered my wits together and had a go at him, taking care to keep my own tone as casual and offhand as I could manage. That way, I thought, my reply would come across as all the more critical and damning.

'My dear chap!' I said, in what I hoped sounded like a

patronizing sort of manner. 'You don't think I do, do you? Approve of killing them, I mean. But fear, instinct and prejudice are very hard to overcome. And in spite of your so-called credo, you Barn Owls are a tiny bit hypocritical about the immigrant question, don't you think?'

'What do you mean?'

'I mean that you don't agree with killing them. The final solution doesn't appeal to your sensitive, educated conscience any more than it does to mine. But, on the other hand, you won't let them settle on your territory and therefore condemn them to no man's land, which more often than not means an inadequate diet, or death by starvation, firestick or pollution.'

Hunter turned his head away from me and did not reply at once. I could see that my words had struck home and I was proud then that my Tawny pragmatism had exposed and confounded his Barn Owl hypocrisy.

'You may be right,' he confessed, at last. 'But what I'm more concerned about at the moment is how I'm going to get to see my father and ask him what's to happen now that Beak Poke's dead. From what you tell me, I'm liable to be torn to pieces if I attempt to cross Ferocity and Ripper's wood without a transit permit.'

'Oh, I'll fix that for you,' I said, relenting a little now that I had won the argument. 'If you like I could fly with you to the Lost Domain when they begin their survey. That way you could get to know them and fix yourself a permanent transit permit, so to speak.'

'That's kind of you,' he said, after a moment's hesitation. 'I'll meet you here at nightfall tomorrow, then? But now I really must be going.'

'Hold on a moment!' I said, wondering why this young white bird was in such a great hurry, at a time when dusk had barely darkened into night. 'Don't be in such a rush!' I insisted. 'There's something I want to ask before you go. What do you think your father will say about your further education? Do you think he'll let you stay on here, at Beak Poke's place?'

'I don't know,' Hunter said, still seeming in a feverish hurry to get away. It was almost as if he had some kind of appointment, though I couldn't for the life of me imagine with whom that might have been, because he had only arrived so recently and as far as I knew had met no other owl in the district apart from myself and the little immigrant. 'There won't be another meeting of the Barn Owl council until the new moon after next,' Hunter continued. 'And all decisions on changes in further education will be taken then.'

'Oh, I know all about that sort of thing,' I said, quite proudly. 'Old Beak Poke used to go on a lot about your Barn Owl education system, all the different subjects that you study, the specialists that you have and all that sort of thing. Frankly, I can't say that I can see the good of it myself.'

'You Tawnies don't believe much in higher education, do you?' Hunter asked me, after fidgeting with his talons on the branch, as if he were now desperately anxious to go. 'I was taught that you leave home and learn to fend for yourselves as soon as you are able. It's called the pragmatic approach and your species is quite famous for it, really.'

'To be quite frank again, that's all a load of crow dung!' I replied. 'You see, the whole point is that we don't approve of higher education for the masses. We don't see the point of having the woods round here filled with poets, philosophers, experts on owlology, learned historians and all sorts of other egg-headed, absent-minded creatures who are so impractical that they can hardly swallow their own food, let alone go out and catch it!'

'You mean that you believe in an élite?' asked Hunter.

'You could put it that way if you wanted,' I replied. 'Though I admit, it does sound rather snobbish. What we don't believe in is a smattering of higher education. It's less useful for Tawny Owl survival than a few experts and decision-makers on the one hand, and a healthy respect for leadership and knowledge on the part of the untutored masses.'

'But too little education produces barbarians like Stoop, Ferocity and Ripper. Only just now you referred to them as chauvinistic thugs and said they were too ignorant and bloodthirsty for your taste!'

Once more stung by the aspersions that Hunter was casting on the habits and the wisdom of my ancient race, I stared at him angrily across the gap that divided our two branches and prepared to counter his Barn Owl hypocrisy once more.

'Obedient barbarians they may be, Hunter,' I riposted. 'But they do have their uses. They'll rid you of your little squatter, and that way your precious Barn Owl conscience will stay clear!'

Hunter held my angry stare for a moment or two and then turned away from me as if in pain. Of course, at the time I put the reason for his suffering down to the simple fact that he had lost an argument. Had I known the real reasons for his evident distress, I might have been much kinder. And then again, I might have been even more aggressive, for I was young and arrogant and some time was still to pass before I heard the alien's song and began to have my first serious doubts about the supremacy of our species and of our Tawny Owl philosophy.

'I must go now,' he said, turning back to me eventually. 'It's late, and I haven't had my supper yet.'

'See you at twilight tomorrow,' I replied, once again feeling more generous in the belief that I had won my argument. 'And by the way, old boy,' I added, as he prepared for take-off. 'I do hope you are allowed to stay and settle in Beak Poke's territory. You're a good chap and I should be sorry to lose you quite so soon. After all, good neighbours are important, and you never know who might take your place.'

He glanced back at me, nodded in acknowledgement, and then took off, rose high above the copse and flew on strong white wings across the meadowland which lay between the willow, the stream and Beak Poke's abandoned farmhouse.

He wasn't heading there, of course. I know that now. If I had known his true destination and what his real purpose was, I would undoubtedly have been shocked and would almost certainly have attempted to dissuade him. But after the event, it is easy to be wise. Innocent of Hunter's true intention, I was glad to have found a companion to fly with me on my dangerous mission to the Lost Domain. Uncertain whether it would be wise or not to tell my parents of this new alliance, I sat for a while on my favourite branch of the willow, looking down from time to time at the muddy stream which slowly flowed below me. I suppose I was searching for some inspiration or guidance, but the water was opaque, not clear and transparent like the spring which gushed from its source in the rock below my home.

Eventually I took off and flew up through the woodlands to report back to my parents, pausing only to kill and eat a scraggy young rabbit for my supper. It did not taste as good as the one I had eaten in the early dawn of the day on which May Blossom saved my life, and this somehow made me miss her with more passion and intensity.

Arriving home I found my parents in a quiet and sombre mood. Though I questioned them, they were not forthcoming about the reason for their worries, and in my youthful innocence I decided they were preoccupied by the dangerous expedition which I was to undertake at their request on the following night. To my relief, they did not question me about Hunter or his little immigrant, and much sooner than expected, I was able to fly to my own oak, above the stream that gushes from the rock, and to perch on the self-same gnarled and ancient branch on which I now sit in the twilight of my nights and days and tell my story to the wind and trees. If I had known then what I know now, the story might have had a different ending. But I will leave that for my silent listeners to decide!

CHAPTER
6

The next episode in my story has been well and accurately told in Quaver's epic ballad entitled 'The Ancient Solitary Reign'. I say accurately but, as I have pointed out before, there are differences, depending on the point of view and on one's own conception of the truth. Quaver describes how Hunter led me to the forbidden territory on the following night and how we flew around the huge, silent house and then across the gardens and the lake. He tells how we flew on across the great stretch of parkland towards the secret forest, and says that his brother felt exhilarated and unafraid, his confidence boosted by my powerful presence flying close behind him. He says that Hunter felt the two of us could take on anything, except the firesticks, though even they now seemed more legendary than real.

Well, that may be true, in a way. Hunter may well have felt confident and brave, but I certainly did not. In actual fact, I was terrified, though of course I put on an outer show of calm and courage in the interests of good form. My silent listeners must remember that this was my first trip to the Lost Domain. Hunter had been there several times before, and for him the firesticks may well have seemed more legendary than real, but as far as I was concerned, flying close behind him across the vast expanse of parkland, I expected to be blasted out of the sky from one moment to the next!

I felt more at home, of course, when we had finally crossed the open space, penetrated the first line of trees, and plunged into the relative security of the secret forest. In this woodland setting I took the lead and, if Quaver's ballad is to be believed, it was now Hunter who felt ill at ease.

He certainly seemed disconcerted as we landed some time later on the branches of a beech tree which stood on the edge of a clearing deep inside the forest. I knew that during the course of their mission, Ferocity and Ripper would never dare to fly beyond the tree line and extend their mission to the parkland, the gardens and the lake. I guessed they would be prowling somewhere in the heart of the forest, not far away from the beech tree where Hunter and I now perched to recover from our long and dangerous flight. I hooted to announce our coming, not loudly, but with a deep, vibrant call that I hoped would not carry to the confines of the forest, where the legendary men with firesticks might be waiting to destroy us.

Two answering calls came almost at once, and from their raucous, unmellifluous tones I guessed that I'd been right and that these replies came from the fearsome Ripper and from Ferocity, who was even more belligerent than her mate and was certainly the most bloodthirsty Tawny I had ever met.

Though I had already warned Hunter about these two and about Stoop, Ferocity's retarded brother, I felt it incumbent on me to repeat my briefing.

'Leave everything to me!' I said. 'They may be hostile to you, but I am their commanding officer; they will obey me and no harm will come to you.'

'That's all very well,' said Hunter, for once sounding

slightly scared. 'That's all very well, but afterwards I have to cross their territory, and you won't be there. What will happen then?'

'Don't worry! I will ensure that they grant you safe passage, though I must confess you may have some trouble with the poor demented Stoop, but I'll brief you about that later. There's no time now. I can hear them coming!'

'So can I!' said Hunter, and though he shifted slightly on his perch, he stood his ground and did not reveal any outward signs of the fear he must have felt.

Moments later Ferocity and Ripper landed on a branch opposite and slightly above us in the beech tree. They were big, vicious birds, and though both were of my own kind I must confess that they presented an awesome rather than a pretty sight.

'Greetings, young master Yoller,' Ripper said, glaring at Hunter with animosity and deep mistrust. 'What be that strange critter you've got with you there?'

Or so the opening exchanges between us are rendered in Quaver's ballad. Whilst he is entitled to poetic licence, I believe he failed to reproduce accurately the rural dialect spoken by Stoop, Ferocity and Ripper. I suppose he did this in order to diminish them and to emphasize the undeniably crude and coarse behaviour of these three loyal Tawnies. Well, I for one do not intend to mock the dead and shall from now on render their speech as more or less educated, even though it wasn't! The truth of the matter is that I was embarrassed, almost ashamed, at the contrast between this cultivated Barn Owl who perched uneasily by my side and our two loyal subjects, who seemed primitive, ignorant and vicious by comparison. I was torn between loyalty to tradition, heritage and my own kind on the one hand, and on the other by an attraction to the brain and different kind of courage exemplified by this white owl by my side – an owl from another culture and another race.

To fend off the problem, I immediately assumed the

accent and the tone of the commanding officer. One might say it came naturally to me, having been in-bred over many centuries. Though still expressing a hostile attitude to Hunter, the two atavistic Tawnies listened carefully while I explained his needs for right of passage across their woodland, both to and from his father's home.

They at once objected to this, complaining that Hunter had flown over their territory before, without advance warning, and that Stoop would certainly have killed the white owl if he'd been swift enough to catch or intercept him. Hunter was obviously embarrassed by this. He had not told me that he'd crossed their patch without asking for permission. However, looking at Ferocity and Ripper as they taunted Hunter and glared at him with the traditional mistrust and contempt they felt for any owl other than a Tawny, I could not help feeling that in his place I might have done the same. I, too, might have cut and run rather than pause and ask for rights of passage, according to Barn Owl and Tawny protocol.

I countered their objections by turning defence into attack, and enquired about the progress they were making in their survey.

'I take it you've already done a reconnaissance of the parkland, the gardens and the lake?' I asked, guessing that in spite of all their chauvinism and aggression, Ferocity and Ripper would never dare fly close to the great house and risk the legendary firesticks, in the way that my Barn Owl friend and I had done this very night.

Incidentally, in Quaver's ballad it is Hunter who is said to have turned defence into attack by putting this question to Ferocity and Ripper. This is not the case. I remember clearly that up to and including this time he remained silent and left things to me, in accordance with his briefing.

'Been to the parkland and the lake? Not on your life, we ain't,' Ripper replied. 'No, my young master. If there be firesticks in this place, that's where you'll surely find them. I'm telling you, wild eagles wouldn't drag us there. We'll check the forest for you, that's our duty, and we'll kill any illegal squatters as we find. But we ain't going near the gardens and the lake.'

'Very well,' I replied, falling back on one of my father's favourite clichés. 'So if you haven't been to the parkland, the gardens or the lake, what information can you give us about your reconnaissance of the secret forest? Have you heard or seen a firestick?'

'Not yet, I ain't,' Ripper replied. 'But these here woods be full of game. Pheasant, partridge, woodcock, hare and rabbit, you name it and you'll find it here. Also, you can tell the men don't come 'ere any more.'

'How can you tell?'

'Because the paths here in the forest be all overgrown, the paths the men must have once used to come in here and hunt.'

'Tell young master Yoller about all those Little Owl pellets as we found,' said Ferocity, interrupting her mate as she subjected Hunter to a particularly vicious stare. 'And tell 'im about all them feathers, too! I reckon these 'ere woods be riddled with blasted little immigrants!'

'There be a colony of them 'ere, I do believe,' said Ripper, glaring at Hunter as if he were in some way responsible for allowing an alien group to move in to what had once been our ancestral territory.

'Ah! And some of us knows who encouraged them to settle 'ere!' said Ferocity, almost spitting at Hunter as she spoke.

'Very well, then,' I said, deciding that the time had come to move. 'Carry on with the good work. I'll be back later on tonight, when I've completed my part of the survey. In the meantime Hunter will be flying home across your territory. I'm sure Stoop will grant him a safe passage if he tells him he has your permission.'

'He'll 'ave to sing a song for his supper!' said Ferocity. 'Or leastways tell a story. You know our Stoop be simple-minded. He won't let no one through unless they can either make him laugh or cry.'

'I expect that can be arranged,' I said. I nodded to them both and then took off, with Hunter following close behind me. I flew swiftly at tree-top height until we reached the next clearing, still not far beyond the heart of the secret forest. Here I landed high in the branches of another beech tree and waited for Hunter to alight beside me. I could tell at once that he was tense and almost boiling over with emotion.

'Is anything the matter?' I asked, rather casually, for I was intent now on scrutinizing the dense and seemingly impenetrable woodland all around us in search of any information that might satisfy my father.

'What is this business about singing, or telling stories?' Hunter asked. He sounded so upset that I turned at once and gave him my full attention.

'Oh, that's nothing!' I said. 'All you have to do is to sing Stoop a song, or else tell him a story, and then he'll grant you right of passage.'

'But I don't know any songs or stories!' Hunter protested. 'My brother Quaver is studying these things, not me.'

'Of course you know some songs and stories,' I replied, a trifle impatiently. 'Everybody does. I admit that some owls are better at telling them than others, but in Stoop's case it won't matter. I've told you before, he's simple-minded due to Ferocity doing target practice on his head. Don't worry, he will be satisfied with almost anything — even with one of the stories or rhymes your mother taught you when you were a fledgling.'

'But you told me he was as fierce as the other two!'

'Listen!' I said. 'If you're really worried about this encounter, I'll fly with you as far as Ripper's wood and introduce you personally to Stoop. That way no harm can possibly come to you.'

'But I shall still have to sing, or tell a story?'

'Yes. In any case, it's something you should practise. My mother once taught me that if you can entertain your enemies, you're much less likely to get killed!'

Hunter fell silent after this, and I could tell that he disapproved of the whole idea. In secret, so did I. Though I would never have confessed as much to Hunter, I found the whole business as demeaning as he did. He was a proud bird and clearly did not fancy the idea of entertaining Stoop, or singing for his supper, as Ferocity had put it. However, though I inwardly agreed with him, I said nothing, but instead continued to scan the ever-more overgrown forest for any recent signs of human presence. What had once been paths were now buried by fresh vegetation, and I judged the place where we now perched to be almost impenetrable by man. I pointed this out to Hunter, who still had not spoken, and he agreed with me, having observed the growing density of the forest as we flew across it from the open spaces of the parkland and the lake.

'What will you report back to your father, when your Tawny survey is complete?' he asked, still seeming very ill at ease.

'Oh, I shall tell him that as far as I can see there are no signs of men with firesticks anywhere in the Lost Domain, and certainly not in the secret forest. When the time is right, I shall recommend that we recolonize the place.'

'And the Little Owls who have settled here?'

'They will be driven out,' I said. 'They will be driven back to no man's land, where they belong.'

'Or killed?' Hunter enquired, with a little shudder.

'Or killed!' I said. 'That depends on whether they vacate the place at once or whether they decide to stay and offer some kind of resistance.'

Hunter shuddered again and I began to become

concerned about his health. At that time I put his shiverings down to the fact that he must soon come face to face with Stoop. It was not until I had heard the alien's song that I realized the true reason for his distress.

'Tell you what!' I said. 'I've had an idea.'

'What's that?' asked Hunter, hopefully.

'Well, when you encounter Stoop, tell him you're coming back across his wood in two or three nights' time. Tell him he'll get an extra-special story then!'

'But I might not be coming back,' Hunter said. 'My father might have found me another place for my further education.'

'Well, in that case it won't matter, will it?'

'No, I don't suppose it will,' said Hunter, sounding rather doubtful. 'It's just that I don't like making promises I can't keep.'

'Don't worry! Stoop is unlikely to remember you from one night to the next. Neither would your memory be up to much if Ferocity had done target practice on your head. And I know what you mean about lying,' I continued. 'One doesn't care for it on principle, and after telling an untruth one is liable to suffer from guilt, remorse or regret. However, I'll tell you what I'll do. I'll fly with you to Ripper's wood, introduce you to him and make your promise for you. That way the responsibility will be with me!'

'That's very good of you,' Hunter said, looking and sounding extremely relieved. 'But will you have time to fly that far with me and then get home again before the sunrise?'

'If we leave now, I might just make it.'

'And the rest of your survey?' Hunter asked.

'I've seen enough,' I said. 'There is no visible sign of men or firesticks. I shall tell my father we can reclaim the forest when we like.'

Though Hunter had a worried look on his face, he nodded his assent, and the two of us took off at once, flew to the edge of the Lost Domain, and then sped on across open Barn Owl country until the land began to slope upward and in the moonlight we saw the outline of Ferocity and Ripper's wood. Soon afterwards we crossed the outer line of trees and landed in the first clearing we came to – a place which would soon become historic, though neither of us could have known so at the time.

I hooted from the elm in the clearing and my call was answered at once from deeper inside the wood. Soon Stoop swooped down through the surrounding trees and landed on the branch opposite the one on which Hunter and I waited. In fact, the retarded bird presented an even more terrifying aspect than I had remembered. His plumage was dishevelled and he had obviously not groomed himself since his sister Ferocity and her mate Ripper had left him alone in the wood to conduct their survey in the Lost Domain. There is something about madness which frightens me, and as Stoop stared at us with those bulging, bloodshot eyes of his, I was glad that I had escorted Hunter thus far to avoid a confrontation which might have ended in serious injury, or worse still, a battle to the death.

In his ballad, Quaver has told how I persuaded Stoop to let Hunter fly across his land with the promise of an extra-special story if he should return in two or three nights' time. What Quaver does not express is my sadness as I watched Hunter take off and wing his way homeward towards the moon, his white shape soon vanishing in the muted light which filtered through the upper branches of Ferocity and Ripper's wood. I felt even then that we had been on the verge of forging a true friendship, and now, as he was swallowed by the distance and the vast night sky, I did not know if and when the two of us would ever meet again.

Quaver also does not say, for he could not have known – any more than Hunter ever did – that I stayed on after my new friend had gone and told Stoop one of the countless stories with which my mother had bombarded me ever since I was a chick.

Most of our education in those days was based on stories. Your mother or father told you a tale, simple of course when you were young, and then becoming progressively more complex as one grew older. Each of these stories had a moral, which one was supposed to interpret when one had heard it. In these far-off days those stories were called fables, and the purpose of telling them was supposed to be to try to teach you how to think. I believe it was called the elliptical approach, but much water has gushed from the rocks since then, and for some time now we Tawnies seem to have adopted the more formal type of lesson practised by the Barn Owl teachers. Anything anecdotal is now frowned upon and seems to be considered academically unsound.

Of course, the simple-minded Stoop was not concerned with the hidden meaning of the story that I told him on that long-gone night. The surface narrative was quite sufficient to absorb the whole of his feeble-minded attention.

As I recounted my tale to Stoop, I felt a hypocrite for having suggested that Hunter would be well advised to learn this rather shallow way of entertaining, and at the same time of teaching one to think according to the commonplace or the cliché.

If I digress again it is only to highlight my own difficulties, and those of any other owl who strays away from his own camp into what some call the middle of the road. When faced with the prejudice of my own kind, I reacted by defending the Barn Owl culture. At a much later date I went as far as to express some degree of compassion and understanding even for the hated aliens. Yet when owls of another race cast aspersions on our glorious Tawny tradition, one sprang at once to the defence of one's own cultural heritage. The longer I live, the more I have discovered that attempting to be open-minded and objective is a curse, leading to conflict with foreigners and ultimately to ostracization by one's own kind.

Perhaps it is both safer and better to accept blindly the traditions of one's own race and to flock obediently with the common herd. Or, as Sage was to put it later, 'Never attempt to destroy an owl's prejudice. For if you do, he will find that he has little left.'

Of course, in those early days I had not yet come to some of these conclusions. I was proud of my Tawny heritage and proud, too, of my burgeoning friendship with the Barn Owl called Hunter. After I had told my simple story to Stoop, I set off on the long journey home in a state of innocence and elation. I had risked the dangers of the forbidden territory and my mission would soon be accomplished.

Little did I realize then that three further stories were to be told before the same time on the following night, and that one of them was so shocking as to ensure a safe passage for Hunter if he, too, had heard it, and if he had told it to Stoop on his journey back across the Lost Domain.

CHAPTER

7

I flew back across the forbidden territory shortly before dawn, pausing briefly to ascertain that Ferocity and Ripper had nothing further to report. Day was breaking again as I crossed the parkland and the lake, but still I saw no sign of man or firestick. I cleared the Lost Domain and struggled homewards, my wings flapping feebly under the rising sun. Having skirted round the village, I crossed the flat Barn Owl territory which Hunter had now abandoned and laboured on across the stream, through the spinney, and then upward through the woods and towards the safety of my ancestral home.

On arrival, I flew straight to my parents' oak, and to my surprise found that both of them were still awake and glaring at each other across the gap between their two favourite branches in the centre of the tree. From their posture, their body language and the way they greeted me, it was obvious that something had gone seriously wrong.

They welcomed me, of course, but absently, as if their minds were still on the quarrel they'd been having. To bring them out of it, I began at once with the report on what I'd observed in the Lost Domain, but to my great disappointment and mounting irritation, neither of them seemed in the least interested in what I had to say. One was naturally more than a little peeved by this. When one has risked one's life at the behest of others, especially one's parents, one feels it incumbent upon them to give one a thorough and enthusiastic debriefing. I dare say my silent listeners will find my use of language slightly pompous, but I believe it sums up the way I felt. The fact of the matter is that I was deeply hurt by their lack of interest. Hurt and indignant. However, indignation is a parasite emotion, like envy or regret, and as I continued to talk, and they failed to listen, this resentment of mine boiled over into a state of flaming anger!

'You send me on these suicidal missions,' I protested, 'and then you don't express the slightest interest when I come back!'

'I'm sorry,' my father said, which astonished me, since I'd never known him apologize for anything before. 'Of course we're glad to see you back,' he continued, blinking at me in the sunlight with a worried and careworn expression on his face. 'The fact is that we've had some very bad news while you've been away.'

'Rumours, not news,' my mother snapped. 'I'm surprised you listen to such rubbish!'

'What rubbish?' I asked, turning back to my father for an explanation.

'We've heard that a monster owl is on its way here from the south,' he replied. 'We have been told that it applies the final solution to all other birds who fly the sky at night.'

'The final solution?'

'Death!' my father said. 'The extermination of any rival species.'

'Who told you this?' I asked, unwilling and unable to believe my ears.

'A Short Eared Owl!' my mother said, voicing her contempt for that species in no uncertain fashion. 'A media bird, a creature of no fixed abode, who gets its living by spreading propaganda, blowing up the news and even by inventing it!'

'There is often an element of truth in what they say,' my father replied gravely. 'We cannot afford to ignore this warning until we get the all clear from our own intelligence service.'

'Nonsense,' my mother said. 'There is no such thing as the monster owl. It is extinct. And even if it were not extinct – and should attack us – we would doubtless bring it down!'

'How?' I asked. 'I have always heard that the monster owl was awfully big, with huge talons and with a wingspan three times as wide as ours. I mean, to my untutored mind, it would seem as if attacking the monster owl, always assuming that it did exist, would be as futile as a dozen sparrows trying to bring down one of us. They would be slaughtered on the wing!'

'They would indeed,' my father said. 'But that is because sparrows have but the tiniest of brains. Being mindless, they would have no strategy and therefore no tactics which would permit them to take on one of us. War is not only about numbers, bravery and strength. It is also about intelligence.'

'And fear!' my mother added. 'The worst thing that can happen to a Tawny Owl, under the night sky, is to become afraid of fear.'

'What do you mean?' I asked, for though young, strong and reasonably brave, I could not see how any sane and well-balanced Tawny could fail to feel afraid of the monster owl, should such a thing exist.

'I will tell you a story,' my mother continued, with the trace of a superior smile on that handsome face of hers – a face I imagined had even when young been handsome as opposed to pretty.

'Don't you think I'm rather too grown-up for stories?'

I asked, resenting what I considered to be my mother's patronizing arrogance. 'After all, I'm old enough to have killed a kestrel and a buzzard and have also been considered mature enough to lead a most dangerous mission to the Lost Domain.'

'And, of course, you've been in love,' my father interrupted with one of his rare, ironic smiles.

'I am still in love,' I said. 'Though from what I've seen of love so far, I cannot say that it appears much connected with maturity!'

'Listen to my story!' said my mother, who seemed secretly pleased by the adult comment I'd just made. 'No one doubts your intelligence or your courage, Yoller, but you must know that none of us is ever too old to go on learning. In fact, for centuries we have been brought up to believe that the day a Tawny Owl stops learning, he is dead.'

'Well, then, tell me the story,' I said, more amenable now to being patronized after the compliments that had just been paid to me.

'Once upon a time a baby Tawny Owl was born here on this very spot and in these woods in which we now live,' my mother began, and I winced – I fear visibly – at the banal and trite opening that was always used as a start for stories told to fledglings. I also flinched at my mother's use of language, because it seemed quite clear to me that if this baby owl had been born here on this very spot it could hardly have been in any other place but in the selfsame wood. This very spot, after all, must be here! But my mother's use of rhetoric and her pleonastic tendencies when telling stories had irritated me since I became aware of them in my early adolescence. Obviously nothing was going to change her now, so I resolved to listen patiently until she'd finished.

'As this baby owl grew up, on this very spot,' my mother continued, seemingly undeterred by the way in which I'd flinched, 'he stared out every dawn and every twilight at what we call the mountain, though of course we know that in truth it is not a mountain, but merely a high hill.'

'Get on with the story,' said my father gruffly. 'Everybody knows now that there are no real mountains in this part of the world. Everybody knows that real mountains have snow on top of them for most of the four seasons. But this is a story, not a geography lesson, so for the Great God Bird's sake, get on with it!'

I was surprised by this unusually aggressive reaction on my father's part. He was usually quite deferential to my mother. Though a brave warrior and a leader of the highest rank, he sometimes seemed almost in awe of her. I wondered then whether he resented the fact that his one and only grown-up son must suffer the humiliation of listening to a fairy tale, but this is one of the many things I shall never ever know, for both of them are long since dead. My mother's only reaction at the time was to counter his outburst by ruffling up her feathers, stretching her neck and gazing down on him with a cold and rather haughty stare – a stare or glare which I believe disconcerted both of us. When she had silently put down my father's minor rebellion, she unflexed her body and continued with her story thus:

'This baby owl was taught when young that he must never fly beyond his own territory and up to the so-called mountain. He was told that on the other side of the mountain, or what we now know is merely a high hill, there lived a dreadful monster owl who would kill any creature who attempted to trespass on his territory. Of course, the young owl was frightened by this tale, as were all other Tawnies in the district. So in his early days he never dreamed of flying up to the great bald hill, let alone beyond it. But the day came when he matured – as you are now doing, Yoller. By this time his curiosity had got the better of him and he made up his mind to find out what the forbidden mountain was like and what – if anything – lived on the other side. So one day, when gloaming deepened into darkest night, he took off from this very spot and flew west in the wake of the drowning sun. He flew up and across the last outpost of the forest until there were no more trees and above him rose the high, bald hill, or mountain, beyond which lived the monster owl.

'Approaching the crest of the hill, the young owl hesitated. It was not yet too late to turn and fly swiftly back to the shelter of his ancestral woods. But curiosity and the desire for knowledge spurred him onward and upward until he reached and overflew the crest of the bald mountain.

'To his horror he saw at once that the legend of his childhood and his adolescence had been true. Emerging from its secret lair in the forbidden territory, the monster owl rose above him, so huge that he blotted out the stars, the moon, and seemed to fill the entire night sky. Knowing that it was now too late to fly back to the safety of his home, the young Tawny Owl flew onward still and ever upward towards this terrible apparition, and to his immense surprise the creature began to recede from him and drop down lower towards the ground, seeming to shrink as the young Tawny Owl approached. Soon the great bird was below him, halfway to the ground, and to our hero's amazement had diminished to no more than the size of a rook or crow. With curiosity now replacing fear, our bold young adventurer flew downward and ever closer. As he did so the sometime monster landed on the ground, shrinking rapidly, first to the size of a sparrow and soon, as the Tawny Owl landed, into a creature tinier even than a wren.

'Perched on the ground above the miniature bird, the young Tawny watched in amazement as the sometime monster looked up at him in terror.

'What is your name? our hero asked, not wishing to

harm this now defenceless and pathetic little creature.

'My name is fear! the tiny bird replied, shrinking still further even as he spoke, and at the same time changing from a bird into a worm. Following this metamorphosis he began to burrow into the earth.

'My name is fear! he repeated, in a fading, whimpering voice, before disappearing deep into some secret hide-out in the womb of the earth.'

Having finished this somewhat long-winded story, my mother resettled herself on the branch with that aristocratic poise, or pose, which was second nature to her. Having settled her feathers, she then stared at me and raised her eyebrows, as if expecting some kind of spontaneous reaction to the fairy story she'd just told.

'What you've just narrated to me is a legend,' I answered, having glanced at my father before replying. 'What you are trying to tell me is that there is no such thing as the monster owl and that fear is merely engendered in the mind.'

'That's the moral of the story, of course,' my mother said. I nodded and said nothing, remembering the two buzzards, who had been real, not legendary, and of whom I had been truly afraid. Perhaps I should have spoken then and voiced the already dawning doubts about my upbringing and conditioning, but I was still very young, and for me these were still the nights and days of discovery and wonder. Long nights of adventure they were then – long nights that led slowly to the dawning of a certain kind of truth.

But I digress again, and of course in those far-off days of my long-vanished, long-squandered youth, I did not think as I do now. In fact, I hardly thought at all. I suppose that like all living creatures I responded to instinct, on the one hand, and on the other to the finely tuned conditioning of my superior class and race.

Would that things had stayed the same! I rue the early

sunrise on which I heard the alien's song and first began to think, for thinking has been the death of me, and now no one will hear my version of the truth – no one but the wind that whispers through the trees and the water that wells up from the rock.

I believe that most of the damage done has been brought upon me by my brain and by the urge I felt so strongly for Mallow and May Blossom. To live long and enjoy a peaceable old age one should avoid all original, creative thought, and above all one should dominate all passion. Had I successfully avoided these two mortal dangers, I would not now be waiting in my third age for those of my own kind to fly through the night sky, destroy me and usurp what remains of my ancestral domain.

But passion came upon me and, later, so did thought, and at the end of my long nights and days I have no one but myself and them to blame.

CHAPTER

 8

At sunrise our first refugee arrived and confirmed the belief I already held, namely that evil does exist and that stories such as my mother told could only cloak reality in the mists of myth and legend.

The shattered refugee reported that he had seen the owls in his own community put to death by the monster owl, which was bigger and more powerful than anyone had previously imagined. Worse was to come! As the sole survivor of his own community, he had flown north and taken refuge in successive Tawny Owl communities, few of whom had believed that the monster really existed, and some of whom considered the refugee to be quite mad. They were soon to be proved tragically wrong when the monster loomed in the night sky, descended on their woodland dwellings and slaughtered them, killing – like the fox – not only for food but for sheer delight and blood lust. Once, he told us, he had even taken shelter in the open country among a community of Barn Owls, whom he described as thoughtful, studious birds. But however thoughtful and however academic, they did not believe him. They, too, insisted that the monster was a myth, took no precautions and were presently decimated by the giant as he flew across their territory on his way north, to the place where I perch now.

According to our pitiful, distraught refugee, the only reason he had been able to stay well ahead of the monster and reach our territory still intact was because the giant owl had found a great man-made estate some two hundred meadows to the south. Here he had paused to glut himself on goose, pheasant, lamb, hare and duck. Our only hope of survival, according to this wreck of a refugee, was that man would kill the great bird with his firestick as a punishment and to prevent him further plundering this vast and well-guarded game reserve.

'You must believe me!' pleaded our near-hysterical refugee, as he stared at us in the early-morning light with his haunted, fear-shot eyes.

'If man does not kill the monster owl and if it pursues its northward path, applying the final solution to all other creatures of the night, you and your entire community will be dead before the rebirth of this crescent moon which at this moment sheds so little light.'

'I believe you,' my father said, after pausing to give my mother a solemn and reproving stare. Solemn because of the coming danger, I imagine, and reproving because of the fairy story she had told me on the night before the dawning of this dreadful truth.

Further interrogation of the Tawny turned out to be quite futile. Terror and fatigue had both taken a heavy toll, and a once sane and healthy bird was now reduced to little more than a gibbering wreck.

My own personal concern was of course for May Blossom, but the shattered fugitive knew nothing of what had happened in the city. He could only recount the tale of the monster's devastation as it flew ever further north.

Soon the exhausted fugitive fell into a troubled, moaning sleep, but as the sun rose higher in the sky my parents and

I stayed awake and pondered on the dreadful tidings he had brought us.

'We must fight,' my father said, eventually. 'We must send out, east, west, south and north, and summon our array. All the Tawnies living in this territory must be called to join us in a great battle, during which we shall bring the monster down.'

'Summoning them is one thing,' I said. 'But supposing they don't come?'

'They will come,' my mother said, calmly, but with great conviction. 'At a time like this, all true Tawnies must stand up and be counted.'

'But even if they did all come, would there be enough of us?' I asked. 'From what this refugee has told us, it would take three score and ten Tawnies to bring this monster down!'

'Nonsense!' my father said. 'It all depends on strategy and tactics. A battle plan is already evolving in my mind. Like all good plans, it will take some time to mature, and after that every detail must be defined. But the nucleus of the plan is in my mind and tonight I want you to fly out east, west, south and north and organize messengers to call all the owls under my command to assemble here on or before the dawn of the following day. If the monster owl is resting only two hundred meadows to the south of here, there is definitely no time to waste.'

'Go to Birch first,' my mother said. 'He is the strongest young bird we have – apart from yourself – and he will be the hardest to convince.'

'Why is that?' I asked.

'Because he is convinced, quite wrongly, that we usurped his family's right to the leadership of this territory,' my father said. 'It is an old story now, long forgotten and much better buried in the past.'

'None the less, it would be better for me to hear about it,' I replied. 'Birch has never liked me and I have never understood the reason why. If my task is to persuade him to join us in this war, the least you can do is to provide me with the history of this feud.'

'Vendetta would be a better word,' my mother said, ruffling her feathers in a manner that suggested complete contempt for Birch and all his ancestry.

'What does vendetta mean?' I asked. I had never heard the word before and somehow to me it sounded foreign.

'It is a word imported by the little immigrants,' my mother said, immediately proving that my intuition had been right. 'It comes from their old language and it does indeed mean feud, but more so! It means feud, but feud suffused by even more blood, revenge and death!'

'Then why, precisely, is Birch conducting this vendetta?'

'Well, if you really insist on knowing, the whole story goes back to more than three hundred winters since,' my father said. 'It all started at the time of our last civil war against the Barn Owls. Up to that time, Birch's ancestors were the oldest aristocracy in this territory, but the leader and his brother were killed in that long-distant war. Their sons were too young to take over, so control of the territory passed from their forebears to ours, and as you know, we have been the ruling family ever since.'

'What shall I do if Birch refuses to fight with us?' I asked.

'You will tell him this story,' my mother said. I groaned inwardly at this, thinking to myself, for the Great God Bird's sake not another story, but my mother subjected me to that haughty stare of hers, so I sat on the branch and listened. It must be apparent by now, to the wind and trees, that there were times I was not as fond of my mother as perhaps I should have been. This was one of them!

'One frozen winter four owls of different species died on the same night,' my mother began, while I sat still and attempted not to fidget on the branch. 'It was a winter's night when snow stood hard as iron on the ground and when the icy wind cut through your feathers like a knife.'

'Will you kindly get on with it!' my father said. 'If you include all those descriptive bits, the monster will have killed and eaten us before you've finished the exposition.'

'It is important to set the scene,' replied my mother coldly. 'It is important to know that when the freezing owls reached that burning forest which is hell, all four of them wanted to get in. Having died of exposure and starvation none of them cared about the burning. None of them cared what happened afterwards, provided they could get unfrozen first.

'But suddenly the great black Satan owl appeared and blocked their entrance to the blazing forest. Wait! he said. You are not the only owls to have died tonight, and it is so cold every one of them has wanted to get in. The inferno is full. There is only one place left, and to fill that I must take the greatest sinner among you.

'You! the Satan bird continued, pointing at the frozen Barn Owl. What sins did you commit?

'Oh, terrible ones, replied the frozen white bird, with his bill chattering as he spoke. The worst one was just recently; when the snow fell and the earth first froze, my eldest son returned and asked for food and shelter. Since leaving home he had not been able to establish himself in a territory of his own. Since my mate and I were on the point of starvation, I told him to go away. There was nothing to eat and no place for him at home, I said. So he left and half-froze, half-starved to death somewhere out there in no man's land. To sum it up, I rejected my own son and sent him to a cold and lonely death, so please, please let me into hell.

'Sorry, said the big black Beelzebub bird, with a slow shake of his massive head. You were only obeying the rules laid down by your Barn Owl tribe – you can't go home again. Isn't that one of the basic lessons that the owls of your species are taught? Young adults must leave the family home to find a new territory and found a lifestyle of their own. I have to confess that I don't like what you did, but since you were merely conforming to the traditions and tenets of Barn Owl philosophy, in the context we can hardly describe your behaviour as a sin. So, sorry, but there's no room for you. You can't come in.

'The place belongs to me! stated the proud Tawny, who was standing behind the Barn Owl in the queue, fidgeting with his talons to avoid frostbite from the frozen ground. When I was young I killed a jackdaw in the early dawn. There was no reason. It was daytime and he had a right to fly across our territory, but I killed him anyway. It was a wanton act of murder, so please let me in to your inferno.

'There must have been a reason, said the Satan owl, frowning down on the Tawny from a great height. Tell me that reason, and I will consider you for the one remaining place.

'Well, he spoke to me, the Tawny said. He greeted me in owl language, a parlance he had learned to imitate. Since I could not – and still cannot – speak the language of the jackdaw, rook or crow, or indeed any bird language other than our own, I felt inferior and killed him out of fear and resentment of this strange intelligence he had. I killed him in the early dawn, but I wasn't hungry, so I didn't eat him. If I had done, it might have justified my action. But after killing him I let the mutilated body of the clever jackdaw fall to the woodland floor to rot and be devoured slowly by worm and maggot. It was wanton murder and for this reason I claim the one remaining place in hell.

'Sorry, said the Satan Bird, shaking his head again. Of course, I do not approve of what you did. You killed the jackdaw in the early dawn, while your Tawny law decrees that you may only kill by night. Yours was a gratuitous and wanton killing, the devil bird agreed. But I cannot classify it as a sin, or even as a crime, for it was born of fear, Tawny Owl conditioning and basic ignorance. You were very young at the time and basically you believed you were defending your own territory. Yours was an error of timing, not malice aforethought, and therefore, tonight, there is no room for you in hell.

'Then let me in! piped up the Little Owl, who in spite of jumping up and down on the frozen ground to stop his small talons from taking root in the stinging ice had so far been dwarfed by the now disappointed Tawny who had stood in front of him in the queue of the four owls desperately anxious to enter into hell.

'Why? asked the Satan bird, looking rather bored. His job was a hard one and on freezing cold nights such as these it was no fun to sit and listen to all species and all manner of owls protesting their innocence, or – as in this unusual case – their guilt. He was bored by their wretched little sins, most of which he could – as the devil he was – consider as little more than misdemeanours.

'Because I poached on the farmland of the Barn Owl and in the Tawny woods. Because I squatted on their land and stole their food. I was an opportunist and a renegade and for this reason I deserve a place in hell.

'No, you don't, the Satan bird replied. Your lot on earth was not a happy one. As an immigrant, despised by the other species, you were forced to live from claw to mouth. Forced to live in no man's land and to steal from the landed owls to keep your family alive. Certainly there is no place in hell for you. I dare say your earthly crime will prevent you from going to the Great God Bird's paradise, which is a boring place in any case. I would guess that your destiny is to wander for ever in limbo, that place between hell and paradise which resembles in so many ways the no man's land you inhabited on earth.

'And you! the Satan bird continued, pointing one of his huge black wings at the Short Eared Owl who stood apart from the other three, shuffling his feet restlessly upon the frozen ground.

'Oh, me? replied the nomad owl. Me, I did nothing. I just dropped by to see if I could get in because it is so cold. I am a media bird, as you know, and I simply have to be there when it happens.

'What do you mean when you say you did nothing? the Satan bird enquired, for the first time raising his eyebrows to show some interest – just a flicker of interest to relieve the boredom of this and so many other routine nights of his eternal duty as the custodian of hell. His only sin on earth had been a personal conflict with the God Bird, and for this difference of opinion he had been condemned for all eternity to manage the dreary, day-by-day and night-by-night administration of his own, self-made inferno.

'I did absolutely nothing! the media bird repeated. I saw a lot, of course. I saw little immigrant owls attempting to poach in the woods – as you rightly said, to keep their families alive – and then being slaughtered by the Tawnies. I saw Barn Owl and Tawny fighting over lines of demarcation between farmland and forest. I saw owls of different species killing one another, and even owls of the same kind fighting each other over some disputed territory. But I myself did nothing. There is no blood on my talons, for I never intervened.

'So you did nothing, ever, to prevent conflict, violence or loss of life? the Satan bird enquired. You did nothing to create understanding among the separate owl species? Nothing to prevent the killing and the violence that you saw?

'That is not my role, the Short Eared Owl replied. My role is to travel and tell stories. Everywhere I go I am well fed, for I have learned the skill of telling each type of owl exactly what he wants to hear. For example, the Tawnies love to hear bad things about the Barn Owls and the Barn Owls love to hear their neighbours the Tawnies described as arrogant barbarians, and of course both species love to hear the little immigrants put down. They like to hear them described as aliens, squatters, feathered vermin, and so on. You see, choice of language is the trick.

'And the Little Owls themselves? enquired the devil bird. What is it that they like to hear?

'Oh, to tell you the truth, I don't visit them very often, the media bird replied. As you know, they are forced to live in no man's land and the pickings there are lean. The fare is so much better in either Tawny or Barn Owl territory.

'So you say you have no blood on your talons? the Satan bird enquired.

'No, but let me in, anyway. Let me in and let me stay until winter has melted into spring. Then I will return to the world of living owls and report favourably on the conditions pertaining here in this very hot inferno that you run. If you like, I will tell the different owl species that I meet that yours is a better place than paradise. You see? You do a deal with a media bird and you will always be all right!

'Come in, oh Short Eared Owl, the Satan bird replied. In my inferno, there will always be room for you!

'The great black bird rose high then into the sky as if to avoid all contact with the media bird as he flew gratefully into the warmth of the blazing forest.

'But remember! boomed the devil bird, as the flames suddenly shot up higher and began to singe the nomad's feathers, Remember that you will never get out of here again. For your sins of omission, indifference and duplicity, you will burn here in agony for all eternity.'

CHAPTER 9

When my mother had finished this story she raised her eyebrows in her complacent, haughty manner and asked me what I thought it meant.

'It means that if Birch does not fight with us, he will go to hell,' I said.

'Excellent!' replied my mother. 'You have understood the message very well. So if Birch refuses to fight with us, tell him the story and the moral will shame him into action!'

'Maybe,' I said. 'But one small problem does occur to me.'

'Yes?' my mother asked, raising those formidable eyebrows once again in what seemed less like an invitation to speak than a challenge, or a warning against any kind of contradiction.

'If Birch declines to fight, I shall of course tell him the story, as you wish. But it strikes me that he might make one very strong objection to the logic of the argument.'

'Which is?' my mother asked, after glancing at my father to judge his reaction to these first disturbing signs of an enquiring mind. Enquiring minds are not welcome amongst our Tawny hierarchy, for thought often leads to disobedience or even mutiny.

'With respect,' I said, 'there seems to be a fatal flaw in the moral of the story. Not from the religious point of view, of course, but a flaw in its effectiveness as a means of persuading a healthy young Tawny to fight against a monster with a weight and wingspan more than three times his size.'

'What is this flaw?' my father asked, calmly, after returning my mother's glance in a manner which suggested he had spotted the weakness too, and had already anticipated what I was about to say.

'Well, the problem here is about going to hell,' I said. 'And whether one wants to get into the inferno or to paradise instead, one can only do so when one is dead. Supposing Birch does not wish to die? What answer will he give me then?'

'You are showing dangerous signs of becoming an intellectual,' my father said. 'And as you well know, Tawny Owl high society tends to frown on them.'

'Be that as it may,' I said, choosing my words very carefully. 'Be that as it may, but given what you have told me about the feud, or vendetta, between Birch's ancestors and our own, if I were in his feathers I would say – or perhaps not say, but think to myself as follows: A monster owl is coming to invade us. My ancestral enemies, those who have usurped and disinherited me, wish me to join with them in fighting it. Why should I? In any case and in all probability, they will be killed. If I join them, I shall also be killed and go to paradise. If I don't commit myself, if I hide somewhere and wait for the monster to move on, I will subsequently be able to take control of the territory, as my forebears would have wished. Listening to the story you have told me, it would seem that much later, when I died, I would have to go to hell. But in your story, that is what all four owls wanted anyway. So why should I object?'

When I'd finished talking there was a long silence as my parents stared at each other and then turned their eyes back on me.

'I cannot dispute your logic,' my father said eventually. 'It may well be that Birch will react in the manner you have suggested. But apart from yourself and from Ferocity, Stoop and Ripper, he is the best fighting owl we have. Therefore your task is to recruit him to our cause. If you wish, you may use the story which your mother has just told you. Conversely, you may use any method you may consider efficacious. The end will always justify the means, as the Little Owls are fond of saying.'

'May I ask a question?' I said, feeling somewhat put down by the way my parents were treating me. 'Having been taught to despise the Little Owls,' I continued, without waiting for permission to go on, 'having been brought up to believe that they were no better than flying scum, or vermin, I have on this fateful night heard two references to what I suppose might be referred to as their culture. First, the word vendetta. Second, this philosophy of theirs which you seem to have embraced and which would seem to mean that the end would always justify the means. Well, with this I have to tell you that I cannot agree. Nevertheless, I will do as you have asked and attempt to persuade Birch to fight with us.'

'How?' my mother asked, submitting me to one of her most glacial stares.

'How?' I replied. 'I will tell you how. I shall explain to him that if he does not fight, Mallow, his mate, will not respect him. I shall tell him that when they breed, their fledglings will be branded from birth as cowards.'

'Do you believe that?' my father asked.

'No,' I said, after a moment's hesitation. 'But then I'm not the one who has to believe it. Birch is!'

'You are right,' my mother said. 'But much will depend on Mallow's attitude. Her influence on him could be decisive.'

'The influence of a female often is,' my father said, glancing at my mother with what I suspected was a touch of irony.

'Well, if she has any sense, she will want him killed,' my mother said, escalating from irony into the dry, sarcastic mode in which she specialized so very well. 'Birch is an abomination, as we all know,' she continued. 'But I repeat that as a fighting owl he has few equals, and if we are to bring down this monster he will definitely be needed. So remember to be very nice to Mallow.'

'I'll do my best,' I said, thinking secretly to myself that the task would not be too difficult, since – in spite of my deep love for May Blossom – I had felt the urge for Mallow on each of the few occasions we had met.

After this long briefing from my parents I slept until twilight, and then, as dusk deepened into night, I flew to the edge of our ancestral territory and down into the neighbouring stretch of woodland which had for centuries been occupied by Birch's forebears. I was about to hoot to announce my arrival when I heard Mallow begin to sing. I guessed she was singing to Birch, and on an instinct I flew down into the branches of a maple tree, perched there silently and listened. Somehow it didn't seem right to interrupt a ballad, even at a time of such dire emergency as this.

I say a ballad, but in fact, as the song developed, it began to sound more like a dirge, or lament. I will now tell the words to the wind and trees, because, as will soon become apparent, the content was to have a profound effect on the rest of my life, and even on the nature of the death that now awaits me. I remember the words more or less exactly, though some of them may have been repeated more or less often than in the rendering I now offer to my silent listeners. I remember the words well, because later, when I asked her, Mallow sang the song again.

> Would you go if they gave a war
> If they gave a war, would you go?
> Before the last big show
> The Barn Owls all said no
> No, they wouldn't go.
> But in the end they did
> And most of them were killed
> But had posthumous honour to show.
> If they gave a war would you go, would you go
> If they gave a war would you go?
> Would you fight for things you were taught to believe
> Would you kill for the sake of your race
> If they gave a war, would you go?
> You would, I know!
> If they gave a war, you would go.
> And *if* you came home you'd have honour to show
> And you'd lack the use of a limb
> But if they gave a war
> You would go, I know.
> If they gave a war you would go.
> And if you came home
> You'd have honour to show
> And you'd lack the use of a limb.

I waited for a while after the song or lament had finished, pondering on the implications of what I'd just heard. I inferred of course that Mallow was singing the song for Birch, that they had heard about the advent of the monster owl, that she thought that Birch would follow the call to war and that my task of convincing him to fight would be simpler than I had imagined.

Subsequent events taught me never to trust inferences again but to go always directly to the source. Had I checked my facts then on that sometime night, the rest of my life might have taken a different course, and after so many winters my coming death might have been a natural one instead of the assassination that I now expect. But at that time I was still young and impulsive and, after only the briefest pause for reflection, I flew into the great oak where Mallow perched.

'I heard you coming,' she said, after we had exchanged the normal greetings. 'Birch is out hunting, but under the circumstances I am sure that he will be back here soon.'

'What circumstances?' I asked.

'The invasion. You see, he guessed you or your father would be coming.'

'So you've heard about it?'

'Of course,' Mallow answered, thereby confirming that the first of my inferences had been correct. As I was soon to discover, it was the only conclusion I had jumped to which subsequently turned out to be true.

As I sat on the branch opposite Mallow and looked into her eyes, I noticed – not for the first time – that in her subdued and modest way, she was most attractive. Mallow was smaller and less assertive and probably less intelligent than May Blossom, but that did not matter, for as I was later to discover almost all other Tawny Owls – male or female – were less assertive and intelligent than the one to whom I was betrothed.

The fact of the matter is that as we sat in the great oak and chatted, awaiting the return of Birch, I began to feel the urge. I was ashamed of myself, but I couldn't help the feelings that I had. 'The feelings you have, you have; and the feelings you don't have, you don't', as one great Tawny poet once put it.

And of course, the issue was made more acute by the fact that May Blossom wasn't there. Like most other owls, we Tawnies are monogamous. Both bigamy and adultery are considered to be sins in the Great God Bird's eyes, and also crimes to be punished by the offended parties in the Tawny Owl community. Be that as it may, as I have just said, I couldn't help the urge and, as I repeat again, it was not my fault if May Blossom wasn't present; as I have frequently had cause to observe, one cannot mate with a bird who is not there.

My unwelcome surge of sexual feeling for Mallow was made more poignant by the fact that I suspected Birch maltreated her. Though an aristocrat, he was the fiercest of all the Tawnies in our local reign, and although female owls have sharp talons I could not imagine how Mallow could defend herself against him if he should choose to abuse her. As we waited for Birch to return, my growing desire to protect her, mingled with the urge, turned my emotions close, I suppose, to that thing called love.

But of course, there was nothing I could do about it. Birch was her mate and according to Tawny lore and tradition there is no such thing as the abuse of a consenting spouse. He arrived as the unwanted urge I felt grew stronger. Settling beside Mallow on her branch in the great oak, he gave me a cold greeting and a most unwelcoming stare. Normally I would have been angered by his rudeness and open animosity, but the urge I felt for his spouse made me feel rather guilty and caused me to react in a friendly rather than a hostile manner.

'I suppose you've come about this invasion by the monster owl,' he said bluntly and at once, before I'd had a chance to state the purpose of my mission. I explained that my father and I were drawing up a battle plan and that all the able-bodied Tawnies in the district would be needed if we were to bring the monster down.

'Well, you can count me out!' he said, immediately and much to my surprise, for after all I had just been listening to Mallow's lament or dirge for a partner who would not refuse to go to war.

'I think you and your father are very foolish,' he continued, with ancient contempt in eyes, which were then still young. 'Those who attempt to fight against this monster will all be killed. The best thing to do would be to hide and let him pass.'

'But where to hide?' I asked. 'We have word that his philosophy is the final solution for all other creatures who fly the sky at night. So where can we hide? We cannot burrow underground like moles. We cannot plunge deep into the water and hide there like a pike. In any case, it is our duty to bring the monster down. Otherwise it will continue to fly north, annihilating all the night creatures in its path.'

'Nonsense!' Birch said, brusquely. 'In my opinion, you and your family have invented this war to give yourselves more prestige and to retain control of the territories you usurped and have malgoverned for many hundred winters.'

I did not react at once to this blatant provocation. I kept my patience, partly I suppose because I was still guilt-stricken by my flowering lust for Mallow. It would be dishonest of me now to say that I remained calm because of the outside threat and because of the mission I had come here to accomplish. However, it did cross my mind that if I responded to the insult and challenged Birch to battle, after the fight there would be one Tawny Owl fewer to defend our territory against the monster.

'The past is another country,' I said, staring at Birch with what I hoped was an icy calm. 'Owl history does not depend on you or me, but our future does. Therefore I suggest that you join us and help to bring this monster down. Otherwise he may return with a mate, breed and proliferate as the Little Owls have done. Then there would be nowhere left to hide. You can fly away, Birch, but from a monster of that kind you can never hide.'

Birch paused for a moment before replying. It was clear that some of what I said was having an effect on him. And also on Mallow, whose eyes had hardly left me as I spoke.

'My advice is this,' Birch said eventually. 'Leave it to the Barn Owls. Let them go to the front line to resist this invasion. That way most of them will be killed and it will save us the trouble of eliminating them later on.'

'Why should we want to eliminate the Barn Owls?' I asked, thinking of May Blossom and remembering that she had hinted at something similar before flying to the city to get knowledge.

'Because as man continues to cut down our woods, and as they continue to build more towns, we shall need the Barn Owl flatlands. You have your ancient woodland territory and I have mine. But what would happen if the men came here and built a town? Where would we go then?'

'That may be a problem some day,' I admitted. 'But at this moment in time, there is a monster on his way to invade, intent on applying the final solution to all creatures of the night. If we don't defend ourselves, there will be no tomorrow, either in these woods or on the Barn Owl farmland.'

Again, I was conscious of Mallow's eyes upon me as I spoke, and it also struck me that Birch's remarks about the Barn Owls might also have applied to my father, myself and all our retainers. If we were killed in this coming war against the monster owl, Birch, his brother and his cousin would be left alive to regain control of our ancient woodland reign.

Birch glanced at Mallow and then stared hard at me. 'No!' he said eventually. 'You talk well, Yoller, but your arguments do not convince me. I shall not fight with you against this invading monster and neither will my cousin or my brother. This I can guarantee!'

'Then you, your relatives and any fledglings you may have will be considered cowards for all time,' I said, reluctantly using my last means of persuasion. I hated doing it, but the monster was coming nearer, we needed Birch, and I remembered what my parents had told me about part of the immigrant philosophy. 'It is the end that justifies the means.'

'If you fight against this monster, you will all be killed,' Birch said. 'And alive, or dead, your opinions are of no consequence to me.'

'Very well,' I said, realizing that my final ploy had failed. 'But remember what I have said. Should we succeed in bringing this monster down – and should we save the district and survive – you and your family will be branded throughout owl history as cowards, as those who hid while others fought to save our ancient community from extermination by an outside threat.'

I left then, after one final glance at Mallow, and flew back up the hill towards what I still believed to be a mountain – the bald hill that towered above the ancestral woodlands in which Birch's family and mine had lived since the beginning of recorded Tawny history.

When I told my father what had happened, he didn't seem in the least surprised or disappointed.

'Well, we had to try,' he said, forming his broad Tawny shoulders into the smallest shrug of resignation. 'Fly now to our loyal subjects, your uncle and your brother, Forster. Summon them here at once, so that we can complete the battle plan, and hurry! You were a long while with Birch, and there is no further time to waste!'

I set off at once, feeling rather guilty that I had paused in the maple tree to listen to Mallow's song. But before I had flown more than a meadow's distance, I heard the cry of a Barn Owl coming from the south, from the direction of the willow where I'd first met Hunter, but now closer and deep inside our woodland territory. I thought it was Hunter's voice but at that distance I could not be sure, so I returned the call, instructing the Barn Owl to wait where he was until I had flown south to identify him and to ask the reason for his presence on our land.

I flew as fast as I could in the direction of the call that I had heard, and presently found Hunter perched high in the branches of a yew tree, some six or seven meadows north of the copse, the willow and the stream. If he had flown so deep into our territory without previously asking for permission, I guessed that this signified an emergency of some kind.

'Welcome to our woods,' I said, as I landed on the branch beside him. 'But I have little time. Tell me at once what ill wind carries you so deep into our forest in the night?'

'I have to cross your territory,' Hunter said at once. 'And I have to warn you at once.'

'About the monster owl?' I said.

'Yes. You have already heard?'

'Of course,' I replied. 'Our intelligence service is second to none. In fact, we had word of this some nights ago, but up until yesterday it was merely rumour. Last night our first refugee arrived, and now we know it's true.'

We stared at each other for a moment or two before Hunter seemed to recover from his fear and told me why he had to fly across our territory.

'I have to warn my younger brother,' he said. 'He is studying as an apprentice to our Bard Owl. Also the poet owl himself must be informed. There is to be an extraordinary meeting of the Barn Owl council, of which he is a member.'

'An emergency meeting, about the invasion?'

'Yes,' Hunter said. 'They will have to decide whether to fight against this monster owl, or not.'

'Tell them they don't have much time,' I said. 'The monster has only one more territory to the south to overcome before he reaches us.'

'What else did your refugee tell you?' Hunter asked.

'The monster is an Eagle Owl,' I said. 'As you well know, this is a species we long considered to be extinct. Its estimated wingspan is approximately three times the size of ours and it can kill almost everything that flies with one stroke of its enormous talons. It takes no prisoners and seems to believe in the final solution, as far as all other owl species are concerned.'

'The final solution?' asked Hunter, who by this time was having some difficulty in concealing the icy fear which I tried hard to hide, but also felt.

'Total extermination,' I replied. 'Complete annihilation of every rival species. No compromises, treaties or pacts of reciprocal agreement such as those which have kept an uneasy peace between Tawny and Barn Owl for more than three centuries.'

'How long?' Hunter asked. 'How long will it be before he gets here?'

'According to our information, he's moving very fast. So fast that so far none of the fallen territories had time to organize effective defences. But the last free territory to the south of here has some very proud Tawny inhabitants. If they decide to fight, it may slow him for a while. Also, their territory is very fertile. There is a lot to look at and an abundance of rich food to eat — hare, pheasant, rabbit and so on. But even so, I don't think he'll stay for long. A barbarian like that is interested in one thing, and one thing only.'

'The final solution?'

'Exactly! So I'd say we could expect him here in two or three nights' time.'

'Where will it end?' asked Hunter, and though he sounded brave and calm I could tell somehow that deep down inside he was as terrified as I was.

'It will end here,' I said. 'We have time to prepare. Not much time, I admit. But we shall stop him here.'

'But surely that's impossible,' said Hunter. 'Our new Owl Owl — the one appointed after Beak Poke's death — says that nothing can stop the monster until he meets another giant, a great white owl who lives far to the north-east of here. He says that the beast you call the Eagle Owl can only be beaten when he reaches the ice and snow, where the kindly white giant will destroy him.'

'What good would that do us?' I asked. 'In the meantime we would all be starving refugees or, much more likely, merely corpses. And our intelligence service has told us that this giant Snowy Owl is just as bad. He's not quite as vicious or as powerful as the Eagle Owl, but in his own way, they say, he's just as big a tyrant and just as interested in total world control. However, your Owl Owl might know something that would help us to draw up the battle plan. Any information about the Eagle Owl could be useful now.'

'I'll do my best,' said Hunter. 'The new Owl Owl will be at the emergency council meeting the night after next. I could have Bardic or my father ask him for you when they meet.'

'So, in a crisis like this, you think it would be in order for a Barn Owl and a Tawny to exchange secret information?' I asked, wondering what my mother and father would think about this conversation I was having with a member of a species that had often been described to me as the enemy within.

'Of course it is in order,' Hunter said. 'In the case of an outside threat like this, all our differences must be temporarily forgotten.'

'That's all very well,' I said. 'But I have heard that your council meetings take all night. I have heard that all the members and the experts discuss every aspect of every issue and nothing is ever decided.'

'That's not true!' Hunter said, clearly stung by the observation I had made. 'It is a system called democracy, which means, among other things, that everyone must be consulted. Then we vote and the majority decides. I must admit that in a case like this, under threat of invasion, it does have its disadvantages.'

'In any case, the night after tomorrow will be too late,' I said. 'The monster may be here by then.'

'Then Bardic is our only hope,' Hunter said. 'If he knows anything I'll report to you when I fly back through here tomorrow night.'

'We shall of course be grateful for any information, but I don't hold out much hope,' I said. 'If this owl Bardic is your head poet, minstrel, or whatever, you can't expect him to be very practical. Artists hardly ever are, whatever species they belong to.'

'You never know,' said Hunter. 'An ancient poem or a ballad from the old days might give some sort of clue to the monster's behaviour pattern.'

'Then let's waste no more time,' I said. 'I'll fly with you to the edge of our territory. I have to enlist two owls there, in any case.'

I took off then and led Hunter swiftly through the woods until the trees began to thin out and you could already catch a glimpse of the open countryside beyond. Just inside the final line of trees I slowed down and landed in an ivy-covered oak.

'You know your way from here?' I asked, as Hunter dropped down on to the branch beside me.

'Yes, I do. My father gave me very clear instructions.'

'Good. It's a long way and a dangerous journey at the best of times. But at least you're flying north, not south, so you won't meet the monster face to face.'

'Let's hope this invasion never happens,' Hunter said. 'But if it does, remember you can count on any help that I can give.'

'You have another choice,' I said. 'You could stay with your brother and with this famous Bard Owl to whom he is apprenticed. Or, better still, you could keep flying north. That way you'd stay two or three nights ahead of the monster. Two, three nights, or even more, because I promise you that even if we don't bring the monster down, we'll put up a better fight than most of the owls he's conquered on his way.'

'No, I'll be back!' Hunter said. 'I am responsible now for Beak Poke's territory and it is my duty to protect it and to stand by the Barn Owl community, my family and my friends. In any case, no one can run for ever. Sooner or later you have to turn and fight.'

'May the Great God Bird fly with you, then,' I said, patting him briefly with my wing. It was the first time in my life that I had touched an owl of any other species. As I left him and flew off to complete my vital mission at dead of night, I wondered what strange impulse had prompted me to show affection to a Barn Owl, one of our sworn enemies. Perhaps it was because in his own spontaneous way he had offered help, though at the time, on that long-vanished night, I did not give much credit to his offer. No, on that night so long ago I did not realize how vital his help would prove to be, and neither did I understand then that I had embarked on a lifelong friendship with an owl of another species – a friendship which, in spite of everything, was to last until his death.

If what I hear is true, his was an honourable death. Mine will be less so. But, partly in memory of Hunter, I shall salvage what remnants of honour I can. Who would ever have thought, so long ago, that the manner of my coming death would have been influenced by a lifelong friendship and affinity with a Barn Owl – and also, to some extent, by the alien's song?

As I flew on that night to complete my mission, I did not understand or realize any of these things. It all came later, much too late, in fact. Which is why I am now branded as a heretic and can tell my story only to the wind, the trees, and to the water that gushes from the rock.

CHAPTER

 10

That night – after I'd said goodbye to Hunter, perhaps for the final time – that night I was shocked by the reaction of certain Tawnies I attempted to recruit. Forster, my brother, and my uncle, Hornbeam, both answered the call at once. It was what one would have expected. But Woody and his brother Nutmeg were both reluctant. Neither of them was either young or strong, and both were considered to be slightly eccentric.

'There's no point in giving a war if you don't win,' Nutmeg said. 'And you stand no chance at all of stopping a monster of this kind.'

Hemlock and his father Vetch both refused point-blank. They had always been isolationist and arrogant and it struck me that night that they must always have resented my father's authority.

'I say welcome to this monster!' Vetch said. 'He will rid us for ever of the immigrants. You say he believes in the final solution? Good! He will rid us of these vermin and help to keep the woodland clean for us.'

'And the Barn Owls,' his son Hemlock said. 'This monster will give them a good going over and save us from doing the same job later on.'

Flying home at early sunrise, I knew I must report to my father that we could count on only half the owls we needed to bring the monster down. I explained the reasons for abstention that I had been given. To my surprise, my father was neither shocked nor disappointed.

'It was ever thus,' he said. 'In times of war the rules are different and only one main rule remains. That rule is called survival.'

'But how can we survive the battle if there are so few of us?' I asked.

'That is what Birch, Vetch, Hemlock and the like are counting on,' my father said. 'They are counting on the fact that we shall be killed and that most of the Barn Owls and the immigrants will be eliminated. Then they and their own will be able to take over the entire territory.'

'Why don't we ask the Barn Owls to fight with us?' I asked. 'Or at least ask them to send a task force to help us.'

As soon as I'd spoken I saw my mother's feathers ruffle and realized that it was not a suggestion she approved of. My father, on the other hand, merely paused for thought.

'It is true that we need more troops,' he said. 'But only troops of quality. Wars are won by brains and courage, not merely by the force of numbers.'

I then told my father about the forthcoming meeting of the Barn Owl council and offered to intercept Hunter on his way back from the mission he had undertaken to warn the Bard Owl and his brother.

'You say they might send a task force,' my father said, after pausing briefly to consider my suggestion. 'In my experience, they are more likely to send a talk force. They will talk all night and then decide nothing. That is the way they are made.'

'But one could try,' I said. 'After all, we are left with no other choice.'

My father glanced at my mother, who gazed back at him

with a haughty and disapproving look, but none the less voiced no immediate objection.

'Very well,' my father said. 'After sunset, fly at once to Beak Poke's territory, tell this young Barn Owl our battle plan and ask him for volunteers.'

'He won't be back by then,' I said, remembering the long mission I had flown for my father. I had expected to be at May Blossom's by midnight but had not in fact arrived there until after sunrise, and even then had almost died in the attempt. 'In fact, judging from my own experience, I don't expect him back till sunrise.'

'You have very little experience of long journeys,' my mother said. 'In fact you have very little experience of anything at all. The timing of long journeys is always unpredictable. Usually, they take longer than expected, but sometimes everything goes well and one arrives sooner than expected.'

'All right,' I said. 'I'll fly to his territory as soon as the sun has set. If I don't find him there, I'll return and intercept him as he crosses our woodland on his way home. But there is one other thing,' I added.

'What's that?' my father asked.

'The battle plan. How can I explain it to Hunter when I have not been told myself?'

'I will tell you at twilight, before you leave,' my father answered. 'While you were away tonight we heard that a second refugee has just arrived. Currently he is resting twelve meadows to the south of here. Apparently he is exhausted and of course in that condition it would be unwise for him to attempt to fly on by day. However, he will be here soon after twilight, just before you leave. I will explain my battle plan to you at dusk, before the refugee arrives, but he may have more information about the monster which will cause me to make changes. If this is so, then you can incorporate these changes in your report to Hunter. Now sleep, for the sun is high and the next few nights will decide our destiny, and you will need all your energy to help us to survive.'

So I slept, and when I awoke at twilight our second refugee had already arrived. He was a strong, handsome bird called Hickory, who at once volunteered to fight with us against the monster.

'He is much bigger and more powerful than you think,' said Hickory. 'In our territory, we tried to bring him down, but we had no proper battle plan and all our troops, except for me, were killed. After the battle, the monster hunted down all those who had not fought against him and slaughtered them one by one. Some had fled before the battle, of course. None to the south or north, but either east or west, in order to avoid the monster's path. So now my territory is peopled only by the dead and by the memories of those who fled in search of safety. I was the last one out.'

'When do you estimate the monster will get here?' my father asked.

'That's very hard to tell,' said Hickory. 'But seeing that there is no further line of resistance between our territory and yours, I'd say he could be here by dawn, or by tomorrow midnight at the latest.'

'Did any of the Barn Owls in your district fight with you?' my father asked.

'No. They raised a small task force of their own, which was immediately wiped out. Some of them went into hiding and a few escaped, but most of them were hunted down, rooted out and put to death.'

'Now listen carefully,' my father said, turning his stately head from Hickory to me, and then back again. 'I shall now give you an outline of our battle plan, which you, Yoller, will explain to your Barn Owl friend if and when you meet him later on tonight. Since so many of our own kind have defected, it is vital to our cause that they provide us with a task force. Vital for us, and vital for them, because it is clear that we must count on numbers if we are to bring this monster down.'

Listening to my father, I was rather peeved. The idea of co-operating with the Barn Owls had, after all, been mine. But Tawny Owl society is hierarchic, which means, among other things, that the father will always take credit for the achievements of his son.

'You will explain to him that if the invasion comes from due south, as we expect, the first place the monster owl will hit will be the Lost Domain.'

'Let's hope so!' I put in. 'At least there's nothing there for him to kill. Except for a few Little Owls, who don't really matter.'

'You are wrong!' my father said. 'There are no Tawnies or Barn Owls there, of course. But there is an abundance of duck, hare and pheasant. My hope is that he will pause there for one or two nights to glut himself on game. If he does, we shall have more time to prepare. But however long he stays, the next place on his invasion path is the Barn Owl territory that lies between the secret forest and Ferocity and Ripper's wood. I believe the present incumbent is a bird called Brook. Tell your friend to warn him. He is especially in danger because I intend to lure the monster across his territory from the Lost Domain and into Ferocity and Ripper's wood. It is there that I intend to bring him down. These two, and Stoop, are the fiercest troops we have, but they do not travel well. They will die to protect their own territory, but abroad they are lost and hesitant.'

Remembering the behaviour of Ferocity and Ripper in the Lost Domain, where they had been sent to conduct the survey, I realized that my father was quite right.

'That means the rest of us must travel to Ripper's wood before the monster hits the Lost Domain?' I said.

'Most of us, but not the decoys,' my father answered. 'If we are to ambush the monster in Ripper's wood, we must be certain that he gets there. So I intend to send a decoy into the Lost Domain to aggravate the monster, who will then pursue him as far as the chosen battleground.'

'What happens if the Eagle Owl catches your decoy on the way?' Hickory enquired.

'Then we shall send another one,' my father said. 'And if he gets killed, we'll have a third decoy waiting to take over and, if necessary, a fourth and fifth as well. When the monster gets to the chosen battle zone he will fly over the wood at well above tree-top height, or so our refugees have told us. His huge wings are much too long and wide for him to manoeuvre through the middle branches of the trees.

'As he reaches their wood, Ferocity, Stoop and Ripper will rise up and ambush him. Their job will be to bring him down among the branches, where the rest of us will stand a better chance.'

I remembered then how ashamed I'd been of Ferocity and Ripper's behaviour in the Lost Domain. Now I was sorry, for if they attacked the monster in the open sky and tried to bring it down, it seemed to me that they would almost certainly be torn to pieces in the attempt.

'What happens if they fail?' I asked.

'If they fail, another three go up.'

'And if they are killed as well?'

'Then we send in a third assault wave. The essence of the battle plan is to bring the monster down among the trees. In the open sky, we stand no chance. The giant thing would pick us off like sparrows.'

'What role in the battle have you planned for me?' I asked, and waited fearfully for his reply. I did not show any fear, of course. That would have been bad form. But now that I am old and soon to die, I can confess to the wind and trees that, as my father paused and looked at me, my heart was fluttering and my stomach churned as if I had swallowed a live toad.

'The third assault wave,' my father said eventually. 'If

Ferocity, Stoop and Ripper fail to bring the monster down, your uncle and his two retainers will fly up into the front line.'

'And then me, with two others?' I asked, surprised at how calm and unafraid I sounded.

'Yes. Which two others I haven't yet decided,' my father said. 'It will depend on how many decoys are killed and how many of your Barn Owl friends volunteer for battle. But in any case, you will lead the third assault wave, because you are the Tawny best equipped for that particular job.'

'And Forster?' I asked, still attempting to sound casual and relaxed.

'Your brother's task is even harder,' replied my father. 'He will be the first – and I hope the last – of our decoys. His job is to fly to the Lost Domain, disturb the monster as he gluts himself on hare and pheasant, and then lead him back across Brook's Barn Owl country to Ferocity and Ripper's wood. If he survives, he will join you as part of the third assault wave.'

'Let me go instead,' I said, suddenly feeling absurdly brave, or fatalistic would be more accurate, I suppose. It was clear that I was going to die in any case, so why not get it over with early in the war and thus give my brother at least some slight chance of life.

My father looked at me and then slowly shook his head.

'No,' he said, eventually. 'I appreciate your valour, but I have chosen Forster as the first decoy because he is the fastest bird we have. Though slighter than yourself and not as strong, he is a fraction quicker on the wing and stands a better chance of staying ahead of the monster and leading him to the point of ambush in Ripper's wood.'

'And my role?' asked Hickory, our second refugee. Outwardly, he seemed as calm as I was, but I wondered whether he, too, might not be suffering from a turmoil deep within. After all, he and our other refugee had actually seen the monster, and seen the monster kill. Quince had gone to pieces and Hickory had not. What did this mean, I wondered. Was it easier to be aware of what you were up against, or was it better to go into battle not knowing the kind of odds you had to face?

'I will decide your role at the dawn of the battle,' my father said to Hickory.

I looked at my father then in much the same way as Hunter looked at me later, when I explained the battle plan. Whilst I admired his ruthless determination and his iron will, I was amazed at his objectivity and at his cold-hearted sense of purpose. Here was an owl prepared to sacrifice his two sons – and probably himself as well – to save Tawny honour and to safeguard freedom of the sky at night, not only for ourselves, but for Barn Owls and Little Owls as well.

At that time, of course, I thought that he was right. The churning in my stomach stopped and I felt brave and free. Brave enough and free enough to give my life for liberty. I wondered how Birch and the other cowards would be able to live with themselves after the coming war. Worse than cowards, they were traitors, and whether we won or lost, honour would be ours and shame would sit upon them for ever more.

Or so I thought then. Now I'm not so sure, and partly for voicing my opinions I have been branded a heretic. But more of that later.

As soon as the sun had vanished below the bald hill, I flew down through our woods and to the copse in no man's land, in search of Hunter. I perched on my favourite branch of the willow above the brackish stream and hooted three times to announce my presence, but no answer came, and for what seemed an eternity nothing stirred in the night sky.

For once my father's judgement had been wrong, I thought. Hunter could not possibly have returned so soon, and in any case, I could have intercepted him as he flew across our woodland on his way back from the north. This was a waste of time! With the monster on its way, my time could have been better spent elsewhere.

Then, suddenly, as I was on the point of leaving the willow, I sensed an owl approaching from our territory. It could have been a Barn Owl, a Tawny or even a little immigrant – at that distance I could not tell. But it was clear that this owl, of whatever species, was responding to my call. But why did he or she come silently, without hooting or screeching – as is customary – to announce its coming?

I watched with rising tension as the bird approached. Could this be the monster, come already? I imagined not, for though I sensed it coming, I could not hear any sound of motion, for it seemed to fly on silken wings. Had it been the monster, then surely the night air would have throbbed with the milling of those giant wings. I turned as the bird entered the copse behind me and saw to my surprise that it was a female Tawny. My surprise grew into astonishment as the silent bird landed on the branch beside me, and I saw at once that it was Mallow.

'What are you doing here?' I asked, without any conventional form of greeting. It seemed that first the tension and then my great surprise had caused me to forget my manners.

'I came to see you,' Mallow said. 'I know you come here sometimes to meet your Barn Owl friend, and tonight I heard your call. I did not answer it, for obvious reasons.'

'What reasons?'

'Well, to start with, Birch,' she said. 'I don't think he would approve of our meeting secretly in no man's land like this, do you?'

'No, I don't suppose he would. But to be quite frank, until now, I didn't know we were.'

'Were what?' asked Mallow, and as she looked at me,

so close this time, side by side on the same branch, her lovely eyes suddenly became more important to me than the invasion and the coming war.

'I didn't know that we were meeting here, secretly, in no man's land,' I said.

'I had to see you. Tomorrow, or the day after, you may be dead. We may all be dead. This may be the last time that we shall ever be together.'

'That would be a pity!' I said, as in spite of myself the urge came upon me and began to rear its ugly head. 'But you and Birch should be all right,' I added, hoping that if I played for time the thing would pass. 'I have been thinking about you and it struck me that you would be safest if you flew to the bald hill and hid inside one of the many hollows in the rock. The bald hill does not lie directly in the monster's path and even if it did, he would be unlikely to find you, hidden deep inside a crevice.'

'Birch has had the same idea,' said Mallow. 'So I suppose that's what we shall do.'

'Strange about Birch,' I said. 'I'd expected him to fight, and clearly so did you.'

'Me? I didn't!' Mallow said. 'I knew he would never fight with you, your father or your brother. He and his family have had a grudge against yours for centuries.'

'Since our war against the Barn Owls, almost three hundred winters since,' I said. 'You would hardly think that a vendetta could survive all those returning blankets of snow and ice and all the melting of it and the coming of the bluebells every spring.'

'He hopes you all get killed,' Mallow confided, looking at me with eyes that were full of a sad, intense feeling that I did not understand. As a matter of fact, I have never understood females very well, though for a time, when more mature, I thought I did. But this illusion did not last for very long, and now, in my third age, I ask myself why the female of the species thinks or feels so differently. I know now that Barn Owl females are different from the males, and as far as I can tell, the same thing applies to the little immigrants. Perhaps this difference applies to all species of animal, from ant to man. I don't know, of course, and now I never shall. And early in the night in the willow tree above the slow-flowing stream the difference didn't seem to matter. What mattered to me then was Mallow and how on earth I could manage to control the growing urge.

'But I don't understand how you knew he wouldn't fight,' I said, still desperately playing for time. 'You see, I heard the song you sang. It was a sad song, almost like a dirge:

'If they gave a war, would you go
Would you go if they gave a war?
You would, I know!

'If you sang like that you must have thought at the time that he would fight.'

Mallow shook her head and looked at me for a long time – an intense gaze or stare which I can never forget.

'Oh, no!' she said, with the liquid look that eyes have before they begin to run with tears. 'Oh, no!' she repeated. 'You see, Yoller, I did not compose or sing that song for Birch. I sang it for you.'

'For me?'

'Of course! I know and everyone knows that you are an honourable Tawny and that if they gave a war to defend our species, you would go. Now, or soon, you are going, and I'm terrified that you may be killed. That is why I am here to tell you that I love you and to say goodbye in case we never meet again.'

'But when did this begin?' I asked, astounded and still trying at the same time to dominate the urge.

'Ever since I met you,' Mallow said. 'You are the most

handsome and intelligent owl in the whole district, and the bravest, too. I adore you, I always have done, and I expect I always will.'

'Then why did you mate with Birch?' I asked, feeling very elated, but also quite perplexed.

'Because you were promised to May Blossom,' Mallow said. 'And in any case, you never even looked at me.'

'Females mature sooner,' I said, remembering something my mother had once told me. 'When I was younger I did not think of love or sex. I wanted to learn to fight and hunt. I wanted to explore our territory. Then I met May Blossom, just at the time when the urge first came upon me. As you probably know, she saved my life, and so I fell in love with her.'

'And you gave your word!' said Mallow. 'All the owls in the district know that when you or a member of your family gives his word, he never goes back on it. That is why I mated with Birch. Because I knew that you would never break your promise to May Blossom.'

'Well, she's not here now,' I said, as the urge within me grew still stronger and that rude part of my body began to dominate my brain. 'She's not here now, and for all I know she may be dead. In two nights' time, I, too, may be dead. In all probability I shall never see either of you again.'

'Then make love to me now,' said Mallow. 'Now, for the first and last time, before the holocaust begins!'

'It is against the rules,' I said, but at the same time moving closer to her on the branch and putting my wing around her shoulders.

'This is a time of war,' she whispered, as I rubbed my cheek gently against hers. 'This is wartime, and in wartime things are different.'

As we embraced and began to make love, very gently, I remembered what my father had said: 'In times of war the rules are different and only one main rule remains. That rule is called survival.'

Well, I survived that night as we made love in the willow tree, and as our loving tenderness burgeoned slowly into passion and then consumed us both like the blazing glare of a noonday sun. Beneath us the brackish waters seemed to quicken and to gush like the mountain stream that I now hear bursting from the rock.

When it was over we stayed on the branch for a long time, our two bodies still intertwined. Looking back on it now, after so many winters, I remember that brief encounter in the willow tree as the sweetest moment of my life, though as I flew home that night I felt full of sin and shame.

I have since come to believe that, like envy, shame and regret are parasite emotions that serve no purpose. In any case, what is done is done and nothing can undo it. So why regret, or shame? They do not help the creature you have damaged, any more than envy will provide you with that special territory or that special tree you covet.

But I was young then and still vulnerable to these parasite emotions. I was also ashamed of having to fly back separately from Mallow. I wanted to take her with me, back to the ancient oak, high up in my ancestral woodland. I could not bear the thought of her returning to Birch and sharing with him what she had just shared with me.

My thoughts and emotions were in conflict as I crossed the woodland and approached my home. My feelings told me to fly straight to Birch, tell him what had happened and claim Mallow for my own. It would probably mean a fight and, though he was strong, even stronger than myself, I knew that he lacked my courage, and I also knew that if I were fighting for Mallow, I might be badly hurt, but there was no way I could lose.

My brain, however, rebelled against this and told me to get on with the vital business of the night. The monster was approaching, we were on the eve of a decisive battle, and selfish matters of the heart must not be allowed to interfere with one's bounden duty. My brain also reminded me of my promise to May Blossom, but the heart refuted this, for it remembered well what she had said: 'It is premature to speak of promises. I shall be gone for a long time and during my absence you may be tempted. If this happens – and if you are sure you have found the right owl – obey your instinct and mate with her.'

'Wait!' my brain replied. 'That is not all May Blossom said. She told you that one day, when your father died, you would probably become leader of the Tawny Owl community in these territories. To do the job properly she warned you that you would need the right partner. She warned you to take care. How can the right partner be the spouse of another owl – and above all the spouse of an owl whose family has been feuding with yours for centuries. If you do this immoral thing, you will merely exacerbate the vendetta and bring even greater disharmony to our district.'

As I approached my parents' home that night, in this state of conflict between heart and mind, I heard a Barn Owl calling from the north, close to the ivy-covered oak in the clearing on the edge of our territory – the place where Hunter and I had last parted. He was clearly on the way back from his mission to the Bard Owl, and it was my duty to collect what information he might have, and also to inform him of our battle plan.

I returned his call at once and flew north towards the clearing and the ivy-covered oak. My brain had won the battle, and the decision I made then was to affect not only the rest of my life, but also now conditions the manner of my coming death. In retrospect, it might have been better if I had obeyed my heart that long-vanished night, and not my brain.

But it is easy to be wise after the event, and no one now will ever know, least of all myself.

CHAPTER

11

'Congratulations!' I said, landing on a branch opposite Hunter in the ivy-covered oak. 'You are back sooner than I expected.'

'I would have been quicker, had our Bard Owl not been so verbose,' Hunter answered. 'I hate to speak ill of my own kind, and especially of the Bard Owl on our council, but I have to tell you that I found him pompous, vain and effete. I don't think he will be a good influence on my brother. He preens himself too much, he talks endlessly, and what he says is always rhetorical.'

'But are they coming to fight?' I asked.

'No!' Hunter said. 'They are coming, but only to witness the battle and then compose an epic ballad for posterity.'

'What good will that do if there is no one left to hear it?'

'My brother asked exactly the same question,' Hunter said.

'And what answer did your Bard Owl give?'

'He said that whatever the outcome of the battle was, there would be Barn Owls left to hear his epic ballad. The most important thing, he said, was to observe history and then render it into art. The monster owl could not possibly kill everyone, he said. Not in this day and age. Only those who opposed him would be killed.'

With an inner shudder I thought of Birch, remembering that he had said much the same thing as this effete and pompous Barn Owl. Only Birch was not in the least effete, and I shuddered again to think what he might do with Mallow, hiding in a crevice on the bald hill while the rest of us fought to ensure his future safety.

'Did he give you any information about the monster owl?' I asked.

'No. At least, nothing useful. He said there were hundreds of old songs and ballads referring to the monster, some as recent as thirty springs ago when there was a great war against him across the salty waters. It seems that very many of our foreign cousins were killed in a dreadful conflict that became known as the war to end all wars. He said that in the end the monster was defeated, but only when he met the snowy giant from the north. Bardic believes the same thing will happen again and that all those who oppose the monster will be wiped out until he reaches the frozen north, where the giant white owl will kill him.'

'Is there nothing in the old songs and ballads that could help us?' I asked. 'We have drawn up a battle plan, but in a war you need as much information about the enemy as you can get.'

'I asked him,' Hunter said. 'But he told me that he was a poet and a minstrel, not a military owl at all. He said that strategy and tactics were best left to the experts and were nothing at all to do with his role as our chief chronicler and artist.'

'A fat lot of use that is, at a time like this,' I said. 'Tell me, does this Bard Owl of yours really believe that the monster will distinguish between combatants, poets and reporters? If he and your brother are in the vicinity, and if we lose, I imagine that the monster will put them to death as well. I don't suppose he'll care much about any epic ballad.'

'My brother Quaver would fight if he could,' said Hunter loyally. 'But he is apprenticed to the Bard Owl and must do as he is told.'

'Did this effete poet of yours give you any idea of what your famous council might decide?'

'He said that in his opinion they would talk all night and then decide nothing. He said that the new Owl Owl would tell us about the genetics and the behaviour pattern of the monster, the Man Owl would tell us what help we might expect from them – from our greatest enemies. Then the Geography Owl would estimate how long it would take for the monster to arrive here and how long it would take him to reach the frozen north where the Snowy Owl would destroy him. The History Owl would then enlighten us about the monster's past and about what might happen in the future, for history repeats itself, or so they say. My father, the Religion Owl, would then be asked to discuss the dictates of ethics and dogma when faced with a conflict of this kind, for as you probably know, it is against our religion to kill any other kind of owl. But according to Bardic, no one on the council will take any notice of what my father says because in these modern times we Barn Owls don't take religion as seriously as we did before. Then the War Owl will estimate the forces at our disposal and advise us whether to fight or to capitulate.

'Bardic says the debate will take at least one night, and possibly two. When it is over, there will be a show of wings and the final decision will be taken. But as my brother Quaver pointed out, it will be too late by then.'

Task force or talk force, I thought, remembering what my father had said. Listening to all this made me proud to be a Tawny. What was the use of all this Barn Owl democracy if in times of conflict you couldn't make decisions?

'So I take it that you're pulling out,' I said. 'It really

doesn't matter. No one asked you to join us in the first place. You volunteered!'

'I'm not pulling out,' said Hunter, angrily. 'I shall bring other volunteers with me, never mind what the council says. I don't know how many – if any – for I am young and don't have much influence. But for what it's worth, you can at least rely on me, personally.'

'Will you go to this council meeting?' I asked.

'Of course not. It's only for elected members, but my father will, and I shall give and get the news through him.'

'Oh, well, just in case you do find any other heroes, I'll explain our battle plan,' I said, and then did so, in some detail. All the while Hunter listened carefully, interrupting me occasionally to ask a question. I must say I was impressed by his courage and intelligence. In a way I was in awe of him, which is strange because I had been brought up to believe that the Barn Owl is an inferior species to ours. Much later Hunter confessed that in that early time he, too, had been in awe of me. How silly when you come to think of it!

Since that long-vanished night I have reflected on all this and reached the conclusion that there are outstanding owls of every species. But most of the others, whether Tawny, Barn Owl or immigrant, are either selfish, cowardly or stupid. Of these three evils I have found stupidity to be the worst. Mine, however, is not a popular view among my kith and kind, and is probably one of the reasons that I have now been branded a heretic.

When I'd outlined my father's battle plan, I paused and waited for Hunter's reaction.

'There won't be enough of us,' he said. 'Your plan is very well thought out, and very brave, but the odds against us are too great.'

'Oh, I don't know,' I said, attempting to sound more calm and casual than I felt, and basically repeating what my father had just said. 'In war, it's often quality that counts. It's no good having a big army or a big air force if the birds in them have no stomach for a fight. I'd rather have a few trained warriors whom I can trust and rely on absolutely than hundreds of amateurs who either change sides or run away when things are beginning to go wrong.

'In any case,' I continued, 'you don't have to fight. You can pull out if you like. Nobody asked you to join us in the first place. You volunteered!'

'I'm not pulling out,' said Hunter, angry again at my second offer to release him from his promise. 'I'm merely expressing my point of view. In my opinion, we don't stand much of a chance.'

'That's negative thinking,' I replied. 'Don't forget that Ferocity, Stoop and Ripper are all trained killers. My brother and I are not quite in their class as ruthless fighters, but I dare say we shall acquit ourselves with some honour. We have it in our blood. We have a great tradition to fall back on and behind us we have the courage and experience of many million winters. Personally, I think that we shall win. And if we don't destroy the monster in Ferocity and Ripper's wood, those of us who survive the battle will go on fighting. We'll fight him in forest, copse and spinney, in no man's land and in your Barn Owl fields and meadows. We'll fight him everywhere, and in the end we'll win.'

'I'm sure I'll find some Barn Owl volunteers to fight with you,' said Hunter, who seemed impressed by my oratory. 'I must leave now, if I am to reach the council meeting in time to give them your battle plan and then to do the necessary recruiting. Will you fly with me as far as the willow in the copse?'

'Of course!' I said. 'And by the way, the willow in the copse reminds me. I was there last night and I spotted that little squatter lurking on your land. Do be a good chap and get rid of her again. My father doesn't like vermin of that kind so close to our territory.'

'I gave her permission to come back,' said Hunter, looking me defiantly in the face. 'I didn't think it mattered any more. Not at a time like this. This is a war, and in wartime the rules are different as you've just said!'

As we took off from the ivy-covered oak and flew across our ancient woodland towards the copse, I did not tell Hunter that these were my father's words, not mine, and I did not tell him that most of our battle plan and strategy for war had been developed by him. I did not tell him then and I have never told him since. I suppose it was because I wanted his approval and esteem. The trouble was that in the epic Barn Owl ballad I am given full credit for the battle plan. Quaver completed his authentic version of the ballad a long time after the war, and by that time my parents were both dead and could not contest it. I should have done, of course. Sooner or later I should have set the record straight. But I never did and now it is too late. Of course, I do not deny that I was once a real hero and that I have made my contribution to both war and peace. However, I should have liked to have been remembered for what I now consider to be my real achievements, or at least my attempts to promote peace and understanding among creatures of the night.

Though vilified now by my own kind, under false pretences I have become a legendary figure in Barn Owl lore and legend.

Soon Rowan and his friends will come to spill my blood. I have a notion that when I hear them coming, I shall fly to meet and fight them in the place where water gushes from the rock. When they have killed me, the stream will wash away my blood and cleanse me at last of my youthful sins of vanity. An odd notion, I admit, but I have faced death many times before, as I did on that night so long ago, before the invasion and the war. I have seen many owls at the extremity of being and noticed that most of them had one thing in common – the desire to believe in something before embarking on the final journey to only the Great God Bird knows where. That long-gone night I had victory and my new love for Mallow to believe in.

Now I have only my memories, the trees, the water and the rock.

CHAPTER 12

'We have more intelligence,' my father said, when I returned home that night after accompanying Hunter to the willow tree. 'A third refugee has just arrived and tells that all resistance in his territory has been put down, or fled. And that the monster is now on his way to the Lost Domain.'

'Will he fight with us, this refugee?' I asked.

'He can't,' my father said. 'The monster caught him a glancing blow as he was trying to flee after they had lost the battle there. The wound is terrible to behold. One wing is half-torn away and half his rib-cage is exposed. And that was just a fleeting scratch from one talon. How he flew this far in his condition only the God Bird knows.'

'Will he survive?' I asked.

'No,' my father answered with a quick shake of his head. 'He will not survive to see another sunrise. And you? What intelligence do you bring from your friend Hunter?'

'The Bard Owl has no useful information for us. He and his apprentice – Hunter's brother Quaver – are now flying to the front line, but only to report on the battle, not to fight. Apparently they intend to compose an epic saga for posterity. In the meantime Hunter is on his way to the extraordinary meeting of the Barn Owl council to explain our battle plan and to ask for volunteers.'

'A fat chance he'll have of getting any!' my mother snorted, with that haughty expression of contempt she wore when referring to any other race of owl.

'Oh, I don't know,' my father said, rather cautiously. 'I once met the History Owl on their council. A brave, intelligent sort of bird he seemed. I mean brave for a Barn Owl. Not brave like us, of course.'

'Don't waste your time in idle speculation about the Barn Owls,' my mother said, impatiently. 'Tell Yoller now about your change of plan.'

'It's not so much a change as a minor modification,' my father said. 'Since the monster is already on his way we have decided to stagger our departure for the battle zone. If we flew as a squadron and he caught us in the open sky above the Lost Domain we would almost certainly be slaughtered. Without the help of Ferocity, Stoop, Ripper and two or three of Hunter's friends, we wouldn't stand a chance. For this reason your brother has already left. He will take up his position on the northern edge of the Lost Domain and wait there until the rest of us have flown past him, one by one or two by two, and reached the assembly point in the clearing just inside Ripper's wood. I shall go next, with Hickory. Then your uncle will follow with his two retainers. You will be the last to leave from this district and your journey will be the most dangerous. For by the time you get there the monster may have ceased feeding on the hare and pheasant in the Lost Domain. But that is a chance we have to take.'

It is a chance *I* have to take! I thought, with an inkling of resentment. But remembering my brother, I said nothing. His was the most dangerous task of all, apart from Ferocity, Stoop and Ripper's role, of course. I wondered at the iron will of my parents who seemed willing to sacrifice both their sons to the Tawny cause.

However, this was the code. You led from the front, by example, or else you did not lead at all.

'Before leaving you will accompany your mother to the bald hill and find suitable shelter for her there,' my father continued. 'Remember that if the monster passes this way he will attack from the air, and though it goes against our nature to hide in crevices underground, in this case it would seem the most sensible solution.'

'Like Birch?' my mother said with great pride and contempt. 'You want me to go to ground like that miserable coward? No, thank you very much! I shall remain here, in my ancient oak. If the monster passes this way, he can have my body, but he cannot take away my dignity and pride. In any case I, too, must set an example to the lower classes.'

'Frankly, that's a load of sparrow shit!' my father said, surprisingly, for he seldom if ever swore. 'I'm in charge of this war, and for once you will do as you are told!'

'Oh, very well, then,' my mother said, with a sigh of resignation and a haughty little shrug. 'I will do as you command, but I want it to go on record that I protested.'

'On or off the record, my dear, nobody who knew you well would doubt it,' said my father, with the flicker of a smile. 'Now, Yoller, my son, I am leaving! Take your mother to the bald hill and find a safe place for her there. We two will meet again, before sunrise in Ripper's wood.'

My father touched my mother very briefly with one wing, and then took off from his favourite branch in our ancestral oak and flew south through the forest in the direction of the Lost Domain. It was a poignant moment. I must confess that I never really liked my mother – at least not since I was a fledgling. All fledglings love their mothers, I suppose, whether they be Tawnies, Barn Owls or even toads. But since reaching adolescence I had found her increasingly intolerant, tyrannical and snobbish. Now, as we perched opposite each other in the great oak, I felt a

125

flood of affection for her. I suppose the source of this flood of emotion was the sudden realization that we might never meet again, and though at times I found her infuriating, I would much rather have had her alive than dead.

With her survival as my purpose, I took off with her and flew across the rising woodland up to the bald hill. Of course, I hoped I might see Mallow there as well, perhaps for the last time. But this was not to be. If she and Birch had already evacuated, there was no sign of them. On the bald hill nothing stirred, and I wondered how many creatures had already gone to ground.

I found my mother suitable shelter in a narrow crevice just below the crest of what at that time I still thought of as the mountain. The entrance was narrow, and she complained that there was barely room for her to squeeze in.

'I shouldn't complain if I were you,' I said. 'It may be uncomfortable, but it's safe! With its giant wingspan, the monster will never flush you out of there.' Seeing her so cramped and undignified inside her crevice, I forgot her selfishness and arrogance and felt sorry for her. Which was odd, really, when one comes to think about it, for she had found an impregnable bunker and safe shelter, while I was the one about to fly to the front line.

'Goodbye, Mother!' I said, as I looked at her for one final time. To my astonishment, I saw that there were tears in her eyes. It was the one and only time that I ever saw her crying.

'Come back soon!' she said, and then turned her head away from me and faced the far crevice wall to hide her tears.

I took off then and flew down the bald hill into the forest and perched for some time in my own oak to say goodbye calmly to my beloved home before I flew off to come to terms with destiny.

I know that my silent listeners may find this passage

sentimental and perhaps even self-indulgent as opposed to Romantic, or truly dramatic, but then the water and the trees never have to fly into battle, as I was to do at dawn the next day. The water flows till man comes to dam it, or else trap its free flow with his false lakes. The trees wait, sighing and moaning in the wind until man comes to cut them down. Only the wind itself seems to be completely free, but for how much longer no one can tell.

As I said goodbye to my ancestral home and prepared mentally to fly into battle, the storm broke. It hit our woodland suddenly, like a thunderbolt. One moment the night sky was serene and the next it throbbed and shimmered as the thunder broke. Forks of lightning flashed and lacerated the night sky with scars of a vivid red, the likes of which I had never seen before and have never witnessed since. The giant oak in which I perched shook with the violence of the storm, the night sky opened, and torrential waters cascaded down and for a while threatened to flush our ancient woodland down from the high hills and into the Barn Owl fields and meadows far below. I learned later that Vetch's elm had been struck by lightning and that he and his son, Hemlock, had been incinerated amongst the blackened, withered branches.

Later I also learned that the storm had been local and had burst only above our wooded hills. Those of the Tawny task force already flying across the Lost Domain said that they could see great weals of fire searing the night sky above the homes they had been forced to abandon, and they feared for those of us who were left behind and must weather the lashing of the storm. It was like a portent, they said later: a portent of the invasion and the coming war. At times like this, I thought as I half-drowned, not under water but high above the ground, even a proud Tawny Owl could come to believe that life was somewhat overrated; at the very best, one might say, a joke in rather dubious taste. At times like this one could not help thinking that it might have been better to have remained trapped and hidden in one's mother's womb.

Cathartic and violent as it was, the tempest did not last for very long. Long enough to kill Vetch and Hemlock and long enough to drench me through every feather and right down to my skin – but then it lifted as suddenly as it had come, and I realized that it was time for me to take off and fly to the front line.

I crossed our woodland territory, resisted the temptation to rest for a while in no man's land, on my favourite willow branch above the brackish stream, and flew on deep into the territory that had once been Beak Poke's and now belonged to Hunter. Of course, Hunter himself would not be there. He had flown along the same route I took now, down from our woodland, across the copse, across his own fields and meadows, past the outskirts of the village and then deep into the Lost Domain. From the Lost Domain, unless the monster had intercepted him, he would have flown further across the territory belonging to the Barn Owl called Brook, through Ferocity and Ripper's wood and then on to his father's territory, where the Barn Owl council meeting was to take place.

Knowing this I was surprised to sense the presence of another owl either in or close to the abandoned farmhouse that had once been Beak Poke's and now belonged to Hunter. For a moment or two terror seized me. Thinking it might be the monster who had paused there to shelter from the storm, I dived into an elm about half a meadow's length from the abandoned building and listened carefully to the vibrations from within.

I soon realized that the creature was actually inside the building, and that it was much too small to be a monster. Then the alien began to sing her song, and though she and her lungs were small, the rich sound of her song filled the night sky with a melody the likes of which I'd never heard before. I thought it more haunting even than Mallow's song, and for the most obvious reasons Mallow's song meant everything to me. These are the words of the song, as far as I remember them. Some of the lines she repeated, for musical effect. I do not remember which lines these were and so now to my silent listeners, the wind and the trees, I will merely tell the essence of the thing.

Eyes of the Barn Owl yours
Eyes of the alien mine

Barn Owl and alien
We fly the same sky at night
And our souls, our two souls
Intertwine

Love knows no class
No class or race
Only the stars
The stars and the moonlight
Give us time and space

Eyes of the Barn Owl yours
Eyes of the alien mine
Why can't it be?

Barn Owl and alien
We fly the same sky at night
Why should tradition
Deny us the right?

We share the same sky
We live for the same sad time together
Why can't we share it in every way
And steal a little time together
When both of us some day,
Some day must die

> Eyes of the Barn Owl yours
> Eyes of the alien mine
>
> Don't ask the reason why
> Why love can always overcome
> But love will always find a way
> To bring us both together
> To leave us free to fly
> Under the same sky
> And I shall always love you
> Love you till I die
>
> And I shall always love you
> Love you till I die

This last line had a most moving, dying fall which I find almost impossible to describe. She clung to the last word like this: 'die -aye-aye-aye-ay!' The melody hung on the night air in the calm after the storm, while through the branches I could see the stars and the moonlight which gave her the time and space for this illicit love affair with Hunter.

I was shocked, of course. To be frank, I would never have suspected such a thing, not even from a Barn Owl. A liaison with a little immigrant? It was unthinkable, even more unthinkable than the act I had just performed with Mallow. I had sinned, yes, but Mallow was of the same species after all! What would happen if Hunter and this tiny alien mated? Could they produce a fledgling, and if so, what kind of hybrid or mutation would it be?

Shocked, I sat on the elm branch for some moments after the song had finished. I did not want to meet the little squatter, but if I flew on above Hunter's farmhouse I knew that she would sense my presence and perhaps intercept me to get news of him. I wondered about making a detour, but realized that there wasn't time. Due to the storm, I was already late, so I took off and flew directly on my course, rising high above the abandoned farmhouse to avoid any contact with the immigrant. But she must have sensed my presence, for as I flew high above the abandoned shack, she was there waiting for me in the path she knew that I must take. At this time I did not know that the aliens could fly so high, and the sight of her ragged little body hovering in front of me was disturbing, to say the least. I could have killed her, of course – killed her and flown on by. But I was flying over Barn Owl territory, not my own, and I had just heard her haunting song. So I stopped and hovered high in the sky opposite her, wondering how Hunter or any other Barn or Tawny Owl could be attracted in any way by an untidy, unruly little squatter such as this.

Then she bounced towards me across the night sky in the characteristic hopping manner of the Little Owl and came face to face with me as I hovered there, uncertain what to do. It was then that I saw her eyes for the first time. And when I saw them, though still shocked, I began to have an inkling as to why Hunter found this little creature so attractive.

> Eyes of the Barn Owl yours
> Eyes of the alien mine!

Well, the eyes of this small alien were in their own way as evocative and haunting as her song had been. In the moonlight on that fatal night, her eyes appeared to have the colour of the sea. I had never seen the sea then and neither have I since, but I had heard of it, and imagined the colour as a deep blue-green, with flecks of hazel caused by the ripple of the waves. This is how the alien's eyes appeared to me that night – less beautiful than Mallow's, but in their own way eloquent and haunting, too, at hidden depths.

'You are flying to the front line?' she asked. 'Across the Lost Domain to Ferocity and Ripper's wood?'

'Yes.'

'Then let me come with you. I want to help you and the Barn Owl volunteers to bring this monster down.'

'I am afraid that is out of the question,' I said. 'As far as I know, there is no record of any Tawny Owl flying anywhere with an immigrant like yourself.'

'Then let us create the precedent,' she said. 'It could be the beginning of a new form of co-operation between our separate races.'

'I don't think my father or any other important Tawny would much care for that,' I said.

'Neither would my own kind,' the little squatter said. 'But we could both set them an example here, tonight. We could unite in the face of an outside threat.'

For a moment or two I hesitated. In one way the idea was not unattractive. One would not have cared to fly across the Lost Domain alone even at the best of times, and with the monster already lurking somewhere by the lake, or in the secret forest, the prospect was even less appealing.

'What is the attitude of your species to this war?' I asked, hoping to gain time.

'They think the giant owl will wipe you out.'

'Is that what they are hoping?'

'I suppose most of them do hope so, yes. I suppose they think that if there are fewer Barn Owls and Tawnies left, there will be more space and food for them.'

'And how do they propose to protect themselves from this invasion?' I asked.

'Most of them will go to ground, or else hide in hollow trees where the entrances are too small for the monster to get in, or else in the nooks and crannies of abandoned buildings in no man's land, where they say the monster will not fly.'

'Then why don't you do the same?' I enquired.

She looked at me for a long time with those deep and seeming sea-green eyes. 'I've told you,' she said eventually.

'I want to help to defend us all against this monster.'

Looking at her small and busy body as she fluttered in the sky in front of me, I wondered what possible contribution she could make in this coming battle against the monster. I was tempted to say as much, but I didn't. It seemed rude. And yet could one be rude to a little immigrant? The concept was a new one and took me by surprise. Up to that night I had always imagined that the only response to these aliens was to insult them, kill them or drive them off one's land. But she, after all, had volunteered to fight, and apart from Ferocity there were no female Tawny Owls in our contingent. If I were killed or badly wounded in the dawn battle, there would be no Mallow, no May Blossom and no mother to staunch my wounds or to comfort me in my dying moments. Yet this little alien was willing to fly with me and face an almost certain death.

'Why?' I asked her. 'You are a female and in any case rather too small to fight. Why do you really want to come to the front line?'

She looked at me with those eyes – alien eyes – which by some trick of moonlight had lost the blue and become translucent hazel and sea-green. She looked at me for quite some time, and seemed to be making up her mind as to whether she could trust me with her true reason for volunteering when the rest of her kind had gone to ground.

'I want to see Hunter again,' she said. 'I want to see him one more time before he dies.'

'What is your name?' I asked.

'Alba. And you are Yoller, commander-in-chief of the Tawny task force.'

'No, I am number two. My father is commander-in-chief, and I very much doubt whether he will allow you to enter Ferocity and Ripper's wood.'

'You can ask him when we get there,' Alba said.

I hesitated and looked once again into those pleading, alien eyes. 'All right,' I said eventually. 'But remember, I can't guarantee anything.' She nodded and gave me a warm, grateful smile. I took off at once, and she followed me with that funny, bouncing flight of hers as we headed through the night sky towards danger and the Lost Domain.

Much later, when his heart was breaking, I told Hunter I had heard the alien's song. Had I told him sooner things might have been different. But I didn't, and that was another sin of omission that I now wait to expiate.

Part Two

A time to love, and a time to hate; a time of war, and a time of peace.

Ecclesiastes, Chapter III, Verse 8

Alas, that Spring should vanish with the Rose!
That Youth's sweet-scented Manuscript should close!
The Nightingale that in the Branches sang,
Ah, whence, and whither flown again, who knows!

The Rubáiyát of Omar Khayyám, Verse 72
Done into English by Edward Fitzgerald, 1859

Armée étrange aux cris sévères,
Les vents froids attaquent vos nids!
Vous, le long des fleuves jaunis,
Sur les routes aux vieux calvaires,
Sur les fossés et sur les trous
Dispersez-vous, ralliez-vous!

Strange army with your stern cries, the cold winds are assaulting your nests! You — along yellowed rivers, over the roads with their old Calvarys, over ditches, over holes — disperse! and rally!

Les Corbeaux
Jean-Nicolas Arthur Rimbaud, 1854–1891
Prose translation by Oliver Bernard, 1962

CHAPTER
13

In his epic ballad Quaver has rendered well the eerie atmosphere in the Lost Domain that night. Of course, he was well able to describe it, for he had flown across not long before, accompanied by his teacher, the foppish Bard Owl.

As Quaver put it in his poetic manner, it was as if all the creatures of the night had burrowed deep into whatever hide-out they could find, waiting with baited breath for the apocalypse to come. It was as if a giant, evil presence overshadowed all the Lost Domain, and as if all the living creatures there were struck dumb and petrified by the monster's presence. We skirted wide around the great house and flew on across the lake and up through the parkland into the secret forest. Even here we did not pause to rest, though I could tell the little alien was tired and had to strain herself to the very limit to keep up with the steady beat of my more powerful and much broader wings. Though I wasn't flying flat-out by any means, I could have slowed down to make things easier, but to be quite frank I didn't dare. There was something uncanny about the stillness in the secret forest that made me more frightened than I had ever been before.

I did slow down a little when we finally flew across the last line of trees and emerged into the open country that lay between the limits of the Lost Domain and our trysting place in Ferocity and Ripper's wood. Alba drew alongside me then, and I felt sorry that I had not slowed my pace before, for the little creature looked exhausted. We flew on steadily, in silence, until in the distance we could see the outline of Ferocity and Ripper's wood, where I knew my father and my comrades would be waiting. The thought of their presence relaxed me and, though the dreadful fight was still to come, I somehow felt the worst part was already over. Die, I might, at dawn, but I would not die alone. At least, that is what I thought until little Alba gave a sudden stifled cry.

'What is it?' I asked, hoping she wasn't about to have a heart attack or some other inconvenient illness now that we had so nearly reached our destination.

'Look!' she said, half-choking as she spoke, and pointing down to the meadow with one rounded wing. I looked down, and what I saw below me made me sick. In spite of the shock and the nausea that this ghastly sight provoked, I forced myself to drop still further from the sky, and then to land on the spot where the carnage had occurred. To do her credit, little Alba came with me, though even an alien could not have been immune to the sight that met our eyes. Bits of the Barn Owl known as Brook were scattered everywhere. He had been decapitated and his head lay separately, some distance away from the torn trunk of what had once been his body. One mutilated wing remained half-attached to the body, while the other lay presumably where it had been severed – close to the dead body of Brook's mate, whom I never knew and whose name I no longer remember. Her corpse was still intact, but slit down the middle from the top of her chest to the very bottom of her stomach. One wondered at the size and power of a talon that could cut a healthy Barn Owl in half with one single blow.

I glanced at little Alba and saw in the moonlight that, although an alien, she was deeply moved by the sight of these brutal deaths. Or perhaps she was merely frightened, I don't know. At any rate, she looked at me with those haunted eyes, which now appeared to have turned from hazel-green to yellow. Whether this was the result of fear or compassion, whether that was the true colour of her eyes, or whether the whole thing was merely a trick of moonlight, I shall never know. All I knew then was that the scattered remains of Brook and the sundered body of his mate were real enough. So real that in spite of myself I had to vomit.

'Please, can we go on now?' asked Alba, after waiting for me to collect myself again. 'I can't bear to be perched here looking at these bodies.'

'Wait a moment,' I said, for my nausea had not prevented me from thought. In fact, possibly because of the horror and the danger, my brain was now racing at twice its normal pace.

'What does this mean?' I asked.

'It means the monster is already here,' she replied, looking perplexed and obviously not following my as yet silent train of thought.

'Yes, of course he's here!' I answered. 'We knew that already. But where is here and where is there?'

'I don't understand you.'

'Don't you? Then let me ask you this. Is this spot where we now perch north or south of the Lost Domain?'

'North.'

'Exactly! And our intelligence service tells us that the monster is flying on a direct path from south to north. He's been here, so what happens next?'

'He flies north,' the alien said.

'And which is the next place north of here?'

139

'Ferocity and Ripper's wood.'

'Yes, so if the monster has followed his predictable pattern, he is already there.'

'There, where we are going?'

'Yes!' I said.

We looked at each other for quite some time in silence. It would have been useless for me to have pointed out what would have happened to those of our forces already assembled there. There were too few of them. They would have been wiped out and Alba knew it. She also knew what would happen to the two of us if the monster was still there. Looking at the corpses of Brook and his mate, it wasn't difficult to guess.

'Do you want to go back?' she asked, eventually.

'No. I can't. I am expected in the front line and I must go, whether the battle is already over, or not. But you can go. Go back into the Lost Domain or, better still, go to Hunter's farmhouse. You should be safe there. It is unlikely that the monster will turn back from his chosen path.'

'No! I'm coming with you. It could be suicide, I know. But I told you, I want to see Hunter again one more time before he dies.'

'He may be dead already.'

'That is a risk I have to take.'

'Very well, if you insist,' I said.

'There is another reason.'

'What's that?'

'Even if I did go back, hide and somehow survive this war, some day the monster would come back. And what should I do then? Some day I want to have chicks and I want those fledglings to enjoy the freedom of the sky at night. I'd rather die now in an attempt to bring the tyrant down than live for the rest of my life in fear and trembling.'

I looked at this little creature and, seeing the blend of fear and passion in those alien eyes, it occurred to me how odd it was that, in spite of being a squatter condemned to live in no man's land, she had just expressed exactly the same feelings about this invasion as had my father.

'Very well,' I said again. 'Let's go. But be it on your head!'

So we took off then and flew onward across the dark Barn Owl meadows towards the looming outline of Ferocity and Ripper's wood. As we approached the woods, I thought of the slaughter I had just seen and of the carnage that was still to come. I also thought of the little alien flying by my side. How strange it was that on what was probably the last journey of my life my companion was not Mallow, whom I loved, not May Blossom, to whom I was betrothed, but an immigrant and an outcast who was in love with Hunter. That night, flying towards almost certain death, I pondered on the complexities and ironies of love. By some chance of fate I remain to tell the story of these loves, but soon I, too, shall be gone. And if anyone remembers the passion of our youth, it will not be Mallow, little Alba or May Blossom. As the great modern Tawny minstrel sang:

'I have heard the skylarks singing each to each. I do not think that they will sing to me.'

That night, in my golden youth and on the eve of battle, I thought that one day they might. One dawn or twilight, I thought the skylarks might sing to me. But they never did, and sadly now they never will.

CHAPTER

 14

Arriving on the outskirts of the wood, I sensed at once that all was well – or, at least, not entirely well, but much better than might have been expected. Leaving Alba to wait in a birch tree on the borders of the wood, I flew on for a meadow's distance through the trees until I came to the clearing where our contingent was assembled. It is at this point that my story – or history – must differ substantially for the first time from the account given in Quaver's epic ballad.

According to his version, I was already aware of the fact that both our refugees had been intercepted and killed by the monster as they flew across the Lost Domain. He also relates that I had reported this to Hunter before he flew to the Barn Owl council meeting in search of volunteers.

This is not true! When I arrived in the clearing that night I had no idea which, if any, of our forces had arrived. The first owls I saw were Ferocity, Stoop and Ripper, sitting in their favourite oak. To be more precise, I should qualify that and say that they were not so much sitting or perching, but rather lurking there among the branches with venomous intent to kill. For the first time since seeing Brook's dismembered body, the sight of them gave me some kind of hope. All powerful as he must be, the monster might have hesitated had he seen those three atavistic creatures waiting there to ambush him.

Next I saw my father sitting in the elm which he had adopted as his front-line headquarters. I flew to him at once and asked how many of our troops had made it across the Lost Domain.

'Not all,' my father said. 'Sadly we have lost both the refugees. The first one is missing, presumed dead, and Hickory was intercepted as he flew across the lake. The monster apparently killed him with one single blow.'

'Where did you get this information?'

'From your brother. He was close behind and saw it happen. He says, incidentally, that the monster is not only bigger than we had supposed, but also flies much faster. To lure him here from the Lost Domain we are going to need more decoys than I had expected.'

'Where is Forster now?' I asked, anxiously scanning the surrounding trees for some sign of my brother.

'Back in the Lost Domain, waiting to flush the monster out before the dawn.'

'There's something I don't understand.'

'What's that?' my father asked.

'Well, when we flew across the Barn Owl territory immediately to the south of here, we found the corpses of Brook and another Barn Owl, presumably his mate. Or to be more precise, we didn't find Brook's corpse so much as bits of him scattered all over the place.'

'Who is we?' my father asked. 'As I perceive it, you are sitting on that branch alone.'

I hesitated then, realizing that I had betrayed myself by use of the plural. I have learned since what my father knew then. I have ascertained that one can learn a great deal by listening to how an owl uses pronouns. I, we, us and them can tell you a great deal about hidden attitudes and feelings.

'I flew here with an alien,' I replied, and then went on to tell my father about little Alba and her desire to see Hunter again one more time before he died.

'Out of the question!' my father said, when I had finished. 'Firstly Ferocity and Ripper would never allow an alien on their land . . .'

'You could overrule them,' I interrupted impulsively. I would normally have let my father finish, but on that fatal night form and etiquette seemed slightly out of place.

'I could, of course,' my father said, nodding, and not even seeming to notice that I'd been rude. 'I could overrule them, but that would set a precedent. After the war there would be little vermin swarming all over our Tawny territories. And if I did let the creature in, what would your mother say? You know she feels more strongly about the squatters than even you or I do.'

'She may never know,' I said, and then pointed out that if we were all annihilated by the monster, the fact would be of no consequence. Not only would my mother never be aware of it, but neither would any of the creatures that survived. They might find the corpse of a Little Owl among the other bodies strewn about the wood, they might speculate as to how she got there, but they would never ever know.

'Wait!' my father said, suddenly seeming to undergo a change of mind. 'You said this little alien was prepared to fight.'

'I did. I told you she has much the same views about the invasion and the aftermath as you do.'

'That's all very well,' my father said. 'But you know it is against the rules for a Tawny to consort with aliens or squatters. By bringing her here, you have placed me in the most embarrassing position.'

'You said that in wartime the rules were different,' I replied. 'And if you had seen Brook's dismembered body, you would realize that we need every claw and talon we can get. Even those of a funny little alien!'

'Actually, I've heard they are quite fierce,' my father said. 'I've never killed one myself, but those of us who have all say they put up a good fight.'

'Then let her come in,' I said. 'If we succeed in bringing the monster down, she can help to kill it when it's entangled in the middle branches of the trees.'

'No, I have a better idea,' replied my father. 'She can act as an extra decoy. I told you we would need more than I had imagined.'

'She can't fly fast enough,' I protested. 'You know these aliens have short, rounded wings. She would be overhauled at once and killed.'

'Well, she has the advantage of being utterly expendable,' my father said. 'If she agrees to act as a decoy, I will overrule Ferocity and Ripper and allow her into this clearing to say goodbye to her Barn Owl friend before the battle commences. However, no Barn Owls have yet appeared, and neither has your uncle or either of his two retainers. If no one else turns up, we shall have to manage with the troops we've got, including your little immigrant. But though I am an optimist, and though I believe in positive thinking, as things stand, my son, I think you should prepare to die.'

'I've been preparing to die for quite some time,' I replied, playing for time, for I was sure that sooner or later Hunter would arrive. He had promised, and even though he was only a Barn Owl, he struck me as the kind of bird who kept his word.

'You haven't answered my question yet,' I continued, as my father prepared to fly off and tell Ferocity and Ripper that in the interests of victory they must for a short time tolerate a little alien on their land.

'What question?' asked my father.

'The question I asked you before we began to talk about

the alien – the question of the monster's path. If his route of destruction lies from south to north, why did he turn back again after murdering Brook and his mate? From the state of their bodies I calculate they were killed soon after midnight. If he'd continued on the flight path we'd expected, he'd have got here well before I did, and those of you now assembled here would all be dead.'

'For that we must thank Forster,' my father said. 'He saw the monster overhaul and kill Hickory in the Lost Domain. Then he realized that the giant owl was proceeding north immediately, without taking advantage of the hare and pheasant he could have butchered and then devoured in abundance in the Lost Domain. Your brother followed the monster, hoping somehow to overtake him and warn us that he would reach Ferocity and Ripper's wood before our forces were fully assembled and we were ready for him.'

'Following the monster? That was brave!' I said.

'True courage,' agreed my father. 'In any case, following, he saw the giant fall on Brook's mate and murder her. According to Forster, Brook attempted to defend her and was torn to pieces, as you saw. However, while this was going on, your brother flew past them unobserved and came on here to warn us. We decided at once that the only hope of survival was for Forster to fly back and try to lure the monster south again to the lake in the Lost Domain where he might be tempted to feast for a while on duck and on the wild geese that are often found there.'

'Did he succeed?'

'I don't know,' my father said. 'Only time will tell. If he did succeed, he will attempt to lead the monster here at the appointed time. However, it is desperately important that we send out other decoys to take over from him in relay from the edge of the secret forest, across Brook's Barn Owl territory to this wood where the killer will be ambushed. Go at once and tell your alien that she may wait for Hunter in that sycamore on the far side of the clearing. But tell her that as a condition for creating this precedent, we require her to act as one of our decoys over open Barn Owl country. Tell her also that she must take up her position as soon as we get the first warning of the fact that the monster is about to leave the Lost Domain. If Hunter has not arrived by then, it will be too late for any final meeting between them. The whole thing is in any case obscene. Who ever heard of a Barn Owl mating with an alien?'

> Eyes of the Barn Owl yours
> Eyes of the alien mine

I heard Alba's song running through my head as my father finished speaking but, since I no longer had any choice, I nodded and set off for the edge of the wood where I had left the little immigrant perched hopefully in the birch tree. But as I flew the short distance through Ripper's wood to the place where she was waiting, other parts of her song came back into my mind.

> Barn Owl and alien
> We fly the same sky at night
> Why should tradition deny us the right?
> We share the same sky
> We live for the same sad time together
> Why can't we share it in every way
> And steal a little time together
> When both of us some day
> Some day must die.

Oh well, I thought, as I landed on a branch of the birch tree opposite the one on which she was sitting, at least the last line seems appropriate for all of us tonight.

'My father has granted you permission to enter Ripper's wood,' I said. 'Normally he, Ferocity and Stoop would tear you to pieces, but under our protection you will be quite safe.'

'Thank you!' Alba said, and her eyes, now hazel-green again, were eloquent with gratitude.

'However, there is one condition,' I added immediately, and then hesitated. I thought of Hunter and then of Mallow, and all at once it struck me as quite wrong to send even an unwanted alien to certain death in exchange for one final meeting with her illicit lover.

'Yes, tell me!' she said eagerly. 'I will do anything.'

That clinched it! This eagerness for sacrifice and death in the name of liberty and love suddenly seemed too much for me. This time I thought of my brother, Forster, whom I suspected I should never see again. I thought of his strong young body, which would shortly be hacked to pieces like poor Brook's, and the whole business of this war and the coming battle began to pall on me to say the very least!

'The condition is this,' I said, lying with what I hoped was a certain, suave aplomb. 'In exchange for being allowed to meet with Hunter on our land, you must help us kill the monster once we have brought him down among the trees. There may not be many of us left by then, and we shall need all the help we can get.'

She smiled at me then. It was such a lovely, radiant smile that for a moment or two I almost forgot that she was not a Tawny.

'Of course I'll fight!' she said. 'I already told you so, didn't I?'

'Very well, then,' I said, using my father's favourite expression. 'Come with me. But don't speak to any of the other owls, especially not the Tawnies. Above all avoid Ferocity, Ripper and my father. You may speak to Hunter and to Hunter only, if and when he gets here, which is now looking more and more doubtful as the night goes by.'

'He will come!' said Alba, firmly. 'If Hunter says he will do something, then he does it.'

'I only hope you're right,' I said. 'As it is at the moment we're well below the strength required. At any rate, we'd better go and see. The night wanes and there is little time left to finalize our plans.'

'Just one more thing before we go,' she said.

'Yes?' I asked impatiently.

'Please don't tell Hunter that I've volunteered to fight.'

'Why not?'

'Because he would not allow it. He told me on no account to come here, but to fly east instead, in search of shelter.'

'Now you tell me this? For the Great God Bird's sake, I thought I was doing him a favour!'

'Don't be angry with me!' Alba said. 'Just promise not to tell him. But you know as well as I do that you're going to need all the help you can get.'

As I flew back to the clearing with Alba, I was astonished to find myself treating an alien and an immigrant as an ally. I was also worried to death about what to tell my father – about what excuse to make for not using Alba as a decoy. Perhaps I could tell him that she had strained a wing on the long flight across the Lost Domain and as a consequence was now lame. I could have told him that she was pregnant, but I knew that wouldn't do. He did not share my mother's passion for anything connected with the process of reproduction, not even in the case of his own kith and kind, let alone what might be taking place in the womb of an unwanted alien.

By the time we reached the clearing, I still had no idea what I must say. However, I led Alba to a sycamore well away from my father's operational headquarters in the elm, and also as distant as possible, of course, from Stoop, Ferocity and Ripper. I then rejoined my father, praying that last-minute inspiration would provide me with some suitable excuse. I remember that the whole thing was rather getting to me at that time. I realized how fond I was of my brother. The thought of Mallow drove me to distraction, and I could hardly wait to mate with her again, although I knew that this might lead to some kind of civil war within our local Tawny clan. And then, of course, there was also the question of my sometime promise to May Blossom. I thought of Hunter, too, and his absurd liaison with this little immigrant called Alba. All this great mess of personal relationships bore down on me almost as much as the thought of the coming battle. Perhaps it would be better if one were to die with honour just before the coming sunrise. At least one would be spared the agonies of one's own and others' prejudices and tangled emotions.

As I landed opposite my father in the elm tree, still not knowing what to say, I heard the distant whispering of almost silent wings.

'Your Barn Owl friend has not arrived and neither has your uncle or either of his two retainers,' said my father, now looking very drawn and worried. For all his much-vaunted optimism, positive thinking and so on, I could tell that now he, too, was having second thoughts about the coming battle. Unless help came soon, we would lose and all be slaughtered. By this time, even my intrepid father must have realized that.

'Has the alien agreed to our conditions?' he asked me, looking across the clearing to where Alba perched alone in the sycamore tree, just out of Ferocity, Stoop and Ripper's sight.

'Listen!' I said, as the whispering wings hummed louder and closer in the silent night. 'It's the Barn Owl contingent. They are coming!'

My father leaned forward on the branch and listened. 'You're right!' he said. 'There are more than two. How many of them can you hear?'

'At this distance it's hard to tell – but at a guess I'd say a number between three and six.'

My father looked visibly relieved, unlike Ferocity, Stoop and Ripper, who were now twitching restlessly in the branches of their oak on the far side of the clearing. They hated Barn Owls almost as much as they loathed the little immigrants, and it is my belief that they would have preferred to fight and die alone rather than co-operate with a species they considered their natural enemies.

By now the Barn Owl contingent was so close that it was possible in the silence to count the separate wing beats. There were five of them. I hooted loudly to attract them to the clearing, flew to meet them and, according to my father's instructions, took them to their quarters in a mighty beech tree on the far side of the clearing.

Hunter introduced me at once to his four companions, all of whom were members of the Barn Owl council. Though they were twelve, only four of them had volunteered to fight. I thought of Birch, Hemlock, Vetch and Woody, as well as other Tawnies who had opted out, and realized that the percentage of Barn Owls and our own species willing to fight for freedom was about the same. Later in life, this gave me food for thought, but at the time my only reaction was one of great relief. With the presence of these five strong, white birds, victory suddenly seemed possible. I say five strong, white birds, but here I exaggerate. Their Language Owl, called Quirk, though obviously agile, was much smaller than the average Barn Owl. Their geography expert was no longer young and so unkempt and dowdy that he reminded me of the decrepit, deceased Beak Poke. However, the other three were splendid specimens. Steeple, Hunter's father, was still a strong and handsome bird, but unfortunately he couldn't fight. Hunter explained that as spiritual leader of the Barn Owl community he was not permitted to engage in physical conflict with any other kind of owl. It was against their Barn Owl religion and obviously, as leader, he could not set a bad example. On the other hand, Steeple himself seemed eager for the fray, and subsequently proved one of the most heroic among us, and is rightly immortalized in Quaver's epic ballad.

That left Hunter himself and the History Owl. Though about the same age as Hunter's father, this expert on their council was still strong, bold and clear-headed, as indeed were the rest of this eminent Barn Owl contingent which young Hunter had somehow persuaded to volunteer for such a frightful mission.

'You will be stationed here until the battle starts,' I said, once the brief introductions had been completed and they were settled in separate ranks in the centre branches of the sturdy beech. 'Our first assault squadron is already in position,' I said, pointing one wing in the direction of Ripper's oak on the far side of the clearing. 'As Hunter knows, our battle plan is to lure the monster here by a decoy system, bring him down among the trees, and then kill him once his huge wings have become entangled in the branches.'

'What about your brother?' Hunter asked, interrupting me before I had finished and before any of his seniors had had a chance to speak. 'Did he get here in the end?'

'He did,' I said, and then explained how, after the murder of Brook, Forster had led the monster back into the Lost Domain. This episode is not recorded in Quaver's ballad, which is of course told from the Barn Owl point of view, but the fact remains that my brother's was possibly the greatest act of heroism in the entire war, and though many died, none knew their fate beforehand as he must have done.

The next error sung – and sung by Barn Owls everywhere on each anniversary of the war – is the question of the decoys, and of who first suggested that the Barn Owls take on this dangerous role, simply because with their longer, slimmer wings they could fly slightly faster than we Tawnies could. Quaver has it that the Barn Owls volunteered. In his version, the History Owl had the idea and voiced it to me in the beech tree.

This is not true. Modestly speaking, the idea was mine. It seemed more logical, for they were indeed faster on the wing, whereas we were perhaps fiercer and certainly more suited to fighting the second and third stages of the battle, first in the open sky above Ripper's wood, and secondly down among the dense branches of the trees.

However, I must be honest with my silent listeners. I cannot lie to the clear spring water, or to the wind and trees. My main motive for suggesting that the Barn Owls take on the role of decoys was to save myself from the consequences of having told an untruth to my father. He had wanted Alba as a decoy because, as he rightly said, she was the most expendable amongst us. Now, by suggesting the evidently more suitable solution of using the Barn Owls instead, I would get credit and my father would at once forget all about the little alien. His purpose, after all, was one — and only one: to bring the monster down and win the war.

So I put it to them and their History Owl at once agreed.

'Yes, we will fly as decoys,' he said, in clear, decisive tones. 'We can take over when your brother has lured the monster from the Lost Domain. We will take over from him in the confines of the secret forest and lead the beast across Brook's farmland until we have brought him here to your trees and to the point of ambush.'

Before I could reply, there was a call from across the woods to the east of us. My father answered it at once from his headquarters in the elm on the other side of the clearing.

'That is my uncle, arriving with his two retainers,' I said, my spirits rising now that we were more or less at full strength. 'I must go now and help to brief the new arrivals, and also to ask my father whether he agrees with your offer to act as decoys. In the meantime you can discuss the matter among yourselves. Obviously, the most important thing is to choose the order in which you are to fly.'

It was only then, on the point of take-off, that I remembered little Alba, waiting patiently in her sycamore for what might be her last chance to say goodbye to Hunter.

'Will you fly with me a little way?' I asked him, attempting to sound as casual and unconcerned as I could. 'I would like a word with you in private.'

'Of course!' he said, and followed me at once to the centre of the clearing where I paused and hovered, well out of earshot of all the other owls assembled there.

'A friend of yours has come here to see you,' I told Hunter. 'At least, she says she is a friend. She's waiting in that sycamore over there.' He glanced in the direction I had indicated, saw the little alien, and half-fluttered one wing in response to Alba's energetic wave.

'I'll have a word with her when we've settled this business of the decoys,' he said bluntly. He seemed embarrassed, and that I could understand, but to me at the time it appeared both ungracious and ill-mannered of him not to show more gratitude. After all, I had gone to some considerable trouble to get the little alien into – of all places – Ferocity and Ripper's wood! At that time Hunter seemed almost irritated by her presence, though of course I could not see deep down into his heart. On the eve of battle, however, I thought of the little alien's haunting song and of the poignant sadness of unrequited love. Of course, I could not see into the future, otherwise I might have decided that – under certain circumstances – unrequited love was less of a danger than the flame of mutual passion.

We parted then, after nodding to each other briefly, in mid-air. He flew back to the Barn Owl beech tree and I crossed the clearing to my father's elm, both of us now caught up in the final, dire preparations for the dawn and for the war that would decide our destinies. Or so we thought at the time, but wars are only a part of destiny, and the heart can sometimes hurt more than the sharpest of all talons.

'Well?' my father said, as soon as I had perched on my branch in the elm. 'What role in this battle do your Barn Owl friends intend to play?'

I told him then that I had suggested they be used as decoys, that they had agreed and were now in the process of working out the order in which they would fly – or die! My father nodded in agreement. He saw at once the logic of my proposal and, exactly as I'd hoped, forgot all about the presence of the little alien.

We then briefed my uncle and his two retainers regarding the part they must play in the now ever more impending battle. I then flew back to the beech tree to ascertain the order of the Barn Owl relay – a relay that seemed likely to lead most of them to sudden, gruesome death.

I have to say at this point that I was impressed by their planning and by the calculations they had made. Their Geography Owl had worked out the exact distance from the confines of the secret forest to this, the battle zone. Estimating the monster's speed of flight – according to the information they had been given – they calculated that three of them would be needed to lead the invader to the point of ambush.

That night I learned that a fit Barn Owl can fly flat-out for a maximum of five meadows' length. Their geography expert had calculated a total distance of fourteen meadows. Each in turn would distract the monster before he over-hauled the previous exhausted decoy and would then lead him on until the next one rose up and took over.

Because Hunter knew the territory, it had been decided that he would take over from my brother on the edge of the Lost Domain. His father, the Religion Owl, would then rise up. Though he was not allowed to fight, there was nothing in their credo to prevent him flying as a decoy. The last lap of this deadly relay would be flown by the History Owl. Should my brother not emerge from the Lost Domain, Hunter – who had typically volunteered as first decoy – would penetrate the secret forest, seek the monster out, and lead him to the edge of the woods, where Steeple would be waiting to take over Hunter's role. In other words, each member of the team would move up one place, and either the Geography or Language Owl would take over from the History Owl in the last position.

I remember very clearly something the Language Owl had said just before I landed in the beech and the Barn Owls outlined their plan to me. He said: 'History, Geography, Youth and Religion shall combine to lure this monster to his death. I like it! It has a fine irony and augurs well for the death of any tyrant.' As I say, I did not hear this personally, but Quaver quotes these words verbatim in his epic ballad. He must have overheard because he was at that time perched on a lower branch of the beech tree with the once pompous and flamboyant Bard Owl who now – in the face of the coming battle – cowered and clutched at the trunk of the tree as if he were attempting to crawl back into his mother's womb!

'We agree with your proposal, and may the Great God Bird go with you,' I said, and then, glancing up at the night sky, I saw the darkness begin to lift, and far to the east a dull and as yet submerged streak of red showed that the fatal dawn was now not far away. 'May the Great God Bird go with you all,' I repeated. 'But if you and he are to bring the monster here before the sun has risen too high for us to fight, then your first decoy must leave at once.'

'We shall all three fly together,' said the History Owl at once. 'Hunter knows the territory and must show us exactly where to take up our positions.'

'I'll be with you in a moment,' Hunter said. 'First I must

say goodbye to a friend of mine.' I looked at Hunter hard, nodded, and then glanced at his father Steeple, and at the History Owl. I could find no more to say to these three brave and suicidal decoys, so I took off without another word and flew back across the clearing to our operational headquarters in the elm. Looking back on my flight across the clearing, I saw Hunter heading in the direction of the part-hidden sycamore where little Alba waited. What passed between them then, in those brief moments, I shall never know.

What I do know is that here in my simple, unpoetic rendering of these great events, I have tried to set the record straight. To sum up in my prosaic way, the true facts that Quaver does not render in his ballad are as follows:

First, I saved the little alien's life by not telling her that she was required as a decoy. I claim no credit for this, and as subsequent events were to show, it might have been better if she had died that night. But that is something for my silent listeners to decide.

Second, the idea of using the Barn Owls to lure the monster to the battle zone was mine. For this, at least, I can take credit. Quaver has it that they volunteered. In his ballad he says their History Owl suggested they should do so because they had longer, slimmer wings and were therefore slightly faster over open country.

However, I do not blame Quaver for this factual error. Volunteering always sounds better than being volunteered – and it is their ballad, after all. It is clear that the more heroic their warriors were made to appear, the more Barn Owl posterity would like it. As my father was soon to say: 'A thousand winters hence, the things your Bard Owl sings of will be treated as mere myth or legend. They will become a sometime thing, a mere hint or stirring from some long-forgotten yesterday, changed and perverted by future owls and by the ebb and flow of time.'

So it is with my own story, and I imagine with the story

of each creature who has lived upon this earth. As I said in the beginning, the truth is relative, and I can do no more now than tell my version of it to the wind and trees.

CHAPTER
15

So now that I have set the record straight as to what happened at the beginning of the war, I can tell of the decisive battle that was now to come, and of the ghastly carnage to take place. I shall tell of it only briefly, however, for from this point on Quaver's account is more or less accurate.

In many ways the Barn Owls were better placed to give an account of the bloody proceedings than we Tawnies were. As decoys, they saw the monster first, and were amongst the first to fall. Secondly, Quaver himself did not join in the fight but flew to and fro from the front line reporting to Bardic, who cowered and clutched at the trunk of the beech tree in terror for the duration of the battle.

Anyway, the now well-known and tragic facts are well reported. Waiting on the edge of the Lost Domain, Hunter saw my brother emerge from the secret forest, followed by the monster owl. As described by his brother Quaver, the sight of the giant almost caused Hunter's heart to stop — and who can blame him? Though we had all been warned by our intelligence services and by the shattered refugees from the south, nothing they said had prepared us for the terrifying reality which Hunter now beheld. When he first saw it, the thing was cruising above the tree tops and above my brother Forster, who was flying below him through the branches of the trees. According to Quaver's account, it was clear that the monster was playing cat and mouse with my brave brother Forster. Rather than risk scraping one of his giant wings by diving deep into the forest to pluck poor Forster from his flight path, the giant was waiting for him to emerge from the trees into the open country where he could kill him without risking a scratch from the rich, late-summer foliage of the secret forest.

According to Quaver's account, Hunter realized this, and also knew at once that to save my brother's life he must rise up and distract the monster as soon as Forster emerged from the trees into the flat Barn Owl country that led from the Lost Domain to where we waited in Ferocity and Ripper's wood.

Tragically for Forster, this did not work out as planned. Though half-frozen with fear at the size of this beast – a beast so big and with a wingspan so wide that it seemed to blot out half of the night sky – Hunter did his duty and rose above the branches of the oak, hissing and screaming his defiance at the fast-approaching giant. Of course, in his ballad Quaver does not mention Hunter's slight delay – an understandable delay, for the sight of this dreadful creature was enough to stop your heartbeat, as the rest of us were shortly to find out. However, he did his duty and risked almost certain death to save Forster and to lead the monster to the place of ambush. But what is not made clear in the Barn Owl ballad is that Forster followed on, obviously intent on taking over again as a decoy if he had to, and then on joining us in Ripper's wood, first for the decisive battle in the sky, and then down among the branches of the trees.

Quaver's account has it that Hunter flew into the forest to intercept the monster and that Forster was killed on the very edge of it, but still among the trees. This is not so, for the remains of Forster's body were found a meadow's length beyond the edge of the secret forest and were scattered there in open country.

Quaver says that his brother turned and saw the monster crash down among the trees with a mighty howl of triumph, a howl so loud that we heard it in Ripper's wood, fourteen meadows' distance from the confines of the Lost Domain. This is true; we heard it. For the first time we heard the monster's voice and trembled. At least, I trembled, but only inside, of course. As deputy commander it would have been bad form to have shown any kind of fear before the coming battle. So the monster turned on Forster, plucked him from the sky and – as Quaver puts it – carried his lifeless, broken body like a toy that dangled from the talons of one giant claw.

After dropping my brother's poor carcass into the meadow, the monster resumed his pursuit of Hunter. Then Hunter turned according to plan, and flew faster than he'd ever flown before in the direction of Ferocity and Ripper's wood. The monster followed, gaining rapidly on his quarry with effortless strokes of those gigantic wings. There was no cover anywhere on the flat ground below him – no chance of shelter until he reached the deserted cowshed that had once been Brook's home and where Steeple, Hunter's father, now waited to take over the role of decoy from his first born son.

At half a meadow's distance from the isolated building the monster had almost caught up with Hunter, who now sensed him rising in the air above him, ready to drop and pluck him in full flight. Then, just as he thought his end had come, he saw his father rising from Brook's cowshed, hurling himself upward into the monster's path. As Steeple launched himself into this suicide attack, the giant hesitated, seeming undecided as to whether he should drop on Hunter first or else turn on this new intruder and kill him as he soared up into this self-destructive assault.

Hunter told me later that the last words his father ever

uttered were: 'Fly on, my son!' Apparently Steeple shouted this as he rose above Hunter and hurled himself with bared talons at the monster's mighty head.

Obeying, and flying on at the very limits of his strength, Hunter heard the giant's thunder-snort of rage, and then the sickening thud of impact as the beast and his father met in mid-air combat. As he strained every nerve and every sinew in the flight ahead, he heard the nauseating sound of lacerating wing and limb, and knew at once that his father must be dead, and that the remnants of his body must now be dropping from the sky to lie scattered in the meadow alongside the butchered corpses of Brook and his mate.

Again much later, Hunter told me that for a while the monster seemed to lag behind him, and it crossed his terror-stricken mind that Steeple might have wounded the giant owl before he perished in his suicide attack. Later, we knew this to be true, and I have always found it odd that there is no mention of the fact in Quaver's epic ballad. Was the poet attempting to conceal the fact that his father – the Religion Owl – had been the first amongst us to wound the monster, and thereby had given the rest of us some hope of proving – as he had done – that the thing was not invulnerable? I sometimes wonder whether Stoop, Ferocity and Ripper would have had the courage to rise up above their wood and attack the beast had they not seen the small scratch and the tiny drops of blood which dribbled from the monster's head and chest.

When I spoke about all this to Hunter – again much later on – he told me that his father had never wanted to study religion or to become the Religion Owl on the Barn Owl council. He had two elder brothers, however, one of whom took over the family estate while the second was sent as an apprentice to the War Owl, which is what Steeple apparently would have preferred. As it happens, he got stuck with religion, and by all accounts he made a good job of it. But judging by his heroic efforts prior to that epic battle in the early sunrise, he might have served the Barn Owl community better in the warrior's role he would have chosen for himself. I have observed that the young are often thrust into things which are not best suited to them, and only discover the error much later when they have mated and produced chicks and when it is much too late to change.

Anyway, before the coming dawn of battle, Steeple did us proud. He saved his son's life, and without his noble sacrifice we others could not have won the war. Who knows, perhaps in the end he fulfilled himself. At any rate, he died a young owl's death and did not linger on as I do now, waiting for time and history to put me down. And the irony of it is that I myself was thrust into the role that Steeple would have chosen – that of warrior, war hero and leader. In retrospect, I would have preferred a life that was more contemplative – perhaps devoted to a comparative study of the separate Tawny, alien and Barn Owl religions, or instead of theology, perhaps even poetry or music. Who knows? I did try to change, but by that time it was too late. In our night world, among owls of all species, one is accepted at face value, or not at all. Once birth and destiny have cast one in a certain role, and once the short story of one's life is under way, it becomes hard or well-nigh impossible to change the part one has been called upon to play. Thinking and the use of intellect confuse owls and are best left to a few harmless experts like Steeple, the theologian, Beak Poke, the Owl Owl or Quaver and Olmo, the two great poets. Now, in retrospect, I would rather have been one of those.

But I digress again, and must now tell my silent listeners of the dreadful carnage that took place so long ago, as the darkness began to lighten slowly on the dawn of that historic day.

CHAPTER

 16

The History Owl took over from Hunter just before the
monster could catch the exhausted hero and cut him down.
The History bird flew on hard and fast towards the clearing
in Ripper's wood where we were waiting to ambush the
beast and bring him down.

As my brother had done earlier, Hunter followed on
behind to take over again as decoy if the History Owl were
caught and killed before he had led the monster to where
it would find its nemesis and we allies would once and
for ever end its reign of terror.

I cannot describe my emotions as I first saw the thing
looming towards us in the night sky. He dwarfed the fleeing
History Owl and was in truth so big that he seemed to
blot out most of the remaining moonlight above the wood
where we were waiting to ambush him. I cannot describe
my emotions, but at the sight of it I remember thinking
that Stoop, his sister and her mate would never obey their
orders and rise up above the tree tops to attack the thing.
But they did! They rose up and flew straight at it, howling
out three of the most bloodcurdling battle cries I've ever
heard. The monster uttered an even louder shriek of anger
and at once climbed higher in the sky to stay in a strategic

position above this first assault force. This allowed the History Owl to escape from certain death and dive down gratefully to join the other members of his Barn Owl contingent at their headquarters in the beech tree.

Watching in awe as the great beast turned on the three of them, I remembered what my mother had said about Ferocity, Stoop and Ripper, and about certain other Tawnies of the lower classes: 'You may consider them to be uncouth barbarians, but I want you to remember this. They are birds who will kill and die for us and for this land of ours.

'Thugs and yobs they may be, but in times of war they are essential.'

These words flashed through my mind as Stoop and Ripper launched themselves at the monster's massive head and chest, while Ferocity rose above him and then plunged down on to his great back and tore away at it with both beak and talons. The giant howled again, but this time in pain and anger as the three of them clung on and ripped away at his chest, belly, back and neck, set above all on the task they had been given – to bring him down among the trees.

At first it seemed as if they might succeed, but then the monster seemed to recover from the shock of this impertinent attack. With a great bellow of rage he tore Stoop and Ripper from his now lacerated belly and hacked at them with one giant claw. Though half torn to pieces, somehow they fought on, thus allowing Ferocity to wreak her havoc on the monster's back. Soon, however, they fell, one with his heart torn out and the other virtually decapitated, with the head now lolling at right angles to the neck.

In his ballad, Quaver has it that Stoop fell with one severed wing and with a gaping wound across his chest. Ripper, he says, was the one to have been decapitated. I remember it as the other way round, but in the heat of battle it is difficult to register every detail. In any case, it doesn't really matter, because before they even hit the ground both of them were very, very dead.

But as our second assault wave flew into the attack, Ferocity still clung to the monster's back, as he writhed in mid-air, attempting to turn and rip her off with one mighty claw. Before he could do so, my uncle's two retainers flew straight at his head and torso. The first was killed at once, but his brave sacrifice allowed the second through to tear at the giant's already wounded chest. As he clung there, with his talons embedded deep in the body of the writhing beast, my uncle rose above the creature and then tore into its back.

As the three Tawnies fought to bring the giant down, I called the Barn Owl contingent from their beech across the clearing to our headquarters in the elm.

'I'm next!' I said. 'I need two of you with me. Decide now.'

'Me and you?' asked the dowdy Geography Owl, with an enquiring glance at Hunter who, unseen by me, had rejoined his contingent in the clearing.

'Of course!' he said at once, though he must still have been exhausted after his long and heroic dash to help lead the tyrant to his appointment with death.

'Good! Then the two of us will attack him from the front,' I said, turning to the Geography Owl. 'You take the back, Hunter, with Ferocity or my uncle, if either one survives.'

We all looked up then in awe, watching the monster heave and writhe to free himself from the three Tawnies who were slowly but surely forcing him down among the tree tops. Then, just as it seemed they might succeed, the mangled, tangled mass of blood and feathers gave a huge convulsion as the badly wounded giant found a final burst of terrifying power and strength. In the course of this frantic spasm he at last tore Ferocity from his back and killed her with one single blow. At the same time, our other Tawny let go of the monster's chest and fluttered downward, not yet dead but very badly wounded and faint from the loss of so much blood. This left my uncle alone upon the monster's back – alone but still forcing the weakened beast further down towards the tree tops.

'Now!' I shouted, and took off with my loudest battle cry, while Hunter and the Geography Owl rose up immediately behind me.

It is hard to describe what I felt in those few moments before impact. I have said before that when badly wounded in battle, one seldom feels the pain. The pain comes later. I have observed that there is a similar phenomenon with fear. Fear one feels before one flies into the attack, but once launched irrevocably towards one's target, the panic disappears and one becomes full of purpose and fully intent on the job one has to do.

So it was on that now long-distant dawn. Though I do not remember the sequence of events precisely, I believe it was the middle-aged Geography Owl who saved my life by flying faster than I had expected and by attacking the monster at exactly the same time. The weakened beast hesitated as we both tore into him, undecided as to which of us to take on first. This hesitation was to prove fatal, for it enabled me to strike the decisive blow in that epic, bloody battle. At the last moment the monster struck out at the Geography Owl instead of me, and I could tell at once that the brave Barn Owl had been badly wounded. However, at the same time, Hunter dived down and ripped at the monster's back, distracting him still further and leaving me sudden access to his huge and horrid face. With one decisive blow, I tore out his right eye. I ripped it clean out of its socket.

In his ballad Quaver says that the monster's howl of agony and his one giant spasm shook the sunrise of that day and was felt and heard all over our territories, even far beyond the Lost Domain. It is said that not one of the many scattered owls who heard that awful cry would forget it until the day he died.

The monster's agonized convulsion shook my uncle off his back. As this brave bird fluttered in the now redstreaked sky, the monster caught sight of him with his one remaining eye and lashed out at him in a frenzy of rage and agony, splitting his body with one dreadful blow.

While I hung on and ripped away in desperation at the creature's chest, my uncle dropped to earth, dead as a stone. But clinging to the monster, I could sense that his strength was now fading fast and that his great wings no longer had the strength to keep him airborne and above the level of the trees. To my surprise, Alba suddenly rose above the tree tops, dived on to the monster's back, next to Hunter, and the three of us began to drag him down. Soon his huge wings began to brush against the upper branches of the trees, and he must suddenly have sensed that he had lost the battle. Maimed as he was — now almost to the point of death — his one chance of survival lay in throwing off the three of us who now clung to him. Bleeding and half-blind, before his great wings became enmeshed in the middle branches of the trees I sensed a final surge of power — a final violent spasm emanating from within him and, though I clung on for dear life, he shook me free and then clawed me just once with those dreadful talons. I saw the same talon rip Hunter from the monster's back, and then I fainted with pain and fell from the tree tops as the final assault wave tore in to finish the tyrant off.

When I came round, I found myself lying under a sycamore — the one in which the little alien had waited for Hunter's coming. Above me stood my father, who seemed unhurt, and the language expert from the Barn Owl contingent who had come from their headquarters in the beech to get news of me. Looking around me I saw bodies and bits of bodies strewn everywhere across the woodland clearing. It was not a pretty sight! Glancing up to take my eyes away from the wounded and the dead, I saw the carcass of the monster grotesquely spread – as Quaver puts it – among the branches of the chestnut into which the final assault wave had dragged him and at last done him to death.

Though this may seem strange to relate, the sight of that giant, lolling corpse, plus perhaps the pain that I now began to feel, caused me to wonder how any war of such a kind could be justified. Looking at the remains of that giant – that magnificent creature whose eye I had ripped out – I questioned whether any such slaughter could be reasonable. Was there no other way, I asked myself, as the numbness wore off and the pain from my wound throbbed harder – was there no other way of settling the disputes of the night sky?

By now, of course, it was no longer night, or even dawn, but broad daylight. Looking down at me in the bright sunshine, my father nodded once and flew unsteadily – as Tawnies do by day – to the beech to confer with the Barn Owl contingent. In his ballad, Quaver has it that these owls were now assembled in a larger sycamore above the place where Hunter lay.

This is not true. Except for the little alien, Hunter lay alone, unconscious but still bleeding, on the woodland floor. None of his own kind were near him at that time. Only Alba perched beside him, waiting for her loved one either to wake or die.

By nodding to me in that rather casual way and simply flying off, my father somehow reassured me much more than he would have done by submitting me to a verbal flood of sympathy or praise. A flood of words at that time might have convinced me that I, too, was dying. That one reassuring nod was enough to make me realize that I wasn't.

However, just to make sure, I asked the Language Owl,

who perched above me in my father's absence, watching the blood ooze slowly from my chest.

'No, you're not going to die,' he said. 'You are badly hurt and it will take you all of the autumn and most of the winter to recover, but you will live!'

'Good!' I said. 'And Hunter?'

'That is not good news,' the Barn Owl replied, after a second's hesitation. 'Hunter may be dying,' this dapper, rather small owl continued, pluming his chest feathers with one talon as he spoke. 'Yet it is also quite possible that he may survive. Much will depend on how he reacts to the trauma of his wound if or when he ever regains consciousness.'

'Why is there no one with him?' I asked, regretting that I myself was not strong enough to fly at once to his side.

'There is someone with him,' the Language Owl replied.

'Yes, but she's an alien,' I said. 'Why is none of your own contingent assisting him?'

'It is a question of protocol,' replied the Language Owl, after a second's hesitation.

'Protocol? What protocol!' I said. 'How can one think of protocol when the ground around us is littered with the wounded and the dead?'

'Ah, but at times like this form and protocol are all the more important,' answered Quirk, with a patronizing and rather supercilious little smile. 'We are well aware of how you Tawnies feel about the immigrants. As you know, we are not over-fond of them ourselves. We know that you never allow them on your land and out of respect for the dead we do not wish to be seen consorting with one here.'

'Respect for the dead?'

'Yes. Especially for Stoop, Ferocity and Ripper. They would turn in their graves if they saw an alien squatting on their land.'

'But they were barbarians!' I said. 'Brave, yes, and splendid fighters. Without them we could not have won this battle. But remember, they disliked you Barn Owls almost as much as they hated the little aliens.'

'We are aware of that,' Quirk said. 'But there is also your father to consider, and your uncle who fell in battle. Would you describe them as barbarians?'

'No, of course not.'

'Well, then, we wish to show them our solidarity. We do not want them to think that we approve of Hunter's unnatural relationship with this little immigrant.'

'What a load of sparrow shit!' I said. One has to remember that I was badly hurt and did not care much what I said, especially to this Language Owl who was later to be immortalized as a hero but in actual fact had not acted as a decoy or even fought in the battle until right at the very end, when I believe he had pecked at the monster's body once or twice after it was already dead. Like Bardic, their false poet, this type of Barn Owl struck me as the worst. They do very little and then take all the glory. In Tawny language we call them opportunists. And what use do they have for a Language Owl on their council, in any case, when they have true poets like Quaver who can compose and sing? Even Olmo, the immigrant poet, has done more for owl language than these so-called experts who cannot soar and sing but are instead obsessed by form and structure.

'There is another thing,' he said, having read the exasperation in my face and having winced at the coarse language I had used.

'What other thing?'

'The question of Hunter's future. He is a brave, strong and intelligent young owl who will one day be called to serve our community on the council. There are some who say that one day, much later on, of course, he might even become our leader. Well, can you imagine a member of the Barn Owl council, let alone the leader, who is flagrantly conducting a liaison with a squatter? How do you think your Tawny elders would react in a similar situation?'

I thought of my mother and involuntarily gave a little shudder. If this same thing had happened to me – the same thing that had happened to Hunter – there would have been hell to pay! This dapper little Language Owl had a good brain and he had made his point. I didn't like him, but I had already learned that in order to succeed in politics, or to govern successfully, one's beak must be kept very, very clean. Or, at least, it must give the appearance of being clean!

For some time I didn't know what to say, so to mask my lack of a suitable reply, I closed my eyes and winced as if I were in the direst pain. To tell the truth, my main wound was now hurting a great deal, but not enough to take the power of speech away. After a suitable pause for reflection I opened my eyes again and glanced across the clearing to where Hunter lay, still unconscious, with the lone figure of little Alba standing over him. For the first time in my young life I thought deeply about prejudice and came then to a conclusion that has stayed with me ever since. If you take prejudice away from owls like Stoop, Ferocity and Ripper, they are left with very little else. It is therefore useless to blow against the wind and against many million years of conditioning. But I was young then and, as I lay hurt among the dead and wounded, a great surge of anger suddenly came upon me.

'Have you no sense of the occasion?' I asked, having now decided that attack would be the best form of defence.

'What do you mean?'

'Look at the dying and the dead,' I said, raising and waving one feeble wing to indicate the casualties and the corpses littered all over the messy floor of the woodland clearing. 'At a time like this, to think or speak of protocol is to my mind quite obscene. That young owl of yours helped us to win the war and now lies bleeding and uncon- scious and – as you have said – possibly at the point of death. Yet none of you will approach him because of form and protocol and because you do not wish to offend my father. Well, I wish to speak to my father now, at once. Please go and call him!'

The Language Owl looked down at me and blinked. 'Are you sure this is wise?' he asked at length. 'You and Hunter are both young – too young as yet to understand these things.'

'That may be true,' I answered. 'But we were not too young to fight, and in his case probably to die. Remember, too, that the little alien fought with us at the end. She risked her life to bring the monster down. For one day, at least, we were allies. Let the truce last at least until the twilight. Then, if you wish, we can all begin to hate again.'

I now remember this scene as clearly as if it had happened yesterday. I don't know where my words came from. It was uncanny, almost as if someone else were prompting me to speak. But speak I did, and the Language Owl blinked again, but listened.

'I will fetch your father, if you insist,' he said. 'But I warn you that he may not be pleased with what you have to say.'

This, coming from a Barn Owl to a Tawny, at this moment, was, I thought, the height of bad manners and impertinence. If this was the way they all behaved, I thought, no wonder Hunter prefers his ragged little alien.

The Language Owl and I stared at each other for what seemed an age. Then he shrugged, took off and flew across the clearing to do my bidding. My father returned almost at once, alone, and perched beside me at the foot of the small sycamore.

'What can I do for you, my son?' he asked, as soon as he had landed.

'You can tell the Barn Owl contingent that one or two of them must fly at once to Hunter and stand by him, in case he ever regains consciousness,' I said. 'And you must fly with them and thank the Little Owl for the part she played in bringing the monster down.'

'Why?' my father asked, sounding not at all angry, but very, very calm.

'Because they are afraid of offending us,' I said. 'Out of respect for Ferocity, Stoop, Ripper and our other Tawny dead, they do not wish to be seen associating with an alien on our land. I want you to greet the Little Owl and also to give my compliments and best wishes to Hunter if and when he wakes. If you do that, the other Barn Owls will feel free to brave the scandal and take care of him.'

My father looked down at me for quite some time without replying. Then he nodded again and without a word took off and flew back to the Barn Owl contingent in the beech tree. After a brief conference, I saw him take off with all of them and fly across the clearing to the large sycamore under which Hunter lay. Shortly after this I saw my father fly down and land at Hunter's side, together with Bardic, Quaver and the History Owl. I saw little Alba move aside, allowing these four to form a semicircle around Hunter's bleeding body.

I did not know at this stage that he had already regained consciousness and, though he could neither move nor speak, he must in his own way have been as aware as I was of what was going on. My father gave Hunter my sincere regards and then gave the little speech that has already been immortalized in Quaver's ballad. Though his words are long well known to my silent listeners, I will repeat them, for in my opinion they have acquired even greater significance in the light of subsequent events.

'We won a great victory today,' my father said, looking up at the enormous, now grotesque carcass of the monster, whose head, wings and body, now hacked half to pieces, were spread out and caught up among the middle branches of the trees. 'The war is over, the enemy is dead, but our losses have been tragically high. Both our refugees were cut down in the Lost Domain, my son Forster died on his mission as a decoy, and my brother and two of his retainers were killed here in the final battle. I have not mentioned Ferocity, Stoop and Ripper, whose suicidal role as the first assault wave must have had a decisive effect on the outcome of the battle and the war. It would be pretty to think that they – and the rest of us who fought here today – would be forever honoured and remembered. We paid a high price, but with our blood we bought freedom for the survivors of this battle and liberty for all the other owls who dwell here in these territories but did not choose to join us in the great dawn battle. As I have said, it would be pretty to think that our deeds will be remembered, but they won't. They will soon be forgotten as a dream that fades and dies at twilight when we wake.'

'You will be remembered!' Bardic said, waving one wing in a flamboyant and rather pompous gesture. 'You will be immortalized in our epic Barn Owl ballad. Your dead heroes will be hallowed and remembered at moonrise and at dawn from this day forth for ever more.'

'I hope so,' Quaver has himself as saying, as he glanced around at the corpses strewn about the woodland. 'I hope so, otherwise what a waste all this would have been.'

My father did not report this to me at the time, and frankly I don't think Quaver said it. It is one of those clever things owls wish they had said after the event. Of course, if you are a poet and the one who tells the story, I suppose you have a licence to invent and to put in what you or someone else might or should have said if it had occurred to him at the proper time. So far I will grant Quaver his poetic licence. His inventions are harmless enough and, although sometimes ironic, there is never any malice in them. What I find harder to forgive are his sins of omission. Why did he never mention the fact that Hunter was ostracized by his own kind as he lay wounded and bleeding on the field of battle?

The fact is, I feel that they were subsequently ashamed of this — as well they might have been. It may be that Quaver included this episode in his first version of the ballad, but that his elders on the council forced him to take it out again. In any case, I have now set the record straight. It was only at my father's bidding that they flew to attend upon their hero, who lay wounded to the point of death, and it was only after my father had made history by nodding once to Alba that they, too, acknowledged the presence of this little alien.

As I watched my father leave the Barn Owl contingent and fly back across the clearing, I wondered whether this war to end all wars would put a stop to some of the prejudice and to some of the senseless killings. If we and the Barn Owls had known then that this was the beginning rather than the end, we would all of us have had much more reason to be ashamed.

CHAPTER
17

As everybody knows, Hunter shocked the Barn Owl community by returning to what had once been Beak Poke's abandoned farmhouse with the little alien, who looked after him during his long convalescence until he was well enough to make his first solo flight early in the following spring. Apparently, after the battle he and Alba stayed in the woodland clearing until nightfall, and then somehow made their way back across the Lost Domain, past the outskirts of the village and on to Hunter's new home. How he managed the flight in his condition, I shall never know, but I heard later that he collapsed again as soon as they arrived and stayed in a kind of coma for several nights and days.

I know how hard it must have been for him! His wounds were worse than mine, and yet there were times during my own return that night when I thought I would never make it back to our woodland home. Crawling and limping through the night sky alongside my patient father, there were times when I thought I must drop and never rise again. On the way we rested several times, but never for too long. During the first of these pauses – in the secret forest of the Lost Domain – my father caught and killed a young rabbit for me, but I could not eat it. In fact many nights were to pass before I could swallow more than the tiniest morsels of food, though my parents brought me more than enough every night to feed an owl of twice my size. News of our victory had reached my mother long before we returned, and she had left her safe crevice and was waiting for us when we arrived shortly before sunrise on the day after that decisive battle.

As I convalesced and slowly grew stronger, autumn mulled the woodland all around me from bright summer hues to more sombre colours, and later still to deepening shades of grey and brown. Unable to fly, I was in a position to observe the change of season in great detail, from the branch I now occupied in my parents' oak. I saw the fruit of the wild guelder rose ripen and then fall, I saw the berries of bitter-sweet or woody nightshade turn from light green to emerald and then via orange into red, while hazel nuts and acorns appeared among the pastel-coloured leaves and crab-apple and sloe made their late appearance on the thinning branches of the trees.

I am not trying to be poetic here. I am merely attempting to show how slowly the change of season seemed to come that year. I had nothing to do but observe. I could not fly and therefore could not hunt, and so for the first time in my life I had time to observe the slow process of change in the natural things around me, mutations that I had previously taken pretty much for granted as the swift stream of youth flowed by. Of course, most of the time I thought of Mallow and sometimes, but not often, of May Blossom.

Thus, as November came and the year lay dying in the evening light, I came to my great personal decision. When spring came and I was fully fit, I would ask Mallow to mate with me. I had realized by now, or thought I had realized, that she was the one true love of my life. Though our mating had been but brief and illicit, I knew that

Mallow was the only one for me. I had to have her, even if this meant a mortal duel with Birch. But if she accepted me, and Birch refused to let her go, I knew that I should win the ensuing fight, because although we were of the same size and strength, I had been born with the greater courage. For the female that I loved, I would be able to sustain any conflict, even unto death. Or so I thought at the time.

The first problem was of course how, what and when to tell my parents. The second dilemma would be how to react to their objection when it came, for object they must, of this there was no doubt whatsoever in my mind.

As the November rains came down, and as the grey skies behind the rain gave dark warning of the coming snow, I carefully planned the method of presentation to my parents.

Birch and his family had been trying to usurp us for centuries, I would say. For precisely three centuries, they had told me – ever since the last successful war against the Barn Owls. Since we had won this war against the monster while Birch and his family had skulked and hidden in the hope that we would die in battle, their stock had fallen very low. We were now the heroes and they were known all over our territory and far beyond as nothing more than abject cowards.

By challenging Birch and by beating him in a battle for his mate, I would be consolidating our position in the community. If Birch did not have the courage to face up to me in a fair fight, then he would be banished to the lower foothills, where rumour had it that the men had started building a new town. There he could live with rat or Little Owl beside the iron tracks and between the confines of our sloping woodland and the hideous and ever-spreading stain of cement and asphalt which man was using to obliterate the Barn Owl country on the plain.

'You can't do this thing,' my mother would reply. 'Owls

are monogamous, or at least Tawnies and Barn Owls are. Once you have mated, the bonding lasts for life.'

'In any case, it would be bad form,' my father would then add. 'We have already explained to you the meaning of *noblesse oblige*. As aristocrats and leaders, it is up to us to set the highest of examples, as we have just done by our conduct in the war. And in any case, you are promised to May Blossom. What would the rest of our family and our retainers think if you were to break such a solemn vow, merely to copulate with a female who belongs to another?'

'But he is an enemy!' I would say. 'You told me so yourself. And Mallow loves me, not him. This I know!' And then I planned to tell them about the song she had sung – the song she had sung not for Birch but for me! I would change the words slightly, to appeal to my patriotic parents, and the last line would run like this:

> If they gave a war, you would go.
> You would go if they gave a war.
> I know you would go for me!

So I weighed the whole thing up for days as I dozed in the thin, cold November sun and fretted all night on my branch in the oak, as the first frosts struck iron into the forest floor below me.

When the early snows fell and I finally spoke, I felt that I had weighed up all their possible objections. Whatever they were, I knew that I would not be dissuaded, for I had realized that my father's ultimate sanction would be to banish me. Well, if he did that, I would go! First I would kill Birch, if he opposed me, and then I would fly off with Mallow in search of a new and fertile territory – a territory where I could find and found a new dynasty of my own.

So I thought I had everything worked out, but when I told them, one late November night, their reaction was not at all what I had expected. When I had announced my intentions, my father and mother first looked shocked, as I had expected. Then, instead of voicing the objections I had so carefully prepared for and was waiting to rebuff, they merely exchanged a glance, conveying something I did not understand.

'Didn't you know?' my mother asked, eventually.

'Know what?'

'Didn't you know that Mallow was dead,' my father said bluntly. He did not beat about the bush. He came straight out with it, just like that. I dare say he, too, had feelings, but he hardly ever showed them, and my mother never did.

'Dead?' I asked, not yet able to grasp what they were saying.

'She died giving birth only a few nights ago,' my mother said, with no hint of the compassion that as a sometime mother she must surely have felt.

'Giving birth?' I asked, still numb and unable to take in what either of them were saying.

'Yes, giving birth. Five or six nights ago she had a son called Rowan. He was born at midnight. She died before the dawn.'

'But that's impossible,' I said, pleading with them to disabuse me of this dreadful truth. 'No chicks are born in November. The mating season is in spring, or early summer.'

'For normal, sane and healthy owls, it is,' my mother said. 'But apparently Birch got her pregnant a night or two before the war, or perhaps the very night you and your father were fighting and he and she were holed up in their wretched little crevice. Sadly, by some mischance, she conceived, produced a chick and died.'

'Unnatural practices,' my father said, with a slow, sad shake of his head. 'His family have been suspected of this sort of thing for centuries.'

Well, I beg my silent listeners to digest this information slowly, as I did then. And as the implications hit you, you will doubtless begin to imagine well what I felt. On the one hand there was the dreadful suspicion that I had unwittingly been responsible for Mallow's death and was now the father of a male fledgling known as Rowan. Much as I loved Mallow – or perhaps precisely because I had loved her so much – I clung desperately to the second and more probable hypothesis. To staunch the guilt of his cowardice, Birch had taken her – against Mallow's will, of course – on the very night of the battle which we fought to save his life, a battle in which so many brave Tawnies and Barn Owls died.

But what if Rowan really were my son? What must I do about it? I must at least see to it that he was being properly fed, and then I must take care of him in memory of Mallow. Mallow! I still could not believe that she was dead.

'Born out of time, how will this fledgling survive the coming winter?' I asked, attempting to sound as casual as I could, while in reality my mind and body were both rocked by dreadful turmoil.

'So far he is doing well,' my mother said. 'His father is taking good care of him, or so they say. I'm not sure that I believe it. Such conduct would be most unusual for a bird like Birch.'

'It is a sense of guilt,' explained my father. 'He realizes that he killed his mate, Mallow, by breeding with her out of season. Now he wishes to make amends and ease his conscience by saving and bringing up her son.'

I could find no words to say, so I merely nodded in reply. My parents glanced at each other and then looked at me again. They looked long and hard, but there was no sign of suspicion in their faces; yet I am sure their minds must have been running along the same lines as my own. This fledgling born out of time, was he Birch's son, or mine? Of course, they did not know that I had made love to Mallow in the willow tree on the night before the war, but now that I had declared my love for her, the prospect of my fornication and her adultery must have crossed their minds.

I hasten to add that I use the words fornication and adultery because that's how my parents would have perceived it. I thought of those brief moments as the climax of my life, moments in which I had soared high above the sordid conflict of the night sky and for once discovered true love and trust.

'In a sense, Mallow's untimely death has done us all a great service,' my father said eventually. 'These are hard words, I know, but words that must be said. By killing Birch, or by driving him away, into exile, you would have sullied the reputation of our family for a thousand winters yet to come. Two wrongs don't make a right. This is one of the principles you were brought up on. You may well consider that Birch was wrong for Mallow, but you must also remember that she chose him. She chose Birch, not you! And once they had mated there was – or would have been – nothing more that a decent Tawny Owl could do about it. Now that she is dead, your path is clear and the meaning plain. As soon as spring comes and you are fully recovered from your wounds, you will fly to the city and find May Blossom. You will bring her back and mate with her, after which I shall abdicate and make you leader of the district. You will need the knowledge May Blossom has acquired in the city to help us to outwit the Barn Owls and to understand the poisoning, the pollution and the future plans of man.'

'Why outwit the Barn Owls?' I asked, in innocence. 'I thought they were our allies now.'

'They were our allies against an outside threat,' my father said. 'But now that the war is over, now that we have defeated the foreign enemy, the internal conflict is bound to begin again. History repeats itself, or so they say. And if it does, then sooner or later there will be conflict between us for the few remaining territories that will survive this ever-increasing encroachment of man upon our ancestral lands. While you were convalescing they began to build a town below us, in the valley. This will first of all affect the Barn Owls, whose farmland will be uprooted to make roads and the thousands of big concrete boxes that men seem to live in. Also, it will affect the Little Owls. Our intelligence service tells us that what was once no man's land is now being reclaimed by man himself, to build on, or else to use for roads. So this means that the aliens will have to depend more and more upon the remaining Barn Owl land, or else move to our dwindling woodland in an attempt to usurp it. All this information came through from our intelligence service while you were recovering from your wounds. So you see how vital it is that you fly to the city in the spring and – as promised – claim May Blossom as your bride.'

While my father pronounced this long speech my mother looked at me intently. Her eyes did not waver from my face. Though I made every effort not to betray my emotions – of which guilt, heartbreak and shame were but three – I found it almost impossible to conceal the turmoil of my feelings. My mother must have sensed this because although she wore her usual haughty look of disapproval, this time I thought I caught a glimpse below the surface of sympathy, compassion or tenderness.

'I will do whatever you ask of me,' I said, some moments after my father had finished speaking. 'But now I am tired and would like to sleep. The wound in my chest has opened again and is hurting me.'

This was true. Though the thing had long since healed, I now felt drops of blood oozing from the deep scar on my chest. At that time I had the sudden and absurd notion that my heart was bleeding. This was ridiculous, of course. Inadvertently I must have scratched myself while listening to the story about Mallow and at the same time trying to stay composed. However, the blood was real enough, and when my parents saw it they were naturally concerned. They must have thought that this superficial pain was what made me wince; not the deeper agony within. Anyway, they asked me no questions and retired at once to their own branch of the oak to let me rest. But as that never-ending grey November day waned into twilight and then crisped with the coming of the sunset frost, I knew neither sleep nor rest. One question nagged constantly at my bereaved and troubled mind. Was this fledgling born out of time Birch's son or mine? The only one who could ever know was now dead, and even if Mallow had survived could she herself ever have been certain as to the true source of this unnatural paternity?

Soon this fledgling, born so long ago, will fly across the woods which separate his territory from mine and then – with the help of his sycophantic retainers – he will kill me and usurp the last of my ancestral land. Could this be my son, I wonder? Could any son of mine be capable of such a crime against his own kind? And in the end does it really matter whose son he is? According to Tawny myth and legend, the first of us came into being forty million years ago, when the world was still very young. Then, they say, there were creatures called dinosaurs and many other species of life which have long since become extinct. According to our lore and legend, we are all sons of Juniper, the first Tawny Owl, and of Orchis, the mate provided by the Great God Bird to create our species and to launch us along the road from the birth of a race towards the inevitability of extinction after fifty or a hundred million winters, or whenever the all-powerful God Bird should decree it. As an individual like myself is born, lives for a few changing seasons on the face of this fragile earth, and then dies when his chosen winter comes, so whole species flourish and then die out when their extinction is decided by the great creator.

So does it really matter, in the end, or in the cosmic

scheme of things? Rowan, son of Birch, or Rowan, son of Yoller. Since he will kill me in any case, does it matter whose son he really is? I ask this of the wind and trees, for I have never spoken of the matter to another living soul. The memory of Mallow must remain unsullied. This I still believe is partly what love means, and love I once knew — passionately and briefly — in the willow tree above the brackish stream on that night so long ago at the beginning of the invasion and the war.

Though long since branded a heretic by my own species, I have, I believe, conserved and cherished my own concept of honour. When the time comes, I shall take that same concept with me to the grave.

CHAPTER

18

That winter was a bad one, but not as severe as Quaver has suggested in his ballad. He says that 'the snow came quickly after the battle and bandaged Ripper's wood with a smooth white sheet of late November snow. More snow came and a thick white blanket soon covered the remains of the bodies scattered beneath the trees. The frost bit deep and froze the earth as hard as iron. More snow fell until the whole of the battle zone took on a silent, ghostly stillness, waiting for new life and new hope to prosper with the coming spring. In the Lost Domain, the lake lay frozen like a stone, while bitter winds howled through the bare branches in the bleak darkness of the secret forest.'

This is all very poetic, but not strictly true. Of course, I am quoting from memory and cannot guarantee that my words are exactly the same as those used by Quaver in 'The Ancient Solitary Reign'. However, the fact remains that the battle took place earlier than he has suggested. When we fought the monster and brought him down, some of the corn in the Barn Owl country still stood tall and golden-brown. The trees were changing colour, this is true, but only just. In reality the battle took place not long after the burning of the blood-red harvest moon, at that aromatic moment on the cusp, when late summer mellows into the season of ripening fruit and falling leaves.

So, contrary to the impression given in his epic ballad, some time passed before winter gripped us all in her icy claws. Had there not been this gentle early-autumn interlude, few of the owls wounded in the war could have survived. And that goes for both Hunter and myself, of course.

As for myself, I began to fly again well before the last of the snows had melted, and by the time the first aspen catkins and the lesser celandine appeared to announce the coming of the spring, I was strong enough to fly to the willow tree in the copse above the stream, in the hope of meeting Hunter. I wanted to see how he was, of course, and also to tell him about my forthcoming mission to the city – an adventure that, to be quite frank, I dreaded! Though there was no question in my mind, at that time, of protest, let alone of mutiny or rebellion, it did occur to me that every time one was called upon to do one's duty as a Tawny aristocrat, it almost always ended in facing up to the prospect of a gory death. *Noblesse oblige* was a fine concept and one that I did not challenge, but I must confess that the putting into practice of this fine principle was something I had begun to question.

So with the coming of the first primrose, violet and snowdrop on the woodland floor, I flew down to the copse in search of Hunter. I perched on my favourite willow branch and hooted loudly to announce my presence. If he did not arrive, I would fly on across the flat land until I came to his abandoned farmhouse.

However, soon after announcing myself I sensed the coming of another owl, but not a Barn Owl, and certainly not Hunter. As far as I knew, no other Tawnies frequented the copse in no man's land, so although still weak, I flexed my talons on the willow branch beneath me, reluctant but still ready for another fight. Moments later, a Little Owl flew in through the upper branches of the copse, fluttered above me for a moment, and then landed on the branch opposite mine – the same branch on which Hunter had perched during the course of our pre-war meetings.

I could have attacked him first, of course, but strictly speaking this was no man's land and he had as much right to be there as I did. So I waited, while he looked at me with his head cocked slightly on one side in the characteristic manner of the alien who is assessing the owl he is about to address, whether that bird be one of his own species or of any other. It is a habit of theirs that has always irritated me, but that night I wished to avoid any kind of violence and so I waited patiently until he spoke.

'You must be Yoller?' he asked eventually.

'I am, indeed. How did you know?'

'Because you sometimes meet here in this very tree with the great white owl known as Hunter.'

'I have not seen him since the war,' I said. 'We were both of us very badly injured and I came here tonight to get news of him. I did not expect to see an alien here instead.'

'Steady how you go!' the Little Owl replied, surprisingly. 'Some of us don't care to be referred to as aliens. We've been here for a long time, you know.'

'You have been here for less than a hundred winters,' I riposted, icily. 'We have seen forty million of this and the other seasons come and go.'

'That is true!' replied the squatter. 'But our species, our race, is an even older one than yours. So old, in fact, that no one can remember.'

'Come to the point!' I said. 'What are you doing here, and above all, what do you want with me?'

'I have been sent to approach you about a truce or treaty,' the Little Owl replied.

'Who are you?' I asked.

'My name is Olmo. In your language that means elm.'

'That is not what I meant. I am not so much interested

in your name. I meant, what are you? What is your official role? What position do you occupy on your Little Owl council, or whatever it is you call it?'

'None,' Olmo replied. 'I have no official position. I am a poet.'

'Then why are you mixed up in politics?' I asked him. 'I have always been taught and have always thought that art and politics were incompatible.'

'Not always,' Olmo said. 'You see, I am not a traditional, chauvinistic poet like the foppish Bardic. Nor am I a lyricist like Quaver.'

'What are you, then?' I asked.

'I am a committed artist. I am what you might call a worker-poet. I use my small talents not only in the service of art, but also in the social interest and in the interests of my community.'

'And which of your small talents brings you here?' I asked, hoping that this sounded ironic, rather than rude or sarcastic. To tell the truth, what he was saying sounded to me, at that time, like a load of crow shit.

'I have told you, I am here on a mission,' Olmo said. 'I have to tell you that a progressive group of Little Owls intends to colonize the Lost Domain. We cannot live for ever in no man's land. We need a territory of our own. I am here to convince you that this would be in your interests as well. There would be no more poaching in your Tawny woodlands. There would be no more senseless disputes and killings over what is no man's land and what is not.'

'But the Lost Domain belongs to us!' I protested. 'It has been ancestral land of ours for many million winters.'

'It was!' Olmo admitted. 'It was once your land, and this we know. But then you abdicated when men built the great house there three hundred springs ago. You were afraid of the men and moved out. In our view you have now become absentee landlords and have thus forfeited your rights to sole ownership of the place. Given this, we intend to move in, colonize the land and create our own republic.'

'What about the men and their firesticks?' I asked.

'As you well know, they have gone away.'

'And if they come back?'

'That is a risk that we shall have to take. The point is, we are not afraid of the men, and you are! That is why we have more right to live in the Lost Domain than you do. Because we are less afraid of the most dangerous animal of all – the animal called man!'

'Sorry,' I said, hoping to sound dry and laconic. 'What you are proposing is quite out of the question. We intend to recolonize the Lost Domain ourselves, just as soon as we are certain that the men with firesticks have gone away. In fact, we conducted a survey to this effect just before the invasion and the war.'

'We are well aware of this,' the Little Owl replied. 'But we are also well aware of the very heavy losses you suffered in the war. In fact, according to our information, your numbers are now so depleted that you would not be in a position to take the Lost Domain, even if it were defended only by a bunch of senile sparrows. The same thing applies to the Barn Owls. After the bloody battle of Ferocity and Ripper's wood, their fighting strength is so low that we could poach on their land without fear of reprisal. But what we want is a peaceful long-term solution. We want to take the Lost Domain and turn it into our own territory – a place where we can live in peace with you in your woodlands, and with the big white owls in their neighbouring fields and meadows. I must warn you, this is our chance and we intend to take it. Given their depleted numbers, the Barn Owls will agree, I'm sure.'

'How can you be sure?' I asked.

'We have our own intelligence service, just as you and the Barn Owls do. Information is power. We are as well aware of that as you.'

'You say that our numbers are depleted and that we are no longer capable of retaking the Lost Domain? At the moment this may well be true. But soon the day may come when we need that land, or at least the secret forest. It was ours once and one day it will be ours again. For my own part, I would hope that we could reach a compromise.'

'What kind of compromise?' enquired Olmo, cocking his head to one side again.

'Well, I could suggest to my father that you should be allowed to settle and live around the lake and in the vast expanse of parkland, but that the forest should revert to us.'

'Do you think he would agree?' asked Olmo, cautiously.

'I don't know, but I could try.'

'And if you were leader now, would you be willing to ratify the proposal – the compromise you have just suggested?'

'Of course. I've just said so, haven't I?'

'Then there is some hope!' said Olmo.

'Some hope of what?' I enquired.

'Of avoiding a pogrom, or a bloody civil war. Only I have to tell you that my revolutionary colleagues are less inclined to compromise than I am. You must understand that we Little Owls have internal conflicts of our own.'

I thought of Birch and the feud that had raged between his family and mine for many hundred winters. I thought of what Hunter had told me about the disagreements on the Barn Owl council, and I nodded.

'One only unites in the face of an outside threat,' I said. 'Once that threat has disappeared, all the internal conflict starts up again.'

'Exactly! Listen, Yoller, I like your idea of the compromise. We take the Lost Domain – all of it – but when the time comes and you need to recolonize the secret forest, we will vacate it and restrict ourselves to the parkland and the lake. I will put this to the executive committee of our new co-operative and I hope they will agree. But, of course, as a mere poet and messenger, I am not in a position to make any kind of promise.'

'Neither am I!'

'We can but try,' said Olmo, with a grin that seemed almost friendly. 'After all, the most important thing would seem to be to avoid future mindless bloodshed. I believe that the younger owls of our three species are now seeking for peaceful co-existence. With the main threat of man to contend with, with the endless competition of the daytime raptors for our scant food supply, it seems more and more absurd to think of civil war. I believe it is time that we younger ones began to challenge the conditioning and the status quo that has kept us either at each other's throats, or at best in a state of cold war, for so many centuries.'

'You are very eloquent,' I said. 'You have great powers of persuasion, but much of what you say is merely rhetoric. When it comes down to the basics, what owls cherish most are their prejudices. They do not care to associate with other, lesser species, and most of all they care about tradition.'

'I am not disputing that,' Olmo said. 'I am merely pointing out that it is up to us to change things for the better. For example, we have great hopes that Hunter will convince the Barn Owl council to approve of our plans to colonize the Lost Domain. He is a forward-looking bird, possessed of some intellect, as well as courage. We are hoping that you will turn out to be the same.'

'In Tawny parlance, intellect is a dirty word,' I said. 'On the whole, we don't believe in it. We believe in common sense instead.'

'You are different,' Olmo said. 'You had the intellect to unite with the Barn Owls and bring the monster down. You also took one of our so-called untouchables to the battleground.'

'I did these things not out of choice, but out of necessity,'

I said. 'As a self-appointed intellectual, you will surely understand the difference between desire and need. And another thing,' I added, feeling ready now to mount a counter-offensive against this undoubtedly intelligent but highly presumptuous little squatter. 'You have mentioned Hunter several times, but you have not told me how he is, or whether you have informed him of your revolutionary designs. Does he know about your plans to colonize the Lost Domain? And where does your female owl called Alba fit into the scheme of things? What will she do if and when you colonize the Lost Domain? Will she go to live in your promised land, or will she stay with Hunter?'

'I don't know.'

'What don't you know?'

'I don't know anything about their relationship. It is a private matter, which concerns only the two of them.'

'But you say that you are hoping Hunter will persuade the Barn Owl council to approve of your plans to colonize the Lost Domain.'

'Yes, in the same way that we hope you will persuade your father to do the same.'

'But does Hunter know?' I insisted. 'Or are you relying on little Alba to convince him at some future date?'

'You seem preoccupied by Hunter,' said Olmo, once again avoiding an answer to the question that was now burning in my mind. 'You must forgive me,' he continued, 'but to me it seems a strange relationship. An unusual affinity, wouldn't you say, between a white bird from the farmland and a brown wood owl like yourself.'

'He is a friend of mine,' I said. 'We fought a war together. As I remember it you and your revolutionary colleagues were not there.'

As my silent listeners may have gathered, I did not care much for this Little Owl called Olmo, but I must admit that he was intelligent. Very intelligent. He sat on his branch of the willow and stared at me for some time without replying, having obviously grasped what I was getting at. Before he'd had a chance to summon up his so-called intellect, I moved into the second phase of my escalating counter-attack.

'And on the subject of unnatural liaisons,' I said, 'how do your revolutionary colleagues – and, indeed, how do the orthodox immigrants among you – perceive this relationship between Hunter and the female of your species known as Alba? Do you approve of it or not? I have to say that it strikes me as even more unnatural than a friendship between two owls of different species who happen to be fighting on the same side.'

'I would rather not comment on that,' said Olmo who, although only an immigrant and a poet, had none the less some notions of diplomacy.

'I will leave you now,' I said, giving the alien messenger a formal little bow. 'I will think on the things you have said and decide whether or not it would be in order to present your proposal to my father.'

'Think carefully!' Olmo said. 'Remember the advantages both for you and for the Barn Owls. Once we have established our own territory – our own democratic republic – we shall no longer need to live in no man's land, or infiltrate your forest or the Barn Owl farmland.'

'You said that before. If I decide to report to my father, I shall of course stress this point as strongly as you have done tonight. I can promise you that it is the only point in your proposal which might appeal to him.'

'Goodnight, then!' Olmo said. 'Shall we meet again when you have made your mind up?'

'Of course. In either case, I shall tell you what has been decided.'

Olmo then returned the bow – little more than a nod, really – with which I had previously taken my leave of him. Then he flew off on his funny, bouncing little wings. Though I could not be sure, I guessed that he was going to the Lost Domain to confer with his confederates. As for me, I sat still on my willow branch and mulled this new information over in my mind and, as I did so, the most horrible suspicion took root and came to sudden flowering, like a voracious, all-devouring weed.

It struck me that Hunter was being used. Perhaps the whole thing had been set up from the very beginning! Little Alba had been sent to seduce and subvert Hunter to the aliens' cause. She was an infiltrator, a spy, and her song, the song that had so moved me, was all part of the same plan. Her song was art, but Olmo had just told me that he believed an artist could use his or her talents in order to further some kind of cause — religious, political, territorial or whatever. Personally, I found this reprehensible. I have always believed — along with one of our most famous Tawny poets — that the expression of any political opinion by an artist represents a most unpardonable mannerism of style. He — or, in this case, she — should be neutral, and by neutral I mean not neutered, but objective. Thus I have tried in this prosaic account of the owl history of my times to be as fair as possible, and to tell things as they happened, or to tell it like it was, as they say these days; to tell it without embroidering, like the media birds, and without striving for aesthetic, religious or political effect of any kind.

Shocked as I was by the suspicion that Alba might be using her art, as well as her body, to subvert Hunter to the aliens' cause, I decided at once to say nothing to my father until I had spoken to the white bird and had ascertained his views on this matter, if indeed he knew anything about it, and I suspected he did not!

This, of course, meant committing yet another sin of omission by not telling my father what I already knew. As it happened, I need not have worried quite so much, for when I returned home well before the dawn after what subsequently turned out to be an historic meeting with the

Little Owl called Olmo, my father broached at once the very topic that the immigrant and I had just been discussing.

'Have you heard?' he asked, as soon as I had landed in the oak.

'Heard what?'

'Didn't Hunter tell you?'

'I haven't seen Hunter,' I replied, and this at least was true enough.

'They say the Little Owls are going to colonize the Lost Domain. As a result of the survey you carried out before the war, we know that some of them are already squatting there. But now it seems that they have plans to turn it into their own, exclusive territory and found some kind of Little Owl co-operative!'

'Who told you this?'

'We have it on the grapevine,' replied my father.

'What is a grape?' I asked, for I had never seen one at that time.

'It is a kind of fruit men cultivate,' my father said impatiently. 'Once upon a time they grew around here, but now they don't. It is too cold. Though another thing that has come through on the grapevine is that the earth is slowly heating up, so one day they may grow here again. However, this is quite beside the point. The point is that these little squatters must at all costs be prevented from usurping our ancestral land.'

'Why?' I asked. 'If they had a territory of their own they wouldn't need to live in no man's land or poach in our own woods and spinneys. In any case, why do we need the parkland and the secret forest? There aren't enough of us left to populate this woodland territory, let alone to colonize another.'

'That is defeatist talk,' my mother snapped. 'You will go to the great city to bring back May Blossom and others of our own kind who are temporarily lodging there. Then we, not the Little Owls, shall recolonize the Lost Domain. It has been known and said for many thousand winters that these Little Owls shall never have a nation or a territory of their own. They were born as wanderers and are destined to live in no man's land for ever. The day they establish a reign or republic of their own, there will be war. War either against us, against the Barn Owls, or even among their own.'

'There is another thing,' my father said, after a brief, disapproving glance at my mother. 'A thing of more importance than any myth or legend relating to the Little Owls. You have said that this woodland territory is more than adequate for all of us. Well, it is now, but as I told you before, men are building in the valley below us and are now creeping slowly up the hill. If they continue, we shall one day need to return to the secret forest. The immigrants' plan to colonize the Lost Domain must be prevented at all costs. The squatters breed like rabbits and once they are established there the parkland and the forest will teem and seethe with them, like wasps or flies around the fallen, rotting fruit in autumn. This is a matter of the first priority and, accordingly, there has been a change of plan.'

'What change of plan?' I asked, with my heart sinking at the thought of another dangerous task with which my father might suddenly commission me. It seemed that every time he gave me a mission, I came home bleeding and half-dead. Though I was still very young, I must confess again that the appeal of all this heroism was palling and falling as the leaves drop at the first touch of winter frost.

'You will not be leaving at once for the city, to fetch May Blossom back. Instead, you will undertake a secret-service mission to discover every detail of the immigrants' plan to colonize the Lost Domain.'

'And how do you suggest one should conduct this mission?' I asked. Though I was careful to show no enthusiasm, secretly I was very pleased, for two most urgent reasons. First, this new task meant postponing the dreaded mission to the city. Second, I already knew more than my parents did about the aliens' plan. Additionally, I now realized that for the first time in my life I was beginning to reason like an adult. This time I would neither volunteer for anything, nor disclose the information I already had. Information was power, according to Olmo, the squatter-poet. So be it! This time I would take credit for researching and reporting what I already knew!

'I would suggest that you start with your friend Hunter,' my father said. 'According to our information, he is now almost recovered from his war wounds and still living with the immigrant you brought to the battlefield in Ripper's wood. Also, we have word that she sometimes hunts in the Lost Domain. If this is the case, she must know the secret plans of her alien race.'

'Very well,' I said. 'I will try to make contact with Hunter tomorrow night.'

'Tomorrow is too late,' my mother said. 'You will fly and seek him out at moonrise tonight!'

This sparked it off! This haughty, half-disdainful edict of my mother's set off my first open rebellion against the role in which I had been cast – the role of a future leader who would ruthlessly maintain all the intolerance and prejudice of our ancient Tawny reign.

'Tonight I have matters of my own to attend to,' I lied in what I hoped was a suave and adult manner. 'And incidentally,' I added, 'from sunset tonight I shall be moving back into my own tree. I thank you both for looking after me during this long winter of convalescence, but now that my wounds have all healed, I intend to return to what I consider my own home.'

My father and mother exchanged a rapid glance, and in my father's eyes I thought I caught a look which said, 'I told you so, I warned you, and now you have pushed your son too far.' I may have been mistaken, I don't know. But in spite of the warning look from my father, and true to the colour of her blue blood, my mother returned at once to the attack.

'If you go now, you need never bother to come back,' she said. 'The mission your father has asked you to undertake is one that is vital for Tawny Owl survival. As future leader, it is your duty to do as you are asked, at once. We have survived so far on the twin bastions of self-sacrifice and discipline. Insubordination, selfishness and ingratitude will get us nowhere. If everyone behaved as you do, we should lose our ancient superiority and sink to below the level of the Barn Owls and even lower than the little squatters. At the setting of the sun and the rising of the moon, we should be no better than the loathsome rook or crow.'

'You did not fight in the war,' I replied, attempting to keep an outward calm, though inside I was seething with emotion. 'You did not fight in the war, you hid in a crevice in the bald hill, not far from that coward Birch. Most of us who did fight were either killed or wounded. One should remember that, I think. One should remember that at the setting of the sun and at moonrise, and one should refrain from comparing us to rook or crow. Now, if it is vital that the survey should begin tonight, why don't you go? Why don't both of you go? Have you suddenly become senile, or geriatric? As for me, I will do as you ask, although I confess I have no stomach for the mission. I will do as you ask, but as from now, I will do things as I decide and in my own time. Goodnight!'

With that I took off before either of them could reply and flew back to sleep in my own tree for the first time since the war. As I winged my way through the wood, it struck me that I had been slightly unfair to my mother. She had not chosen to hide in the crevice. It was my father who had obliged her to do so. None the less, I was not sorry. I felt that at long last the time had come. As I flew back to my own oak, and as the first red weals of sunrise began to sear the dark night sky, I thought to myself, this is the dawn of the first day of my new life. From now on things will be different. From now on I will do things my way.

Well, I was right. It was the dawn of a new life, but it was also a prelude to my coming death. As Quaver put it, in his rather biased account of these same events, the paths of love, honour and success lead always and only to the grave.

But on that night so long ago I was still young, strong and full of hope for a better life, not only for myself, but for all the owls who fly in hope from sunset until dawn, under the same sky.

CHAPTER

 19

I slept all day, untroubled by remorse about what had passed between myself and my parents, and at dusk I took off, flew down to the willow in the copse, and hooted to announce my coming. I had decided that if Hunter failed to answer my call, I would fly on to his abandoned farmhouse and confront him in the home he had made with little Alba – the place where he had been convalescing since the war.

However, I was relieved when he answered my call at once, with a message to the effect that he was on his way to meet me in the copse. In view of the delicate nature of my mission, I obviously preferred to avoid the presence of the little alien.

I waited on the willow branch with very mixed emotions as the handsome white owl winged his way across the meadows that separated the broken-down house in which he lived from the confines of his territory and mine. We had not met since the war, as my silent listeners already know. If they have the feelings one hopes they have, the wind and the trees will be able to imagine the state of my emotions as I waited for my former friend and wartime ally – a friend and ally I had been sent to spy on; an owl of another species who had proved himself to be a more loyal comrade than many of my own so-called superior kind. But what troubled me most about our first post-war reunion was the fact that I now had to question his relationship with little Alba, the alien who had taken care of him throughout the long months of winter. I had to establish whether he knew that she had been hunting in the Lost Domain, and whether he knew that she might have had the most insidious and far-reaching ulterior motive for what might have seemed to her lover a risk and a self-sacrifice of the most noble kind.

As I waited in the willow, Hunter flew in on silken wings and settled at once on the branch opposite me. I saw at once that he looked fit and well, and that there were no visible signs of the dreadful war wounds he had sustained.

After we had exhausted the conventional form of greeting, enquired after each other's health and so on, I decided to come to the point at once. I had too much respect for Hunter to stoop to any kind of duplicity.

'What do you know about the Little Owls and the Lost Domain?' I asked, as soon as the first formalities were over.

'Very little,' Hunter replied in his usual frank and open manner. 'I know that some of them are living there, as indeed they were before the war, when we flew there together to conduct the survey for your father.'

'And did you know that little Alba often went hunting there?'

'Of course. I wouldn't say often, but from time to time this winter she was obliged to fly there to feed herself. The food on Beak Poke's land was not sufficient for the two of us. I could not hunt, of course, so she would bring me whatever was available here and then fly on to the Lost Domain to get what she could for herself.'

'Did she not tell you about the revolutionary committee?' I asked.

Hunter looked back at me with such frank and blank

surprise that I knew at once that he must be innocent of all complicity in the alien plot to take over and usurp the Lost Domain.

'What committee?' he asked, and as he put the question to me I saw a sudden flicker of doubt begin to blur the candid and open expression in his eyes.

'We have it on good authority that they intend to form a republic there,' I said. 'Though it is generally accepted that these immigrants have been condemned by the Great God Bird to live always and for ever in no man's land, despised and held in contempt by all other owl species, it now seems that some of them have decided to establish a territory of their own. I have heard it said that Alba is aware of this and has attended some of their council meetings, but this is merely hearsay. I wasn't there myself and so I can't be sure.'

'I'm sure you're wrong,' Hunter replied at once. 'As you well know, Alba saved my life this winter. She fed me through the frost and snow, she licked my wounds and helped me back to health and strength. If and when she went to the Lost Domain, it was in search of food for herself, not to attend the meetings of some revolutionary committee.'

'You must forgive me!' I said. 'I hate to stir up trouble or to bring bad news, but we have it on the grapevine that she is one of them, and that as soon as this co-operative, or republic, is established, she will go there and live among them.'

'I don't believe it!' Hunter said, after a moment's pause. 'If there were any truth in the matter, Alba would have long since told me.'

'Talk to her about it,' I suggested. 'Ask her why she flies to the Lost Domain to hunt. Since the war, your numbers and ours are so depleted that even on this run-down territory of poor old Beak Poke's, there is more than sufficient food for the two of you.'

'I don't care for your insinuations,' Hunter said. 'I respect you because we fought together in the war and you proved to be a loyal and courageous friend. But to implicate Alba in a plot of this kind is quite simply ridiculous! If you must know, she loves me and she will stay with me until the end! She cares nothing for the traditions and the prejudices of her own kind, and I care even less than nothing for the worn-out Barn Owl dogma on which I was brought up. I believe that younger owls like you and me should set an example, and by doing so should help to set our separate species free from the chauvinism and the blind hatred that has been fed into us for centuries.'

'That is more or less what Olmo thinks,' I said.

'Olmo?'

'Olmo is a poet and one of these new revolutionary Little Owls who want to establish this co-operative or republic in the Lost Domain.'

'When did you meet him?'

'He came here the other night with a message for my father.'

'What was your father's reaction?'

'I haven't told him yet. First I wanted to talk to you and find out what you knew about it.'

'I know very little,' Hunter said. 'I know only that Alba has two cousins living in the Lost Domain – male cousins that she is not over-fond of. Apart from that, it would seem that you are the one with all the information!' Hunter said this without sarcasm, and even the touch of irony that he had attempted did not come across. There was hurt in his voice and in his eyes, and I believe he realized then that he had been betrayed.

'Go home and speak to Alba,' I insisted. 'Get her to tell you all she knows. It may be that she knows nothing, as you say. But if she is involved in this plan to colonize the Lost Domain, your Barn Owl friends will want to be informed. In fact, maybe they have heard already, in which case your position could be embarrassing, to say the least! They won't believe that Alba neither knew nor told you. You will be accused of complicity in the little squatters' plot to take over the Lost Domain, and your chances for the future will be severely damaged.'

'I don't give an ounce of sparrow shit for my future chances!' Hunter said, with some considerable feeling. 'I just want to live the rest of my life in peace, and live it preferably with little Alba.'

I looked at him for a moment or two, wondering whether I dared ask him the question that was now uppermost in my mind. Well, we had flown together on that dangerous mission to the Lost Domain, and afterwards we had fought side by side and both been injured in that bloodiest of wars. In wartime things are different. One gets to know the other more quickly and more intimately than in times of peace. So I took the plunge!

'If Alba decided to join this new co-operative and live with her own kind in the Lost Domain, would you go with her?' I asked.

Now it was Hunter's turn to pause and reflect. Before replying, he shifted slightly on his branch of the willow tree, glanced down to the brackish stream and then up to the stars. Then he looked back at me and, though he was outwardly composed, I could see that the hurt still lingered and that I had begun to sow the seeds of doubt.

'The question has not arisen,' he said, eventually. 'The question has not arisen and I don't suppose for a moment that it ever will. But if it did, at some future date, I would give the matter my consideration.'

'You would consider living among a colony of Little Owls in the Lost Domain?'

'I have said that I would give the matter my consideration.'

'You would be an outcast!' I said. 'Your own kind would

reject you, for now and for ever. There is nothing owls hate more than a split with their ancient traditions.'

'Speak for yourself!' said Hunter. 'You are a Tawny. I am not. All Tawnies are tradition-ridden, as I believe many of the Little Owls are ridden with the God Bird.'

'Everyone is ridden with something or other,' I agreed. 'But you and Olmo may be right. It may be that the post-war owls of all our species will love each other, co-operate and create a new millennium. I must admit I have my doubts, but I must accept that it all remains to be seen. In fact, the more one thinks about it, the more you might be right! A great white owl – a war hero and a future leader – abandons his own kind and goes to live among the pygmies in what most of your own species must consider a jungle. Yes, indeed! You could make history. You could become a legend in your time!'

I didn't like saying this, but I was quite clear as to what I was doing. I was being cruel to be kind – cruel so that in time my friend should see the folly of his ways and not throw his whole life away for a highly suspect little alien who could sing. However, if Hunter was stung or angered by what I'd said, he showed no sign of it. Instead, he looked at me calmly, though traces of pain and worry still lingered in his eyes.

'I will do as you suggest,' he said. 'I will speak to Alba and attempt to learn the truth, if any, behind these allegations. In the meantime, please say nothing to your father, or to any other owl. So far all is hearsay, and hearsay can escalate out of all proportion, as you probably know.'

'Very well. But I can't wait too long. My father has asked me to investigate this matter, and although one does not care for the task, investigate one must. I suppose the best thing would be to fly directly to the Lost Domain, but for obvious reasons, I'm not at all keen on that course of action!'

'Give me time,' Hunter said again. 'Give me time and I

will get this information for you, not only from Alba, but from its source, deep inside the Lost Domain. After my long winter of convalescence, I must go home to see my mother. On my way I shall visit the place where my father fell in Brook's meadow, and I shall fly to the battlefield to salute both the Barn Owl and the Tawny dead. As you are well aware, my journey will take me right through the heart of the Lost Domain. If there are secrets there, then I will find them for you. But first you must tell me exactly what it is you want to know.'

'First I need to know whether it is true or not.'

'What Olmo told you?'

'Yes. Then, if it is true, I need to know the numbers and names of these revolutionary immigrants who intend to colonize the place. Not all the names! Those of the leaders will do. But my father will want to know each leader's specific role.'

'Anything else?' asked Hunter, whom I admired for successfully concealing the emotion he must have been feeling at this time.

'Yes. Details of the constitution of this new republic. If they have such a thing, of course. Being aliens, I don't suppose for a moment that they have made any proper plans. But then again, one never knows.'

'I will find out what I can,' said Hunter. 'However, I am not yet strong enough to undertake the journey that I have in mind. It will take until at least the next full moon before I am fully ready. In the meantime, I suggest you trace this poet, Olmo, and talk to him again.'

'That is my intention,' I replied. 'And also in the meantime, I will try to satisfy my father by feeding him one piece of information at a time. However, how long he will stand for these delaying tactics, one doesn't really know.'

'I would have thought he had very little choice,' Hunter riposted. 'Unless he wants to go himself, of course!'

'He is too old and much too valuable to be risked on a

mission of this kind,' I said at once. But this time Hunter's irony had touched me, since for quite some time I had formed the distinct impression that my father was now leading from behind. This is what happens to most of us, I fear, as we grow older.

Hunter said goodbye to me then in a manner that was rather cold, but not surprising in view of what I had just told him. He flew back in the direction of his broken-down farmhouse, doubtless intent on a preliminary confrontation with the little squatter who had half-saved his life and then nursed him back to health. As for me, I also took off soon afterwards, and winged my way slowly back to my own oak. I needed time to think before the next meeting with my father.

As I flew out of the copse and up into our sloping woodland, up towards the bald hill which I had always fondly thought of as a mountain, I must confess that I was assailed by considerable doubts. Had I been hypocritical? Had I been wrong, or not, to warn Hunter about his infatuation with the little immigrant? I had been so nearly on the point of throwing my own future away for Mallow. In fact, had she not died in giving birth to what might well be my son, I would almost certainly have done just that! And so how could I now sit in judgement on another who loved not wisely, as our ancient Tawny poet says – on another who loved not wisely, but too well?

The question disturbed me deeply that night as I sat in my own oak and thought about it all. No, I correct myself! I did not think so much as brood, and in the midst of this brooding I began to feel sorry for Hunter and sorry for myself. Supposing I had killed Mallow by mating with her out of season? How could I ever respect myself again? Yet I had done it, and I knew that if she still lived, I would do the same thing again. So what right had I to perch in judgement on my friend Hunter for his love affair with the little squatter? She had fought in the war, after all, which was more than Mallow, my mother or May Blossom had done. And now it seemed she was a spy, in the service of the revolutionary Little Owl co-operative!

My silent listeners will understand that all this was a lot to take, so soon after the war. One wanted peace now, and not the eternal setting of one race, one species or one religion against another.

But then again, there was one's duty. Oh, yes, always one's duty. But duty to whom, and for what, I asked myself as the sun thrust up through the blackness of the night and began to rise above the bald hill, the stream and the woodland which I loved so well. Ferocity, Stoop and Ripper had done their duty and were now dead. One had never liked them, and to be honest, I can't say it really mattered. But I suppose it did to them. And I had been very fond of my brother, Forster, who would – I believe – have been a stronger and firmer leader than the one I was shortly destined to become. And he, too, had died, in the service of what? Tawny Owl supremacy, freedom to fly the night sky? Only the Great God Bird knew why he and so many others had died, and why so many others had derived the benefits without making any kind of sacrifice.

I dozed then, as the first light began to break and the red streaks of dawn began to feed the first spring leaves on the trees around me with those magic, pastel colours which few other creatures ever see.

How will this ever end, I thought, as at daybreak I drifted into sleep. Must there always be more strife? Why can't we live in peace together and enjoy the ever-changing rhythms of the countryside? What would happen to Hunter and Alba? What would happen to me on my most dangerous forthcoming mission to the city? If and when I returned, would the Little Owls have colonized the Lost Domain? And if they had, would this mean war again?

Had I known the answers to these questions then, I would not have slept so well on that day in early spring.

Had I known the answers, I think I would have fled in search of some safe place where no other owls were to be found. I would have searched for some safe haven with only the wind and trees for friends. But at that time I was still young and curious, and could hardly wait to find out what might happen next.

As it happened, and as my silent listeners already know, my questions were answered much sooner than I had expected!

CHAPTER

20

In Quaver's chronicle, or epic ballad, there is no account of what passed between Hunter and myself in the willow tree on that distant night in early spring. In 'The Ancient Solitary Reign' it is mentioned that we met, and that immediately afterwards he confronted little Alba. But there is no record of our conversation, and I have often wondered why. In the long intervening winters, and in view of everything that has happened since, I have come to the conclusion that his fellow Barn Owls were ashamed of him. They did not like the idea of one of their own kind living with a little alien, any more than my father or mother would have approved of my relationship with the lovely Mallow had she lived.

In Quaver's version of these historical events, credit is given exclusively to Hunter for discovering the immigrants' plot to colonize the Lost Domain. There is no mention of the fact that he, their wartime hero and potential leader, had been duped by an alien spy.

It is my belief that in his original version Quaver would have told the truth, as reported to him by his brother. But I dare say that when he presented his first draft to the Barn Owl council, they forced him to make certain changes. In particular, they would have wanted to eliminate anything that threw a bad light either on Hunter, or especially on themselves as the elders of the Barn Owl community.

This is pure speculation, of course – a hypothesis which I ask my silent listeners to analyse and then breathe further down the winds and rivers if they wish. Other such anomalies will become apparent as my tale progresses, and though I strive always after truth, my own version of things must also be subjective. Though I have long since outgrown any racial, religious or political commitment, I am still a Tawny Owl and, as such, I cannot pretend to fathom the hidden longings or aspirations of other species, be they immigrants or the white owls who live below us on the plain.

But enough of this barren conjecture and back to the narrative, which our expert storytellers say should be swift and sure as the water that surges below me from the rock. After my meeting with Hunter, I reported back to my father well before the dawn.

'Very well, then,' he said. As you will have gathered by now, 'very well, then' was one of his favourite expressions.

'Very well, then, but we cannot wait for him to return from this first journey home. In the first place, we don't know what may happen when he gets there. Now that his father is dead and his brother back with their pompous Bard Owl, working on their so-called epic ballad, his mother may want him to stay.'

'You can't go home again!' I said. 'That is one of the Barn Owl rules. It is something they believe. I know because both Beak Poke and Hunter told me.'

'Rules are made to be broken!' my father said, uncharacteristically.

'Especially after a war,' my mother added. 'After a war the old values are always called into question. Generally there is a decline in the standards of morality.'

'There is usually a decline in all standards, both during and after any kind of war,' continued my father. 'When death has stared them in the face — when they have lost their loved ones — owls forget for a while about form and tradition. So any post-war period is a dangerous time — a time when discipline is slack and great mistakes are made. It is also a time when those who did not take part in the war are most likely to profit from it.'

'Like the Little Owls,' my mother said. 'They would not have dared to attempt this colonization of the Lost Domain unless our own and the Barn Owl numbers were so tragically depleted. And there's another thing to bear in mind about your friend Hunter,' she added, leaning forward on her branch.

'What's that?' I asked.

'His mother and his elders on the Barn Owl council will do everything to stop his liaison with this little alien. Now that Beak Poke is dead and the war is over, they will offer him a new tutor — a new territory — anything to get him away from the clutches of that little squatter.' My mother paused for a moment and then leaned back again and began to pluck fastidiously at the feathers on her chest. 'Or else, as I've already said, his mother will ask him to stay at home and become head of the family territory.'

'But first he must conform?' I asked.

'Of course!' my mother said. 'Even Barn Owls would never entertain the idea of a council member or a major landlord living in squalor with a little alien.'

'So you don't think he'll come back?' I asked.

'No!' my father said. 'Not unless he is very stubborn, or else very foolish. They will make it worth his while to stay.'

'And if he doesn't?'

'Then he will be ostracized,' my mother said.

'Ostracized?'

'Yes. Cut off without any hope of becoming a future leader in the community.'

'Like me, if I'd taken Mallow?'

214

I saw a quick glance pass between my parents – a brief glance of complicity.

'Yes, more or less,' my mother said, turning back to me at once. 'You see, Yoller, there are things the establishment will tolerate, and things it will not.'

Then sod the establishment, I thought. But, of course, I didn't say so. I still needed to play for time.

'So you see how essential it is,' my father said. 'It is essential that you discover the subversive plans of these little aliens so that we can counter them at once. To this end, you must fly at once to the Lost Domain. Be perfidious, if you wish. Pretend to be representing us on a diplomatic mission. Gather all the information you can and then return to us at once. Above all you must discover their strong and weak points – the strengths and weaknesses of the aliens' plan to colonize the Lost Domain. On no account must we become complacent, merely because we won the war. That would be fatal. To survive, one must be able to sustain conflict. And conflict there will be. Do you understand?'

'Yes, but I regret it!'

'So do we all,' my mother said. 'But conflict is part of life. It is part of what we call survival.'

'It is also part of death,' I said, remembering the bleeding corpses strewn about the mossy floor of Ferocity and Ripper's wood. 'However, I will do what you consider to be my duty. I will fly to the Lost Domain tonight and bring back whatever information I can find. However, I must warn you that I don't know how long it will take me to carry out an investigation of this kind. If you want a thorough survey and an exhaustive report, then you may have to wait.'

'If the Little Owls have already settled there in any numbers, your mission may be dangerous,' my father said. 'You had better take another Tawny with you, just in case.'

'You mean a bodyguard?' I asked. 'A brute like Birch,

perhaps? How do you think I can gain the confidence of these immigrants and infiltrate their secret society if I arrive there with a Tawny thug like Stoop, Ferocity or Ripper?'

'Do not speak ill of the dead!' my mother said. 'And you know very well that Birch cannot go with you. He has his fledgling to look after.'

His, or mine, I thought, but naturally said nothing. In any case, Birch was the last owl I would have wished to accompany me on a mission as dangerous as this.

'Yoller's right, this time,' my father said, surprising me again. 'His mission is that of a diplomat, and therefore he should fly alone.'

'Do you mean a diplomat, or a spy?' I asked. 'If I fly and risk my life in the role of a diplomat, I must have some powers of negotiation. I must have something to offer in return for the information I receive. If I fly with nothing to barter with, they may kill me as a spy.'

My father and mother glanced at each other again and this time it was clear from the expression in their eyes that my point had struck well and truly home.

'Very well, then, what do you suggest?' my father enquired.

'Under the circumstances – and I mean our straitened circumstances at this time – I would offer them the gardens, the lake and the parkland in which to found their new republic. I would suggest that they set up the co-operative there, whilst we retain all rights to resettle in the secret forest.'

'No!' my mother replied immediately. 'You don't understand the immigrant mentality. If you give them one meadow's length, they will take ten times as much at once. You may pretend to negotiate with them, if you wish, but only in order to extract the information we require. As soon as we know their plans, their numbers and, as your father says, their strengths and weaknesses, we can send in a task force to destroy them.'

216

'What task force?' I enquired. 'After our heavy losses in the war, there aren't more than half a dozen Tawnies fit to fight in the entire district.'

'Yoller is right,' my father said, thus surprising me for the third time in one single night. 'The important thing at the moment is information, not action. It is essential that we monitor the progress of these aliens, so that when the right time comes we are in a position to destroy them.'

'And when will the right time be?' I asked, with my eyebrows raised, expressing what I hoped was a sophisticated kind of irony.

'When you return from the city, bringing reinforcements,' my father replied at once. 'May Blossom is not the only distant cousin we have living in that place. There are others, many others who must be longing to return to their rightful habitat in the wild. And it is these Tawnies who will eventually take not only the secret forest, but the entire length and breadth of the Lost Domain.'

'And what if the men with firesticks come back?' I asked.

'If they come back in the short term, they will kill the Little Owls who are attempting to settle there,' my father said. 'If they return later, they will in any case first kill the owls living closest to the great house, around the lake and in the parkland that slopes up to the woods. This will give the Tawnies living in the secret forest advance warning and they will be able to escape.'

'Where to?' I asked. 'The Lost Domain is surrounded by Barn Owl country. Their only refuge would be here. You say the men are already creeping up the hill with their roads and buildings, so our ancestral territory is shrinking. Would there be room for all these Tawnies from the city, assuming that they came and then were forced to abandon the Lost Domain?'

'You are thinking too far ahead,' my mother said. 'You may have to think ahead when you become leader of this community, but not before. As your father pointed out quite recently, you occasionally show signs of becoming an intellectual. It is a fault in you that I deplore!'

'I am only trying to connect,' I said.

'Do not attempt it!' my father said. 'At any rate, not yet. Remember only the old code of honour for all young Tawny officers: Mine not to think or say, mine only to obey.'

'So you want me to fly to the Lost Domain, ostensibly on a diplomatic mission, but in reality to spy on them, and then report back to you?'

'Yes!' my father said. 'Now is our way clear and our meaning plain,' he continued, using a quotation from one of our relatively modern Tawny poets. 'You will negotiate and offer them, as you yourself suggested, use of the gardens, the lakeside and the great expanse of parkland in which to create their new republic. But you will insist that at all times we must have access to the secret forest, which will be colonized by us on your return from the great city.'

'And will you honour this agreement?' I asked. 'Assuming, of course, that I am able to negotiate such a settlement with the Little Owls? Will you leave them to live in the great parkland, in the gardens and by the lake, or will you attempt to drive them out once we have recolonized the secret forest?'

'That will depend on the ensuing circumstances,' my father said. 'If the men return from their war and kill the Little Owls, there will be no need for us to do it. The men will start their killing near the great house and the lake. The Tawnies living in the higher woodland will have time to escape. The aliens will be trapped, as it were, in a ghetto of their own making!'

'You have not answered my question. If I negotiate this agreement with the Little Owls, namely that they occupy the gardens, the lakeside and the parkland only, and leave us the secret forest – and allow us, of course, free passage across what will by then have become their territory – we in return will never attempt to reclaim the district in which they have built their new republic?'

'We will destroy them when the time is right,' my mother said. 'For the moment, what we require is diplomacy. We must ensure that they do not infest the secret forest before our cousins return from the city and reclaim it as their own.'

'Then you are asking me to lie? You are asking me to negotiate an agreement which I know in advance will be broken, if and when it suits our imperialistic plans?'

'That is known as diplomacy,' my father said, with a curt little nod. 'Go now and negotiate this agreement, but remember that your main task is to gather information. Your diplomatic mission is merely a cover to enable us to gather the necessary intelligence.'

'In other words, you have cast your son, the sometime warrior, as a spy?'

'In the interests of our Tawny Owl survival, yes!' my father said. 'I would send another owl, but I cannot, because you are the one best suited to the job. You know the territory, you know Hunter, and you are acquainted with Alba, the little immigrant on whom he is squandering his youth. You have also been approached by Olmo, their messenger, so in a sense you have been cast in your present role by time and circumstance.'

'How did you know that I had already met with Olmo?'

'You met him in the copse, on a willow branch above the brackish stream. Why have you not told us what passed between you that night?'

'Nothing passed between us,' I lied, trying to sound casual, though in actual fact I was in a state of shock. Had my own father begun spying on me now? 'I merely asked him if he had news of Hunter. But I repeat, how did you know that he and I had met?'

'It was reported to us,' my father said.

'By whom?'

'I do not wish to reveal my source of information at this point.'

'So you want me to be a spy, but in the meantime you've set someone to spy on me!' I said.

'Don't be impertinent!' my mother snapped. 'How dare you accuse your father of such a thing!'

'Take it easy, Yoller,' my father drawled, in the most aristocratic of his tones. 'It was pure coincidence that the two of you were observed together. However, your mother and I did think it rather odd that you should not have felt it incumbent on you to report back to us on the subject of an encounter with a Little Owl who appears to be invested with the role of their official messenger.'

'Who told you this?' I insisted.

'It doesn't matter,' my father said. 'What matters now is that you should fly at once to the Lost Domain, seek this Olmo out and obtain all the information we require.'

'Very well!' I said, knowing that this use of his favourite cliché would please him. 'I will go at once and conduct negotiations with the Little Owls along the lines you have suggested. And I will return with all the information you require. But I will do this on one condition, and one condition only.'

'And pray what might that one condition be?' asked my mother, leaning back on her branch and preening her feathers in haughty disapproval.

'I want to know who is spying on me,' I said. 'And when you see him next, tell him this. As soon as I know his name, I shall kill him. Is that clear?'

With this, I took off from my branch and flew in a blaze of fury down through our woods in the direction of the willow in the copse that stood above the brackish stream. I seethed with shame and indignation as I flew – shame because I had been chosen to negotiate a treaty which might be broken at any future time, in the interests of the Tawnies, and seething indignation because my own father and mother had set another owl to spy on me. Me! A war hero, a future leader and, now that Forster was dead, their one remaining son. When one's blood is boiling with anger, one tends to fly faster than at other times and one does not tend to notice the passing time or the woodland and countryside along the way. I therefore flew on in my inner rage, oblivious to the snowdrop, primrose and violet sleeping in the woodland carpet below my driven wings.

Descending from the woods, I did not pause to take notice of the pear blossom in the hedge or of the daffodils and moss cups, or of the first daisies which burst from the floor of the copse below the willow tree and beside the brackish stream.

I flew into my favourite branch and sat there seething until dawn came and went, and then I slept until woken at noon by the call of the first cuckoo. Under the high sun one could smell the coming spring, and on the Barn Owl land nearby I could hear the bleating of young lambs, and thought I could smell the marsh marigolds which had begun to push their way up on the banks of the slow-moving stream below me.

I slept again, and then, at twilight, I made a sudden decision! I would not do this thing. I would not act as a diplomat and negotiate a treaty that I knew would be broken at our earliest convenience. The counterparts to this agreement were only Little Owls. As such they were a lower form of life, hardly better than magpie, rook or crow. But none the less they were owls of a kind, and above all there was my honour to consider.

'Honour!' Sage was to taunt me when I met him later in the city. 'What is honour? Can you eat it? Can you mate with it? Will it give you shelter from the hail and wind?' he asked me then, as we perched in a huge cypress tree in the park, close to the compound in which men kept so many species of bird and animal imprisoned in their cages. 'What is honour, then?' Sage continued, spotting my ears prick at the sound of howling and wailing which rose up from that dreadful prison, lacerating the night sky around us with the lament of creatures who had been trapped by man and would never more be free. 'Why don't you go and ask the owls incarcerated in that prison. Ask them what honour is! If any single one of them has a shred of honour left, I bet he would trade it just for the chance to perch with us here, under the open sky, in the freedom of this cypress tree! More than that, I bet that if the most honourable owl among those prisoners had a mother, a mate or a female fledgling, he would trade either one, or all three, to fly as free as we do, under the same sky – the same night sky the God Bird created as our natural habitat. Honour is for those who can afford it, dear boy. It is not for the likes of you and me!'

Of course, all this came much later. I was warned about Sage well before I met him – warned that he was a real intellectual, whilst I was always torn between accepting the ancient values, the lores and mores to which I had been conditioned, torn between accepting or questioning and contesting them as I did that night so long ago, perched high in the willow tree above the slow-running stream.

However, at that time I believed in honour, and in spite of the subsequent lessons that I learned from Sage, I have never entirely abandoned my belief in it. One has to cling on to something, I suppose, and although I have at times behaved dishonourably, I like to think that this was due to misinformation, or to genuine misjudgement on my part, not to cowardice or dishonesty.

In any case, as the moon rose that night above the willow and the stream, I decided that I would not do my father's bidding and carry out my mission as a spy. Instead, I would wait in the copse for Hunter to return, or for Olmo to come back and enquire as to what had passed between myself and my father regarding resettlement of the Lost Domain.

222

I was certain that one or both of them would come, and in spite of what my parents had told me, I was especially sure about Hunter. I had fought with the big white bird, side by side, and I knew that his sense of honour was, if anything, more keenly honed than mine. I had seen the hurt in his eyes when it was suggested that Alba, the little immigrant, had duped him. I had seen the hurt in his eyes and, prior to that, I had heard the alien's song:

> Eyes of the Barn Owl yours
> Eyes of the alien mine
> Why can't it be?
>
> Barn Owl and alien
> We fly the same sky at night
> Why should tradition
> Deny us the right?
>
> Love knows no class
> No class or race
> Only the stars
> The stars and the moonlight
> Give us time and space
>
> Don't ask the reason why
> Why love can always overcome
> But love will always find a way
> To bring us both together
> To leave us free to fly
> Under the same sky
>
> And I shall always love you
> Love you till I die
>
> And I shall always love you
> Love you till I die.

I don't remember the exact words, of course, but the alien's song had haunted me ever since I first heard it. It had a ring of truth about it, and it made me think of Mallow and the song that she had sung for me. Had I not heard Alba's song, I would have been certain that the little alien was a spy. But having heard it, I could not be sure, and so I settled down to wait. So much of one's life is spent in waiting, when one comes to think of it. And in the end one is waiting for one thing only – a thing called death. But now, at the beginning of my third age, I grow morbid. Then I was young and strong, as Hunter was. Though my parents had suggested it, I knew instinctively that he would not give in to any attempted blackmail perpetrated on him by those of his own kind. No, Hunter would not be blackmailed, and soon, at dusk or at dawn, he would return.

And I would wait here, in the willow tree, in reluctant sympathy with his strange, illicit love affair, but above all out of respect for his still strong and untarnished sense of honour.

CHAPTER
21

After resting up in the willow tree for one whole, glorious spring day, I flew to Beak Poke's farmhouse, in search of little Alba. I wanted to interview her personally, before Hunter returned. But as I had guessed, she wasn't there. I searched the meagre fields and meadows on the territory which the wise old Owl Owl had once inhabited and which now belonged to Hunter, should he choose to return and claim it as his own. As already stated, I was sure he would. It was only a question of time. But I would use this time to find out more about the little alien with whom he was obsessed.

Since she was nowhere to be found, I guessed that Olmo had been right, and in the absence of her loved one, she had returned to the Lost Domain, not to hunt, but to be present at the plotting and the planning of the new Little Owl co-operative. In spite of Alba's haunting song, my suspicions deepened as I flew across the fields and meadows under the crescent moonlight.

Below me in the meadows the green grass surged and rippled, bursting with the advent of new life. Moles poked their heads up unsuspectingly, and I took two of them during that long spring night. The budding corn fields were alive with field mice and the hedgerows teemed with shrew and vole. Whatever Alba's motives for returning to the Lost Domain, clearly a lack of food on Hunter's territory could not be counted among them!

Well before dawn, I flew back to the willow in the copse and settled down to wait again. As the sun rose, I decided to fly home to my own oak, avoiding my parents until I'd had a chance to talk with Olmo, Alba or Hunter on the following night. If my father and mother thought that I had flown to the Lost Domain, on my mission as a spy disguised as a diplomat, then so much the better. As for me, I intended to wait, in the certainty that Hunter would return to what was now his only home.

Shortly before dawn, I took off from the willow branch and headed slowly back up the sloping hill that led to the heart of our ancestral woods. However, I had not flown more than a meadow's length when I heard a call coming from the trysting place which I had just left. I turned and flew back at once, to find Hunter waiting for me, perched on his favourite branch of the willow tree.

'I say, old boy, are you all right?' I asked at once, for the big white bird did not look at all well. He was shivering slightly and seemed to be suffering from some kind of shock.

'Oh, I'm all right,' he said. 'Something nasty happened to me just now, that's all.'

'What happened, if you don't mind my asking?'

'Oh, nothing much,' said Hunter. 'There was a kestrel hunting on my land and so I killed him.'

'You killed him?' I said, in great surprise. 'How and when did it happen?'

'Only a few moments ago. It was just before dawn, so I was well within my rights. But now I have to say I wish I hadn't done it.'

'Did you eat the creature afterwards?' I asked, for I had often wondered what a kestrel tasted like.

'No!' said Hunter, shivering a little as he spoke. 'I couldn't eat him. In many ways he was too much like one of us!'

'Ferocity ate one of the several that she killed. She told me it tasted delicious. But I'm like you. I'm too squeamish. I don't think I could ever bring myself to eat another bird of prey.'

'I wasn't hungry,' Hunter said. 'And that's another thing that worries me. You know that our religion does not permit Barn Owls to take life unless it be for food or self-defence.'

'Or else in the defence of your territory,' I added, scrutinizing Hunter carefully as I spoke. Having fought beside him in the war and seen his heroism in action, it struck me that the depths of his current emotion were due to something more than to the killing of a kestrel on his land. Remembering the mission on which my father had sent me, I decided to probe further.

'Yes, we are allowed to kill in the defence of our territory,' Hunter agreed, after a long pause. 'But in that case we're supposed to give a warning first. I didn't, and now the kestrel's death is on my conscience. Anyway, it's over now, and I suppose it's just one more thing I'll have to live with till the day I die.'

'Are you sure the kestrel is your only problem?' I asked.

'At least I did it cleanly,' Hunter said, completely ignoring my question. 'His body is lying on a hedge near here, close to the place where Beak Poke died. Do you want to see it?'

'Yes,' I said, after a swift glance upward at the brightening sky. 'Let's go now, before the sun rises fully and impedes my flight.'

So we flew off together, silently and swiftly, to the spot where many considered that Hunter had laid his second claim to fame. But much later he told me that it was a place that he tended to avoid, for he was one of the few who never came to believe in the legend that grew up around him, and for ever after was to associate the hedge on which the dead kestrel now lay with feelings of guilt and shame.

As we circled above the creature's headless body, I hooted to myself in amazement, and for the third or fourth time that early morning glanced sideways and studied Hunter in surprise.

'My God, you did kill him cleanly,' I said eventually. 'My guess is that he didn't know a single thing about it. Big, fierce brute he was, too, by the look of his ugly carcass, yet you did such a perfect job that anyone who saw the remains of him would think the monster had come back!'

'Don't mention it to anyone,' said Hunter, as we ceased circling above the gruesome sight and winged our way back to the spinney, side by side. 'It was just something that I felt I had to do, and that's all. I'm not proud of it, and I don't want the word to get around.'

'Don't be ridiculous, old boy,' I said. 'The night has a thousand eyes and the day but one. You know that as well as I do. By midnight tomorrow, most of the owls in this district will know, and so will the daytime raptors. And I dare say that once they've seen your headless kestrel, they'll keep well out of your way from now on and for ever more!'

'I know the sun has already risen,' said Hunter, as we flew back silently into the cover of the copse and landed in our favourite willow. 'But I have something to tell you. Something that cannot wait!'

'I'm all ears!' I said, as we settled on our favourite branches. 'You won't mind my saying so, old boy, but I knew you were holding something back.'

'You were right about the Little Owls,' Hunter blurted out. 'They have colonized the Lost Domain. They intend to settle there and turn it into what they call their promised land!'

'I am aware of that.'

'But how did you know?'

'Bad news travels fast,' I said. 'And our intelligence service still functions pretty well, in spite of our depleted numbers.'

'What are you going to do about it?' Hunter asked. 'Are you going to drive them out, or let them stay?'

'And you?' I asked, practising my role as a diplomat and avoiding a direct reply to Hunter's question. 'What action is your Barn Owl council going to take?'

'That remains to be seen. The next scheduled plenary meeting is not until the full moon rises once again. No official decision can be taken until then.'

'But you must have some idea of the way the wind is blowing,' I said. 'You must have some idea as to what the outcome of the council meeting will be!'

'I did speak to the History Owl,' Hunter admitted. 'He said that on the whole he approved of the idea.'

'Why?'

'Well, first of all we shouldn't have to put up with any more squatters on our land. Neither would you Tawnies. Then Rivers thought that in the event of a second invasion by a monster owl, or the like, the little immigrants would be more inclined to fight with us, as allies, to repel the outside threat. After all, for the first time in history, they would have their own territory to protect.'

'And what did your mother say?'

'She said no good would come of it. She said that the myth and legend associated with these Little Owls have decreed that they must never own a territory of their own. The Great God Bird intended them to live for ever in no man's land. If they were ever to settle in any one place and form a co-operative, a republic – or even a nation, as some of them are now beginning to call it – then there would be war.'

'My mother says more or less the same thing,' I confessed, not, I admit, without a sense of shame. 'And what is more, she tells me that many of the Little Owls themselves believe it.'

'They do!' Hunter answered. 'According to little Alba, many of them do. It is mainly the bolder, younger ones who are taking this initiative. Many of the older or more timid birds are terrified and believe the whole enterprise will end in disaster. In fact, they will face much opposition from within.'

'But surely they have nothing to fear from the older or more timid birds among them?'

'Not so,' said Hunter, with a sad shake of his head. 'These aliens have a strong and rigid sense of religion. I have heard that most of you Tawnies pay beak service to the God Bird, but don't really believe in Him. Well, among us Barn Owls it is more or less the same. There are some who believe passionately, of course, as doubtless there are among your own kind. But on the whole the God Bird tends to be invoked by us in times of dire distress, or when a bird is dying and has no idea where he is about to go, or what is about to become of his mortal soul. But according to Alba, with the little aliens it is different. They believe all the time, and they tend to practise what they preach. Or rather what the great vicar bird preaches.'

'Does this great vicar bird live here, or in their old country?' I asked.

'The greatest of all their vicar birds still lives in the old country, but he has a deputy here in these territories who is said to be the most influential Little Owl alive. The faithful among them maintain that he gets telepathic messages from the infallible one. How these messages cross the high, snow-capped mountains and the wide expanse of salty waters, no one knows. But the faithful believe it, and I suppose that is all that really matters.'

'And this vicar bird, here in these territories, is against the idea of his own kind setting up a republic in the Lost Domain?'

'Apparently, yes.'

'But why?' I asked. 'Surely if he represents their God Bird, he must have the best interests of the Little Owls at heart.'

'You would have thought so,' Hunter agreed. 'But according to Alba, this is not the case. According to Alba and her friends, these vicars of the God Bird work on an old adage that also exists in Barn Owl language. Namely, united they stand, divided they fall. According to the revolutionary leaders who wish to create this republic in the Lost Domain, the leaders of their religion are afraid that the aliens will come to place more faith in the new state that they have created than in continuing to strive for a heavenly state of grace, as they always have done whilst condemned to live in no man's land.'

'What do you think about it, Hunter? After all, you have a personal involvement in this matter, and I don't.'

'You mean my relationship with little Alba?'

'Of course!'

'Well, it's over. Finished!'

'How so?' I asked, attempting to stay calm and collect information for my father. After all, apart from wishing to see my friend Hunter again, that is why I was here, perched on the willow branch above the slow-flowing stream.

'Because she is going back to live with her own kind, in the new republic they are creating in the Lost Domain.'

'No!'

'Yes,' Hunter said. 'And worse than that, she's going to mate with their new leader.'

'What's his name?' I asked, hating myself for taking advantage of my friend when he was off his guard and clearly bleeding from a wound that was deeply embedded in his soul.

'His name is Renato,' Hunter answered. 'He himself is not so bad. He has some vestige of culture – of cross-cultural understanding, if you can follow what I'm trying to say.'

'You mean that you, a Barn Owl, and me, a Tawny, can perch here in this willow tree in no man's land and talk about the future and co-existence of our various species. Is that what you mean by cross-cultural understanding?'

'Yes,' said Hunter, after a brief pause for reflection.

That 'yes' seemed to be torn out of his very soul, against his will, against his every instinct, yet he pronounced it, and the true pain – the source of the grief that caused him to do so – was shortly to be made plain to me. When I heard the source of his sorrow, I remembered the alien's song, I remembered Mallow's lament, and my heart bled on the willow branch above the brackish stream for an owl from another species who had loved and been betrayed – betrayed not only by his little alien, but also by those of his own kind.

'Who are the other key figures in this provisional government of the new republic?' I asked. 'Are they also concerned with cross-cultural understanding?'

'No! Quite frankly, they are thugs.'

'Like Ferocity and Ripper?'

'More or less. Possibly even worse.'

'What are their names?'

'One is called Falco, and the other Primo.'

'In their old language, Primo means first one and Falco means falcon?' I asked.

'Yes, how did you know that?'

'Never mind!' I said. 'What I want to know is the meaning of the leader's name. Renato, isn't that what you said he was called?'

'Renato means born again,' Hunter replied, and the pain flooded back into his eyes as he thought of this alien leader who was about to mate with his beloved little Alba.

'And he is not a thug?'

'No. He is hard, mean and ugly, but not a thug. He is also much better educated than the other two.'

'What about their messenger, the poet called Olmo? What impression have you formed of him?'

'None,' said Hunter. 'We haven't met, as yet. And now I don't suppose we ever shall.'

'What are you going to do now?' I asked. 'Are you going to study under the new Owl Owl, or not?'

Hunter shook his head and looked away from me, but not before I had glimpsed a new wave of pain behind the expressive eyes set deep in that magnificent white head.

'No,' he said. 'I am not going to study under the new Owl Owl. Winger has chosen my sister instead.'

'Winger?'

'Winger is the new Owl Owl, appointed by the council after Beak Poke's death.'

'I didn't know your sister was interested in owlology,' I said.

'She isn't, or rather wasn't,' said Hunter, rather shortly, as if he did not wish to discuss the matter any further.

'But you think she may be interested in him, instead?' I asked, determined to push the matter as far as I dared, under the delicate circumstances.

'How should I know?' Hunter snapped back at me. 'Dawn Raptor does not confide in me. Though brother and sister I have to confess that we have never got on very well.'

'And I suppose you will get on even less well, now that she has usurped the position that was yours by right.'

'That's nonsense,' Hunter said sharply. 'There are no such things as rights when it comes to being chosen for higher education. The tutor, or expert, merely chooses the student or apprentice whom he believes has given evidence of the greatest aptitude.'

Or is the prettiest, I thought, but said nothing, for that evening Hunter was clearly in no mood to be trifled with.

'It seems a bit hard, though,' I limited myself to saying. 'I mean, here you are, a war hero just recovered from your wounds, and yet your own kind seem to have nothing in particular to offer you. No place on the Barn Owl council, not even an offer of higher education. What are you going to do?'

'My mother asked me to stay at home,' Hunter said.

'And aren't you going to?'

'No!' said Hunter, very firmly. 'You can't go home again. That is one of the very first lessons that she taught me. No, I shan't go home again. I shall stay on here, in Beak Poke's abandoned farmhouse. I shall hunt his meagre fields and meadows and educate myself as best I can.'

'And that way you will still be close to little Alba?'

'What good will that do me, once she has gone into the Lost Domain and mated with Renato?'

This was naturally a question that I couldn't answer. But while there was life, there was hope, I felt – hope for him, at least. If Alba were not happy in the place where she was going, he might one time – at dawn or twilight – hear the little alien's song again. I should never more hear the song that Mallow had once sung for me, for my loved one was dead.

'Listen, Hunter,' I said, acting on an impulse that was driven from my young soul for my friend who clutched tightly to the willow branch to hide his heartbreak from me. 'Listen,' I repeated. 'I have a proposition that I want to put to you. There is a dangerous mission I have to undertake, involving a long and dangerous but exciting journey. I wondered if you'd care to join me?'

'Where are you going?'

'To the city,' I replied. 'I have to go and tell my cousins there that they can come home and repopulate Ferocity and Ripper's wood. And if there are other displaced Tawnies there, I must tell them that the secret forest in the Lost

Domain is theirs for the taking. We cannot allow it to be transformed into a dominion of the little aliens.'

'What is a city?' Hunter asked, and the big white bird suddenly looked vulnerable, as well as sad, as he clutched bravely to his perch on the willow branch.

'The city? It is a massive place where countless thousands of men herd together like mindless starlings or peewits in a single patch of meadow. The city is like ten thousand villages, all lumped together, all full of noise and lights and other things that no owl could possibly imagine.'

'We call that a town,' said Hunter. 'I heard about them in my basic human studies.'

'Well, it's the biggest of them all that I must go to. It seems the journey will take me six whole nights, if I am lucky and nothing delays me on my flight. When one gets there, they say the dangers are appalling. I don't suppose you would care to come with me, would you?'

'Oh, yes! I'll come with you,' answered Hunter, without the slightest hesitation.

'Think about it very carefully,' I said. 'It is a long journey from which neither of us may return. As for me, I have to go. It is one's duty. For you, the expedition would be pure, unadulterated folly.'

'Folly is the best antidote for pain,' said Hunter, and smiled across at me from his willow branch. I have to say that this was one of the saddest smiles that I have ever seen, either before or since, and as the years rolled by from youth into the beginning of my third age, I remember still the words and the way he looked as he said them to me.

'Folly is the best antidote for pain.'

'When do we leave?' he asked, and the expression in his eyes had now lost the sorrow and taken on the steely glint that I had seen in them on that famous dawn when we fought the monster owl.

'Let's say in seven nights' time,' I suggested. 'I'll meet you here at twilight. And remember, I shan't be offended if you don't turn up. If you do come, I suppose you'll be the first Barn Owl ever to set out on such a journey, and I suppose that in the dreadful city you will learn more about the men that your species live so close to on the land. Incidentally, did you know that men had been having a war of their own?'

'We had rumours of it,' Hunter said. 'Why would that be, do you think?'

'One doesn't know,' I said. 'One can only presume that there are different species of men, and that they have the same kind of territorial conflicts as we owls do.'

'But I haven't seen men fighting one another in this district,' Hunter said.

'No. According to our information, the men from here have gone across the great salty waters to fight on the other side of them. One doesn't know for certain, of course. It may be just a rumour. But there has been no fighting among the men living here, except for fire falling from the sky.'

'On the towns and cities?' enquired Hunter.

'Yes,' I said. 'We know this from our Tawny cousins living in the biggest of all towns – the place to which we fly in seven nights' time. But our latest information is that though much of the city smoulders still, the fire has now stopped falling and the men are slowly beginning to clear the rubble and the ruins away.'

'Do you think many of the owls living in the city will have been killed?' asked Hunter.

'I don't know. It is one of the things that I am being sent to find out.'

'You must go now!' Hunter said. 'The sun has already risen high and you will find it difficult to fly back home by daylight.'

'It's not far and I know the way,' I said. 'It is agreed then? We meet here in this willow tree in seven nights' time. And then we take off for the city.'

'It is agreed,' said Hunter, with a solemn little nod. By

now I knew him well enough to know that a nod was as good as a promise. What I did not know, of course, were the dreadful things that were to happen in the seven days and nights before we were to meet again. Some of these things I might have prevented. I don't know. I must leave this for my silent listeners to decide and to pronounce judgement on in their wisdom and in the fullness of eternal time.

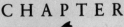

22

I did not fly home that morning under the rays of the rising sun. I let Hunter go back across the flat fields and meadows to his lonely farmhouse, and then dozed off gently in my favourite branch of the willow above the slow-running stream.

Sod them all, I thought, possessed now by a slowly growing resentment of my parents and of the entire Tawny Owl establishment. *Noblesse oblige*, indeed! Very well, then! Let them think that one was still deeply ensconced in the Lost Domain, engaged in vital and dangerous matters of espionage, whilst I was in fact dozing away in my favourite willow, letting the warm spring breeze massage my feathers and caress the scars beneath them – scars which had still not entirely healed since the monster owl had torn me with his dreadful talons.

At noon, I heard a rustling on the slow-flowing stream below me. Looking down I saw a young moorhen who had clearly been carried from her family pond, or backwater, beside the brackish stream, and now floated with the gentle current towards some confluence with a swift-flowing river, and from there to be torn in an ever-flowing torrent towards the mighty sea.

Of course, one could not allow a thing like this to happen. It was against all the rules of nature for moorhens to abandon their backwaters and be torn by swift currents which would take them eventually into salty waters where none of their kind could survive.

By this time I was very hungry, and so to do this small water bird and myself a mutual favour, I fell from my willow tree, plucked the succulent little creature from the water, killed it as cleanly as I could, and then carried it back to my willow branch to lunch upon this unexpected delicacy.

Afterwards I dozed again until the sun began to set above me behind what seemed then to be the vast expanse of our ancestral forest. Under the first light of the crescent moon I took off and flew back to my parents' oak, where I found them waiting for me with ill-disguised anxiety.

'Well?' my father asked me at once. 'What news do you bring from the Lost Domain? What intelligence have you to report?'

'My trip has been an arduous one,' I answered. 'And dangerous, too, as you may well imagine. In the Lost Domain it is not permitted for aliens to eat. And remember, they define us as the aliens now! The food there belongs entirely to the Little Owls – to those who have colonized the place. So with your permission – or without it – I intend to feed myself before reporting to you the information that I have obtained.'

'Then fly directly to Cleaver's wood,' my mother said at once. 'It is teeming with young rabbits, with far more than he and his scraggy wife and ugly fledglings will be able to digest between now and the bursting of the next harvest moon.'

Cleaver was a friend of Birch, an uncouth creature who had attempted to bully me when I was young and who since the war had done little more than pay sneering lip service to the heroism of those who had saved his own miserable self and his unlovely kith and kind from extinction under the giant claws of the Eagle Owl.

'I shall go there at once,' I said, relishing an encounter with this brutal coward. 'As soon as I have eaten the juiciest of his rabbits, I shall return and tell you what I have learned.'

Having made my point I flew into Cleaver's territory and plucked a baby rabbit from the forest floor. Having enjoyed this illicit meal all the more because it was poached from the land of an uncouth barbarian, I then flew back to the heights of our ancestral woodland, where my mother and father were both waiting for me, as before.

'Well,' my father said at once. 'Now that you have filled your belly, what report do you have to make on the events that are taking place in the Lost Domain?'

'Don't be vulgar,' my mother said. 'Yoller did not fill his belly, as you so grossly put it. Instead he ate an elegant sufficiency of that coward Cleaver's rabbit.'

'The information you require is as follows,' I said, fixing my father with a steelier glare than I had hitherto been able to confront him with. I then told him what information I had received from Olmo and from Hunter, but without quoting them as direct sources. I must confess now to the wind and trees that I took credit then for what I had not in fact achieved. I made it appear as if I had penetrated the Lost Domain alone and gathered all this vital intelligence at great risk to my psyche and to my very life itself. But as I have observed since, one often gets more credit for the lesser things one does, whilst any truly courageous, original or creative effort is met at best with suspicion and at worst with derision and contempt.

'Splendid,' my father said when I had finished. 'So now we know their strengths and weaknesses, the names of their leaders and the numbers they have already assembled there. Thirty or forty birds, you said?'

'That is a mere estimate,' I admitted. 'I counted fifteen

of them and was told by Olmo, their poet-messenger, that there were at least twice as many planning to move into the Lost Domain. But I repeat, this is merely a guess. In the time available, there was no way that I could verify the numbers.'

'You have done well, Yoller,' my father said. 'Better even than I had expected.'

'And now?' I asked. 'What action do you intend to take on the basis of this information which I have brought to you?'

'None!' my father said.

'None?'

'None! In the light of our latest intelligence, no action will be necessary.'

'And what is this latest intelligence?' I asked, attempting to sound more casual than I felt.

'We have it on very good authority that the men with firesticks are returning from their war. They will reclaim the Lost Domain and kill all the predators who have occupied it since their departure.'

'Including owls?' I asked.

'Including owls, of course,' my father said.

'But why?' I asked. 'What harm do we do to the men?'

'They think we eat their pheasant chicks, the ducklings on their pond, the young chickens and the baby rabbits – all food they like to kill and eat themselves.'

'But we do, don't we?' I asked. 'I mean, I've just killed and eaten one of Cleaver's rabbits.'

'Exactly!' my father said. 'But you are stronger than Cleaver and he doesn't have a firestick. The men do! When they find their abandoned domain infested by Little Owls, foxes, weasels and the like, they will kill them all. Or at any rate, as many of them as they can find.'

'But shouldn't they be warned?' I asked, rather shocked by my father's sanguine attitude to the coming holocaust.

'Of course not,' he replied at once. 'If the men get rid

of the blasted little squatters, it means that we won't have to do it later on.'

'But if the men have come back, we can't return to the forest in the Lost Domain,' I said. 'It would be just as dangerous for us as it would be for the Little Owls.'

'Obviously,' my father said. 'But ask yourself this! What do you think would happen if we warned them?'

'They would escape,' I said.

'They would escape! And where would they escape to, do you think?'

'Back into no man's land?'

'Precisely! They would fill every copse and spinney here for miles around, poaching the voles, moles and shrews which the lower form of Tawny has to eat. They would not come up this high, of course. They would not dare to penetrate our ancestral woods. But what about our cousins down below? Do you think we can wittingly expose them to an army of hungry refugees?'

I hesitated a moment or two before replying. I thought about the song I had heard the little alien singing – 'The Same Sky':

> Eyes of the Barn Owl yours
> Eyes of the alien mine
> Why can't it be?
>
> Barn Owl and alien
> We fly the same sky at night
> Why should tradition
> Deny us the right?
>
> Love knows no class
> No class or race
> Only the stars
> The stars and the moonlight
> Give us time and space

> And I shall always love you
> Love you till I die

Before I replied to my father, Mallow's song also flashed through my mind:

> If they gave a war would you go?
> Would you fight for things you were taught to believe
> Would you kill for the sake of your race
> If they gave a war, would you go?
> You would, I know!
> If they gave a war, you would go.
> And *if* you came home you'd have honour to show
> And you'd lack the use of a limb
> But if they gave a war
> You would go, I know.

'Well,' said my mother, who had remained silent for what in her case amounted to an inordinate amount of time. 'You have done well and we are proud of you. Your next task must be to fly to the city and bring back May Blossom to be your bride. Also bring back any other worthy exile who may help to repopulate our lands.'

'But not Sage!' my father said. 'Not Sage or Dodger! You must on no account encourage either of these two to return.'

'Who are Sage and Dodger?' I asked, thinking still about the twin concepts of Mallow's song and of 'The Same Sky', but none the less making every attempt to keep a straight face and appear to be concentrating on these new duties which my parents were preparing to foist upon me.

'In the first place, Sage is an intellectual,' my father said. 'He was banished from these territories some fifteen springs ago for preaching all kinds of heresies against this great land of hope and glory, and against those Tawnies like ourselves who have been chosen to rule the night sky.'

'Chosen by whom?' I asked, attempting to make the

question sound more innocent than I truly intended it to be.

'By the Great God Bird, of course,' my mother snapped back in reply.

'I have never truly understood the concept of this Great God Bird,' I said, digging my claws firmly into the branch I was occupying in my parents' family oak. 'I have never truly understood your seemingly possessive concept of the God Bird. If He truly does exist, then He must be the leader and protector of all birds – Tawnies, Barn Owls, eagles, buzzards, nomad owls, little aliens – and even protector of the ugliest starling and the most humble of all sparrows. Otherwise, what kind of God Bird would He be?'

'I will explain,' my mother said, puffing her feathers out and assuming that haughty and arrogant posture of hers which I had long and slowly learned to hate, as I hated the sluggish waters in the brackish stream below my favourite willow tree. Me, I loved the pure water that gushed from the mountain rock, like the fresh and clean ideas that might burst from a pure and unadulterated brain.

'I will explain,' repeated my mother, with that condescending way she had of looking over one's head and almost pretending that she wasn't there. 'We Tawnies are a superior race of bird. Of creature, even. We are probably – almost certainly – the highest form of life on earth. We have forty million years of history to prove it. Now you in your puerile and immature fashion are attempting to challenge the wisdom of your father and his forebears, owls who have defended our territories for centuries, not only against renegade Tawnies such as Birch and his unspeakable ancestors, but also against rook, crow, buzzard and, in more recent times, this vermin from across the salty water – this alien vermin known as the Little Owl. As if this was not enough, you mention the Great God Bird in the same breath as the starling or the sparrow! I might have understood you if you had mentioned the robin or the wren. Though small and insignificant, these creatures do have a certain aesthetic appeal. And in the want of more substantial food, they can, especially in winter, provide a very appetizing snack. But what I have to tell you now is this. You have been chosen as the future leader of this district. You will take over from your father on your return from the city with your mate, May Blossom. The knowledge she will have acquired there will prove invaluable in controlling and containing the persistent and continuous erosions made into our ancient forest and woodland territories by both man and other, lower forms of bird life. You will do your duty and keep the night sky clean for Tawnies, not only superior Tawnies like ourselves, but birds like Stoop and Ferocity – thugs, peasants if you like, but loyal, and who fell for us on that early dawn in Ripper's wood.'

It was then, for the first time in my young life, that I realized how much I hated my mother and every single thing she stood for. I loathed her at that moment with a deep hatred that I had never felt for any living being up to that point in my life, and I am happy to say that a loathing of this particular kind I have never experienced since.

My father was different. He was old and rusty and, perched proudly on his branch of the family oak, he seemed to know that the time of his own demise was near. So he wanted a son to take over. But what son? The son of a bitch? Incidentally, and to digress again, I have never understood why the female of the canine species should be singled out as the most horrific form of life. 'Son of a bitch', we Tawnies say, referring to a coward or a renegade like Birch, Hook or Cleaver. Well, I realized then, at that precise moment, that I was precisely that. Nothing more and nothing less. I was merely the son of a bitch.

At that same moment – as this terrible realization came upon me – I felt a great compassion for my father. Had he hated my mother as much as I did now, detesting her more than anything that lived or moved on earth – more than the slugs we ate when food was scarce, more than the men who were slowly preparing to tear down and transform the ancient woodland in which we had lived for centuries?

Yes, I knew then that I hated my mother more than anything that lived or moved on earth. She was evil personified, or so I saw her then, and so I have remembered her ever since that long-gone night. Truly evil, she was, and I vowed to myself that the rest of my life would be dedicated to bringing down and utterly destroying the chauvinist tradition built up and fostered over so many centuries – a chauvinism on which she and her kind had thrived by somehow convincing other birds that she and her class had been invested by the God Bird with the divine right of kings.

Looking back on it all now, I can see that this was the beginning of the end for me. One cannot hate one's mother and expect to get away with it. Apart from being branded an ungrateful heretic by one's own kind, there are the parasite emotions of guilt and remorse to contend with.

Everyone agrees that remorse and guilt are quite useless and unproductive as emotions, but one can hardly help being affected by them where one's mother is concerned.

However, all these problems were to arise and torment me later. My most immediate dilemma was whether or not to warn the squatters – or at least little Alba – about the return of the men with firesticks. On the one hand I now considered her a traitor who had been planted to dupe my friend Hunter into negotiating some advantageous deal with the Barn Owls; on the other, I knew how much he loved her and, above all, I had heard the alien's song. Back in my own oak, I battled with these concepts of loyalty and of betrayal – loyalty to the interests of my own kind, the proud and ancient Tawnies, loyalty to Hunter, a friend of another species, but a friend who had saved my life and lost his own father in what we had thought then was the war to end all wars.

I had no reason, of course, to feel any loyalty whatsoever to little Alba. But why betray her and her kind to the arch-enemy of all of us, called man? Could there be no way that we creatures of the night could combine against this greatest predator of all, combine against man and bring him down in the same way as our united efforts had brought down the monster owl? Was there no way we could all listen to the little alien's song and learn to share the same sky at night?

Dawn approached and, though still torn, I was no closer to making any kind of decision. Then, as the sun rose high above my ancestral oak, I knew I had to do it. I knew I had to fly to Beak Poke's abandoned farmhouse and pass on to Hunter the secret information that had come into my knowledge.

I personally cared nothing for the Little Owls – this I must confess. I do not wish to present myself here to my silent listeners as some kind of peace-maker, saint or phil-anthropist. But I did care for Hunter, I had cared very much for Mallow, and I imagined that if Hunter's feelings for little Alba had been the same as mine for Birch's mate, then spy or not, his heart would break when he knew that she was dead. His heart would break even though he knew she had duped him and betrayed him. How, for example, did I know that Mallow had not betrayed me by mating out of season with the insatiable Birch in that wretched little crevice where they had gone to ground and hidden to avoid the invasion and the war?

Perhaps I was young and feeble-minded then, but Alba's song still haunted me, especially the words:

> Eyes of the Barn Owl yours
> Eyes of the alien mine

Don't ask the reason why
Why love can always overcome
But love will always find a way
To bring us both together
To leave us free to fly
Under the same sky

So as the light faded and twilight fell, I took off, and flew
down across our sloping woodland, the floor of which
was now burgeoning with bluebells, anemones and the red
stalks and pale green flowers of wood spurge. The colours
of these plants were muted by twilight, but their aroma
sang with joyful harmony and eloquence of the coming
spring – no, not only the coming spring, but the rebirth of
all natural life, which had stolen out from beneath the ice
and snow and come upon us unawares.

I flew low that night, through our ancient woodland,
and drank in with great delight the subtle aromas and
the muted twilight colours of flowers and plants of whose
existence I had always known, but whose exact identity
had hitherto remained blurred by the half-light of dusk or
dawn, or more likely by the selfish unconcern of all young
creatures for the other animals and plants among which
they live, move and have their being.

That night, for the first time in my life, I identified marsh
violet and ground ivy. I had seen them a dozen times
before, of course, but now in this late twilight, which was
to herald such a black and tragic night, I recognized these
living things for what they were, and as I flew low above
them I dreamed of the peace and happiness they exemplified which, according to the poet Olmo, might soon
become a norm – something to be shared like dusk and
twilight by all the different creatures who flew the sky at
night.

Hunter was not in the willow tree when I arrived, and
neither did he answer any of the three or four successive

calls I made to announce my coming. It was therefore with a sense of foreboding that I launched myself from the willow branch above the slow-running stream and flew across the flatland towards the broken-down farmhouse which had once belonged to the wise old Beak Poke, but which had, since his death, become the lone resting place of my friend Hunter and of the little squatter – the little alien who had first healed Hunter's wounds and then abandoned him to live among her own and alien kind, in our ancient Tawny territory once and forever known as the Lost Domain.

My sense of foreboding grew as I sped across the flat fields and meadows between the willow in the copse and the broken-down building in which Hunter and Alba had been shacked up since the war, and in which they had shared the stars and the moonlight, allowing no tradition to deny them the right to live and love each other under the same sky.

When I got there the building was deserted, and at once I feared the worst. The Barn Owl intelligence service was at least as good as ours, and Hunter must have learned, as I had, of the return of the men with their firesticks. He must have flown to the Lost Domain to warn the Little Owls – a mission I knew I should have flown myself the night before.

Not knowing what to do, I waited, first outside the abandoned farmhouse and then inside. It was the first time I had ever entered a human habitation, even though this one, of course, had been deserted by man long before Beak Poke moved in. It had been deserted and derelict, in fact, for longer than any living owl could remember.

I flew in through a gap in the upper wall – a gap that I supposed had once been a window. No thinking Tawny would claim to have as much knowledge of men as the Barn Owls do – not, one must stress, because the Barn Owl is any cleverer than a gifted Tawny, but simply because the big white bird lives in much closer proximity to these vicious two-legged creatures and therefore in theory has more knowledge of their poisonous days and ways.

At least, this is what one continued to believe until one had been into the great city. It was only there that one realized that of the three main owl species living in this land, the Barn Owl is in fact the least adaptable to the ways of man. For example, they cannot live in what they call a town. We can, as I was soon to discover. Also, as soon as I had flown in through this gap which I realized must once have been a window, I saw one of those long, horizontal perches on which men sleep by night. At the head of this long, horizontal sleeping-thing there was a kind of board. Below this headboard there were traces of owl blood and several Barn Owl feathers. It was therefore clear to me at once that this was the perch on which Hunter had chosen to rest and cling to life during the long period of his convalescence.

Significantly, I found no Little Owl feathers near Hunter's perch, but discovered them instead on a large wooden object whose purpose at that time I could neither comprehend nor imagine. I later learned from Sage and May Blossom in the city that these wooden objects were boxes in which men kept their plumage, which for some extraordinary reason they removed at night and put on again the following morning. Sage explained this extraordinary phenomenon to me as being due to the fact that men have not been equipped by nature with a natural, integral plumage such as all owls have, but are in fact born naked and remain naked until the day they die. They thus require the skins and pelts of other animals, or plumage made from plants, to keep them warm, and also to adorn themselves according to whatever status they enjoy in the human world.

But on that dreadful night none of this was yet known to me. All I deduced from finding little Alba's feathers on a ledge in this wooden object was that she had perched there during her long winter vigil as nurse and companion to the wounded Hunter. It therefore became clear to me that during this period of hospitalization they had not attempted to submit to the urge – as I had with Mallow.

For some obscure reason this innocence and abstention impressed me, and it was precisely at the moment when I pondered why tradition should deny the possibility of love between two different species that I heard the first blasting of the firesticks tearing the stillness of the night sky. The firing came, of course, from the direction of the Lost Domain, and though distant enough and safe in the upper storey of the abandoned farmhouse, I have to confess that I was terrified. I knew then that my father had been right, and I also knew that I should have flown to warn the little immigrants on the previous night.

Now it was too late! Hunter, I guessed, had gone in any case. It was in his nature. Betrayed by the little spy or not, at the last moment he would have wished to save her life. As we all know from Quaver's ballad, this is exactly what he had done, wishing to see her for just one more time, perhaps hoping, though knowing she had betrayed him, to bring her back with him to the safety of the flat Barn Owl country and to the abandoned farmhouse where I perched now and trembled at the thought of the slaughter that must be taking place around the lake, in the parkland, and perhaps as high up as the secret forest.

I was torn then between the brave impulse to fly in the direction of this carnage and to risk my life as I should have done the night before. I was torn between this altruistic impulse and the desire to escape and fly back at once to my ancient woodland home, which rose high and still remained unthreatened by the ravages of man.

To my dying shame, I chose the latter course and fled. I have pondered since on the cowardice of my action – or non-action. But I put it now as a final plea to my silent listeners that my response may have been based on an instinctive and overwhelming desire for survival. It is all too easy to blame one's parents and one's conditioning for one's moments of cruelty or cowardice. 'I was brought up that way', one might have thought, and this justified any kind of action, whether brave or cowardly. I knew that no credit or approbation would accrue to me for any kind of suicidal effort made to save those who were not of my own kind. On the contrary, as my parents had pointed out, the men were now performing a task of extermination that would save us the trouble and the pangs of conscience for carrying out the same form of genocide at some later date, when our own forces had been reassembled and retrained.

So I flew home, through the darkness, back to the safety of my woodland oak. It was only on the following evening that I found the courage to return and to discover the full extent of the bloodshed that the men, having returned from their own war, had perpetrated on the innocent and natural inhabitants of the Lost Domain.

I hunted little that night, ate less than usual, and spent most of the time until early dawn huddled against the branch of my oak. Though now out of earshot of the Lost Domain, I imagined that I heard another burst of firing, and wondered whether any creature of the night would be left alive by the time the first streaks of dawn began to lighten the night sky. I wondered also what would happen to us if what my father said was true, and the men in the valley continued cutting down the trees below us and moving slowly higher through the foothills towards the heart of our ancient woodlands. Would they bring firesticks, like the men who had returned to the Lost Domain? Would they try to exterminate us in the same ruthless way my father had told me they would attempt to eliminate the Little Owls?

I wondered, too, about Alba, and about whether I would ever hear the alien's song again. But my main concern was for the missing Hunter. Had he really flown to seek out his little immigrant on that fatal night?

Shortly before sunrise my father flew into my oak and perched on the branch opposite mine. I told him at once what I had heard.

'I know!' he said, nodding gravely. 'Bad news travels

fast. Last night the first refugees arrived not long after midnight.'

'Little Owls?' I asked.

'Yes, two of them.'

'What did they say?'

'There has been a holocaust, as I had expected.'

'How many dead?'

'They don't know, but many, including the alien called Renato, who was supposed to be the leader of their new co-operative.'

'Did they mention a Barn Owl among the dead?'

'No, they mentioned two dead foxes, but no white owls. However, they were in shock and their account of the events was garbled, to say the least. At times it bordered on the incoherent. And I don't suppose one's powers of observation are at their best when men are blasting away at one with firesticks.'

'Where are they now?' I asked. 'I'd like to talk to them.'

'Oh, I've sent them on their way,' my father said, with an indifferent little shrug. 'They asked for asylum in these woods, of course. But you know what your mother's like. If I'd let them stay for a few nights, she would have made a dreadful fuss.'

'Where did you send them?'

'To the no man's land that lies below our foothills.'

'To the place where you say men have begun to build this new town?'

'Yes. It's still classified as no man's land. They might survive there for a season or two, but if the men continue they'll be forced up into our foothills. Of course, I told them that if they were caught poaching there I would have them killed.'

I merely nodded in reply to this. There are times when one's thoughts are best kept to oneself. But as my father spoke, the words of the alien's song, 'The Same Sky', kept running through my mind:

Barn Owl and alien
We fly the same sky at night
Why should tradition
Deny us the right?

Love knows no class
No class or race
Only the stars
The stars and the moonlight
Give us time and space

We share the same sky
We live for the same sad time together
Why can't we share it in every way
And steal a little time together
When both of us some day,
Some day must die

I also made a silent vow that if and when the time came,
I would not be the one to execute these creatures. In
fact, I would use my influence to grant them asylum in the
foothills until they had found somewhere else to go.

'As I have told you, their account of the proceedings was
incoherent,' my father continued. 'Therefore your next task
is to fly as close as possible to the Lost Domain and find
out how many of the immigrants were killed, and whether
those left alive intend to emigrate *en masse* or whether they
plan to elect a new leader and continue setting up their
new republic.'

'But why?' I asked. 'Now that the men with firesticks
have come back, no Tawny would be mad enough to settle
in the secret forest, let alone in the parkland or around the
lake.'

'Men come and go,' my father said, with another dis-
missive shrug. 'So far we've stayed for forty million springs,
and it is said that in their old country the Little Owls
survived for even longer. So in the interests of our

long-term future it is essential that we prevent them from settling in the forest of the Lost Domain, providing that that is their intention. Remember that the men with firesticks went away before. They may go away again. It is said by some that in any case they are poisoning themselves slowly and one day may become extinct.'

'Said by whom?' I asked.

'Amongst others, by Sage, the owl you will meet when you go to bring back May Blossom from the city.'

'But you warned me against him,' I protested. 'You said he was a dangerous intellectual and on no account to be trusted.'

'We shall wait and see what May Blossom has to say,' my father continued, without attempting to respond directly to my protest. 'She went to the city to get knowledge, and when she returns, we must use it. If we are to survive for another forty million years, we must monitor the progress and the habits of all our rival predators, be they Barn Owls, Little Owls or men. In fact, I want you to undertake your mission to the city as soon as you have ascertained exactly what happened in the Lost Domain, and also the future plans of the immigrants, if any!'

'Couldn't you send Birch, or someone else, for a change?'

'What! To the city?'

'No. I realize that must be my task and mine alone, because of May Blossom and because of my reputation and prestige as future leader. But to the Lost Domain again? If the men with firesticks are still there it's hardly likely that I shall need any reputation or prestige. Dead owls don't, you know!'

'No, but their families do,' my father at once replied. 'And as I have told you before, we must always be seen to be leading from in front, never from behind.'

He paused for a moment and looked up as the first pink streaks of dawn lit up the night sky.

'In any case,' he said, turning back to me, 'Birch is a

256

coward and he wouldn't go. So what would be the point of asking him? And there isn't anyone else who can be trusted, at least not yet. We lost most of our heroes in the war against the monster, as you well know. But there's no need for you to go at once. We will wait and see if more refugees turn up. If they left after the holocaust, instead of in the middle of it like the first two, they may be more coherent and may be able to provide the information we require. You may even find that your friend the white owl knows, and his territory is well outside the danger zone.'

'I believe Hunter may be dead.'

'Why?'

'I think he flew to the Lost Domain last night in search of the little alien you met once in the war.'

'Men don't shoot Barn Owls as a rule,' my father said, after pausing to reflect for a few moments. 'But from what I can gather, they were killing everything else in sight, so it may well be that he got himself into the line of fire. Or it may be, of course, that these men were too ignorant to distinguish a white owl from the vermin they were attempting to extinguish. However, it would be worth trying to find him before you fly closer to the Lost Domain itself.'

'Thank you! I'll bear that in mind,' I said, remembering that last dangerous reconnaissance flight I had supposedly undertaken into and across the Lost Domain, whereas in actual fact I had obtained the necessary information separately from Olmo and from Hunter in no man's land – in the copse that stands above and around the slow-running stream. In any case, I had got the results, and that's what counted. In later life I have learned that this is nearly always true. Never mind the methods, the philosophy or the tactics. Just carry out the task assigned to you – in a brave or cowardly fashion, by fair means or foul – and on successful completion of the project you will be considered a successful creature or, as in the case of owls like Hunter and myself, even a hero. But if you fail, for whatever reason, however noble, you will be downgraded, despised and held in contempt.

But yet again I digress! The narrative must flow fast like the water that bursts from the rock close by, as it did on that sunrise so long ago when my father left me and returned to his own abode in his even greater and more stately oak — an oak and an abode that one supposed one day might be one's own.

But first I must survive this dangerous mission to the Lost Domain. I dozed and slept fitfully in my oak until dusk, and in my waking moments I willed the Great God Bird to send us more refugees — refugees who could provide the information that I must otherwise risk my life to obtain. But none came, and shortly after twilight my father visited me again.

'Are you ready?' he asked me.

'I suppose so,' I said, affecting a bored little yawn to mask the fact that I was scared. 'I shall take your advice and seek out Hunter first, in case by some miracle he survived the holocaust and is still alive. If I can't find him, I shall fly on towards the Lost Domain in search of Olmo the poet, or any other Little Owls who might have survived the holocaust and will therefore be able to give me the information you require.'

'Good luck, Yoller,' my father said. 'Fly high and free, but be wary and don't take any senseless risks!'

I nodded without replying as my father patted me briefly with one of his broad wings, and then I took off, flying downward in the direction of the willow in the copse, wondering how an owl could perform a task like mine without taking any risks. Leading from the front was a concept that my conditioning had now caused me to accept. What I neither understood nor appreciated was why the most dangerous missions always seemed to devolve on me. *Noblesse oblige*, preparation for future leadership, perhaps? Setting an example to lower forms of Tawny life, such as Hook and Cleaver? In any or whichever of these cases, as I flew down towards the willow that stood above the brackish stream, I decided that after this assignment and the following, even more perilous journey to the city, I must either become leader or else abandon the ambitions of my family, abdicate and decline any further opportunities for heroism in the front line. Others were welcome to the glory! Either I would lead from behind, as my father and most other ageing Tawny generals in other districts did, or else I would eschew for ever those same paths of glory, which lead but to the grave, and settle down with May Blossom – or preferably a female like Mallow – leaving other creatures of the night to plot, to struggle and to fight for their own species and for domination of the night sky.

These were my premature and subversive thoughts on that late twilight as I drifted down into the copse and perched on my favourite branch of the willow. Once settled, I hooted loudly, twice, but there was no reply from across the flatland that lay between the copse in no man's land and the abandoned farmhouse in which Beak Poke had once lived and in which, after his death, the little alien had slowly and patiently nursed Hunter back to health.

'He is dead!' I thought, and my heart sank. But before abandoning hope, I filled my lungs and tried again, sending out a call louder than any I had ever emitted, save for the one battle cry that had burst from me spontaneously as my assault wave rose up to make its near suicidal attack on the Eagle Owl.

For a time there was no reply, but then I heard a faint call, coming from beyond the flatland fields and meadows. It was the call of a Barn Owl in distress, unable or unwilling now to fly. It came from the direction of Hunter's derelict farmhouse, and I jumped to the conclusion that he had been badly wounded by a firestick, but had somehow managed to fly back from the scene of the holocaust to a place where he could either die in peace or else slowly recuperate without further threat from man.

I took off at once, flew fast across the fields and meadows and hooted just once more before I reached the abandoned building and flew in through the gap that must once upon a time have been a window.

I saw him at once, perched on the headboard of the long, horizontal thing that men sleep on. He was leaning back against the wall and his eyes were closed. His body seemed lifeless and his feathers were unkempt and dishevelled, but at first glance I could see no sign of injury or blood.

I fluttered for a moment, uncertain what to do, and then perched opposite him on top of the wooden object I have described before – the container or box men use to store their plumage in at night. From here I could see his chest heaving deeply, and as I stared down at him in great concern his eyes opened and he looked back at me with the dull, glazed expression of an owl who has seen things that he either cannot or does not wish to describe. He was clearly in a profound state of shock, but after further scrutiny I could still see no signs of wounds or blood.

'Are you hurt?' I asked, as he gazed at me with the blank look of one who has been to hell and back. He shook his head just once and then closed his eyes again, as if he could not bear to look on anything, not even at a friend who had come to visit him in the safety of his own home.

'What happened?' I asked, realizing that somehow I must try to bring him through this state of shock. There was a long pause before he opened his eyes again.

'She's dead!' he said, eventually, in the flat, dull tones of one who has been stunned and not yet fully regained his senses.

'Alba?'

'Yes.'

'How? Where? In the Lost Domain?'

'I don't want to talk about it,' Hunter said, closing his eyes again.

'You must talk about it! You are in a state of shock. You must come through it! You must talk about it and tell me what you saw.'

'I can't,' Hunter said.

'You have to!' I insisted. 'You have been through some nightmare which has put you under a kind of spell. To break the spell you must talk to me and tell me what you saw.'

There was a long pause while Hunter rested the back of his head against the wall, with his eyes still closed, as the implications of what I'd just said to him filtered through the mists of his suffering until they tapped the source of some survival instinct hidden in his brain.

'You went to the Lost Domain last night, in search of her?' I said, prompting him again. He nodded once in answer, but did not choose to speak.

'Were there many killed?' I asked. 'For the Great God Bird's sake, talk now or you'll bury yourself ever deeper in this trance!'

He looked back at me then, and for the first time that evening there was a flicker in his eyes that suggested that I had touched the source of survival, and he had begun to realize at last that I was making sense.

'I went there to get her back,' he said, after another long pause. 'Or if I couldn't get her back here to live with me, then at least to see her again one more time.'

'But you knew she had mated with Renato?'

'No. I knew she intended to, but I thought I might be in time to stop it and to persuade her to come home again. But even if it proved too late, I had to see her again. Just once more, to tell her that I loved her and to wish her well.'

Now that he had started talking, Hunter's eyes had brightened a little, and his head moved as he gazed around this part of the abandoned farmhouse, which he had once considered to be his and Alba's home. From the expression in his eyes, I saw it was a place where he must no longer stay. If he did, he would be torn by memories of the alien who had nursed him back to health, then used him and finally betrayed him to return to her own kind.

'Tell me what happened,' I insisted, partly – and shamefully – because I needed this information, and partly because I knew that he must exorcize the terrible things he had seen by recounting them.

He glanced around once more, then his head went back against the wall and he began to talk. I tell this story in his own words, as well as I can remember them. It is a shorter, less lyrical account of these same events than that rendered by Quaver in his epic ballad, but it differs, I believe, only in detail – detail which only my silent listeners may decide is either significant or not.

'I took off soon after twilight and flew to the Lost Domain. All went well until I reached the stretch of woodland that screens the great house, the gardens and the lake, and hides the Lost Domain from the rest of the outside world. It was only then, as I flew on through these woods towards the great house, the gardens and the lake, that I realized there was something wrong.'

'What was wrong?'

'The light! The moonlight was much too bright. At least, that's what I thought at first, but then I realized that this uncanny daytime glow – almost as strong as the blood-red heat of a noonday harvest sun – was generated from the great house itself, where all the windows were ablaze with light. My first impulse was to turn and fly back through the woods, skirt round the village, and then bury myself in Barn Owl country and the safety of this abandoned building. But then I thought of little Alba and remembered that this might be my last chance to persuade her not to mate with Renato, but to come home and live with me here, in comparative safety, as before. So I plucked up all my courage, emerged from my hiding place, and began to weave my way through the upper branches of the trees towards the edge of the lake, where I knew that the bright light blazing from the great house could no longer reach me.

'I paused on the edge of the wood and perched for a while in a willow overlooking the lake. I was now enveloped mercifully in darkness, though the full moon ahead of me was reflected in an eerie, silver shimmer from the waters of the lake, and behind me the lights from the mansion still burned like a great beacon in the night sky. As I perched in the darkness of the willow, attempting to summon up yet more courage to enable me to fly on across the lake and up into the parkland, it happened!'

'What happened?'

'All hell was suddenly let loose,' Hunter said. 'A great ray of man-made light suddenly lit up the centre of the park and then, immediately afterwards, four shattering explosions burst the stillness and shattered the ear-drums of the soft night air. Almost immediately, a second man-made beam lit up the edge of the forest far beyond, and immediately four or five more shots rang out in quick succession.'

'I heard them!'

'You heard them, even at that distance, in the heart of your native woodland?'

'No, I heard them here, where I am sitting now. You see, last night I flew down to look for you. I heard them – and even at this distance they scared me so much that I took off and flew home again. Only the Great God Bird knows what effect they must have had on you!'

'I was frightened!' Hunter confessed at once. 'So frightened that I shrank back into my willow tree and watched as the two different groups of men began shouting to each other, one from the centre of the parkland and the other from the edge of the secret forest. I watched as these two man-made rays of light converged on the centre of the parkland and then began to bob downward, showing the men their way to the lake, and to the willow trunk to which I still clung, struggling against the impulse to escape before they came too close.'

'But you stayed?'

'I stayed and watched the bobbing rays of light come closer and closer until they passed beneath the willow tree in which I remained hidden, clinging to the trunk. At that point, before they passed beneath me, I was curious and very much afraid, but my purpose still held to find little Alba and bring her back to live with me here. The terror hit me as the men passed beneath on their way back to the house, when I saw what they were carrying.'

Hunter paused then and leaned his head back against the wall, eyes closed, as the recent nightmare took him in its grip again.

'What were they carrying?' I asked, determined to keep him talking until he had begun to exorcize the events of that dreadful night by recounting them to another living being.

'They were carrying dead Little Owls,' he said. 'Not in what we call their arms – the wings with which they cannot fly – but around their waists. Two lifeless birds dangled head downward from the first man's waist. Their legs had been tied to some kind of belt around his middle, and their round bodies, blunt wings and lolling heads bounced grotesquely against the man's bottom as he strode on below me towards the blazing pool of light around the house. A third owl was dangling from the waist of the last man to pass below me. The sight in itself was sickening enough, but the thought that one of them might be Alba drove me almost frantic with despair.'

'You couldn't see?'

'No, and to my shame I was afraid to fly closer and

investigate. Each of the four men carried a firestick on his shoulder and, as I have already said, I was terrified. I watched them move on across the gardens towards the blaze of light, and then saw them swallowed up by the great house. Ahead of me, across the lake and in the parkland, I sensed the presence of a dying dog fox and heard the faint cries of other wounded animals. One of them was a Little Owl, and the thought that this might be little Alba drove me almost to distraction. In spite of this, I still dared not move from my hide-out in the willow tree. I waited for what seemed an eternity until one by one the blazing lights in the great house behind me were extinguished and darkness returned to the Lost Domain.

'Sometime between midnight and dawn the signals from the dog fox began to fade, and I knew that he must now be close to the point of death. Soon they ceased altogether, but the faint signals from the Little Owl lingered on and wafted to me through the silence and the darkness of the night air. It was only then, as I have said, sometime between midnight and sunrise, that I found the courage to take off again and fly across the lake and then upward through the parkland towards the spot from which these muffled signals came. My flight path took me above the dog fox, whose rank smell still emanated after death, and then on to the centre of the parkland and to the great oak which men had flooded with their instant light. Below this tree lay the body of a murdered male immigrant. I did not stop to identify the body and only later discovered that the corpse was all that remained of Renato, the owl they had elected as their leader.

'I flew on until in the higher parkland I came to the point from which faint signals of the wounded owl still came. I hesitated, fluttering above the ground on which the creature lay. I was afraid of what I might find when I flew down. But I knew that I must, so I dropped from the sky and landed in the grass beside the prostrate body.'

'It was Alba?'

Hunter did not answer me at once. Overcome by emotion, he merely nodded, and then began to shake his head from side to side as if what he had seen was too horrifying to relate. I knew that I must keep him talking, for two reasons. First for his own sake – I knew that he would never come through the trauma and the shock unless he could share it with another living soul. And also, of course, I had my ulterior motives. I needed the information for my father, and had no wish to risk my own life by flying to the Lost Domain.

'Was she badly hurt?' I asked, prompting him to go on with his story. He had already told me she was dead, and it was therefore self-evident that the wounds she had sustained had proved fatal. But I asked the question anyway, and my ploy worked, for he came out of his trance and began to talk again.

'It was horrible!' he said. 'One of her wings was shattered, there were holes in the left side of her body, and half her face had been so badly damaged that it was almost shot away. She was unconscious and, as I bent over her, I knew without the shadow of a doubt that she was dying.'

'How awful!' I said, as Hunter choked and began to dry up again. 'Was there nothing you could do?'

'Nothing!' he said, picking up my cue again. 'That was the worst part. There was nothing I could do, not even to help her survive those last few moments of misery and pain that might be left between her and all eternity. And I have to tell you this, Yoller. As I looked down at her shattered face and body, I felt not only sick and sad, but also bitter. Bitter because if only the world had been a slightly better place – if its pressures and prejudices had not driven us apart – she might not have been lying there in such dreadful suffering with her face and body blown apart.'

Here Hunter choked and paused again, his mind clearly full of the dreadful sights that he had seen.

'Did she not regain consciousness before she died?' I asked, determined now that he should bring the story to an end. At first Hunter did not reply, but merely nodded.

'Yes,' he said eventually. 'She opened her eyes once more and even managed to speak to me.'

'What did she say?'

'She said she loved me. She said she knew that one day I would come to fetch her, so she had mated with Renato to free me and to save my reputation. Now I'm dying, she said. Poor Renato is already dead and no fledglings of mine will ever see the sunrise or the silver moonlight on the lake. I told her to be still and to save all her strength for getting better. But she went on talking and with her last breath she begged me to make a promise.'

'What promise?' I asked, as gently as I could, while Hunter's chest heaved and he choked once more with the fullness of what he was trying to express.

'She made me promise not to change. She made me promise to work with young owls like you and Olmo to make the night-time world a better place.'

'And did you?' I asked.

'Yes, I did. She smiled at me, her chest gave one final great convulsion and she died.'

As he spoke these final words Hunter's own chest heaved once, his eyes closed, and his body slumped back against the wall. I no longer knew what to say or how to prompt him. He was scarcely breathing now, and one might have thought that he, too, had embarked on his own final journey to the great beyond.

Then his eyes opened and he leaned forward as if anxious to make some kind of confession.

'I spoke the final words for her,' he said. 'The words we say for the dying and the dead.'

'The words you taught me? Hoard and covet not, but be brave and free . . . ?'

'No, that is our credo. The last words, as we call them, are different.'

'But you can say them for an alien?' I asked. 'Even if they have a God, it surely can't be the same one as yours – or ours,' I added, thinking of how shocked my mother would have been if I had spoken our simple Tawny prayer for the dead over the body of an alien.

'Alba once told me their God was the same. She believed that there was only one God Bird – the same one for all creatures who fly at night. The only difference was that the separate species worshipped Him in their different ways.'

'Do you believe this?'

'I don't know,' Hunter said. 'But I believe that if our last words are true, then they must be true for everyone. They must be true for Tawnies, immigrants, and for all other species of owl that live and breathe upon this earth. So I changed the words to include little Alba.'

'What did you say?'

Hunter looked at me for a moment, then leaned back again and began to recite the Barn Owl prayer for the dying and the dead.

'As you depart this sky and earth and go at last to rest, know that you are not alone. Know that your species will survive for all eternity, beyond the barnyards, fields and meadows where we live, and also in no man's land. Beyond the twilight and the dawn, beyond the pale moon that glimmers and the stars that shine for ever in the black and vibrant night. Through knowledge and self-sacrifice you will survive until the sun no longer sets and until the moon fails to rise and give us light. Know that with us and among us still you will survive for all eternity and beyond the boundless limits of all wisdom and all time.'

'That's longer than our prayer for the dead, and more poetic,' I said, when Hunter had finished speaking and opened his eyes again. 'Tell me, which were the words you changed?'

'I said your species instead of our species and I added no man's land because that is where most of the immigrants live. In our Barn Owl prayer, we mention only fields and meadows.'

'I think you did the right thing,' I said at once. 'But weren't you afraid that the Great God Bird would consider it a blasphemy – to pray above the body of a dying alien?'

'No,' Hunter said. 'Not if He is as compassionate and forgiving as He is said to be.'

I hesitated for a while, wondering whether I dared ask Hunter any more questions. Now that he had unburdened himself of the worst part of his ordeal, he looked exhausted. But in spite of this, I persisted. If he could not give me the necessary information, it would mean my flying to the Lost Domain.

'Do you know how many were killed, or what the remaining immigrants intend to do now?' I asked. He looked at me for some time and then shook his head.

'I sat by her body until dawn,' he said, now choking on his words again. 'Then, at sunrise, I flew back here and have seen or heard from no one since.'

I nodded, realizing that this time there was no escape, no easy way out of the task that I had been set. This time I must fly to the Lost Domain myself. I looked at Hunter as he slumped back against the wall, his eyes now closed again, and knew that he was in no fit state to come with me. And even if I waited until the following sunset, I guessed that he would still be loth to fly across the place where little Alba's body lay.

'Have you eaten?' I asked him in concern, as he sagged back against the wall.

'No,' he said, with a slow shake of his head. 'I'm not hungry. But you go. You must have nourishment. You can hunt here, of course. There's plenty of food about at this present time.'

'You must eat as well!' I said. 'I will catch something for you and bring it back.'

'No,' Hunter said, shaking his head again. 'Feed yourself and then get home before daylight breaks. When the time comes, I will eat. For the moment I prefer to be left alone with my grief.'

'I'm not going home,' I said, and told him then about the information I must obtain for my father. 'This means, I suppose, that I must go to the Lost Domain?' I asked him, when I'd finished my explanation.

'Go to the secret forest,' Hunter said. 'Skirt round the gardens and the house, as I did, and fly across the parkland shortly before dawn. That is your best chance of avoiding the firesticks.'

'But why the secret forest?'

'Because Alba told me that in the event of an attack such as took place last night, the survivors would settle there. Some would be terrified and fly away, like the two refugees your father saw. But the hard core would remain and settle in the secret forest. They would not give up the chance of establishing their own republic and in no way would they return to no man's land.'

I thought about this for a moment. It was late to start the journey now, but if I took off at once I might just make it before the risen sun; my size and staggering daytime flight made me almost a sitting target for the firestick. But as I have told my silent listeners before, this time I knew I had to go, and go alone. So why not now? The longer I waited, the more apprehension would prey on my mind. Half-fatalistic and half-reckless with bravado, I made my decision and told Hunter that I would leave at once.

'And don't forget to eat!' I added. 'You must be strong, if we are to fly to the city in four nights' time. Such an expedition is pure folly, of course. But you will remember what you said?'

'No,' Hunter replied, slowly shaking his head. 'Tell me, what was it that I said?'

'You said that folly was the best antidote to pain.'

'Oh, yes!' he replied, leaning back against the wall again. 'Very well, Yoller! When I am ready I shall eat. In four nights' time I will meet you at twilight in the willow above the stream and we will fly south together on this suicidal mission. Thank you for inviting me to join you.'

'Goodbye, then!' I said.

'Goodbye, and be careful,' he replied. 'If you don't turn up at the appointed time and place, I shall assume that you were shot in the Lost Domain!'

'Thanks very much, for nothing!' I said, and looking at him, to my immense relief I saw the flicker of a smile in those eyes which up until this point had either been glazed with shock or else, in his lucid moments, filled with a pain and sadness more acute than the grief and guilt that I myself felt after I had heard of Mallow's death.

I smiled back at him and left through the gap in the wall, heading towards the Lost Domain and my encounter with the beginning of a new destiny – or perhaps merely the confirmation of a fate that had already been decided by the Great God Bird in the sky. I don't know. As Sage was to say later, it is easy to be wise after the event. But though the seeds of doubt, already sown, were to take root as a result of what happened on those long-gone nights, many winters were to pass and much blood was to flow before I came to believe that little Alba, Hunter and even Olmo, the alien poet, though perhaps naive, had all in their separate ways been right, whilst we had been over-zealous in our ancient Tawny pride. I still don't know, and now I never shall. Now it must be left for fickle history and for my faithful but silent listeners to decide.

CHAPTER

24

Much later, when I first heard Quaver's ballad, I wondered why he made no mention of my visit to his brother the night after the men with firesticks returned and perpetrated their slaughter in the Lost Domain.

Perhaps his brother never told him, but knowing Hunter I suspect he did. I think it is more likely that Quaver omitted this episode so as not to show the legendary Barn Owl hero in his moment of pain and weakness after little Alba's death.

One can't be sure, of course, but I suspect that this must be the case, for his account of the holocaust itself is accurate, fuller and much more lyrical than mine. I say accurate, but there are some anomalies, of course. As I remember it, the second tree in which Hunter hid that night was a willow, and not a black poplar as Quaver has it in his ballad. This is, of course, a minor detail, and of no consequence at all in what Sage was later to refer to as the cosmic scheme of things. However, though of no consequence in itself, this detail, like so many others, is significant in that it underlines the enormous difficulties in rendering an accurate account of times past. For example, the dialogue between Hunter and little Alba, as she lay dying, is longer and made more romantic in 'The Ancient Solitary Reign'.

I think there could be two reasons for this. Either Hunter was no longer in shock and therefore more articulate when he told the story to his brother at a later date, or else — and this is more probable — Quaver used poetic licence and embroidered what he'd heard. All Bard Owls tend to dwell on and embroider such events as suit the purpose of their ballad. They also tend to eliminate or cut down on any happening which does not contribute to or enhance the story they are telling. This is probably why the Barn Owl ballad makes no mention of my solo flight to the Lost Domain in an attempt to gather the information for my father. Either Quaver forgot or else left it out on purpose, because it is more strictly part of the Tawny saga than it is of the white owls' history. For whichever reason, my silent listeners have never been told how I left Hunter alone to nurse his grief and flew as fast as I could towards the confines of the Lost Domain.

Though hungry, I knew I had little chance of reaching the secret forest before dawn if I took time out to eat. In spite of this I made the same mistake again — the mistake I had made when May Blossom had to kill the female buzzard to save my life. Foolishly, I allowed the pangs of hunger to get the better of my brain. Sensing a young rabbit in a copse beyond the village, I swooped down, devoured it, and then rested for a while in the branch of a maple tree. Though I ate quickly and took less than the proper time to digest my food before setting off again, the delay proved fatal, for the giant red fingers had appeared to smear the night sky even before I reached the woodland that hides the lower half of the Lost Domain from the outside world.

Pressing on regardless, I skirted round the gardens and the house, using the woodland as cover until I reached the borders of the lake. Here I paused, in a willow, possibly the same one in which Hunter had perched and witnessed the tragic events of the night before. In the meantime the red streaks of light were now fading into pink as the sun emerged from behind the secret forest and began to rise in the sky ahead of me. It was already dawn, and I still had to fly over the lake and then cross the vast stretch of parkland that swept up to the shelter of the forest.

For a while I hesitated, struggling against the kind of panic that begins to numb one when one realizes one has made a bad mistake and as a consequence is in grave danger. There was still time to struggle back to the copse where I had eaten and then sleep there, or at least rest up until the blessed twilight restored my full powers of flight. This would have been the wiser course, but as fear continued to numb me, I realized that, once having escaped, I might lack the courage to return again. Then, as the sun rose higher and the light grew brighter, a strange kind of madness overtook me. A kind of pulsing or throbbing started deep inside my body and spread outwards until my wings and talons tingled with a kind of fever or a flush of devil-may-care bravado.

My brain, too, was racing with nonsensical thoughts as I screwed up my courage to the sticking place and prepared to take off for the secret forest. One of the absurdities that I used to motivate myself was based on the studies we had made of the arch-enemy, man. Men, I knew, slept by night and hunted or did the other futile things they did by day. But the night before last, and maybe last night as well, they had gone hunting with their artificial light in the parkland of the Lost Domain. Did this mean that they had reversed one of their basic behaviour patterns by using the night-time for activity and the day for sleep and rest? Did these men differ from the norm? There are different types and species of owl. Little Owls, for example, could fly and hunt by day. Barn Owls lived mostly in disused buildings. We lived mainly in the woods or forests and the Little Owls in no man's land, whilst the nomad, or media birds, lived everywhere and rested on the ground! So if there were different species of owl, with different habits, why should there not be different types of men?

Clutching at this faint hope, and feeling the adrenalin pump through my body and my wings, I hooted in defiance – a stupid thing to do – took off and headed for the lake. I crossed it safely, barely pausing to glance down at the succulent selection of duck, mallard and half-grown geese floating on the water below my flight path. My rush of bravado lasted till I had cleared the lake and set out across the last stretch of upward-sloping parkland. As I did so, I suddenly became conscious of my size. We Tawnies are big birds, and I was bigger and stronger than the average for my species. Now, for the first time, my size, my strength and my very race put me at a disadvantage – my species, because Tawnies cannot fly fast by daylight, and our swift and silent flight by night is replaced in the sunlight by a slow and clumsy flapping; my size, because I could so easily be seen from the ground. I needed woodland to protect me, but here there was none. The fear and the feeling of numbness returned, but I flapped onward across the park and through the ever-brightening daylight towards the uncertain sanctuary of the secret forest. My flight path to the centre of the park must have been much the same as Hunter's, but though I glanced down from time to time, I saw no bodies. Perhaps the men had been back by daylight, found them and buried them underground, as they do with their own kind, presumably to prevent the stench of rotting flesh from fouling up the environment in which they live.

But then I remembered what Hunter had told me about the dead and dangling Little Owls being carried back to the great house. For what purpose would they do this, if not to eat them? To feed them to their human fledglings who were still too young to hunt?

There was no record in our long history of any owl ever

being eaten by a man, but times change. Over the past fifty or sixty seasons men had acquired ever brighter light at night. They had put up more and more buildings and caused poisonous smoke to pour up into the sky. They had even begun to drop fire down upon each other from the artificial birds they used to fly about in. Whilst our own way of life remained much the same, many things in the world of men had changed. Perhaps they had also modified their eating habits to include Little Owls or even Tawnies amongst the many other animals and birds they ate. Perhaps they had taken to eating foxes as well, though I could not imagine how any creature could bring itself to consume anything that, after death, emanated such a rank and pungent smell.

It was with such strange, uncanny thoughts running through my head that I came within striking distance of the secret forest and breathed a huge sigh of relief as the shelter of the woodland loomed ever closer in front of me.

But my relief was premature! As I approached the tree line, two men emerged from the woodland directly below. At night, I would have picked up their presence sooner and changed my flight path accordingly, but in the daylight our sensory powers are impaired, so that now I found myself flapping above them in the open sky, in bright sunshine, with nothing to shield me from the firestick which one man carried on his shoulder. However, it was not he but his companion who spotted me and pointed up into the sky at once, as I instinctively struggled to gain height with all the strength and rhythm I could cull from my sluggish daytime wings.

Below me, as I glanced down again, I saw the first man tugging frantically at his companion who carried the firestick, pointing up at me again as I fought the air and wind around me to gain height. I saw the second man follow his comrade's gaze, shielding his eyes against the dazzle of the early-morning sunlight as he traced and immediately located the spot above him where my broad wings beat on upward, carrying my big but vulnerable body slowly higher towards the risen sun. The second man unslung the firestick from his shoulder, still staring up into the sky. Then he turned to his comrade, shook his head, and replaced the firestick on his shoulder.

Moments later, my efforts had carried me above and beyond the edge of the woodland, and I dived down, instinctively craving the cover of the trees, and then drove myself onward among the upper branches, heading for the densely wooded centre, or what was soon to become known as the inner sanctum of the secret forest. When I had reached what I judged to be the heart of this ancient, thickly wooded haven, I collapsed into the middle of an oak and camouflaged myself close to the trunk on a big branch which sprouted from the centre of the mighty tree. There I perched, hidden and slowly recovering my composure, whilst the early-morning breeze whispered through the smaller branches high above me and ruffled the fresh spring leaves which danced around me in the unaccustomed daytime light.

I don't know how long I sat there, perched in what struck me as the safety of this ancient oak, buried and hidden deep in a cluster of surrounding trees in the depths of the secret forest. I heard no sound of men approaching, only the rustling on the forest floor below me of a hundred different creatures, some small, some medium-sized, like squirrel, weasel or mole, and some relatively large, like buck rabbit, hare or fox. Secure as I was, high in the middle of the massive oak, none of these creatures presented any kind of threat to me. They were no more of a menace than any of the dozen or so daytime birds that flitted in and out of the branches now burgeoning with green foliage all around me. I say these creatures presented no threat, but as the afternoon wore on, these common daytime birds began to mob me. Sadly we Tawnies are subjected to this kind of thing from time to time. In fact, my parents had warned me about it when I was young.

'They do it to get rid of us,' my mother had explained. 'If they find a Tawny sleeping or resting in their territory by day, they will attempt to drive him out, knowing that he will be a threat to them by night. It only takes one of them to discover you and you will be persecuted by these mindless creatures as the buzzard by day is mobbed by rook or crow. The first one to discover you will then spread the word to most of the lower forms of bird life that fly the sky by day. When enough of them have been assembled, they will perch in the branches all around you and then set up a cacophony of twittering and shrieking in an attempt to prevent you from sleeping and ultimately to drive you away. If this happens, do not be afraid. They will not come too close, and will certainly never dare to make a direct attack, however great the number that they have assembled to pester a higher form of life whom they, in their ignorance, consider an intruder. So, if this should ever happen to you, stay where you are and wait. If one of these hecklers comes too close, kill it, and you will find that the rest of the mob will fly away. One must on no account give in to this kind of pressure, or passive resistance, as they call it. One must, I repeat, simply sit quite still and wait, kill one, if necessary, eat it, and then wait again until the others have gone away. You will find that the leader of the mob will probably be a blackbird. They are the worst and most militant agitators among the common daytime birds.'

'Do I really have to eat it?' I asked, for at that time in my young life I was still fairly squeamish about consuming other birds.

'You must!' my mother said. 'To kill any creature and then not eat it is a sin, or at any rate we consider it bad form. When you kill and begin to eat the bird, make sure the other mobsters are all watching. In this way our proud and ancient Tawny image will remain intact. We're not barbarians, like man or fox, who kill not only to feed themselves, but for some perverse kind of pleasure known as sport.'

As I have already said, I had never been subjected to this tiresome ordeal before, and had therefore never taken much notice of my mother's warning. When one is young, one tends to think that the natural disasters and irritations that others undergo will never actually be experienced by oneself.

Now, remembering what my mother had once said, I sat quite still in the middle of my oak, in the centre of the secret forest, while this ever-growing legion of pesky sparrows, starlings, blackbirds and even several tiny wrens perched and shrieked in the branches all around me and kept me from either sleep or rest. However, I sat quietly and made no move, as I had been advised, until a particularly plebeian-looking blackbird moved down from a branch above me and perched within what I considered to be easy striking distance, even allowing for the fact that in daytime my hunting faculties were limited.

For some time I pretended to ignore him, and took no notice of the incomprehensible insults that he shrieked out at me through his ugly orange bill. Presently other birds came closer, and I found myself surrounded by a howling mob which was obviously determined to get rid of me. Still I hesitated, not so much reluctant to kill as loth to obey our Tawny rules and eat the wretched blackbird afterwards.

Encouraged by the other mobsters, the blackbird moved still closer to me. Suddenly my patience snapped. I lurched upward from my branch and killed him with one single blow. As soon as I moved, the other rioting birds flew off in panic, but to my great disappointment they did not disappear, but took up positions at a safer distance in the mighty tree. I took the blackbird back to my perch and sat there with its body trapped on the broad branch by the talons of my powerful right foot.

For a time there was silence, and then the chorus of protest began again, soon building up into that same unbearable cacophony of sound. So, with great regret and some revulsion, I began to eat the creature. As I started, the heckling died down, and by the time I had swallowed the last of the blackbird, the rest of the mob had first fallen silent and then fled, just as one had been told they would.

I sat there for a while, enjoying the peace and quiet but, frankly, feeling sick, or queasy to say the very least. I was also rather dejected. How depressing it can be, indeed, to discover that one's mother has been right! One would much prefer to re-invent the world according to one's own ideas, but as I have subsequently discovered, habit and tradition take many centuries to die, and even after formal death they linger long in the owl subconscious, and however unpleasant or unfair, these instincts can never be entirely suppressed and are bound to break out again from time to time.

Mobbing, war with other night birds, competition with the daytime raptors, when would it ever end? I wondered. Would there ever be a time when one could live in peace, or were danger and violence endemic to all forms of life?

Brooding on these existential problems, I suddenly became aware that a Little Owl had flown into the tree above me. Looking up to the branch on which he'd landed, I thought I recognized Olmo, the poet, but it was hard to tell. I had only seen him once and, in any case, all Little Owls looked much the same to me. As a matter of fact, all creatures of another species did. It wasn't until one came to know them well that one was able to distinguish one from another. This is of course a disadvantage, and I worked hard at the business of distinguishing one alien or one Barn Owl from another. Later, this acquired ability stood me in good stead, and later still it was one of the minor reasons for my being branded a heretic, for in a moment of anger I attributed our inability to distinguish between individuals of other races to the twin factors of Tawny ignorance and arrogance. This did not go down too well, as my silent listeners may well imagine!

At any rate, Olmo seemed to have no difficulty in recognizing me, for he greeted me by name, at once, without the slightest doubt or hint of interrogation in his voice.

'Olmo?' I replied and, when he nodded, I took off from my branch, slowly so as not to alarm him, and flew up to join him higher in the oak.

'What are you doing here?' he asked me, as soon as I had perched opposite him on a branch which was uncomfortably slender for my greater weight.

'I came to look for you.'

'Why?'

'Firstly to console you for your losses, and secondly to ask you what you and your comrades intend to do next.'

There was a pause while Olmo subjected me to a long, hard look.

'You are saying you came here as a spy?' he asked, when he'd had time to take in and process what I'd said.

'I don't know what you mean.'

'Oh yes you do. Your father has sent you to see how many of us were killed by the men and their firesticks and how many of us intend to remain here in the Lost Domain.'

'You are right, to some extent,' I admitted. 'After all, this secret forest by right belongs to us. If you should decide to settle here, and not in the parkland and the gardens, as we discussed before, at some time in the future we might have to repossess this territory, which has belonged to us for centuries.'

Olmo stared at me again for quite some time before replying.

'I must say I admire you,' he said eventually. 'You fly here the night after the holocaust, risking death by firestick, to count our dead and monitor our future plans. Few birds of your species would be brave enough to undertake a mission of that kind.'

'I can't say I'm enjoying it,' I replied. 'But I'm very glad you found me. I didn't relish the idea of flying all over the secret forest in search of you.'

'I heard the mobbing,' Olmo said. 'I guessed it would be a Tawny and that that Tawny would be you!'

'Don't Little Owls get mobbed?' I asked.

'Not often. At any rate not as often as you Tawnies do.'

'Why is that, do you think?'

'I don't know,' Olmo replied. 'Perhaps because we are smaller and therefore seem less of a threat.'

'But you are more of a threat to the daytime birds than we are!' I protested. 'You hunt by night, but also when the sun is high. We kill only by night, and even then seldom kill and eat another bird unless there is an acute shortage of food on the woodland floor.'

'I suppose you had to kill a blackbird to stop the mobbing?'

'Yes,' I said. 'How did you guess?'

'It is the only way. On the rare occasions when it happens to us, we are obliged to do the same.'

'How many of you died the night before last?' I asked, bluntly. I was brusque not out of any desire to be rude, or because I lacked compassion, but because I was anxious to get the information as soon as possible and then set out for home as soon as dusk had deepened into night.

'We don't know, exactly,' Olmo replied, looking at me bravely, but with a crack in his voice that showed how much he must have suffered, and I wondered whether the panache with which he now confronted me might not be a Little Owl equivalent of the bravado which I was using in an attempt to outface him!

'We don't know how many managed to escape,' he continued, attempting to show no more emotion and to shrug off the tragic losses they had suffered. 'There were sixteen of us. So far we have accounted for six bodies, and three of us are still missing.'

'That means there are only seven of you left.'

'Yes.'

'Yet in spite of the men with firesticks, and in spite of the fact that if and when they leave we shall come back and claim the secret forest – in spite of everything, you still intend to stay?'

'That is your father's intention?' Olmo asked, without replying directly to my question.

'Yes. He says that our traditional woodlands are still being eroded by man, and that it is our duty to preserve what's left of it for future generations and for the survival of our race.'

'But your father is old, and soon must either die or abdicate. You will succeed him then and the decision to invade us and take over will be entirely yours.'

'Well, in that unlikely eventuality, I can say quite frankly that I don't think seven, eight or even a dozen of you would present any great problem for a Tawny task force.'

'Do not delude yourself!' Olmo replied, and his bright, sad eyes shone with conviction as the sun sank lower and the first shadows of twilight dimmed the daytime light. 'Do not delude yourself,' he repeated. 'There are only seven of us now, but more will come. Little by little we shall attract more refugees or settlers. Here, we have established our own territory and have sworn never to go back to no man's land. We shall breed here, flourish and, as time passes, we shall prepare defences that will be guaranteed to protect our promised land.'

'Do you want me to tell my father that? I mean, is this some kind of ultimatum, or not?'

'You may tell him what you wish. We know that you would never send a task force to the Lost Domain as long as the men with firesticks remain. No one knows how

283

long that will be, or what events may occur in the mean-time to make you change your mind. This is our promised land, and here we intend to stay, whatever sacrifice that may entail.'

'You know that little Alba is dead?' I asked, not wanting to confront him any further on the territorial issue. I knew in any case that what he'd said was right. We would never attempt to reclaim the secret forest while the men with firesticks remained. We had neither the stomach for it, nor sufficient forces to colonize the place and to protect our own ancestral woodlands at the same time.

Olmo hesitated for a long time before attempting to answer my question about Alba. For the first time he seemed overcome by the tragedy and by the losses that had befallen them. In fact, he looked so upset by my question that I wondered fleetingly whether he had been in love with her as well. But that seemed hard to credit. Olmo, Renato and Hunter all in love with the same scruffy little alien? But then I remembered that she was not an alien to them.

'Hunter is very cut up about it,' I added, since the poet had still not replied to my question. 'In fact, he's quite distraught. You know he flew to the Lost Domain that night, found her dying, and then kept vigil by her body till the sun began to rise?'

'I know!' said Olmo, choking on his breath in much the same way as Hunter had when recounting this sad episode to me.

'How do you know? Did you see it happen?'

'No, but one of our community was hiding in an oak close to the place where she was killed. She saw the big white bird come to comfort her, and when she flew here just before the dawn, he was still sitting by her body.'

'And you know that Renato was killed as well?'

'Yes. I saw that happen.'

'Who will be your leader now that he is dead?'

'We don't know. There will be an election as soon as

we have settled and begun to recover from the shock.'

'Could it be you?'

'No,' Olmo said. 'I am a poet. A committed poet, yes! But never a politician. I would imagine that either Primo or Falco will take over. They were both founder-members of the community, along with Renato.'

'What are they like?' I asked.

'Militant,' replied Olmo, with a slight shrug of his rounded shoulders. 'I'm afraid you won't find much space to negotiate with them.'

'Well, for the moment at any rate, I wish you luck,' I said. 'I am sorry for your losses and I hope you live safely here until the time comes for us to retake the secret forest. But I have to say that I hope the Tawny invasion does not happen in my lifetime or in yours.'

'In our lifetime,' Olmo replied, nodding slowly. 'If it does happen in our lifetime, you will almost certainly be leader of the Tawnies. It will be within your power to prevent a bloody war.'

'And you?' I asked.

'I told you when we first met, I will do all I can, and as far as the Barn Owls are concerned, I know that Hunter will do the same.'

'This has nothing to do with Hunter,' I said. 'The Barn Owls live on farmland, not in woods or forests.'

'And when there is no farmland left?' asked Olmo, raising his eyebrows slightly as he spoke.

'Don't be ridiculous!' I said. 'There will always be farmland left. Otherwise, how would the men eat?'

'That's not what I meant. Of course there will be farmland left – for men – but will there be so much of it? Remember that two thousand springs ago man began to cut down your precious woodlands and turn them into farmland. Who says they won't turn the farmland back into woods, or else build new towns on it? If either of these things happened, the Barn Owls would have to adapt and learn to live in the forests, as we Little Owls are learning now. Otherwise, they would slowly become extinct.'

'So you think all three species could be in conflict over the woodland that is left?'

'It's possible,' Olmo said. 'And in that case, Hunter's mediation would help to prevent war breaking out between us. Hunter's mediation, yours and mine. The older owls in all three species are too ridden with the past and with tradition. They don't perceive the changes that are taking place around them.'

'From what you are saying, it sounds to me as if all three species may soon be competing for a place in no man's land!'

'The Barn Owls would not survive there,' Olmo said. 'They need wide open spaces. Likewise, they could never live in a town. You Tawnies might adapt to either. We Little Owls would manage even better. After all, we've survived in no man's land for half a century or more. But I want to make it quite clear that none of us here has the slightest intention of returning.'

'I think you've already made that point,' I answered. 'And I'm glad – since you have repeated yourself, so shall I. I repeat, I wish you well for the time being, and if there must be conflict between us, then I hope it will not occur in your lifetime or mine!'

We looked at each other steadily for a moment or two, and then, without saying goodbye, I took off and flew through the secret forest in the deepening twilight until, as the last of the sun sank behind me, I reached the edge of the parkland where I paused and perched, wondering whether to brave the dangers at once, or to wait until dusk had thickened into night.

After a few moments I decided to go on. At least even in the semi-darkness my full flight powers would stand me a better chance. Crossing the vast expanse of open land I neither heard nor sensed the presence of a man, but as I approached the lake I saw that the great house was once more lit up by a blaze of light. I crossed the lake, dived into the woodland beyond, flew through it, and soon emerged in safety on the other side. Only then did I slow down and begin to ponder on what Olmo, the Little Owl, had said. Woodland constantly eroded by man, farmland swallowed by new roads and buildings – would this eventually lead to a territorial war between the three species? And without ample farmland, would the white owls eventually become extinct?

At that time, to my conditioned way of thinking, these hypotheses seemed doubtful – no, fanciful to the degree of being almost absurd. Little did I know then that much worse was to come, and that the real danger had yet to be discovered!

Part Three

. . . a time to keep silence, and a time to speak.

Ecclesiastes, Chapter III, Verse 7

With them the seed of Wisdom did I sow,
And with my own hand wrought to make it grow:
And this was all the Harvest that I reap'd –
'I came like Water, and like Wind I go.'

The Rubáiyát of Omar Khayyám, Verse 31
Done into English by Edward Fitzgerald, 1868

Nel mezzo del cammin di nostra vita
mi ritrovai per una selva oscura,
che la diritta via era smarrita.
Ah quanto a dir qual era è cosa dura
esta selva selvaggia e aspra e forte,
che nel pensier rinova la paura!

Dante Alighieri, 1265–1321
La Divina Commedia, Inferno

CHAPTER

25

Having returned home, I told my parents everything, which I now realize was a grave mistake.

'It is a sign!' my mother said, after I had told them of my narrow escape from the firestick. 'A sign that men consider the immigrants to be vermin, just as we do. And they obviously look upon us Tawnies as a higher form of life.'

'I wouldn't be too sure,' my father said, reluctant as ever to contradict her and mumbling a little as he spoke, so that his words seemed to lack conviction. 'There could be many reasons why the men made no attempt on Yoller's life. For example, if they had studied our habits as the Barn Owl has studied theirs, the men would have known that our traditional territory is the forest and that we are therefore much less of a threat to the animals and birds that breed in and around the parkland and the lake.'

'Nonsense!' my mother said. 'We know that man is an upstart creature, but he is not entirely witless! He knows that the aliens have been here for fewer than a hundred springs. He knows that they are not a natural part of our environment. So, like us, he is anxious to destroy them.'

'You may be right, my dear, but we have no evidence of this,' replied my father. 'I think, Yoller, that you should be advised on this matter by May Blossom. She went to the city to get knowledge and also to observe at close quarters the habits and attitudes of man. In the meantime, apart from her direct experience, it is also to be hoped that she has learned much from Sage. I think we should assess any information they can give us before attempting to recolonize the Lost Domain.'

'But you told me Sage was seditious!' I protested.

'So he is,' replied my father. 'But one must always be ready to learn from one's enemies. As your mother rightly says, we are indeed a higher form of life and right is unquestionably on our side. But to survive all the swift dangers of these modern times, I believe that we must learn humility. We must be prepared to learn, not only from the enemy within, but also from such low-life birds as magpie, rook or crow.'

I was amazed to hear my father talking in this way, and concluded that he must be growing slightly senile. At the same time I could see that my mother was even more shocked than I was.

'Learn from the magpie!' she said. 'What nonsense! Whatever next? Next I suppose you will tell us that we must study creatures like the toad, or take lessons from the ant, the cockroach or the worm!'

'We could do worse,' my father said. 'The worm knows how to dig deep down into the earth to protect itself, and in some ways the ant is a model of cohesive social behaviour. It seems that with this idea of a co-operative the Little Owls are trying to learn from him. For us, this could be very dangerous. In fact now, as my third age approaches, I am convinced that we should learn from any creature that we can!'

I have already said that I was astonished, but it was quite clear that my mother's reaction exceeded this and bordered on disgust. However, she said nothing, but merely ruffled her feathers and expressed contempt both by her body language and by the haughty, offended expression on her face.

Now, of course, so much later in my life, as old now as my father was then, I wish I had never divulged this information to my parents. But at that time I was still relatively young and innocent. I had not yet realized that information is power, and that the giving or withholding of what one knows can mean the difference between survival and death.

Although I did not say so at the time, I must also confess to having been disturbed by the fact that my parents did not seem in the least perturbed by the massacre that had just taken place, whilst I, on the contrary, could not help feeling that a touch of compassion for the murdered Little Owls would not have come amiss. In fact, the seeds of doubt, already sown, had now begun to take root and grow, so that although I dreaded my forthcoming mission to the city, when I left home that night it was with very few regrets.

In the late twilight I flew down to the willow in the copse, wondering whether Hunter would turn up at our trysting place, or whether he had chosen the wiser course and flown home to his mother to enjoy his well-earned status as a war hero, certainly destined at some future time to become a leading member of the Barn Owl community. But to my surprise he was already there, waiting in the willow tree in which we always met, above the brackish waters of the same slow-running stream.

'How are you?' I asked, after landing on my usual branch opposite the one on which he always perched.

'All right,' he said. 'And you?'

'All right. But of course I'm not looking forward to this suicidal mission to the city.'

'Don't worry,' Hunter replied, sounding very calm and almost fatalistic. 'I'm coming with you, as I said.'

'Do you think that's wise?' I asked. 'No Barn Owl has

ever been known to survive long in a city, or what you call a town.'

'Well, we shan't be staying there for long, shall we?'

'That depends,' I said.

'Depends on what?'

'On May Blossom. As far as I'm concerned my mission is to bring her home at once, along with any other Tawnies willing to return and reinforce our depleted rural population. But these other town birds must be notified, and I don't know how long that may take.'

'It doesn't matter,' Hunter said. 'I know this expedition is folly, for both of us, but as you say I said, folly is the best antidote for pain!'

I looked at Hunter long and hard, and saw that his purpose was fully set and his resolve to accompany me held firm.

'Then you are ready to leave?' I asked, eventually.

'Of course! I take it you have some sort of route, or directions on how to get there?'

'We must fly south for six nights above the iron tracks,' I said. 'According to my father's information, that will bring us to the outskirts of the sprawling city.'

'Let's go then. And the devil take the hindmost!' Hunter said.

Of course there was no question of the devil or the hindmost. During the long nights and days that followed, we formed an almost perfect combination. Most of our route lay over open Barn Owl country, and here Hunter taught me to catch food in the fields and meadows that lay on either side of the iron tracks. Conversely, when we crossed copse or spinney, and on the rare occasions when we were able to hunt in rich, dense woodland, I took the lead and showed my travelling companion how to quarter the forest floor in search of substantial food like brown rat or baby rabbit.

Once, at the end of the fourth night, dawn broke quicker

than expected and caught us unawares. We were still flying over open country with no copse, abandoned building or any other daytime shelter in sight. There was no choice but to carry on, and Hunter slowed down to stay with me. He could have flown faster than me, and sooner sought a safe daytime base, but he cut his speed to keep me company as I laboured to keep pace with him on my clumsy daytime wings. He stayed with me as we crossed what seemed to be an endless plain, where the green wheat rippled like waves below us, slowly ripening in the morning sun.

Suddenly two giant buzzards appeared from behind the fireball of the rising sun, wheeled high in the sky above us, and then paused before plunging down into the attack.

'Turn away from the light!' Hunter shouted. 'It's dazzling us. Dive down to the shelter of the hedgerow. If we have to we'll take them on the ground.'

I took his advice without hesitation, and followed Hunter's white shape downward as he plummeted towards the only area of shade afforded by the one remaining hedgerow that had not been ripped out by prairie-farming man. Diving downward in Hunter's wake, I remembered that the decrepit old Beak Poke had told me about such places – vast tracts of land, mainly to the south of our territory, tracts of land that man had turned into barren deserts with hardly any remaining vegetation, except for the never-ending wheat which rippled on towards the edge of the horizon.

As soon as I had crashed down next to Hunter in the meagre protection of the hedgerow, I followed his upward glance at the buzzards, who had checked their downward dive and were now wheeling quite close above us, obviously assessing the position and waiting for the moment to dive in and attack. It was then, as they hovered close above us, that Hunter began to undergo the most incredible transformation, in front of my very eyes. His feathers suddenly began to puff up, his eyes dilated as he glowered up at the buzzards, his body began to pullulate, and the whole of him suddenly seemed to inflate to almost twice his size. Then he began to rotate his bloated wings so that they turned over forwards in a grotesque and aggressive motion that I'd never seen or believed possible before. At the same time he began to shriek obscenities up towards the circling buzzards, and his voice sounded so shrill and bloodthirsty that for a moment or two I was terrified – terrified, until I remembered that he was on my side!

This display of aggression had the desired effect, shocked the buzzards and drove them higher up into the sky, so I attempted to imitate Hunter, swell up and rotate my wings forward as he had done. However, it didn't work and, having almost toppled over in the attempt, I tried to do my bit by flapping my broad wings and swearing upward at the buzzards in the toughest, roughest tones that my vocal cords could find.

The daytime raptors continued to circle higher above us for quite some time, but Hunter kept up his performance, howling more bloodcurdling and violent expletives up into the skies. By now he had blown himself up to an even greater size, until I became afraid that soon he might suddenly explode. Then, to my immense relief, the soaring buzzards suddenly took wing and sped westward, high above the wheat fields and away from the still-rising sun.

For a while neither of us spoke, and I watched in awe as Hunter slowly deflated to his normal size.

'I say, how did you do that?' I asked, when his eyes had ceased to stare out like fiery beacons from his face, and he had once more become the composed, polite and well-mannered Barn Owl whom I knew, or thought I knew!

'Oh, it's nothing,' he said with a tired little shrug, seemingly drained by the incredible aggression that he'd just displayed. 'It's something my father taught me. Something we've copied from the Short Eared Owls, or media birds, who usually nest on the ground. It's called the static defence mechanism, and it's meant to scare your enemies away.'

'Well, it certainly succeeded!' I said, peering up into the western sky where the two buzzards were now mere vanishing specks on the distant horizon. 'Could I learn it, do you think?'

'I suppose so,' Hunter said. 'It's just like anything else. To do it properly you need lessons and then lots of practice.'

I thought about this for a while, and then decided that when the right moment came I would ask him to give me lessons. It was all very well for my mother to look down on Barn Owls as a lower form of life, but it struck me then that the lesson Hunter's father had taught him was a lot more useful than having to listen to long-winded stories about how to avoid fear, or hell!

'What shall we do now?' I asked, feeling uncomfortable with only the scant and mutilated hedgerow to protect me from the morning sun.

'We'll fly on!' Hunter said. 'We'll take it slowly and sleep for the rest of the day in the first shelter we can find.'

So we took off and flew across the seemingly endless flatlands until we came to a small but expanding town beside the iron tracks. In skirting round this new man-made scar on the landscape, we discovered a deserted copse where we dozed and slept for the rest of the day, taking off again at twilight. On this, the fifth night of our journey south, the landscape began to change again. Instead of the barren prairie land, we found ourselves flying over districts ever more populated and despoiled by man. Now the distance between small towns and villages grew even shorter, the man-made lights began to multiply, and seemed to burn brighter and ever later into the night. By now the two iron tracks we had followed from the beginning of our journey had multiplied beneath us to four, to six and now, on the dawn of the fifth day, to eight! There was no more shelter for us on the ground, and by common consent we decided to strike out either east or west of these spreading iron tracks that were now leading us towards the centre of the great, satanic city.

In the end, we opted for the west, to avoid being dazzled by the rising sun, and flew with the warmth on our backs in search of one final countryside haven in which to rest before the final stage of our dangerous journey. Just as my wings began to fail and flap in clumsy daytime flight, the buildings ceased to sprawl beneath us and we came upon a sheltered, rural valley which spread below us like an oasis in what the media birds refer to as the desert. Beyond the valley and further to the west, the land rose up into a sweep of wooded hills that reminded me of my ancestral home.

'Here?' Hunter asked, nodding down at the unsullied Barn Owl countryside, which was still split by full-grown hedgerows into a patchwork of fields, meadows, copse and spinney, very like our own rural territory which we had left far behind us to the north.

Of course, I would have preferred to have flown on up into the forest further west, but I agreed at once, for it was obvious that this lightly wooded, undulating valley would provide ample protection for us both. I nodded in agreement, and then followed Hunter as he dived swiftly from the sky, heading for a thick copse in the centre of the valley. As if he had read my thoughts, he took me closest to the kind of shelter where I felt most at home, ignoring the ruined buildings and abandoned sheds to which his instinct would otherwise have drawn him. I had compromised, and so had he. We were searching for a common denominator that might help both of us survive. Now, as the end of my life approaches, I still think it is a pity that most owls do not attempt to do the same.

We found a decent-sized oak in the centre of the copse and, well hidden from the hurly-burly of the outside world, we settled on our separate branches and went to sleep. Or at least, I went to sleep at once, and did not wake until the sun was falling fast behind the range of wooded hills which stretched upward to the west of us. As I blinked at the red ball of fire about to sink below the tree line, I was surprised to see Hunter perched on the upper branches of a maple tree, about thirty owl-lengths between myself and the setting sun.

Still fuddled by sleep, I jumped to the conclusion that he had woken early, gone off to explore the territory and to find himself some food, for neither of us had eaten anything since the early hours of the day before. I blinked again, opened my bill wide in a contented yawn, and then called up to him with a sleepy early-twilight hoot.

To my surprise, he did not respond as expected, but fluttered his wings briefly in a shy, almost effeminate manner, as if for some unknown reason he had suddenly become bashful and wished to keep his distance. All the time he seemed to be staring down below me at the branch on which he'd settled to sleep through the noonday sun and the long afternoon of the previous day. Following his gaze I looked below and saw to my astonishment that Hunter was still there. He had not stirred since perching there that morning and was obviously still asleep, with his head half-tucked beneath one protective wing. The drowsiness of early twilight in this seeming oasis left me as instantly as if I'd been drenched by the torrent of a sudden storm, for as I sat there, bolt upright on my branch, I realized that I was no longer in the presence of one Barn Owl, but two! Not knowing quite what to do about it, I hooted louder, this time directing my call downward with the intention of waking Hunter. In this I succeeded. His head emerged from the protective wing, he looked up at me into the sun, and blinked in much the same way as I had done on waking a few moments before.

'Look!' I said, pointing with one wing towards the other Barn Owl, who was still perching above us in the maple tree. 'I thought it was you!' I said, as he struggled to surface from his sleep.

'Well, it isn't me. I'm here!' he said, and even though he was still half-asleep, the logic of his words seemed quite irrefutable.

'Well, then, ask him what he wants!' I said.

'It's not a he, it's a she.'

'Well, then, ask her the same question.'

'I expect this is her territory,' he said. 'She'll want to know what we are doing here.'

'Well, why doesn't she come any closer?' I asked, feeling quite uncomfortable at having confused Hunter with a female of his species.

'I expect she's afraid of us,' said Hunter, who was now wide awake and gazing up at our unexpected visitor with considerable interest.

'Then why not call out to her and explain that we have no hostile intentions?'

Hunter nodded and at once did as I'd suggested. The female fluttered her wings once more, hesitated, and then took off and flew the short distance that separated her maple from our oak. However, she did not land close to either Hunter or myself, in the centre of the tree, but perched in one of the upper branches, presumably so that she could make a quick getaway if the need arose. In spite of my difficulty in distinguishing between individuals of species other than my own, it struck me at the time that this female was the most attractive Barn Owl that I had ever seen.

Hunter asked her name, which was Holly, introduced her to me, apologized for our trespass on her land, and briefly explained the purpose of our mission.

'I've heard of you!' she said, visibly relaxing as her fear began to ebb away. 'Aren't you from the district far to the north of here, where the monster owl was brought down?'

Hunter glanced at me and I glanced back at him. One could not brag, of course, so what was one to say?

'We were involved in it,' Hunter replied, nodding in a very modest sort of way.

'But how did you know?' I asked, speaking directly to this female Barn Owl for the first time.

'A media bird!' she answered. 'A Short Eared Owl flew through here in the middle of the winter. He told us that you had brought the monster down, though your casualties were very high. He said that in your district co-operation between Barn Owls and Tawnies was unique. He told us that even a female immigrant took part in the final battle.'

Glancing back at Hunter I saw him wince at the memory of little Alba. To save him further pain, I quickly changed the subject.

'Who is we?' I asked.

'We?' enquired Holly.

'We or us,' I said. 'You mentioned us, and obviously there must be more than one of you, in a fertile valley such as this. It could support how many? I'd say a dozen at the very least!'

'There were almost a dozen of us once,' said Holly sadly, her eyes misting over with pain in much the same way as Hunter's had done at the mention of the little alien he'd once loved – not wisely but too well! 'Now only two of us are left,' she said. 'Just my mother and myself, but she is sick, partly with grief, and seems to have lost the will to live.'

'What happened to the other members of your community?' I asked.

'It wasn't a community, in the normal Barn Owl sense,' said Holly, still troubled by what I took to be the most acute and painful memories. 'This territory belonged to one of the last aristocrats. He let my father and mother settle here because their territory to the south had been destroyed by man.'

'How destroyed?' I asked.

'Built on,' Holly said. 'Buildings, roads, smoke and men everywhere. And zoomerangs, of course.'

'What are zoomerangs?' I asked.

'The things that men race up and down in on the iron tracks, or else along the roads,' said Hunter, who now seemed more composed.

'Were you born here?' I asked.

'Yes,' Holly said. 'I was born here and later promised to the son of the aristocrat who owned this valley. You see, my parents were grateful for the land they had been given, and they were pleased and flattered when Westwood showed an interest in me.'

'Westwood was the son?' enquired Hunter.

'Yes.'

'And were you in love with him?' I asked.

'No. I was only a fledgling. I mean, I'd been brought up to be grateful, but that was all. At the time I was much too young to mate with him or with anybody else. And in any case, first I wanted an education.'

'What happened?' I asked. 'What happened to Westwood, his parents, your father and the other Barn Owls who lived here, in this oasis?'

'They were killed by the monster,' Holly said. 'That is all of them except for Westwood, myself and my mother.'

'How did you escape?' asked Hunter.

'My father told my mother and myself to hide away at home.'

'And where is home?' I asked.

'A ruined building. A place we call a church. It's where men take their dead and bury them in wooden boxes in the ground.'

'Does it have a steeple?' Hunter asked.

'Yes, that's where we live,' said Holly. 'In the crumbling pinnacle on top of the deserted church.'

'My father was called Steeple,' Hunter said. 'My family,

like yours, used to live in the roof of a church, until one day the deserted building collapsed, and my ancestors moved into a nearby isolated barn.'

'Come with me!' Holly said. 'Come with me and meet my mother in the steeple above the ruined church. It would make her happy. Since the invasion she has pined for our dead and seen no other owl but me!'

'And the owl called Westwood?' Hunter asked. 'How did he escape? Did he hide with you and your mother in the steeple?'

'Oh, no!' Holly said. 'He left this valley some time before the invasion.'

'Why?' Hunter asked.

'Because he didn't like the idea of aristocracy,' Holly said. 'He believed that all owls should be equal.'

Thinking of Stoop, Ferocity and Ripper, I knew that this was nonsense. Owls are no more equal than foxes or badgers are. Like modern Barn Owls, they might enjoy equal opportunities, but between the opportunity and the fulfilling of it lies the shadow, as one of our modern Tawny poets said.

'What did his father think about these notions?' I asked, guessing how my own parents would react if I had dared to voice such a revolutionary idea.

'They didn't get on!' Holly said. 'His father expected him to stay on and take over the dynasty when the patriarch died or grew too old and decrepit to lead and protect the small community.'

'I don't understand,' Hunter said. 'If this Westwood wanted to reform the valley and introduce a democratic system of government, with an elected council of experts, along the lines of ours and most other Barn Owl communities, why didn't he wait until his father died and then introduce the necessary changes?'

'He was too impatient,' Holly said. 'He wanted to influence the lives of other owls. He wanted to go much further than most other Barn Owl communities and to abolish all forms of privilege. He wanted a revolution, and most of all he wanted power.'

'So he abandoned you, his family and his ancestral territory to pursue these mad, missionary intentions?' I asked, having formed a very unfavourable impression of this owl called Westwood. It may be that my disapproval was rendered more acute by the fact that, in one sense, I envied him. He had rebelled against the old order and struck out on his own, spurning a position of power and privilege to pursue this revolutionary or missionary ideal.

'He didn't exactly abandon me,' Holly said. 'In some ways, I wish he had, but the truth of the matter is that he gave up his rights as future leader of this valley and promised that he would return to claim me when he had established himself in a territory far to the north. A place in which he could gain power and use his influence to reform the existing community according to his New Apostasy.'

'What does that mean?' I asked.

'Abandonment of one's own religion, or tradition,' replied Hunter at once.

'Hunter would know that,' I explained to Holly. 'You see, his father was Religion Owl on their council. Tragically, he was killed during the great battle to bring the monster down.'

She looked up at Hunter, he looked back at her, and for a moment I saw them feed deep into each other's eyes. This shared grief – both fathers killed, both lovers lost – created the ideal conditions for what is known as love at first sight. I recognized it because I had known the same thing once myself, with Mallow. With May Blossom it had been different. Love and the urge had come upon me more gradually after she had saved my life and then cared for me as I convalesced in the home she had now abandoned in search of knowledge in the city.

Now my task was to bring her back and keep the promise I had made so long ago. But would I even recognize her, I asked myself. And would Holly recognize her Westwood in the unlikely event that he should some day return home and claim her for his own?

Whilst I pondered on these things, Holly and Hunter had progressed from their long, lingering eye contact into a deep and intimate conversation of their own, rather excluding me, I felt, though not deliberately, of course. However, it was now time to eat and then to set off at once on the last leg of our journey into the infernal city. So I looked at Hunter and raised my eyebrows in order to remind him of our purpose.

'Do come and visit my mother before you go,' I heard Holly saying at that moment. 'Since the invasion she has seen no other owl but me and the media bird I told you about. She is old now and almost without hope. It would do her so much good to meet two of the owls who brought the monster down – the monster that killed my father and most of the other owls in this territory!'

Hunter looked long at her and then glanced back at me. I could see that he was torn between the choice of staying on for a while in this fertile valley with his new-found friend and leaving with me on what might well prove to be the last journey of his life! If Hunter was torn, then so was I, for had I been in his position I would undoubtedly have wished to stay. The mission, after all, was mine. I had asked him to come with me out of one selfish and one altruistic motive. The selfish one was obvious. On a dangerous, possibly fatal sortie of this kind, one could wish for nothing more than to be accompanied by a tried and trusted friend. The unselfish motive was equally clear in my mind. I had asked him to come in order to distract him from his grief for little Alba, and from the temporary lack of a central purpose in his life. In this it seemed that I had suddenly and unexpectedly succeeded.

Racking my brain in search of a compromise, I remembered what my father had told me on the briefing for this, the longest journey of my life. He had told me that a Tawny owl would be waiting for six nights on the roof of the great building in the centre of the city where the iron tracks came to an end.

'The journey should take six nights,' he'd said. 'But that's only if you have no major setbacks. A town owl will be ready to receive you at dawn on day six, day seven and day eight. From day nine you will be considered missing and presumed dead.'

'I'd like to stay a little longer and visit your mother,' Hunter said, reluctantly declining Holly's invitation. 'But I'm afraid we must eat and then leave at once. You see, Yoller's friends are waiting for us in the city.'

Holly looked so crestfallen at this that I decided to make it easy for her, for Hunter and also for myself. I must say that the idea of stealing a march on the world and on my own destiny by staying an extra night and day in this oasis was a temptation I found difficult to resist. One day and one night snatched from duty and from the talons of time. Of course, by then I had been conditioned to do my duty, but I was also beginning to discover that duty carried to excess is much the same as masochism.

'I don't see why we shouldn't spend tonight and tomorrow here, if Holly doesn't mind,' I said. 'So far we are on schedule. Tomorrow's sunrise will see the beginning of day six. If all goes well for us, we should still reach our destination by the dawn of day seven or eight, and still not be declared missing and given up for dead.'

'Oh, I'm so pleased! And so will my mother be,' said Holly, whilst Hunter stayed silent and looked at me steadily, doubtfully, as if he were trying to read my mind.

'Come with me now and I will show you where to eat,' said Holly eagerly. 'Then I will take you to the ruined church in which we live and introduce you to my mother.'

'Just a moment!' I said, pursuing my plan to make things easier for the two Barn Owls. 'Tell me, in the woodland territory we saw rising above the east of this valley, are there any Tawnies left?'

'There was one,' said Holly, doubtfully. 'I heard him calling out almost every night for some time after the invasion. He called every night but no one ever answered, so I suppose he must have been the sole survivor.'

'And you didn't respond to his calls yourself?' asked Hunter.

'No,' Holly said. 'Now I wish I had. Now that I've seen the two of you together, I realize that Tawnies and Barn Owls can be friends. But I was brought up to avoid any kind of fraternization with the woodland owl.'

'By whom?' I asked.

'By both Westwood and his father. In fact, the only thing they had in common was a deep mistrust of you Tawny Owls. From their different points of view, they both considered you to be the enemy within. But I don't believe it! You, Hunter and the other owls in your territory have just proved the opposite of Westwood's theory by co-operating and uniting to bring the monster down. But I'm talking too much, and you must both be hungry. I'm sorry! It's just that I haven't talked to another owl for so long that I feel I could perch in this tree and listen to you both all night!'

'I'm sure both of us take that as a compliment,' I said, attempting to sound as gracious as I could. 'But you are right. I am hungry and I regret to say that I must decline the invitation to visit your mother. You see, unfortunately I feel the call of duty coming on.'

'Duty?' asked Holly, suddenly looking crestfallen again.

'Yes. Take Hunter for some food and then home to meet your mother. In the meantime I will fly up into those hills and see if I can find any trace of your lone woodland survivor. The purpose of my mission is to offer resettlement to Tawnies whose communities were ruined by the war, or who now wish to return to their origins and help us repopulate after their ghastly experience of attempting to scrape a living in the city.'

Having completed this noble discourse, I sat back on my branch and watched while Hunter and Holly exchanged an almost furtive glance. Whilst they were obviously happy to have this opportunity of developing their relationship in private, it was clear that, being sensitive young birds, they did not wish me to feel excluded. Though this was of course an unselfish ploy on my part to leave the two of them alone together, I must confess that I was glad of an excuse to avoid meeting Holly's mother. Three Barn Owls and one Tawny in the roof of an abandoned church sounded to me like a recipe for claustrophobia. I myself preferred the freedom of the skies and the chance to hunt in woodland territory one more time before being engulfed by the asphalt jungle which was waiting to swallow both Hunter and myself at the end of our long journey.

'Do you want me to come with you?' Hunter asked.

'No!' I replied. 'This is something that I can best deal with on my own.'

'Then at least fly with us as far as the ruined church,' Holly said. 'There is a great chestnut tree to which you can return when your mission's over, and where you can meet Hunter again before the dawn.'

I agreed to this, and almost at once we took off and flew to the dilapidated church in which Holly and her mother lived. They left me in the chestnut tree on the verge of the abandoned, overgrown graveyard, and I watched as their two white, silent forms flitted across the sometime cemetery and then disappeared into the crumbling steeple of the church.

I did not leave at once, but waited for a while and mused on the bones of the human dead who lay buried here and in countless other places like it all across the land. I wondered what a man might feel if obliged to perch above a place whose surface soil concealed the bones of many a long-gone owl. These were futile and rather morbid thoughts, I must confess, but perhaps not quite so unnatural at a time like this. Though satisfied with the unselfish gesture I had made in leaving Holly and Hunter alone, on the eve of the last stage of our journey, I too would have liked to have hunted with them and then spent the whole night talking about life, love and about separate and yet common destinies.

Had I known how turbulent and painful these growing destinies would be, I might have turned, gone back to my ancestral oak, and never flown abroad again!

CHAPTER

26

In the Tawny woodland to the east I ate well that night but found no trace of any remaining creatures of my own kind. The woods were less extensive than they seemed when viewed from Holly's valley, for beyond the crest of hills men were building a new town which threatened to creep slowly up and erode the remaining Tawny territory, just as my father had warned might happen some day at home, even in the heartland of our ancestral domain.

As I have said, I found no trace of another Tawny Owl, not even a feather or bones picked clean by maggots but still not yet swallowed by the new growth of the woodland floor in spring. Though I was saddened by my failure to find the remains of this lone survivor, I felt gratified to think that when my own end came I would not have to be put into a wooden box and buried in the ground. At this time in my life I found this habit of man's to be bizarre, if not perverse, and it was not until I reached the city that I understood the reason why. In the asphalt jungle nature cannot take care of her own, so bodies must be disposed of in this artificial way.

I apologize to my silent listeners for these further speculations into the macabre, but I was lonely that night and very much afraid of meeting death myself sometime between midnight and the dawn of the following day. I arrived back early, perched in the great chestnut overlooking the abandoned graveyard, and waited impatiently for Hunter to put in an appearance sometime before the coming sunrise. It seemed an age before he came, though to be fair he flew out of the ruined steeple and across the churchyard just as the first giant fingers of pink smeared the sky with dawn.

'How did you get on?' I asked, determined to sound as casual as I could and conceal any fear or self-pity that I felt.

'Quite well,' he answered, in a non-committal manner, and I wondered whether he, too, was determined to keep his private feelings to himself.

'How is Holly's mother?'

'Not too good,' he said. 'Between you and me, I don't think she has long to live.'

'Why don't you stay here?' I asked on an impulse. 'Why don't you stay here till her mother dies and then take Holly back with you to your home territory?'

'Did you find your lone surviving Tawny?' Hunter asked, proving by this rebuff that he intended to keep his feelings to himself.

'No!' I said. 'But what I did discover is that this fertile valley is surrounded by man. To the east, south and west they are spreading everywhere. It is time for you and Holly to get out and go back to where you once belonged.'

'She wouldn't go without her mother,' Hunter said. 'And an old bird like her would never make the six nights' journey down the iron tracks.'

'What about this Westwood character?' I asked. 'I hope you're not being put off by the sometime promise that Holly's father made to him?'

'Of course not!' Hunter said. 'And yet in a certain way it is a question of ethics.'

'Gnat's piss to ethics!' I said. 'You want to get Holly back to your home territory as fast as possible!'

'What for?' Hunter asked.

'To mate with her, of course!'

'I don't know that I want to mate with her,' Hunter said. 'These things take time. They don't happen overnight.'

'They do!' I said, remembering Mallow. 'And in any case, even if you don't want to mate, you could take her home and arrange for some kind of further education. That's what she said she wanted and she certainly won't get it here!'

'And how do you expect me to do that?' Hunter asked. 'Remember, I haven't even got a place myself!'

'Nonsense!' I said. 'You are already a legend in your time and after this trip to the city you will return home as a prophet!'

'We haven't got there yet.'

'It's close enough for you,' I answered. 'You know no Barn Owl can survive in the asphalt jungle for any length of time.'

'There's another problem,' Hunter said.

'What's that?'

'Holly wants to study poetry and singing.'

'So?'

'So my brother Quaver is currently apprentice to the Bard Owl, my sister is studying under the new Owl Owl, and so in the departments that interest Holly and me there are no more places left.'

'Has she any talent?' I asked.

'Talent?'

'For music and singing!'

'I don't know.'

'Then get her to sing to you,' I said.

'When?'

'Well, I suppose you're going to see her again before I go?'

'Before we go!' Hunter said.

'So you're still determined to come with me?'

'Yes.'

'You're wrong, you know!'

'Allow me to be the best judge of that,' Hunter said. 'I agreed to accompany you to the centre of the city and then back again. That is what I intend to do.'

'To see it through to the finish, just like the war?'

'Just like the war,' Hunter said.

After this I kept silent for a few moments and blinked upward as the rising sun began to bathe the trembling leaves of the chestnut tree in early-morning light. It would soon be time to go to sleep and store up energy for the folly of the coming night. Even so, I decided to try one last unselfish ploy that would keep Hunter here with Holly and thus allow him to avoid this last leg of our suicidal mission to the city.

'I know you Barn Owls think that everything can be learned from a tutor,' I said eventually. 'But most Tawnies believe that a poet or a musician is born rather than made. Don't you think you have a duty to discover natural talent? To give her a chance, at least?'

'She's coming to say goodbye before we leave at twilight,' Hunter said. 'If you insist, I will ask her to sing to us then, though I don't see the point of it, and in any case, she'll probably be too shy.'

'A true artist can never be too shy,' I said. 'A true artist must have confidence. Look at your wretched, flamboyant Bardic. As far as I can tell, the only thing he has going for him is the entirely mistaken belief that he's the best. So if your Holly has confidence, which is a must, then she will sing to us tonight.'

'Yes, all right!' said Hunter, who appeared to be half-irritated and half-pleased by my persistent efforts to bring him closer to this lovely Barn Owl called Holly. 'But I've already asked you, what's the use of it? She's promised to this ex-aristocrat called Westwood. What if he comes back?'

'He won't,' I said. 'My theory is that he had early news about the invasion and got out while he could, leaving his kinsfolk here to die. And this business about a New Apostasy is a load of – well, a load of you know what!'

'There are some owls with ideals,' said Hunter, sounding rather pompous. 'Ideals that transcend mere power-seeking and material comfort.'

'Oh yes?' I asked. 'And would you give up an oasis like this and a delightful creature like young Holly to find and found your New Apostasy?'

'No,' Hunter said.

'Neither would I! And on the topic of this bird called Westwood, is it not true that the revolutionary Owl Owl on your local council – the one who took on your sister as a pupil instead of you – is it not true that he also immigrated from the south?'

'Yes.'

'Well, I bet it's the same bird,' I said.

'Impossible! The new Owl Owl on our council is called Winger, not Westwood.'

'But he holds the same beliefs?'

'As far as I can gather, yes. But it's only hearsay from my mother and from my sister, who seems obsessed with him.'

'Well, if it is the same bird, and your sister is obsessed with him, where does that leave Holly?'

'Listen,' Hunter said, staring up at me with a startling blend of resentment and sadness in his eyes. 'Listen, Yoller, it's good of you to be concerned about my private life, but you must understand that I've just been through a major bereavement, and in any case it's much too soon for me to think of mating.'

'You mean the killing of Steeple?' I asked, wondering how I would feel when my own father died.

'That as well,' Hunter said.

'As well as what?'

'As well as little Alba's death. I know you never approved of my relationship with an immigrant, or an alien, but believe it or not I loved her, and I believe that she loved me. At any rate, she took care of me after I was injured in the war, and for a long time she was my best friend. You can't expect me to forget her as one forgets a moontide dream at twilight.'

'Sorry, old boy, I've been rather tactless.'

'You meant well. And I agree with you that Holly is attractive. But what have I to offer her? Nothing!'

'Yourself,' I said. 'But I'm sorry that I mentioned it and I promise not to interfere again.'

'Don't!' Hunter said, but this time in a more kindly tone. 'Just get some sleep and save up your energy for tonight. To get to the centre of the city, you're going to need it all.'

'All right,' I said, and then watched while he tucked his handsome white head under one strong wing. Would he sleep tight, I wondered, or would he be woken by dreams of Alba and of the way she had betrayed him before she died? In his sleep, would he hear the alien's song? If he did, might it not convince him that he and Holly, too, were free to fly under the same sky?

Don't ask the reason why
Why love can always overcome
But love will always find a way
To bring us both together
To leave us free to fly
Under the same sky

Speculating on these things I drifted into sleep and did not wake until the sun had sunk halfway below the wooded hills to the west of us. Hearing the murmur of two voices

I blinked into the last rays of the dying sun, and then saw that Holly had come to say goodbye to us and was already perched on the branch below me, opposite Hunter. I closed my eyes again, pretending to be still asleep, and listened to them talk.

'Yoller wants you to sing to us before we go,' Hunter was saying.

'Do you think I should?' asked Holly.

'That depends. It's entirely up to you. Yoller says that all artists need confidence. Some of the worst have too much and some of the best lack all conviction.'

'The best lack all conviction and the worst are full of passionate intensity!' Holly said. 'I know it well. It was composed by a Barn Owl poet who came from across the salty waters, from the same place as my parents.'

'Was it?' Hunter asked. 'I always thought that he was one of ours.'

'Ours, yours, what does it matter in the end,' said Holly. 'The truth cannot be restricted to any one place, one culture or one time.'

I wondered about this as I perched there with closed eyes, not wishing to interrupt them and therefore still feigning sleep. I wondered how Hunter felt about time, place, truth and culture. He had lived with Alba at the same time and in the same place, but in the end their love had been broken by different concepts of the truth and by the question of different races and cultures.

'Will you come and see me on your way back?' Holly asked him after a pause during which she had obviously summoned up the courage to put this leading question. With Barn Owls, as with us, it is normally the male who does the courting.

'I shall, if I can,' Hunter said. 'But what if your Westwood came home to claim you in the meantime?'

'I shan't mate with him. I've told you, it was a thing my parents wanted, not me!'

316

'Arranged matings!' Hunter said. 'It is a forbidden thing in the territory where I live.'

'Quite right!' Holly said. 'A female should be allowed to choose for herself, in just the same way as a male. And I would choose you, if I could.'

'Why?' asked Hunter, after a slightly tense and embarrassed pause.

'Because you don't push me, or crowd me, as Westwood used to do. You don't edge down the branch closer to me all the time, with bulging eyes that show that the thing uppermost in your body and your mind is not love, but simply the urge.'

At this point, embarrassed by the turn their conversation was taking, I decided that the time had come to make my presence felt, so I yawned ostentatiously, opened my eyes wide, and peered down at them.

'Ah, good evening,' I said. 'How nice to see you both. I'm so sorry, I appear to have overslept.'

'Don't worry,' Hunter said. 'There's time for us to eat here and still get to your destination before daybreak.'

'And time to hear Holly sing, as well,' I said, hoping they would not suspect that I'd overheard a substantial part of their conversation.

They glanced at each other then; a long, lingering look it was, and one that made me feel as if I should have been anywhere else but there.

'All right!' Holly said, suddenly plucking up her courage. 'I'll sing for both of you. Shall I do it now, or when we've eaten?'

'How many songs do you know?' I asked.

'Oh, several,' Holly said.

'What are they about?'

'About everything, but mainly about other animals. My father taught me most of them when I was a fledgling. He believed that we owls could all learn from other living creatures.'

'So did mine!' I said, much to Hunter's surprise. 'He said we had much to learn from the lower forms of life.'

'And your mother?' Hunter asked.

'She didn't agree,' I admitted. 'She said that attempting to learn from creatures such as the magpie and the worm was a waste of time.'

'I have a song about the magpie,' said Holly, shyly. 'If you'd like to hear it . . . ?'

'Of course we would!' I said.

She glanced at Hunter, as if seeking his approval. He nodded, she wriggled once on her branch, composed herself, and then began to sing. As far as I remember the words, they went like this:

Oh Magpie
Why do you fly so low, so low
Why do you steal
The fine lady's rings
Why do you steal the rings
The trinkets and things
And why do you fly so low?
Bright, shiny things
Things you cannot eat
Things you cannot eat?
Is it because they glimmer
And glitter so, and shine
The hard shine
Of useless things
Of things you cannot eat?
Or do you steal to show
To the rook and crow
That though basically
In the same family
You are a higher form of life.
Like the fine lady
With her rings and things
Rings and things

A higher form of life?
And why do you fly so low?
Do you wear the rings
The trinkets and things
To show off to the crow
To show you are superior
To him, or to the rook?
Tell me, magpie
Why do you fly
So low, so low?
And why are you black and white
Black and white
Because God made you so?
Why can't you be
Different shades of grey
Like me.

These were the words, some of which I did not understand. But the most interesting thing was the quality of her voice, which was less strident and raucous than those of the other Barn Owls I had met. It was even softer and more lilting when she sang than when she spoke. In his ballad, Quaver says that I described her voice as 'having a lilting cadence that soothed one like the song of a nightingale in some quiet glade, but at the same time laughed and bubbled with the clear sparkle of a mountain stream. It sang of woodsmoke and summer flowers and Hunter fell in love with it at once.'

Well, this, of course, is nonsense. I said nothing of the kind! Having no bent or talent for the lyrical, I couldn't have produced a stream of image and metaphor so rich as to border on the sentimental. And if Hunter did fall in love with her voice at once, he certainly gave no sign of it at the time. In my opinion Quaver was resorting to poetic licence, a thing he frequently succumbs to in the seemingly interminable course of his epic ballad. Either it was poetic licence, or else it reflected his own feelings when he met

Holly much later and for the first time heard her songs. In my opinion he was describing his own reaction to her voice, not mine, and probably his own love for her, not Hunter's.

The fact of the matter is that as soon as Holly had finished her song Hunter congratulated her politely and I asked at once what the word trinket meant. She explained that it was a worthless ornament that humans used to adorn their bodies or else to embellish the places where they lived. She also taught me what ring meant, in the context of the song. I knew what a ring was, of course, but I had no idea that humans and especially the female of the species had metal ones which they wore on things called fingers, which as my silent listeners may or may not know appear to be a rather ineffective equivalent of our talons, though no owl in his right mind would fly around encumbered by senseless ornaments that impeded the use of his natural faculties.

Of course, I followed the surface meaning of the song. We all know that magpies steal bright, shiny things – I myself had once seen one flying in the early twilight with an object in its beak, a silver-coloured trinket which glinted in the last rays of the dying sun. But I suspected that there was more to the song than this – a hidden meaning which I had failed to detect. Unless, of course, it was supposed to be a satirical comment on the absurd amount of time and energy that birds of different species waste on trying to create an image for themselves, both within and without the confines of their own class and race. Personally, I was already well aware of this message, and it left me rather cold. I couldn't see why we owls, the most intelligent of animals, couldn't get on with the essential business of survival and stop harking back, like my mother, to higher and lower forms of life and to the endless and futile quest for status.

'Please sing us another song!' I said to Holly, feeling

that Hunter's response, whilst civil, had been less than enthusiastic.

'Not now!' Hunter said. 'Now it's time to eat. And if you don't mind, I'd like to say goodbye to Holly's mother.'

'Of course!' I said, thinking that it would be a far, far better thing to leave the two of them together. 'I'll meet you here at midnight; Holly will sing to us once more and then we'll leave.'

'Well before midnight!' Hunter said. 'I don't want you to be caught out again at dawn, attempting to fly on in the face of the rising sun.'

'As you wish,' I said, rather stung by his reference to my limping daytime flight. I nodded politely to both of them, took off, and headed back to the large copse in which we'd first met Holly. Here I caught a very young rabbit, carried it up into the oak and ate it slowly, wishing that I could stay on here with Hunter and Holly in this last oasis, in this last fertile valley which was teeming with food, for there was no one left to eat it except for Holly and her mother.

For the first time in my life I envied the nomadic existence of the Short Eared Owl, who had no fixed abode but was free to search for oases such as this, where he could eat to his heart's content in exchange for telling stories about distant wars and other events he had observed, but in which he himself had not been required to risk his life or to take any direct part. I know they were despised as media birds, but I reflected now that, apart from their enviable freedom, they also served a purpose. When we arrived here, Holly had already heard of us, which made this last fertile valley seem even more of an oasis.

How pleasant, I thought, to have no territory to protect, but to come and go from distant places where you are welcome and where everybody knows your name. Fly in, entertain them, and then fly out again, without commitment to any race, creed or cause – without having to sweat and spill blood in pursuit of ancient and parochial feuds. But I was a Tawny, not a Short Eared nomadic owl. My destiny was to become a leader, and I had little choice but to get on with it and do my duty to my own class and race.

Having pondered on these things and digested the young rabbit, I flew back to the chestnut tree on the edge of the graveyard to find Holly and Hunter already waiting for me. Having sensed my coming, they had moved apart on the branch where they'd been perching side by side. Though I had not seen it, I suspected that they had been even closer before my arrival, and had rubbed cheeks together in private before the time came to say goodbye. To part is to die a little, as our foreign cousins say, and with my memories of Mallow I thought I knew how the two of them must be feeling.

'Have you eaten?' Hunter asked me as soon as I had perched on my own branch.

'Yes, I've eaten well. And you?'

He nodded and flapped his wings twice as if winding up for the long flight ahead.

'Hold on a moment!' I said. 'I want to hear one more song before we go!'

I saw Hunter grasp the branch tightly with his talons and then glance upward at the still-rising moon.

'Is there time?' he asked.

'Of course there is. It's still well before midnight and there must be time. You have to remember, old boy, that this might be the last song one ever hears!'

I said this of course partly in jest, trying to be flippant, but I could see at once that my attempt at humour had not gone down at all well with Holly.

'Oh, don't say that!' she pleaded. 'You must come back safely from the city! If the rest of us are to survive, we need owls like the two of you.'

'That's kind of you,' I said, feeling secretly quite flattered.

'Sing to us now!' Hunter said, glancing up at the moon which was now drifting higher and closer to the point of midnight. 'The sooner we leave, the better chance we have of coming back again at twilight or at dawn on some future day.'

'What would you like to hear?' asked Holly, directing her question at me.

'Something like last night,' I said. 'Another of the songs your father taught you, with a hidden message. My mother used to tell me stories like that – it's part of our Tawny education. But your song was in a way deeper and more subtle. Or less didactic, shall we say.'

'Would you like to hear a song about an owl?' asked Holly.

'What kind of owl?'

'Any kind of owl,' said Holly. 'It's an owl seen from a man's point of view, and we don't know whether men can distinguish one kind of owl from another, any more than we can distinguish between different types of men. Assuming that there are different types of men, of course.'

'There must be,' Hunter said. 'Otherwise they wouldn't have wars.'

'You say this song is sung from the point of view of a man?' I asked. I wanted to be sure that I had heard correctly, for the notion to me seemed bizarre in the extreme.

'Yes. It's one of the first songs my father taught me,' Holly said.

'He taught you a lot, didn't he?' Hunter asked.

'A lot of songs?'

'A lot of everything!'

'He taught me what he could,' said Holly. 'Especially the songs. Where we come from originally, across the salty waters, the Barn Owls sing a lot more than they do in these territories.'

'Let's hear it, then,' I urged. 'It's true that we often

323

wonder about men. It may be an odd notion, but who's to say that they don't wonder about us?'

Holly gave me another shy smile, did her little wriggle on the branch, composed her soft, well-plumed feathers, and then began to sing:

> Owl
> Why do you fly by night
> Out of sight, out of sight?
> We hear you cry and cry
> Out of sight, out of sight
> And we smell, we smell
> The blood you spill
> At night we hear your cry
> We know that creatures die
> In the night, out of sight
> So that you can eat
> So you can eat your fill
> Killing as you fly
> Out of sight, out of sight
> Killing in the darkest night.
> We kill by day
> You kill by night
> Owl, which is right
> To kill by day or kill by night
> Out of sight, out of sight.
> Owl, which is right
> To kill by day or kill by night.
> Which is right? Which is right?

This time, when Holly finished, I was the first to congratulate her. The song had a dying fall that pleased me. As with 'Magpie', it asked a question that was left unanswered. To me at that time it seemed natural enough to kill certain things in order to eat them, but why was the world divided into day and night? Because the Great God Bird, or the man God, had decreed it so? It made one think, and sadly the first thing that sprang to mind was that man could not only kill by day but also in the deepest darkness. All I could suppose was that Holly's song was one that dated back to the old days, the old days and safer nights before men had invented artificial light.

Of course, I did not point this out to Holly. It was clearly better that she should think that her new friend would reach a safe journey's end before the coming dawn.

I watched while she and Hunter said goodbye. They did not rub cheeks this time, but Holly clung to him with her eyes and fed deep into them, as if begging him to stay, or at least to promise a swift and safe return. Visibly, Hunter betrayed no evidence of suffering, but thanked her for her hospitality, as I did, and bade her farewell in a manner that was if anything less emotional than mine. A few moments later we were on the wing and heading back east towards the dreaded iron tracks. Though neither of us spoke or turned to wave, we did, as if by tacit agreement, turn back once before we were out of range, and for a fleeting moment I saw the dim outline of the lovely white owl as she stared after us from the top branches of the chestnut tree – the tree that overlooked that ancient resting place of human bones.

Still in silence, we made good progress under the midnight sky, soon left the fertile valley behind, and found ourselves heading south above the widening tracks and the thickening buildings towards what might well prove to be our point of no return. From time to time a zoomerang would thunder beneath us, making the most shattering noise and belching nauseous, acrid fumes up into the night sky through which we flew. Beside us the buildings along the iron tracks grew taller and seemed to crowd ever closer together. Soon we were swallowed entirely by man-made buildings which below us and ahead of us glowed with an eerie artificial light. The deeper we penetrated down the line towards the centre of this burning man-made hell, the more I realized that, had I been on my own, I would have turned and fled back to sanity – first to Holly's last oasis and then to my ancestral territory to the north, where the grinding noises, the smoke, the soot and the glaring lights, though moving slowly closer, were still but a distant reminder of this nature-raper known as man.

'Stop!' I said, realizing that to take Hunter any further would be both selfish and unfair. 'Look!' I said, pointing downward with one wing at a church topped by a steeple, which was none the less dwarfed and engulfed by the spread of tower blocks which rose up all around it, and suffused the stillness of night with an eerie, unnatural pall of unhealthy yellow light. 'We're going there!' I said, pointing down again to the graveyard, which seemed to be the last open space that we would ever see.

'Why?' Hunter asked.

'Because I need to talk to you.'

'Are we nearly there?' asked Hunter.

'Where?'

'Near our final destination. You must get there before dawn, you know. In the daytime you'll never make it.'

'Yes, according to my briefing we've made good time and we're nearly there. For the Great God Bird's sake come down with me. I need a rest!'

Hunter looked at me, nodded, and then followed as I picked my flight path, plunged down, skirted my way through the tops of the tower blocks and landed on a branch of a stunted plane tree which stood on the edge of the small and barren cemetery.

'What have we stopped for?' Hunter asked, as soon as he'd perched opposite me.

'You must go back,' I said.

'Why?' asked Hunter, who now reminded me of the Magpie's song, because under the eerie, yellow light that filtered down from the surrounding tower blocks he no longer appeared to be white, but merely a pale shade of grey. Who knows, perhaps I, too, had turned a lighter shade of brown under the muting influence of this man-made light.

'You must go back for two very basic reasons,' I declared, speaking I hoped like one bred painstakingly over many centuries to take the initiative and to command.

'What are these basic reasons?' Hunter asked.

'One, survival! You can already tell what it's going to be like in the centre of the city. Sheer hell! So turn back now and get out while you can.'

'And what is the second reason?' Hunter asked.

'The second reason is that Holly needs you!'

'Please!' Hunter said. 'I asked you not to bring that subject up again.'

'I must!'

'Must you?'

'Yes, you have a duty to her. She is one of your own kind. Soon her fertile valley will be engulfed by man. And in any case, you must see her again for another reason.'

'What reason?'

'Because you are the first male she has ever loved.'

'How can you tell that?'

'You get to know a female better when you listen to her voice,' I said, remembering Mallow's lament and, of course, the alien's song. These had told of love and hidden passion, whilst Holly's were songs of innocence. I said as much to Hunter, though without mentioning little Alba who had so deeply affected Hunter's life, or Mallow, about whom he knew nothing. 'Holly's is not the music of a bird who has been torn by love,' I said. 'Her songs are riddles, fables, songs of learning like the stories they tell us Tawnies when we're young. You must visit her on your way back. Don't forget that her mother may be dead by then, in which case she would be left entirely alone.'

'Except for Westwood.'

'He won't come back!' I said. 'And even if he did, it

would only make things worse because she doesn't love him.'

'You surprise me!' Hunter said.

'Why?'

'Because in spite of your facile, aristocratic sense of humour and your in-bred qualities of leadership, you are at heart a Romantic.'

'I'm not at all romantic,' I protested.

'Oh, but you are!' Hunter said. 'Not romantic in the sense of sentimentality, but romantic in the tradition of our Barn Owl poetry.'

'And what is that tradition?'

'Romanticism is about the search for the unobtainable. It is about unrequited love. But it is also concerned with the inner eye, and about seeing where science has no light.'

'It doesn't sound very practical to me!'

'It isn't, and you aren't,' Hunter said. 'If you were more practical, we wouldn't be sitting here in a small urban graveyard, on a branch of this stunted tree and exposed to all and sundry by this ghastly artificial yellow light. We are here because of your mad, romantic quest for May Blossom.'

'I am here because my father sent me and it is my duty. You are here because you volunteered! How many more times must I tell you to get out while the going is good and go home?'

'You tell me something!' Hunter said. 'Since you appear to be an expert on my private life, let me ask you this. Will you even recognize May Blossom if and when you ever meet again?'

I paused for a moment and looked at him. I must confess that this counter-attack of his had taken me by surprise, and also touched a nerve almost as raw as the one that bore his memory of little Alba. The truth of the matter was that I didn't know. I didn't know whether I would recognize May Blossom or not.

'Shall we go now and get on with it?' he asked after a moment's pause in which I had failed to reply.

'All right,' I said. 'But remember that, from now on, things can only get worse.'

'We kill by day, you kill by night. Tell me, owl, which is right?' Hunter said, slightly misquoting Holly's song.

'They also kill in the hours of darkness,' I said. 'You and I both know this to our cost.'

Hunter winced then as I touched once more on the raw nerve of little Alba's death. In fact, the pain in his eyes was too much for me to bear, so I spread my wings suddenly and took off, with Hunter following close behind me. I took off and flew south towards the centre of the throbbing city – that great brick and concrete desert which never, ever slept. I should have pleaded with him once more, persuaded him to return before final commitment to the bowels of that man-made hell. I should have, but I didn't. And given what happened to him and to us all, I shall never forgive myself, not even now, as my own nemesis awaits, and the moment will soon come when I am called upon to pay for all my sins of omission and to settle my final debts.

27

We got there just before the dawn, not soon after midnight, as Quaver has it in his ballad. In fact, from now on his account and mine differ drastically. From now on most of the events I must relate to my silent listeners are almost too painful to recall.

Though already recounted in the epic Barn Owl version of recent history, some of the so-called facts are not merely inaccurate but totally untrue. I must confess to the wind and trees that much of this is my fault, because on my return from the city I not only omitted certain vital evidence, but also lied. I lied, however, at the request of the lost Hunter, and in order to save his family and friends from needless suffering. Of this, more soon. First, briefly, here are the main facts as they have never been told before.

When we eventually reached the termination of the ever-widening iron tracks, both of us were exhausted and over-whelmed by the lights and the stench from the city which it seemed never, ever slept. Unnatural it was, to a degree. 'Owl, you kill by day, we kill by night. Which is right, which is right!'

Of course I do not wish to comment on the *modus vivendi* of human beings, but they were clearly different here from in the country, where man switched off his lights and went to bed, leaving the night sky to those of us who had inherited it from the Great God Bird himself.

Even in the pre-dawn darkness the whole of the city was lit by an eerie pall of smog and suffocated yellow light. When we arrived on the roof of the huge shed where the iron tracks terminated in the centre of the city, we were both terrified, but neither one of us would show it. We perched on the roof of this huge shed, where it seemed dozens of the steaming, smoking zoomerangs rested for the night. But even as we paused for a moment and attempted to recover from our long flight, the clanging and banging from below us broke out again, and the zoomerangs began to move once more beneath us, even before the sunrise attempted to break through the darkness and the ghostly mist of artificial light.

According to my father's briefing, I hooted to attract the attention of May Blossom or of any other city owl who had been delegated to meet us on arrival. I hooted twice, and then we waited on that roof as the man-made lights waxed so many and so close that they suffused into one single, artificial moon which lit up the lifting darkness with an uncanny, translucent glow.

My call was answered much sooner than expected, and presently a city owl called Dodger arrived on the roof of the zoomerang terminal to take us to the place where my long-lost love, May Blossom, awaited us. At this point I must confess that I was scared – not only scared by the smog and by the muted city lights at dawn, but also by the worry that Hunter had either sown or confirmed in my mind. Would I even recognize my sometime love, or had the memory of her been entirely obliterated by my one night of passion with Mallow?

This emaciated, soot-ridden town owl called Dodger led us from the roof above the zoomerangs to a great park in the centre of the city. At first it seemed like an oasis – a green haven in the midst of screaming traffic, foul smells and more human beings than I ever hope to see again. But before moving on to describe the sinister disadvantages of this seeming paradise, I must at once point out that the scraggy town owl who took us there was not in fact named Welkin, as Quaver has it in his ballad. The bird in question was called Dodger.

Why did Quaver alter this? Why did he change so many things that happened from then on? Was it partly out of a desire to protect his brother, to honour me, and above all to exalt the Barn Owl image? I must leave this for my silent listeners to decide. The truth of the matter is that as soon as we arrived in this great park, this wide expanse of woodland and lake, we were at once introduced to Sage, the town owl philosopher, and not to May Blossom. While making the acquaintance of Sage we heard the screams. They were the most blood-curdling cries for help that I have ever heard. Some came from owls, birds and other creatures which I recognized. Others emanated from unknown species, some obviously so large and potent that they appeared more terrifying even than the fog, the smog, the smoke and the clanging in the man-infested jungle into which we had flown. Some of the beasts I heard howling and bellowing on that long-distant dawn sounded uncannily like giant cats – cats so huge that they could easily kill and consume a bull!

'Don't worry, it's only the prisoners,' said Sage quite calmly, after he had seen the shock on Hunter's face and mine.

'What prisoners?' I asked.

'The incarcerated animals,' Sage said. 'Birds and beasts from all corners of the earth are kept here in captivity by man.'

'Not to eat?' I asked.

'No,' Sage said. 'To study them and their habits and to exhibit them to human beings. May Blossom has learned much from the captive birds. She visits the prison frequently, at night, when the guardians are asleep. She has gained much knowledge in this way. Knowledge that will be of great use to you when she returns to your rustic territories.'

'Incidentally, where is May Blossom now?' I asked. To be truthful I was slightly peeved that she had not been present to greet me, even if we had arrived one night later than expected.

'There!' Sage said.

'Where?'

'In the prison, talking to some of the inmates. One, incidentally, is a Barn Owl like you,' he said, turning suddenly to Hunter.

'Like me?' Hunter enquired.

'Well, no, not exactly like you,' Sage said.

'What is the difference?' I asked.

'The difference is that your friend here is free. It is the first time that I have ever seen a Barn Owl in liberty. Normally his species is incapable of adapting to life in the city.'

'Then how has this one in the prison managed to survive?' I asked.

'Because he believes himself to be partly human,' Sage replied.

'Partly human?'

'Yes. If you are interested, May Blossom will tell you more about him later on.'

'How can an owl come to believe that he is part-human?' Hunter enquired.

'Because he was reared by a human female,' Sage said. 'As a chick, he fell out of the nest and was picked up by this surrogate mother who cuddled, fed and protected him from then on.'

'Then why is he in prison?' I asked.

'Because when this human female moved away from her home and set him free, he attempted to mate with them.'

'With whom?' I asked, using the accusative to show this so-called wise owl that even a rustic Tawny knew some grammar.

'With other human females,' Sage replied.

'Can you imagine such a thing,' I asked, turning to Hunter, who up to now seemed to have been rather left out of things.

'No, I can't,' he said. 'Quite frankly, it sounds to me like the tallest story that I've ever heard.'

'Oh, does it?' Sage said. 'If that's the case, why don't you both go and see him while you're here. I'm sure he would be delighted to receive a visit from two rustic owls, and perhaps if you hear the story from his own beak you will believe it!'

'That may be the case,' I said, liking the venerable Sage less and less as I tentatively got to know him. 'But in the meantime, if you wouldn't mind, I'd like to ask three fairly fundamental questions.'

'Ask away!' Sage said.

'Right! First of all, when is May Blossom expected back?'

'Any time now.'

'I see. I am to take it that she sleeps here with you in this cedar tree?'

'She does when she is not otherwise engaged,' Sage said.

'Will she be otherwise engaged tomorrow?'

'That I cannot say. She is a young female of extraordinary intelligence and, as I have already told you, will go far.'

'Thank you. Then under these rather unexpected circumstances, where do you suggest that Hunter and myself should spend the night?'

'Oh, the park is full of trees,' said Sage. 'Full of safe trees, as one might say. The only problem here is the howling of the animals incarcerated in the prison. There is no danger to any of us outside.'

'Firesticks?' I asked.

'No firesticks here!' he said. 'Firesticks are things men use in your rural territories. Here in the city we are safe.'

'You may be safe, but what do you eat?' I asked, for since arriving I had not heard the rustle of a single rat, mole, vole or rabbit.

'Mainly pigeons,' Sage said. 'And sometimes the odd seagull, always supposing that one is strong and fit enough to kill them. Otherwise there are starlings, sparrows and all sorts of other low-life birds. Really, here in the city, if you are street-wise, you can eat almost anything you like.'

'What does street-wise mean?' Hunter asked.

'A street is the town name for a road. Street-wise means that you know your way around it, presumably as you know your way around your native fields and meadows.'

'Has May Blossom become street-wise since she arrived here?' I asked.

'Oh, very much so,' Sage said. 'I've already told you, she learns very fast and should be a great asset to your tribe when she finally returns.'

'Ours is not a tribal society,' I said. 'The fact that we come from the countryside does not mean that we are entirely ignorant.'

'Oh, no, of course not!' Sage said, spreading his wings in a conciliatory manner. 'I can assure you no offence was meant.'

'And there's another thing,' I said. 'What do you mean by when she finally returns? Hunter and I were thinking of going back as soon as possible.'

'Oh, really?' Sage said. 'I think you'll find that May Blossom is not quite ready yet.'

'But I've come all this way to fetch her!' I protested. 'And to offer refuge to any other tenant owls like yourself. As you probably know, since the invasion and the war our rural population has been much depleted. There is space now for owls like yourself to resettle – owls who previously had no territory of their own.'

'It is considerate of you, but I personally must decline the offer,' Sage said. 'I shall stay here in this great city where there is so much knowledge to be got.'

Secretly I was pleased by this refusal, partly because I had begun to suspect that Sage's relationship with May Blossom might not always have been entirely platonic. Though I was irritated by his suave, intellectual manner, in sense I felt relieved, and therefore held back from a direct confrontation. I was jealous, yes! This I openly confess. But at the same time I had my own conscience to contend with. There was, after all, the question of my one dalliance with Mallow, a night that could never be forgotten. There was also the fact that Hunter had previously pointed out. So much water had gushed from the rock since our last encounter that I might not even recognize May Blossom when I met her.

Of course, I mentioned none of my vague suspicions to my Barn Owl friend at that time, but when May Blossom arrived soon afterwards I noticed that his greetings were very cool. One might almost say that he looked at her askance. As for me, I felt the urge instantly, as soon as she landed in the cedar tree. I brushed her cheek with mine and at once felt inflamed with passion. One must remember that I was no longer quite so young, and that I had been celibate since my one night of illicit passion with the lovely, fallen Mallow.

Watching as Sage introduced Hunter to May Blossom, I felt the incipient jealousy surge up and well through all my veins until it set even my external feathers trembling and tingling with resentment. Looking at him I could see that, though ageing, he was still strong and handsome, in an ascetic sort of way, in spite of the shades of grey which now suffused his well-groomed feathers. He had a certain style, there was no doubt about that. As my father had pointed out, he might have been an intellectual outcast from the traditional Tawny stream, but there was no denying that he was a rebel with a certain charisma and status.

'Well, now, have you already eaten?' asked May Blossom, looking away from Hunter and turning her radiant smile on me.

'Not yet,' I said. 'As you can see, we arrived later than expected.'

'Then you must both be starving! Come with me at once and I'll show you where there are at least a dozen sleeping pigeons. Then we'll find a comfortable tree nearby and you can settle for the remainder of your stay here in the city.'

Decisive as ever, May Blossom took off almost at once, and I barely had the time to nod goodbye to Sage before Hunter and I followed her out of the cedar tree and up into the night sky. We flew high across the park until we came to a damaged building where these pigeons were sleeping in the eaves. Swiftly and silently May Blossom dropped from the dark sky and dived through a gaping hole in the roof. She killed the first bird as it woke, and I took a second before it had time to escape out into the reddening rise of dawn. Hunter was third through the roof and failed to catch his prey at once. As we watched, he turned, sped in pursuit of the fleeing birds, and brought one back before I had begun to sample the strange food which now lay spread out on the rafter below my talons.

'Well, *bon appétit*!' May Blossom said, as Hunter found himself a convenient rafter of his own, deposited his prey, and prepared to join us.

'What does *bon appétit* mean?' I asked.

'It means enjoy your meal!' answered May Blossom.

'Where did you learn it?' I asked. 'I've never heard the expression before. Neither have I ever heard one owl say to another, Enjoy your meal.'

'I learned it on my visits to the prison,' May Blossom said. 'In their language, our cousins from across the water use it all the time.'

'Well, then, *bon appétit*!' I said to her and Hunter, as I

addressed myself to the pigeon. 'I've never eaten one of these before and I only hope I'm going to like it!'

'Amongst town owls it is considered a delicacy,' May Blossom said, turning away from me and treating Hunter to one of her radiant smiles.

Well, delicacy it might have been, but for such a large bird it had hardly any meat on it. It was also messy to eat, or maybe it would be more accurate to say that Hunter and I made a mess of ours because we were not aware of the correct etiquette, or the technique of eating it. May Blossom obviously was, and put us both to shame by the neat and elegant manner in which she carved her bird, and then polished it off with great panache.

Panache was another foreign word she had learned in the prison and which she used later on as the sun climbed in the sky to describe the intellectual town owl Sage.

'He has not only great learning, but wonderful panache,' she said, as the sun rose above the open rafters of the roof and the cacophony of the great city began to swell around us into a mighty roar.

'And what does panache mean?' asked Hunter, who had by now demolished his first pigeon in a rustic fashion almost as clumsy as the manner in which I had disposed of mine.

'Oh, it means style, charisma – or perhaps sometimes, on the slightly more negative side, great swagger!'

Whilst on the one hand I was relieved to hear that May Blossom had noted a negative side to Sage, I was put out when she announced that she would presently be returning to the cedar tree to spend the coming day with him.

'There are some very pleasant lime trees back towards the centre of the park,' she said. 'If we leave now you should both be settled in and well hidden before the sun rises too high and the first human visitors arrive here in the park.'

'Why can't we stay here?' I asked. I had no wish to fly

over human territory by daylight, and I knew that Hunter would be far more at home in a partly ruined building than in a tree beneath which men might wander, glance up and disturb his privacy.

'Well, of course you may stay here if you wish,' May Blossom said. 'But I must warn you that here, too, you will be increasingly surrounded by humans as the day goes by.'

'At least we shall be less disturbed here by that frightful howling and wailing from the prison,' I replied. 'We can still hear the cries, but at least they are muted and, at this distance, very faint.'

'During your time in the city you must get used to it,' May Blossom said. 'And you must get used to a great deal else as well.'

'This is becoming increasingly apparent!' I said. 'Thank you for helping us to feed and for showing us this place, but we have had a long and tiring journey, so if you're ready to leave now, I think it's high time that Hunter and I tried to get some sleep!'

'As you wish,' May Blossom said. 'Shall we meet again at twilight? You see, I have various activities planned for you during the time you spend here in the city.'

'As I have already told your friend Sage, Hunter and I intend to spend hardly any time here at all. I had planned on flying back with both of you very soon. In fact, as soon as sunset on the day after tomorrow.'

'But I'm still putting the final touches to my higher education,' said May Blossom. 'And what a waste it would be if, after your long and dangerous journey, you did not get some elementary learning too!'

'You may be right,' I replied, remaining calm on the surface, though inwardly I was seething at May Blossom's assumption that whatever learning I had gleaned was elementary. It was pretty basic, of course, but one does not wish to have this pointed out to one by the female with whom one is supposed to spend the rest of one's natural life.

When she'd left us to return to the cedar tree and her mentor Sage – a teacher with panache – Hunter and I sat in silence for quite some time.

'Thank you for that!' Hunter said eventually.

'For what?'

'For suggesting we stayed here.'

'Don't mention it, dear boy.'

'But I know you would have been happier in a tree!'

'One can't have everything,' I said, tempted at this point to confide to my friend my suspicions about the relationship between Sage and May Blossom, but of course I didn't. It would have been bad form. Instead, I asked him how he had enjoyed his pigeon.

'I didn't,' he answered calmly but without any hesitation.

'Neither did I!'

'I suppose it's a question of getting used to it,' he continued. 'And in a way May Blossom is right. If you stayed here longer, you could learn a great deal.'

'What, learn from Sage?'

'Why not?'

'Do you like him?'

'No,' Hunter said. 'If you must know, I don't care for him at all. But he has something that you need, and so does May Blossom.'

'What's that?'

'Knowledge, or at least information,' Hunter said. 'Knowledge means survival of the mind, but information means power.'

'Then you think I should stay here and learn to say things in foreign languages, like *bon appétit*? Frankly, I don't see how that would help me to survive or to retain power once I take over the leadership from my father.'

'It might be useful,' Hunter said.

'Might it? When I met Olmo, the Little Owl poet, he

taught me something very important about other languages. He told me to ask myself a question.'

'What question?'

'If you have nothing to say in your own language, why learn to say it in another?'

'Ah, but it's obvious why he said that.'

'Why?' I asked.

'Because his father made him learn the old language, the native tongue of the territory in which the Little Owls originated.'

'How do you know that?'

'Because Alba told me.'

'She knew Olmo, then?' I asked, remembering my earlier suspicions concerning the poet's love for the little alien.

'Of course she knew him. And he told her that the main stress in his young life was not so much growing up in no man's land as having to learn the dead language of his ancestors.'

'In that case, why do you think it's so important that I should learn to say *bon appétit*?'

'Because of the concepts,' Hunter said.

'What concepts?'

'Well, take *nemo propheta* for example. *Nemo propheta* means you can never be a prophet in your own country. That's a concept that comes from Olmo's old language. In a way it's like what I imagine *bon appétit* to mean.'

'What's that?' I asked.

'Possibly the idea that one should enjoy a shared meal and not thrust food down one's gullet merely in order to go on living.'

'So you think I should stay here?' I asked, highly surprised at the unexpected trend that Hunter was taking in our first conversation at dawn in a bombed-out building in the dreaded city.

'Yes, I do!'

'Why?'

'To get knowledge, like May Blossom. Or even more important for your future role, to get information. You told me once that I had become a legend in my time. So are you, or so you could be. It all depends on knowledge and in your case on information. As I have already said, information means power, and if May Blossom has more of it than you, she will be perceived as the prophet and will eventually take over.'

'Take over what?'

'The leadership of your community. Your entire life!'

'Nonsense!' I said. 'She will be my partner, she will share her learning with me and, most important, she will produce my son and heir. And that will be the end of it!'

'I wouldn't be too sure of that,' Hunter said.

To tell the truth, I was not as certain as I sounded, even then, when I was still young, arrogant but also undesiring of any kind of change and incapable of envisaging any sort of future that was not bogged down by prejudice and by negative tradition. So I continued with my attitude of *laisser faire*, another foreign expression which May Blossom taught me later. To translate it into Tawny language is difficult, but we do have an expression which is more or less similar: let sleeping dogs lie! So I did! I let things slide out of my control. I should have listened to Hunter's words of counsel, but I didn't. I continued with my ineffectual attitude of *laisser faire*, which brought upon us all the subsequent and tragic consequences of which my silent listeners will already be well aware. As one of our relatively recent Tawny poets said, the saddest words e'er spoke by owl or sparrow: 'It might have been.' Or as Olmo once said: 'Life is a random business. It is what happens to you while you are making other plans.'

'So be it,' as May Blossom used to say. And so was it, though neither Hunter nor I could have guessed quite how badly things would turn out as we finally went to sleep under the risen sun in the smoke-ridden city on that now long-forgotten night.

CHAPTER

 28

For the next few days things went from bad to worse. By day, we stayed on and slept in the damaged building in the confines of the park. By night we ate pigeon, starling, sparrow or whatever form of low-life bird we could get hold of.

Whilst I adapted quickly to this new diet, Hunter did not. He had little appetite and at the rising of the sun each day he seemed thinner and paler than he'd been at sunset on the night before.

During the waking hours of darkness we were taken by May Blossom or by Dodger to visit the city and to be shown the manner in which these urban humans lived. To tell the truth, it was not a pretty sight! They flocked like sheep, swarmed like bees or ants, and at all times generated the most appalling noise with their machines. Whilst it was true that in the small city gardens there were rich pickings for a bird of prey, the fact of the matter was that the very ease of killing things and eating them seemed to rob one of one's atavistic instincts. Killing sparrows and pigeons in the city seemed almost too easy. There was no competition. One simply found out where they were and then went in to slaughter them, always being careful, of course, to say 'after you' and '*bon appétit*'. To be frank, it did not seem worth risking one's life to acquire the kind of information offered to us by Sage, Dodger or May Blossom.

To me it soon became apparent that Hunter could not survive much longer under such conditions. His species was simply not adaptable enough. In the meantime, it had become obvious that May Blossom was not yet ready to return home with me. So what was I to do? Since she spent the day in Sage's cedar tree and not with me, I suppose I might have been justified in going home at once with Hunter and leaving her to return on her own. But I must confess to my silent listeners that I was somewhat in awe of her and also, in the meantime, I had come to believe that she was holding something back. There was something she wanted to tell me but either couldn't or wouldn't.

As the sun rose at the end of the third night, I suggested that Hunter should go home alone.

'Go back the way we came, find Holly and take her home with you,' I said. 'Or else stay for a while in that small oasis and wait till her mother dies. Then you can go back with her and take up your rightful role among your own as a legend in your time.'

Hunter thought for some time before replying. Even then he did not speak at once, but merely nodded slowly as dawn rose on the third day above the damaged building which had become our temporary home in the city.

'You may be right,' he said eventually. 'I don't think I can live much longer on this diet of pigeon, starling and sparrow. But even worse is that awful howling and screaming from the prison. I'd rather be dead than trapped in there. I can't sleep by day because of the noise of men and their machines. Only the Great God Bird knows how many of them there are!'

'I did not know death had undone so many,' I said, quoting one of our relatively recent Tawny poets.

'All right!' Hunter said, suddenly. 'I'll go back on my

own. You stay here with Sage, May Blossom and Dodger and try to get more knowledge.'

In retrospect, this was the beginning of the end. At the time I did not know what to do or say. My loyalties were divided. May Blossom was my first sweetheart, she had saved my life and perhaps – and this is a big perhaps – perhaps above all she was one of my own species. But Hunter had also saved my life, had fought beside me in the war, and had gradually become my most trusted friend.

But I had made my fatal decision by then and compounded it by asking Hunter if there was anything I could do before he left.

'As a matter of fact, there is!' he said, at least outwardly not showing any sign of resentment at what I considered to be my betrayal. The agreement between us had been that we should fly to the city and then back again – together. Now I was abandoning him to stay here with May Blossom who, when not providing Hunter and myself with almost useless information, spent all her time with Sage.

'What is it?' I asked. 'Tell me! I will do anything I can.'

'Well, then, try to find out where we can get a decent meal before I leave. There must be edible mammals somewhere in this gigantic wasteland.'

'I will fly to Sage and May Blossom now,' I said. 'They will help. If not, I am certain that Dodger will know somewhere you can eat well at least once before you leave.'

'Wait till twilight!' Hunter said. 'The sun has already risen and your powers of flight will be impaired!'

'I'm going anyway. And tonight I promise you that we shall eat a proper meal!'

I left then and flew straight across the park to the cedar tree in which Sage and May Blossom lived. To tell the truth, I was glad of an excuse to poke my beak in and find out why May Blossom had spent most of the time since I arrived with her middle-aged tutor and not with me. I was burning to know whether they perched and slept on the same branch together, and sunrise was the perfect time to find this out!

When I got to the cedar in the centre of the park, Sage had disappeared and May Blossom was alone. Of course, he might have heard me coming and left for devious, expedient reasons of his own. This I shall never know. But May Blossom's reception was such as to suggest that this might well have been the case.

'What are you doing here?' was the greeting I received as I landed on the branch opposite her.

'Hunter is leaving,' I said. 'And he wants a proper meal to see him on his way.'

'What do you mean, a proper meal?'

'I mean something of substance. Not pigeon, starling or sparrow. We aren't used to this kind of food, you know!'

'You are rural, or even worse, provincial!' May Blossom said. 'Here in this park there is an abundance of cosmopolitan food available. You cannot enjoy it because you are limited by your own experience and tradition.'

'That may well be the case,' I said. 'But one thing interests me and one thing only. Hunter needs a proper meal and I am determined that he shall get one before he leaves.'

'Very well!' May Blossom said, reminding me more and more of my parents. 'I will send Dodger to you shortly after sunset and he will show you a place where you can feed on vermin, or junk food, as you are accustomed to do in the country. I must warn you, though, to be aware of the feral cats.'

'What does feral mean?'

'Wild!' May Blossom said.

'Then why not say so. Why must you use foreign words all the time?'

'I can see you are resentful. That is a pity. I came here to get knowledge, to help us to survive. It is beginning to seem to me that your purpose is merely to drag me back

347

to the rustic ignorance in which your ancestors have so long thrived.'

'My sole purpose is to get my friend what he conceives of as a decent meal. He came here of his own free will. I should be leaving with him but I'm not. The least I can do is to grant the one request he's made me after such a long and loyal friendship.'

'You should never have brought him in the first place!'

'Why not?'

'That's obvious!'

'Not to me it isn't.'

'Hunter is a Barn Owl,' May Blossom said. 'And as you will shortly discover, Barn Owls are the enemy within.'

'How so?'

'If you had any sense of history, you would know!'

'I take it that this sense of history is something you have learned from Sage?'

'Partly from Sage, partly from others, and mainly from my own powers of observation,' she said.

'And what, in particular, have you observed?'

'That history repeats itself,' she said.

'Meaning?'

'Meaning that the Barn Owls are our traditional enemies and that uniting with them to bring the monster down has a well-known historical significance.'

'Which is?'

'Which is that creatures in perennial conflict will combine and unite to fight off an outside threat. But as soon as that external menace has been dealt with, those temporary allies will find themselves at war again. This is the main reason why you should never have brought Hunter here,' she continued. 'It is also the reason why we have kept back the most important information and limited ourselves to teaching you the meaning of expressions like *bon appétit*. Do you think I have spent all this time in the city to get knowledge only to share it with our future enemy?'

'Nonsense!' I said. 'Far from being an enemy, Hunter is my best friend.'

'Be that as it may!' May Blossom said. 'In any case, tomorrow he is going home, and all I can say is good riddance to bad rubbish. Perhaps in the course of time you will reflect on these things and realize that I was right.'

'If not impossible, I find that extremely unlikely,' I said. 'But he is going in any case, and in the meantime I would be glad if you could help me find a place to get some of the food we are used to before he leaves. Given the vicissitudes of time and chance, tonight may be the last occasion on which Hunter and I ever eat together. For this reason, for the sake of old memories, I would like to get it right.'

'Very well,' May Blossom said. 'I will send Dodger to you at twilight. He will know a place where you and your Barn Owl friend can glut yourselves on the plebeian food you seem to prefer to the delicacies available here in the city, to higher forms of life.'

'Don't talk to me about higher forms of life,' I said, remembering my mother's obsession with Tawny excellence, and also recalling the splendid irony of Holly's song about the magpie. 'I'm sick to death of hearing about how superior we Tawnies are. Where is the evidence that we are innately superior to the rook or crow, or even to the sparrow?'

'You are not making any sense,' May Blossom said. 'It may be that you are still exhausted and slightly unhinged after your long and dangerous journey. Go back to your temporary home and get some sleep. I'll send Dodger to you at twilight, and tomorrow, when your Barn Owl friend has gone, we can get down to the serious business of your learning, and of how to shape the future of our Tawny Owl community when we return and take control of our ancestral territory.'

So now suddenly it's ours, not mine, I thought to myself,

but said nothing. To tell the truth I was thinking of the little alien's song – 'The Same Sky':

> Love knows no class
> No class or race
> Only the stars
> The stars and the moonlight
> Give us time and space
>
> Don't ask the reason why
> Why love can always overcome
> But love will always find a way
> To bring us both together
> To leave us free to fly
> Under the same sky

Well, so be it, as May Blossom would have said. Under the circumstances there was very little I could do except abandon her, now and for ever, fly home with Hunter and try to find another female, perhaps less intelligent and more loving, like Mallow. But Mallow had betrayed Birch. Why? Because she loved me and hated him, or because, as an ancient Tawny poet phrased it, 'Nowhere lives a female true and fair.'

So I decided to keep my long-given promise to May Blossom, who was as good as her word, at twilight sending Dodger to the damaged building where Hunter and I were now squatting together like two aliens in no man's land.

The devious, emaciated town owl arrived as the sun fell in a ball of fire behind the gigantic tower blocks which rose high above the park to the west of the temporary shelter we had found.

'So, I hear you want to feed on mammal junk food?' he asked, as soon as he'd flown in through the roof and landed on an exposed beam opposite the ones where Hunter and I were huddled, each of us separately trying to pretend that we were not suffering from the appalling cacophony of sound that battered one's ear-drums all day and continued only slightly diminished throughout the hours of darkness.

> Owl, we kill by day,
> You kill by night
> Which is right?
> Which is right?

'If you could show us somewhere to go, we would be grateful,' I said, secretly loathing Dodger but not wishing to compromise Hunter's last chance of eating proper meat.

'Well, if you are so fixated and set in your rustic ways, I will take you to a place near here where fire fell from the sky and razed all the buildings to the ground – the same falling fire, incidentally, that damaged the roof of the building in which we are perching now.'

'What kind of food can we get there?' I asked.

'Rats. But I must warn you that they are not the relatively innocuous sort of rodent that you are accustomed to in the country. These are sewer rats!'

'What is a sewer?' I asked.

'I haven't time to explain that now,' said Dodger, almost as if he were acting under instructions not to give away any kind of secret information that might be picked up by my friend Hunter. 'I must just warn you that they are very big and very vicious. Also, having consumed mainly human excrement, they do not taste as well as you might expect.'

I glanced at Hunter with my eyebrows raised. He looked back at me and nodded.

'We'll take our chance,' I said. 'Even in the country we are becoming accustomed to pollution.'

'That's fine by me!' Dodger said. 'I merely felt it my duty to advise you. And I must also warn you about the feral cats.'

'The wild felines,' I said.

'How did you know what feral or feline meant?'

'Because May Blossom told me. Hunter and I may come from the countryside, but we both learn quicker than you think.'

'All right, then. Are you ready?' asked Dodger, sounding slightly peeved.

'Of course we're ready,' I said. 'You lead and we'll follow. From what you told us, it can't be very far!'

And if from now on the account of events given in Quaver's ballad corresponds exactly with my own rendering, it is no mere coincidence. My silent listeners must know that the Barn Owl poet got his account of that dreadful night from me. Hunter never mentioned it. He could not or would not for reasons that will subsequently become apparent. And if on this occasion I not only committed sins of omission, but also lied, I shall, I hope, be judged by posterity to have compromised my integrity on behalf of another owl – a white owl, not one of my own species, but none the less my very truest and best friend. So when I lied, it was at his request. The explanation for this comes later, but in the meantime I wish to recount the tragic events of that night to the wind, to the trees whose leaves sigh in the wind, and to the water that gushes from the rock.

If the events are almost identical to those told by Quaver in his ballad, it does not matter. As I have already said, and for reasons that will soon be revealed, the author of 'The Ancient Solitary Reign' got all his information about this episode from me! The truth about subsequent events was never known to him. Neither were the reasons for Hunter's silence. Now is the time to set the record straight, and that I shall attempt to do as soon as I have repeated the chronicle of that tragic night so long ago, beginning from the moment when we flew out from the edge of the park and across the brightly lit roads and houses until we came to this devastated area full of burned-out buildings whose entrails spilled out over what had once been gardens, and where town grass now sprang up in its weedy way above the rubble on the ground.

Having circled above this dark patch of wasteland, I was the first to plunge down and catch a huge rat as it scuttled below me through the undergrowth of what once might have been a cultivated garden. I killed the thing at once, but as I drove my talons through its neck I felt those on my right claw catch and become enmeshed in something on the ground. I tried to pull them free, at first gently and then harder, but nothing happened. My right claw remained trapped in this wire mesh which had been half-buried by the wild vegetation that had replaced the garden so carefully cultivated by man. While I was trying to free my claw, I heard both Hunter and Dodger swoop down, catch their food, swallow it and then take off again. So I ate my own meal and waited for one of them to come down and find out what was wrong.

But then I sensed the feral cat, and saw it sneaking stealthily across the wasteland towards the place where I was trapped. It was a very fierce but mangy creature, which I guessed to be a female. Her yellow eyes gleamed bigger and brighter as she crept closer to me, lusting for my flesh and blood.

Just before this creature got within pouncing distance of me, Hunter plunged down from the sky with his talons bared and aimed directly at the wild tabby's neck. She sensed him coming, though, and twisted at the last moment, so that he missed his target and ripped a great, gaping hole in her back instead. The feral cat screamed and ran for cover as the blood spurted upward from the massive wound in her back.

Hunter hovered for a little while and then landed beside me when he was certain that the killer wasn't coming back. I told him what the trouble was and he did his best to help. We got two talons free but the centre one had got enmeshed and twisted right round in the thin wire net, and while we were still trying to work it loose we saw two more wild cats creeping towards us in the darkness. Both of them were males and much bigger than the she-cat Hunter had very nearly killed.

'Go now, Hunter,' I said, as they crept closer towards us on those cruel, feline haunches. 'Take off while you've still got time.'

But he wouldn't move. He stood his ground in front of me, and we both watched as the first of the two scraggy cats moved to within striking distance of us. Then Hunter used his static defence technique, flared his plumage till he looked nearly twice his size, clappered his bill ferociously, and rotated both wings forward like a giant fan. The first cat sprang back in alarm, hissed, and then crouched down on its haunches. The second one stole up to join him, and they both sat there with their necks stretched forward, watching us and waiting to attack again.

Soon the two cats closed in once more. They crept forward to within pouncing distance, and Hunter puffed himself up again, howled at them, and whirled his wings round even more wildly than before. They sprang back a bit and crouched among the rubble, but you could tell that next time, or the time after that, they'd come in for the kill.

'Go now!' I said. 'I've got one free claw and my bill to fight with. I know that I can't win, but I promise I'll take at least one of those killers with me to the Great God Bird in the sky.'

But Hunter wouldn't listen. He just sat there, looking at the cats and waiting for them to move in again. There was no sign of Dodger or May Blossom, so when they began to creep to within striking distance, I made my big decision. I knew I had to do it when I saw the wild cats moving in. It took me all my strength and courage, and as I finally tore the talon from its socket, I must confess that I howled out in pain and almost fainted. But maybe that was just as well. It shocked the cats and stopped them at the very moment when they were poised to spring on Hunter for the kill. Blinded by pain, I took off and flew low across the wasteland, expecting Hunter to follow. I gained height, crossed the dimly lit street beyond the wilderness of burnt-out houses, and then looked back to see if he was coming. He was. To my great relief I saw his white shadow flying fast and low across the wasteland towards the road. And then, to my eternal sorrow, I saw the dreadful thing that happened.

As he was about to gain height to fly across the road, a machine swept fast round the hidden bend and blinded him in its blazing beams of light. It was horrible to watch. He simply hovered there, quite mesmerized, and though the machine slowed down a little, it struck him in mid-air and flung him sideways to the ground. I saw the machine slow down and stop, and so I waited, hovering in the sky above. Two men got out, walked back, bent over him, picked his body up, walked back down the road with it, and put it inside their machine. Then they got inside themselves and immediately the machine started up and moved away. I suppose I should have followed, but I was still in too much pain to think, and also half-stunned by what I'd seen. In any case, it would soon have disappeared among all those other man-made lights. Just one machine among so very many.

Much later, when I gave this account of that dramatic night to Quaver, he asked me why the men had taken his brother's body.

'To eat it, do you think?' was the horrific question that he put to me.

'No,' I said. 'I've never heard of humans eating any kind of owl, have you?'

'Not in the country. But you tell me that you ate sparrows and pigeons in the city. So if you Tawny Owls survive on a different diet there, perhaps men do also.'

'I never thought of that,' I confessed to Quaver on that

much later occasion. 'To tell the truth, old boy, the idea of an owl being eaten by a man is too horrible to think of.'

Of course, in this last sentence the operative word is truth. By that time I knew the truth, but I never told it. Now I shall, so that when I go to meet the Great God Bird in the sky, though still a sinner, I shall at least have confessed and – who knows, if He is as gracious as they say – I may at last be partially absolved from blame.

CHAPTER
29

For several days and nights after Hunter's death I was stunned. I had, after all, lost the best friend and companion one had ever had.

Though obviously relieved that the bird she conceived of as a Barn Owl spy was no longer around, May Blossom tried her best to be caring and compassionate. So, surprisingly, did Sage, and even Dodger behaved with a touch of grace that I had not suspected he possessed.

During the long nights that followed Hunter's dreadful accident, we flew around the city contacting other town Tawnies who might wish to leave the conurbation and return to their native countryside. To my great surprise, most of them, like Sage and Dodger, seemed quite happy to stay put.

'Once you are well established in the city, life is easy,' one of them said to me. 'Why should I go back to the primitive life now that I know where there are rich pickings to be had. There may be millions of men here – who make the most dreadful noise, I admit – but at least they don't carry firesticks. It's merely a question of getting used to the diet. Once you've become accustomed to the cacophony and the cosmopolitan food, there's really no longer much motivation or incentive to return to one's rustic origins.'

I must say that the reaction of the town owls I met made me very sad. After all, one had risked one's life to come here and offer them a territory in the country, which no one who lived there could have imagined they might decline. But most of them did, and of the very few who accepted, hardly any could have been described as very bright. A couple were what one might describe as contemplative. Sick and tired of the noise, the hurly-burly and the city hassle, they wished to return to their origins and to a more natural way of life. But these were the exceptions to the rule. Most of the others who wanted to return were merely those who had failed to make it in the metropolis. They were the born losers, one might say, and one sensed instinctively that when they came home to us they would be losers too.

The thing I had been most dreading happened on the fifth night after Hunter's tragic accident. May Blossom and Sage decided that I must visit the prison – in the dead of night, of course. Dodger was delegated to take me there, for the other two had one last mission to fulfil before I could return to my own country home with the bride to whom I had committed myself so many sunsets and twilights before.

They told me they had to fly to something called a suburb to contact the last of the town owls who might be interested in taking up my offer. While they were away, I must take my final opportunity of visiting this ghastly place, they said.

And so, against my will, I went, though now of course I wish I never had! Apart from the screams, the groanings and the moanings of animals I could not identify, which was in itself quite terrifying, it had been agreed that I must first visit the bird house where owls from both home and abroad were imprisoned for life and rotting away towards certain death.

In the first cage that Dodger took me to there was a monster owl of the most terrifying proportions. Though behind bars, the very sight of him frightened me half to death. Dodger himself did not seem in the slightest bit perturbed, but of course he had only ever seen one in captivity, and had never had to fight against a liberated Eagle Owl in the way that those of us in the home territories had. Though the creature was asleep when we arrived, it sensed our presence and at once opened its huge, luminous eyes.

'Do you want to speak to it?' asked Dodger, obviously not in the least frightened by the enormous beast who now stared out at us from its small, inadequate cage.

'No!' I said. 'I met one of these before, under very different circumstances, and that particular encounter was enough to last me for a lifetime!'

'Then let's go and talk to the Tawnies and Barn Owls behind bars,' Dodger said. 'According to May Blossom, that is one of the main priorities.'

'All right,' I said, casting one glance back at the brooding monster in its cell. Though obviously cowed to some extent by its period in this human prison, the great beast looked back at me with a malevolence that almost made my feathers stand on end. The arrogance and hatred in his eyes was something that I shall never, ever forget, and it made me wonder how Hunter and I had ever managed to bring such a huge and vicious creature down.

'Which first?' enquired Dodger, as we took off and left the monster trapped and lurking in its cell. 'Barn Owls or Tawnies?'

'Barn Owls!' I said, feeling that it might be slightly less painful to witness a white bird in captivity as opposed to one of my own kind. Little did I know the shock that was in store for me!

'All right, then,' Dodger said. 'I'll take you to see the Barn Owl who believes he is part-human. The others they have put in his cage have all died. Having been brought up by a female human, he doesn't mind the daytime visitors who ogle at him through the bars of his cell. The white birds who grew up in the wild cannot stand the proximity of man, and very quickly pine away and perish.'

When we got to the cage, I could not believe my eyes. It contained two incarcerated Barn Owls, one of whom was fast asleep.

'That is the one they call Humanoid,' Dodger said to me. 'The one who thinks he is partly a human being. The other one – the one who is awake – seems vaguely familiar. He reminds me of someone I met quite recently.'

'Of course he does!' I said. 'That's Hunter, my best friend.'

'Are you sure?'

'Of course I'm sure!'

'Well, then, ask him to identify himself.'

'I don't need to! Can't you see that he recognizes me?'

And indeed Hunter did!

'Hello, Yoller,' he said. 'What ill wind has driven you into this abysmal place?'

'May Blossom sent me,' I said. 'Visiting the prison is supposed to be part of my education. But what in the Great God Bird's name are you doing here? I thought that you were dead.'

'So did I!' Hunter said.

'How did you get here?' I asked.

'The men brought me,' Hunter answered. 'Or, to be more truthful, I think they did. I really don't remember because I was suffering from concussion after being stunned by the machine.'

'You saved my life and I thought that you were dead!'

'Not yet, but I soon shall be,' Hunter said.

'Won't they ever let you out?' I asked.

'No!'

'Why not?'

'Only the Great God Bird knows. During the day the humans come in droves to peer at us. To stare at me and poor old Humanoid. You remember when Sage told us about the one Barn Owl in captivity?'

'The one who was brought up by a human mother?'

'Yes. That's him, up there asleep. Unlike any other owl I've ever known, he sleeps by night. I can't and it is killing me. From shortly after sunrise until dusk the humans pour into this place and boggle at us through the iron bars of this cage. I can't sleep in the day, I can't sleep at night. There's simply nothing I can do. Fortunately quite soon I shall be dead.'

'No you won't!' I said. 'Sooner or later you will escape.'

'How can I?' asked Hunter, nodding down to indicate the iron bars of the cage.

'I'll get you out!' I said, and began to peck furiously at the hard metal bars that penned him in. Though in those days I was still young and strong, my full-blooded attempts to tear my way into the cage came to nothing. Well, not quite to nothing, for I bruised my bill and my forehead and gave myself two black eyes. But I tried! Only the Great God Bird knows the frustration that I felt that night as I hurled myself at the bars of the cage to set my best friend free. I did everything I could, but nothing yielded. The metal, the bars and the cage remained intact.

'You might as well forget it,' Dodger said. 'No one ever escapes from here.'

'Let it be, Yoller,' Hunter said. 'I am as good as dead.'

'Nonsense! Somehow or other I'm going to get you out of here!'

'You can't!' Dodger said. 'Others have tried before, but the only time any bird or animal escaped was when fire fell from the sky the time the men were in the middle of their war. Some got away then. One of them was like the monster you've just seen. In fact, he was probably the one you fought against.'

'Don't give up hope!' I said to Hunter. 'It may be that the men will have another war and that fire will fall from the sky again. Then you will be able to escape!'

'No, I shan't live long,' Hunter said. 'I can't eat the food they give me here – dead day-old chicks which taste of nothing. But that's not the worst of it. The worst thing of all for an owl like me is to be locked up. To be locked up in this cell and to have humans gawping at me all day. No one could or would want to go on living under these conditions.'

'You must!' I insisted. But Hunter merely looked at me through the bars of his cage and sadly shook his head.

'There's nothing left for me,' he said. 'Nothing except a slow, lingering death. But there is something you can do for me.'

'Anything!' I said.

'When you get home, tell them that I am dead.'

'No!'

'Why not?'

'Because you aren't and I won't allow it. I'll find some way to get you out.'

'You can't!' Dodger said. 'No one ever escapes from here unless fire falls from the sky.'

At this point I lost my patience and told Dodger to go away.

'Piss off!' I said. 'And leave me here with my best friend!'

'All right, if that is the way you want it,' Dodger said. 'But you might as well resign yourself to the fact that your white owl friend is right. He is as good as dead!'

I turned on Dodger then with every intention of killing him, but Hunter stopped me by calling out from behind the bars of his tiny cage.

'Leave it be!' he said, as Dodger took off and escaped from me. 'Let him go. He's nothing but a town owl wanker,

362

anyway. And there's another thing I want you to do for me,' he added, after I'd restrained myself from flying in pursuit of Dodger and cutting off his head.

'What's that?'

'On your way home, fly through the place where I met Holly. Tell her what happened and explain that we two shall never meet again. No! Don't tell her that. Tell her as well that I am dead.'

'Why?'

'Because I'm afraid that if she knew where I was she might try to come and visit me in the prison. Tell her I am dead so that when her mother dies she can get on with her own life. If you don't, she may hang about waiting for me in vain.'

'I don't want to do these things. I'd rather tell the truth,' I said.

'Don't!' Hunter implored me. 'It would be terrible for my mother, my brother Quaver and even for Holly if they knew that I was locked up here and destined to die in this prison. Just say that I was run over by a machine and died instantly. Tell them I died a young owl's death. And remember, this is the last thing you can do for me!'

'All right!' I said. 'I'll do what you ask, but I don't like it.'

'And I don't much care for being in this prison!'

'It's my fault! If you hadn't come with me, none of this would or could have happened.'

'We all have to die some day,' Hunter said. 'Just tell them I'm already dead. They will get over it in time and no one will have to worry about me. Go now!' he said. 'Go now and don't come back again. Just promise me that you will tell Quaver and Holly that I am dead.'

'I promise!'

'Good!' Hunter said. 'Goodbye, old friend. Live well, live free, and live a little bit for me!'

I turned and flew off then with tears in my eyes. I have

tears in my eyes now as I tell this story to the wind and trees – tears because I never kept the promise that I made to my best friend.

How could I? How could I tell them he was dead when he wasn't? Or at least, when he wasn't yet. So when May Blossom and I flew back some days later I did not take her past the place where Holly lived. That way I broke my promise, but I also avoided lying. And when we got home the first thing I did was to contact Quaver to tell him that his brother had got lost in the city. I was a coward and what I did involved not merely sins of omission, but also downright lying. I only hope my silent listeners will forgive me for my lack of courage and understand that at least to some extent I was trying to respect the wishes of my friend.

Part Four

A time to be born, and a time to die;

Ecclesiastes, Chapter III, Verse 2

Said one among them – 'Surely not in vain,
My substance from the common Earth was ta'en,
That He who subtly wrought me into Shape
Should stamp me back to shapeless Earth again?'

The Rubáiyát of Omar Khayyám, Verse 91
Done into English by Edward Fitzgerald, 1868

Death be not proud, though some have called thee
Mighty and dreadfull, for, thou art not soe,

. . . .

One short sleepe past, wee wake eternally,
And death shall be no more; death, thou shalt die.

John Donne, 1572–1631
Holy Sonnets, X

CHAPTER
30

When I got back I found that many things had changed. Firstly, my father had fallen ill and gone into what seemed to be an irreversible decline. In fact, during the long winter that followed our return, he died. In the spring our one and only son was born. One might say it was a question of new life for old.

May Blossom had made it clear from the beginning that she did not want to breed. First, she said, she must put her learning to the use of our ancient Tawny Owl community. Survival of the species, she pointed out, came before the self-indulgence of producing offspring of one's own.

I disagreed with her, of course, especially because I had long been plagued by the nagging suspicion that I might already inadvertently have fathered. Rowan, son of Birch, could quite possibly have been a son of mine.

'I have a duty to my ancestors,' I said, as we perched in my stately oak and watched the sun sink in a red ball of fire behind the western hills. 'My father is dying. If I do not produce a son, the dynasty will end.'

'Do you care?' May Blossom asked.

'Of course I care!'

'Why?'

'Because I do!'

'Well, if you care about the survival of what you describe as your dynasty, you should pay more attention to the affairs of leadership and spend less time brooding on the possibility of producing a son and heir.'

'You don't seem to understand,' I said. 'We have been here for centuries – no, longer than that, for millennia. My family has ruled these woods since recorded history began. Now that my father is dying, it is our duty to provide the family with a son and heir!'

'Very well,' said May Blossom, who since her return from the city had come to remind me more and more of my parents. Even her use of language seemed to me to hark back to the bad old days, when we Tawnies believed ourselves to be invincible – chosen by the God Bird to dictate to all other species who dared to share the sky at night.

'Very well,' she repeated. 'But I must warn you that there will be only one. There is too much work to do. I cannot dedicate the rest of my life to producing your fledglings.'

'And what if the first fledgling is a female?' I asked.

'So much the better!' May Blossom said. 'Your mother would agree that it is high time we females took a major role in government.'

In a sense this worried me more than anything May Blossom had said since our miraculous return from the city. Having ingratiated herself with my dying father, she was now proceeding to bend my mother to her will. This was relatively easy, since they both shared an innate belief in the superiority of our species and in the just purpose of our cause.

Another thing that worried me, in terms of fatherhood, was the increasing amount of time she spent with Birch. She consulted him frequently on what she considered to be the Barn Owl threat to our territories. Ferocity and Ripper's wood had been vacant since the war, and there were rumours that Winger, the new leader of the Barn Owl council, was planning to annex this traditional Tawny territory and use it as part of an experiment to discover whether his species could survive, breed and prosper in the woods as well as on the farmland plains.

Other rumours filtered through about this new leader, who had apparently usurped the power and influence of the History, Geography and Language Owls, all three of whom had fought beside us in the war. The socialist or co-operative measures to which Winger seemed to be subjecting the local Barn Owl community reminded me of the story Holly had told us about Westwood, to whom she had been promised by her father. But I did not care to think often of Holly, for she reminded me of Hunter and the vow I had broken. When I did think of her, it made me wince with guilt at the thought of that lovely, young white owl waiting in her steeple, in the churchyard, the copse, or even beside the distant iron tracks – waiting for Hunter, who would never, ever come.

My own guilt, too, cancelled out any resentment I might have felt for the amount of time May Blossom spent with Birch and Rowan. I often tortured myself by wondering whether he knew what had passed between Mallow and myself before she died in giving late, unnatural birth to her son. If he did know, or if he merely suspected it, had he told May Blossom? Did this explain the growing affinity between them? Did one ever really know or could one ever really trust another owl? There are so many things that make one shudder and twitch with guilt when experience touches one of those raw nerves that bite with the memory of past errors.

Such troubled thoughts ran through my mind in the never-ending winter which saw my father's death, and during the early spring which, with opening buds and the burgeoning of nature, greeted the coming of my son. From the night of his birth my own life changed. For the first time I had a single, solid, central purpose – to provide for my son; to make sure that he survived and, in the course of time, became a wise leader, an owl who could grasp the concept that all creatures of the night one day must learn to co-exist and live together under the same sky.

In his early days I spent most of my time with young Hunter, leaving May Blossom to occupy herself with the leadership of our community. I taught my son to fly, and told him the stories that I had heard from my mother in the great ancestral oak where I had fledged from an owlet into my first blooding in the field, and my first experience of that rarest combination, both love and the urge, with Mallow.

In fact, my relationship with May Blossom was quite different. First, we had argued furiously about the name. My mother and May Blossom had agreed to call him Sage. I asserted myself and insisted that he should be known as Hunter, in memory of the most valiant friend I ever had.

'Hunter is not a Tawny name,' May Blossom objected, the first time we seriously discussed the matter.

'Neither is Sage,' I said. 'Or Saage, as you pronounce it.'

'Oh yes it is!' May Blossom said. 'It comes from our cousins across the water and in their language it means wise.'

'Sage taught you a lot, didn't he?' I asked, with old suspicions welling up again as to the exact nature of her relationship with the venerable town philosopher.

'As a name, Hunter is banal,' May Blossom replied. 'It is a commonplace. All owls have to hunt, like men, foxes and even worms, who burrow into dead flesh to keep themselves alive.'

'Let's leave our first choices out of this,' I said, deciding to probe now into my other suspicion concerning the relationship she was currently conducting with Birch. 'You say you want a traditional Tawny name for our fledgling.

Then why not call him after one of our most common trees or plants? Why not call him – if it is a him – Rowan, Birch or Ash, after my father. If it is a she, why not call her May Blossom, after you. Or Holly, Hyacinth, Violet or Marigold, or even Ivy Perch?'

'Male or female, I don't want to call our offspring after any tree or flower,' May Blossom said. 'I want him or her to have a name that hints at a higher form of life, touching not only on the trees and plants that surround us or, even worse, on the banal assumption that nature is merely red in tooth and claw.'

'What name would you suggest then, if our fledgling were a female?'

'Felicity!'

'Happiness!' I said. 'Well, that is an abstract concept, I agree. As abstract as Sage or Wisdom.'

'How did you know that felicity meant happiness?'

'Oh, for the Great God Bird's sake, you seem to think I'm some kind of rustic idiot! Just because you went to the city to get knowledge, it doesn't mean that the rest of us are totally deprived of any kind of learning.'

'Very well, then,' May Blossom said, reverting to the supercilious, almost dictatorial manner that she had assumed since returning from the city and consorting with my mother. 'Very well, then,' she repeated, 'if the fledgling were a female, what would you call it?'

'Alba,' I said spontaneously, never having envisaged the possibility of the creature now waxing inside May Blossom to be anything but male.

'Why?' May Blossom asked, fixing me with eyes that reminded me more and more of my mother's.

'Because of "The Same Sky",' I said, having been caught very much unawares.

'What do you mean, the same sky?'

'It was a song I heard.'

'What song?'

'A song sung by the Little Owl Hunter was once in love with.'

'What was it about?'

'About the need for co-existence. About love, but also about tolerance. Above all, it was about avoiding senseless conflict.'

'That is nonsense and you know it,' May Blossom retorted. 'The conflict will never cease. There will always be periods of peace and war; as with the relationship between two owls, there will always be a time for love and a time for hate. You must never allow your sense of history to be corrupted by do-gooders.'

This comment cut me to the quick.

'I am not a do-gooder! I detest them just as much as you do. But this little alien Hunter was in love with risked her life to fight beside us during the invasion and the war. And I was always taught that actions speak louder than words.'

'You mean like when I saved you from the buzzards?' May Blossom said.

'I kept my part of the bargain, didn't I? I came to the city to fetch you back. What more do you expect of me?'

'Your former courage,' May Blossom said. 'Everybody knows about your heroic deeds during the invasion and the war. However, that is now history. It is the present and above all the future that we must look to. And I have to say that since losing your talon in the city, you appear to have gone into a decline. To me, and to others, you seem to be growing old before your time!'

'Decline or not, I have seen sufficient bloodshed to last me for a lifetime. All I want now is to live in peace, here in my ancestral woods, and to bring up my only son. For so you have decreed. One and one only was what you said. But because there will be one and one only, his survival is imperative to me. I must make sure that he has all the help and support a young one needs.'

'Or she!'

'Or she,' I conceded.

'Shall we compromise?' May Blossom asked. 'If it is a male you may have your way and call him Hunter. If it is a female, she will be called Felicity. Do you agree?'

'Yes.'

'Good. It is good that we have decided because you know my time is near.'

'Of course,' I said.

'There is one more thing that I require from you!'

'What's that?' I asked, surprised and gratified by what seemed to me to be a happy compromise.

'I want you to go and see Quaver.'

'What for?'

'We have word that he is involved in a Barn Owl resistance movement aimed at deposing Winger.'

'Why don't you send Birch? Given that he seems to have taken control of things!'

'You know Quaver. You were his brother's best friend. If we are to live in peace with future Barn Owl generations, it is essential that we support this counter-revolution. The old order cannot simply disappear. This owl called Winger with his New Apostasy is a threat to all of us.'

'If Hunter had been here, none of this would have happened,' I said. 'He would have respected our territory, and even the right of the Little Owls to live in no man's land.'

'You may be right,' May Blossom said. 'But Hunter is no longer here, and we must therefore act on his behalf by supporting the Barn Owl counter-revolution.'

'What do you want me to say to Quaver?'

'You will take him an ultimatum. You will make it clear to him that if Winger is not overthrown from within, and if he persists with his plans to colonize Ferocity and Ripper's wood, we shall send a task force to destroy him.'

Here I heard shades of my parents and of ancient traditions which would, it seemed, never ever change. They would always oppose the wisdom of a bird like

Hunter, and militate against Mallow's song about war, or against the concept of living together under the same sky.

'I will deliver your ultimatum after our son is born. I want him to grow up in a time of peace, not war. In my opinion it is much too soon to deliver an ultimatum of this kind. I believe that you, Birch and your other advisers are overreacting to rumour and to hearsay. For the moment Ferocity and Ripper's wood has not been occupied. It is still free, vacant Tawny land.'

'*Laisser faire!*' said May Blossom, sarcastically. 'Is this your new philosophy – to do nothing until it is too late?'

'Yes, in this case my philosophy is *laisser faire*. Let the Barn Owls do it! The rumours you heard about a resistance movement and a counter-revolution are quite true. Quaver told me when we returned from the city and I visited him with the sad news that his brother had gone missing and was presumed dead.'

'And what exactly did he tell you?'

'First, he said that he had joined the resistance movement because Winger had rejected entirely the epic ballad that Quaver and Bardic had been working on since the war, which the Bard Owl believed would commemorate and immortalize the efforts both Tawnies and Barn Owls made to bring the monster down. The pompous fool believed that he was rendering history into art. Winger told him that this did not serve the purpose of the New Apostasy. He and Quaver must begin the ballad again, excluding any reference to our Tawny and Barn Owl alliance and to the fact that without our sacrifice the war could not have been won.'

'Why didn't you tell me this before?' May Blossom said.

'You didn't ask. And, in any case, I was at that time under the illusion that I was still leader of this community.'

'If you continue to abdicate,' May Blossom said, 'though you may remain as leader, it will be leader in name only.'

'Is that so?'

'You have reneged on your responsibilities and on the leading role your family played for centuries.'

'Very well,' I said, deciding that for the first and possibly the final time I would emulate my father and May Blossom and play the role to which I had been born and bred. 'But for the moment I am still leader and I will do it my way. I've seen too much, and while I'm still in charge I shall do everything to avoid the spilling of blood and the senseless slaughter that you propose.'

One of the banalities influential Tawnies tend to use is the phrase 'I told you so'. Little did I know how soon May Blossom would be able to use this commonplace to put me down. None the less I tried and, if I was wrong, I hope my silent listeners will attribute my failure to the fact that I fell victim to a form of idealism, a dream – a dream that has waned and died in the twilight of my days.

CHAPTER

 31

Soon after that, young Hunter was born, and from the first moment I was quite sure he was mine. From the time of his birth onward, my life changed. For the first time it had a central purpose, or what May Blossom and Sage would have called a *raison d'être*.

There is an old Tawny Owl proverb which says that the life of a male is effectively finished when he gives up his own aspirations and begins to live vicariously through the intelligence and achievements of his fledglings. I don't know whether this is true or not, but the fact remains that during his early days the traditional roles of male and female were reversed. I spent more time with my son than May Blossom did. She was absorbed with the pressing affairs of leadership, and flew often to see Birch, Rowan and other Tawnies to discuss with them the three main issues of those times.

The first, of course, was Winger's threat to take over and colonize Ferocity and Ripper's wood. Connected with this was the drastic change in the Barn Owl policies of government since the extremist had been elected as their leader. Co-existence with this Winger's New Apostasy and its revolutionary policies had become well-nigh impossible with what I now considered to be chauvinistic Tawnies, such as Birch, May Blossom and my mother. Therefore, as far as possible for an owl in my position, I kept out of it, and concentrated on the welfare of my son.

In this respect I think it interesting to note that one's own ignorance is first well and truly exposed when one attempts to provide one's own offspring with some kind of education. The basic things do not present enormous problems. Teaching them to eat, to fly, to clean themselves and to preen their feathers is simple compared to the time when they begin to communicate and to ask one what I call the 'why questions'.

From the dawn of his birth, I had taught my son to call me Yoller. It seemed less formal. So as soon as he had learned to speak, what one might call the interrogative phase began. For example:

'Please, Yoller, why do we fly by night and not by day?'

'Please, Yoller, why do most other birds fly by day and not by night?'

'Please, Yoller, why do Little Owls live in no man's land?'

'Please, Yoller, why is your father dead?'

'Because.'

'Because what?'

'Because he's dead.'

'What did he die of, then?'

'Old age.'

'Then why is your mother still alive?'

And so it went on, as any parent will have experienced.

'Please, Yoller, why do men live in brick, stone or concrete boxes? Why don't they live in trees? Why do worms burrow underground and eat dead things whilst we only eat fresh meat? Why is the moon yellow and the sun pink or red? Why does the sun rise in the east and set in the west? Why are snowdrops white, like hawthorn or apple blossom, when cherry blossom is pink? And why do moles live underground?'

Many of these things I had asked myself as a fledgling, and I did my best to answer them as truthfully and sincerely as I could. But even though I tried my best, the questions my son put to me constantly revealed my own limitations and made me ashamed of my own ignorance.

To avoid answering the most difficult of these, I resorted to the telling of stories, though I tried to make them more entertaining and less didactic than the ones I had been told in my own days as a fledgling. My basic aim was to allow young Hunter to draw his own conclusions or, in other words, not so much to teach him, but to help my son to learn.

In spite of all these difficulties, the main one being the daunting responsibility of trying to shape or form a fledgling's future, these agonizing nights, dawns and twilights when I cared for him will be remembered by me from now on as the happiest time in all my life.

So absorbed was I by my son that I took little notice of the changing world around me. This, I fear, was a mistake. If you like, it was partly self-indulgence and partly indulgence of young Hunter, who had from his first sunrise become the most important factor in my life.

So when May Blossom returned one early sunrise from an all-night meeting with Birch, my mother and various other militant Tawnies, I was irritated and resentful of the demands that she and they now made on me.

'We have decided that the ultimatum must now be delivered to the Barn Owls,' May Blossom said. 'Either they abandon all attempts to take over traditional Tawny land, or we send a task force to annihilate them and retake our ancestral land.'

'Whose ancestral land?' I enquired.

'Ours!'

'Oh! I see. I was rather under the impression it was mine!'

'Mine, yours, Birch's, it belongs to all of us,' May Blossom said. 'We have decided that you must contact Quaver and arrange for his resistance movement to overthrow Winger and his New Apostasy. Then, when they have re-established their ancient solitary reign, we may begin to co-exist with them again.'

'But why me?' I asked. 'Since you seem to rely so much on Birch, why don't you get him to do it? That way, I can stay here and take care of young Hunter while you conduct your endless meetings and plan the future for us all.'

'I suppose you think that's funny,' May Blossom said.

'There is always a thin line between tragedy and comedy,' I replied. 'It is merely a question of language and of style.'

'That is not true,' May Blossom said. 'It is a question of history, race, class and tradition. Language and style compared to these other factors are a frivolity.'

I listened to May Blossom. I heard what she said. As I grow older I have learned to listen and to get knowledge not only from my peers but also from lower forms of life such as the Little Owl, the magpie or the worm.

Presently I was to discover that ideals of this kind can never counter the prejudices and traditions that Tawnies cleave to and without which they cannot live.

CHAPTER

 32

'Well, you have to let him go some time,' May Blossom said, as yet again my ideals and those of the mother of my son clashed, and once more brought to light the ultimate incompatibility between the traditions of our ancient solitary reign and the need I felt for a new beginning which would include all creatures of the night. 'He can't stay here and hang on to our tail feathers for ever.'

'It's too soon,' I answered. 'Wait till the next full moon. Wait till he's a little more fully fledged. There are risks out there,' I said, remembering the various dangerous missions I had undertaken for my father. 'Risks we both know about too well. Don't you remember saving my life, when you killed that female buzzard?'

'We can't hold him back,' May Blossom insisted. 'You fought in the war, I flew to the city to get knowledge. Both of us did our bit.'

'But why?' I asked. 'Why do we have to do our bit? Why can't we retire to our ancestral woodland hills and live with our son in peace?'

'There will never be peace,' May Blossom said. 'There will always be conflict and striving for survival.'

So May Blossom and young Hunter got their way, and

he set off for his first solo flight as dusk deepened into darkness and the fading crescent moon rose high in the night sky.

I hunted by myself that night and ate off vole and shrew. There was no mole or succulent young rabbit to be found. It seemed that most of the creatures in our woodland habitat had gone to ground. It was an uncanny feeling, and one that I had known, especially on the night before the invasion and the war – the night that was riven by a storm, by thunder, lightning and a deluge from the skies that were perhaps all portents of the coming apocalypse.

Sure enough, as I headed back to the oak in which May Blossom awaited me, black clouds swiftly obscured the crescent moon and total darkness blotted out the distant stars. Next there was a roll of thunder, followed by the brightest flash of lightning I have ever seen. The heavens roared once more as I homed in on the oak tree; the sky was once more forked by brilliant light, and then the deluge came. And on that long-gone night it came like nothing I had ever known before. The very oak in which I perched shook and trembled in the storm. Then began a series of shocks, accidents and misadventures from which I never fully recovered.

May Blossom was waiting for me when I arrived and, though she preserved her outer air of calm and composure, I could tell she was as consumed by worry for our son as I was.

'Don't worry, Yoller. He'll be all right,' she said. 'He'll find a spare branch somewhere and rest until the storm is past.'

'In this weather, on his first solo flight, he could so easily get lost,' I said. 'I must go and look for him!'

'You can't fly into the eye of this storm,' she said. 'You would be risking your own life and wasting energy you may need to search for him if he has failed to return before the dawn.'

'No, I must go now. If anything happened to him I would never forgive myself.'

'But you don't know which direction he took,' May Blossom protested.

'I believe I do. I believe he flew down to the copse in no man's land, beside the slow-running stream.'

'Why should he go as far as that?'

'Because I told him about Beak Poke, Hunter and little Alba. You know how adventurous he is. He was curious to see something of what lay beyond the confines of these woods, and also to meet another kind of owl.'

'You didn't tell him about the Lost Domain?' May Blossom asked, sounding suddenly alarmed.

'Unfortunately, I did. But I told him that on no account must he attempt to fly there. It would be a long way for a fully grown male, let alone a fledgling.'

'Did you tell him about the danger of the firesticks?'

'Yes.'

'And about the vicious colony of immigrants?'

'I told him he had no rights of passage and might be attacked by the Little Owls. He won't have tried to get there, I'm quite sure.'

'You said he was adventurous.'

'Adventurous, yes. But not stupid. I believe he's flown down to the copse in no man's land between the territory that once belonged to Beak Poke, then to Hunter, and is now inhabited by the Barn Owl poet and his apprentice, Quaver. My only fear is that in this storm he may have got lost and strayed too deep into Barn Owl territory beyond, into the flatlands where I have never flown.'

As I spoke there was a flash of lightning, though no longer from directly overhead. We waited for the clap of thunder, which was more muted this time and came from a greater distance than before. I guessed that the epicentre of the storm was now shifting towards the new town rising in Barn Owl territory, close to the place where Hunter had been born. This meant it was moving in the opposite direction to that which I must take in search of my only son. Without staying to listen to May Blossom, I took off and flew through our woods towards the willow in the copse. Within moments I was drenched, and the howling headwind slowed my flight to a stunted daytime crawl.

I called but no answer came. I flew on and called again, but still there was no reply. So, with fear mounting, I struck out across the unknown Barn Owl territory, skirting the edges of the forbidden forest. I followed a course between the road on which Beak Poke had been killed and the brook that bordered the Lost Domain, until I came to a church with a tall steeple close beside a tiny village. At this time of night there were no human lights to be seen. The thunder and lightning lay far behind me and the rain had abated to a mere drizzle, which stopped soon after I'd paused to rest on a recess in the wall of the lonely derelict church. As the first sign of a clear dawn suffused the vanishing black clouds with the first touches of the palest pink, I called out again for help, knowing that even now I was too far from home to get back before daylight.

At first there was no answer, but I tried again and this time heard the distant response of what I took to be a Little Owl, though at that distance it could have been confused with the cry of a young Tawny who has not yet learned to hoot. With hope in my heart I took off and flew back towards Bardic's territory from whence the call had come. I tried again, the Little Owl replied, and soon I located him below me in a meadow between the brook and the country road, quite close to the first line of trees that stood like outer sentinels guarding the thick forest of the Lost Domain.

I hooted again, and then plunged downward towards the alien, whose posture reminded me of the time I had observed little Alba attempting to provide some comfort for the dying Beak Poke. In fact, as I dropped down towards the ground, I saw the body of an owl, either dead or dying, half-hidden from the sky by one of the Little Owl's wings, which was spread out as if to protect the injured body, or else to comfort the soul of a dying bird.

Even before landing beside them, I recognized both creatures. One was Olmo, the alien poet, and the other was my son and heir, who had been named after my lost friend Hunter.

'I'm sorry,' Olmo said, as I squatted beside him on the ground. 'He was dead before I got here. I gather he is one of yours?'

I hopped closer to the body then, half-hoping to find some signs of life. There have been many cases of owls given up for dead who, in spite of dreadful wounds, have made the most miraculous recoveries. I had been mortally wounded twice, first by the buzzard and then by the monster owl in the battle that brought him down. Hunter, too, had survived even worse injuries than mine. So I bent over the torn body of my son, still clinging to the hope that he might be alive.

He wasn't. His neck had been severed by a powerful blow from the talons of a raptor bigger than Olmo, who still held out one protective wing above the dead body of my son.

'You didn't do it?' I asked him, wanting to make sure.

'Of course not,' Olmo said.

'Who did?'

'I don't know. I was flying from the Lost Domain on a mission into this Barn Owl territory when I heard the sounds of a fight between two owls. I came closer to investigate. This young Tawny here was clearly trespassing, but probably not on purpose. There had been the most horrendous storm, and the chances are that he got lost. By the way, do you recognize him? Is he one of yours?'

'He is my son,' I said, looking down at Hunter's wet and bedraggled body.

Olmo looked at me then, and I saw at first surprise and then compassion well up into his eyes.

'Your son?'

'Yes. It was his first solo flight.'

'For the Great God Bird's sake, I'm sorry,' Olmo said.

'So am I!' I answered, trying to cling to the last vestiges of self-control. 'But tell me how you found him, and give me some clue as to who his murderer might have been.'

'It was a Barn Owl,' Olmo said, after a moment's hesitation. 'Of that I'm certain, but which one it was I don't know.'

'Whose territory is this?' I asked.

'Bardic and Quaver's,' replied the Little Owl without the slightest hesitation. 'But it borders on the flatlands where various Barn Owls live.'

'You're sure the killer was a Barn Owl?'

'Yes. I saw the white shape fly up into the sky shortly before I arrived upon the scene.'

'And was my son still alive when you got to him?'

'No,' Olmo said. 'If it is any consolation to you, I can guarantee that he died instantly and without pain.'

'It is what I would have wished,' I heard myself saying. 'A young owl's death. Death in the midst of risk and adventure. Not lingering, rotting decay in the decrepitude of old age!'

Looking down again at the body of my son, I was strangely relieved to see that Olmo had been right. Death must have been instantaneous, for the incision was quite clean. The Barn Owl responsible for this crime must have been an adult in his prime. No novice killer could have struck home so surely with one single blow.

'How can I help you now?' asked Olmo, looking at me with pain and concern in his alien's eyes.

'Leave me alone with my son,' I said. 'I need time. You see, he was the most important thing in all my life.'

'I realize that and I'm sorry,' Olmo said, making ready to take off.

'Don't go yet,' I said. I was in a state of intense shock, a state in which one does not feel the gravest battle wounds at once. Yet as the numbness began to wear off and the pain came, I realized that I now had to come to terms with the worst thing that had ever happened in my life. 'Though young, you are a poet,' I continued. 'Tell me, how should I break the news?'

'To his mother?'

'Yes.'

'You must tell the truth.'

'But I don't know the truth,' I said. 'I don't know who killed Hunter, my only son.'

'The distance was too great,' Olmo said. 'Had it been a Little Owl, one from our community in the Lost Domain, I could have told you which of them it was. But to me, from a distance, birds of other species all look much the same.'

'I know,' I said, nodding slowly and promising myself that in the future I would never generalize again. It was clear to me from then on that all species are composed of good and bad, and that it was our duty to serve the God Bird by distinguishing between them, as one distinguishes between good and evil among one's own class or race.

'If I can, I will help you to find out who did it,' Olmo promised.

'If this is Bardic and Quaver's territory, they must be the prime suspects,' I said.

'No, I don't think so. At any rate, not Quaver. Quaver is a true poet, not a killer. In my opinion he would only fight in self-defence.'

'But what if my son attacked him?'

'That would be a different matter,' Olmo admitted.

'And Bardic?' I asked.

'Bardic once crippled one of my best friends,' said Olmo, after a moment's pause for thought. 'But that was because she had flown into the inner sanctum of his strange home in the abandoned building beside the iron tracks. He was frightened and reacted instinctively to defend himself. Personally, I don't think he would have had the inclination or the courage to attack your son in open country.'

Listening to Olmo, and staring down at the lifeless body of my son, as the shock wore off and the pain bit deep, I decided to act at once.

'I could fly there and kill them both,' I said.

'And what if they are innocent?' Olmo enquired.

'They allowed this thing to happen on their territory. For me, that is sufficient.'

'No, it isn't,' Olmo insisted. 'You have an enviable reputation among both the Barn Owls and the immigrants, as you call us, of being a thinking Tawny. Not just a chauvinistic bird who believes in and fights to defend his ancestors' rights. Take my advice. Stay by your son's body for a while and then go home and tell his mother. That is your bounden duty. Afterwards, when you are calmer, visit Bardic and Quaver and find out if they can provide any information about the movement of Barn Owls in this territory on the night your son was killed. If your son did attack Quaver, and Quaver killed him, I think he would admit it.'

'And Bardic?'

'No! Bardic is too pompous and flamboyant to admit anything. And worst of all, in my opinion, he is a bad poet. But none the less, as I have already told you, I don't think he was capable of doing it.'

'I will accept your advice,' I said. 'Leave me now to sit here by the body of my son until dawn has broken. Do your best to find out who killed him.'

'I shall!' replied Olmo, glancing down once more at the lifeless, bedraggled body soon to be devoured by worms and maggots, who would grow fat on the seed of my sperm and the product of May Blossom's womb.

He left me then, and I perched by Hunter's body until the sun rose high and the wet remains of him were bathed in daylight. Then I took off and flew homeward, blinded not only by the risen sun, but also by grief and by the knowledge that I must now face the most difficult task in all my life – to tell a mother that her son was dead.

CHAPTER
33

'This means war,' May Blossom said, after I told her what had happened. From then on, in fact, to my great distress, she seemed to grieve less for the death of her son and dwelt more on the idea of revenge.

'The Barn Owls have already given us a perfect excuse by usurping Ferocity and Ripper's wood,' May Blossom said. 'Our intelligence tells us that Winger has three females living there. Three females with whom he intends to breed.'

'Nonsense,' I said. 'Barn Owls are monogamous, like us.'

'Well, evidently Winger is an exception.'

'Who are these three females?' I asked.

'One is your dead friend's sister, Dawn Raptor. She is a disciple of Winger's and only too ready to submit herself to this foul experiment. One of the others has recently arrived from another territory, and the third is the mind-less, idiotic Ivy Perch, daughter of Winger's so-called amanuensis.'

'What is an amanuensis?' I asked.

'A kind of slave,' May Blossom said. 'Or, if you prefer it, a lackey. A time-server. A so-called revolutionary who is said to believe in the New Apostasy but who would be just as happy maintaining the ancient Barn Owl reign. Only nobody would ever have asked him to do it. Under the old Barn Owl order, he would simply have remained a peasant. Dirge is the kind of owl who would serve any system for his own self-advancement.'

'Do not declare war!' I said. 'Let me go to Quaver and get him to help us identify the white owl who murdered our son. Then I will kill the culprit. I will kill to do justice, but I have seen war before and I do not want the blood of innocent Barn Owls on my talons. I seek personal revenge, not genocide.'

'You are not the Tawny you once were,' May Blossom said. 'Since losing your talon in the city, you have become less of a heroic figure.'

'I never intended to be a heroic figure,' I said. 'There is a time to love, and a time to hate; a time of war and a time of peace.'

'Then now is the time to avenge the death of our son,' May Blossom said. 'Go to Quaver and give him an ultimatum. Tell him that unless Winger and his female acolytes vacate the wood that once belonged to Ferocity and Ripper, we shall kill them and reclaim our land.'

'Very well,' I said, sensing shades of my dead father both in the vocabulary and in the voice I used. 'Very well, I will do as you suggest. But my objective is to find the killer, not to destroy the Barn Owl community, or start another senseless war.'

'Go now!' May Blossom said. 'I am losing patience with you, Yoller. I repeat, you are no longer the intrepid male I met and with whom I mated.'

'Maybe you'd have been better off with Sage,' I said.

'That is very possible,' May Blossom admitted. 'The fact is that I kept my promise, waited, and finally mated with you, perhaps because I was proud of once having saved your life.'

I felt that this comment was unfair. To be constantly

beholden to another owl is a pain. It is a pain when one's parents constantly demand gratitude, and even worse when one's mate chooses to dredge up her heroics from the past.

But, in any case, I flew to deliver the ultimatum to Quaver, as May Blossom had requested – or ordered. Things between us were coming to a pass where I could not distinguish between the two – a request and a command. Even before the death of my son, our relationship had become almost intolerable. Now that he had died under such tragic circumstances, instead of uniting us his untimely and heart-rending decease seemed to have driven us still further apart.

I hooted on arrival in Bardic's territory, which had first belonged to Beak Poke and then to Hunter. I perched on the same branch of the willow tree and, not long after, Quaver came.

'Who killed my son?' I asked, as he landed on the branch where his brother had perched so many times before.

'I don't know!' he said, and from the tone of his voice I could tell he was sincere.

'Was it Bardic?' I asked.

'No!' Quaver said. 'Bardic could never have killed a son of yours. He is too much of a coward.'

'None the less, he must be the first suspect,' I said.

'And me the second?'

'Yes. The third is Winger. I understand he visited you on that fatal night.'

'He did, but that doesn't necessarily mean that he is guilty.'

'Olmo was perched beside the body when I arrived. He was the one who told me that a white owl did it. Do you think he could be lying? Do you think he was the one who murdered my son?'

'No!' Quaver said. 'Like me, Olmo is a poet, not a killer. Though I am sure that if he had to he would kill – to protect his loved ones, or else in self-defence.'

Quaver's words reminded me of what I had just said to May Blossom. I could not imagine the foppish Bardic killing anyone, and Olmo was more likely to compose a ballad about violence than commit it himself.

'Very well, then,' I said, disturbed as I heard my own voice remind me yet again of my father. 'I will go now and interview this Barn Owl you have elected to be your leader. I know where he lives. I shall fly there at once and confront him.'

'Don't do that!' Quaver said. 'You must know that those of us who fought with you against the monster have created a resistance movement to bring Winger down. The History, Geography and Language Owls are all involved in this.'

'And you?' I asked.

'Me too!' he said.

'But not Bardic?' I enquired.

'Not Bardic,' Quaver said. 'Bardic is a time-server and a sycophant. He will serve whoever happens to be in power at the time.'

'But what do the Barn Owls in your resistance movement intend to do?' I asked. 'Overthrow Winger, kill him or what?'

'The exact strategy has not yet been defined,' Quaver said. 'But the substance and the purpose are very clear. Sooner or later, he will be overthrown. He must be! He is turning himself into a dictator.'

'Using the excuse of his New Apostasy?'

'Exactly. He is even dictating to Bardic and myself what kind of ballad we should compose. He wants us to change the true historical events to show that the war against the monster was unnecessary and that you – our Tawny allies – were in truth the war-mongering enemies within.'

'I have bad news for you,' I said.

'What's that?'

'An ultimatum from May Blossom. Either Winger and

his female friends vacate Ferocity and Ripper's wood, or else they will be killed.'

'But I've told you!' Quaver said. 'The History, Geography and Language Owls are preparing for a counter-revolution. The problem is that Winger has a majority on the council. I am trying to help with the resistance, but I don't like bloodshed and, barring that, there doesn't seem to be a great deal I can do.'

'Leave it to me! Let me find out if Winger killed my son. If he did, then I will deal with him. You won't need a revolution. I'll do the business for you.'

'You can't presume he's guilty,' Quaver said. 'If you killed him without proof, it might cause a war between the Barn Owls and the Tawnies.'

'Unless Winger and his three females vacate our land, there will be a war in any case.'

'How did you know about Winger's experiment? He was hoping to keep the thing a secret.'

'Not a chance!' I said. 'Our Tawny Owl intelligence service is still extremely efficient, in spite of our depleted numbers.'

'Most of the Barn Owls don't know,' Quaver said. 'If we told the council about Winger's plan to mate with three separate females, it would help to bring him down.'

'Then why don't you do it?'

'Because of the big problem,' Quaver said.

'What big problem?'

'Infertility, and the breaking of the eggs. Surely, if your intelligence service were so good, you would have known about it.'

'*Touché!*' I said, using a foreign word that I had learned from May Blossom in the city.

'What does that mean?'

'It means you have scored a point. But tell me more about this infertility.'

'For some time past Barn Owls in this district have been

finding it hard to reproduce,' Quaver said. 'Either no eggs are produced, or else the shells are so thin that they break before the time of gestation is complete and the fledglings are still-born.'

'How dreadful!' I said, stung by a stabbing spasm of pain for my own son's death. Still-born chicks were a tragedy for the parents, I thought, but it was even worse when a father and mother had nursed the son or daughter almost to the age of maturity – had seen the fledgling acquire an identity and then die before his or her own independent life had really begun.

Quaver must have sensed something of my pain, for I was conscious of his sensitive, sympathetic eyes on me while he waited for my convulsions to cease and for my spasm of grief to pass. Of course, it did not leave me altogether, and it never has. But on that early morning, as Quaver waited patiently and watched, my sudden agony slowly subsided to that dull ache that I knew then would never fade, and never, ever has.

'Tell me about this experiment of Winger's,' I said, when I had recovered my composure. 'What is the purpose of it, do you think?'

'I should have thought that was self-evident,' Quaver said.

'Not to me it isn't. The only obvious thing about it seems to be that he is using his position and his power to mate with three females at the same time. Only the Great God Bird knows how he can manage it. Personally, I find one female almost too much to deal with.'

'He has a theory about pollution,' Quaver said. 'He thinks the infertility crisis might be due to some kind of contamination caused by man. For that reason he wants to try breeding in a place as far away from them as possible.'

'Then why not in the Lost Domain?'

'Because of the Little Owls,' Quaver said. 'You know

they've colonized the place and that their numbers have multiplied since you went away?'

'I had heard that, yes.'

'Well, Winger doesn't think we're strong enough to take them on. And then, of course, the territory tradition-ally belongs to you, as does Ferocity and Ripper's wood, which is at least vacant and perfect for his so-called experi-ment.'

'If you want to know, I think this so-called experiment is like the belch of hot air that a crow makes when it breaks wind after eating something dead and half-rotten that it found upon the road. As I've already said, in my opinion Winger is merely using it as an excuse to justify his appetite as a libertine. What he's trying to do is to revive the old, discredited tradition known by our foreign cousins as *droit de seigneur*.'

'What does that mean?'

'Basically, it means the top owl can mate with anyone he likes. Because of his position he's not bound to the common code of morality. The Little Owls used to have a similar practice, which in their old language was called *jus prima noctis*, the law or right to take away the virginity of any female subject on the night before she mated.'

'You seem to have learned a lot in the city,' Quaver said, after cocking his head on one side and then thinking for a while.

'One does,' I replied modestly. 'In the city one can't help it. There is an abundance of opportunity for learning.'

Having said this I felt rather ashamed of myself for sounding so pompous. It was the kind of remark one might have expected a town Tawny like Sage or a Barn Owl like the effete Bardic to make. I remembered my own resent-ment at the condescending air of superiority that I was obliged to endure during my time in the city. Now here I was flaunting my own rather superficial knowledge to put down Quaver, who, though a Barn Owl, was after all an apprentice poet, and almost certainly possessed of as much learning as my own.

However, to do him further credit, he did not seem the least upset by what I'd said, and perched thinking on his branch for quite some time before replying.

'Have you ever been in love?' he asked eventually.

'Yes, twice,' I said.

'How would you feel if on the first night your bride-to-be was deflowered by the leader of your tribe?'

'First of all our society is not tribal, and secondly I would kill him.'

'I've never been in love,' Quaver said. 'Only perhaps with the idea of love. I hate violence, but if someone abused my future mate in such a way I think I would do the same.'

'What, kill him?'

'Yes!'

'And what if someone murdered your only son?'

'Then I would do what you are doing now. I would seek him out and exact my own revenge. But I would try not to generalize. I would try not to hate or to punish other, innocent creatures of the killer's species.'

'That is exactly what I believe,' I said. 'But I have May Blossom to contend with. As a bereft mother, she hates all white owls now. Unless I can find the killer quickly, she will send a task force to eliminate or drive out Winger and his females from Ferocity and Ripper's wood.'

'Can't you stop her?' Quaver asked. 'I thought you were in charge!'

'In name only, since losing my talon,' I replied. 'Unless I can find out who murdered her son and punish the individual, I fear that she and Birch will kill as many Barn Owls as they can. I don't want war between us. That is why I'm going to Winger now, to find out if he did it. In the meantime, you tell your revolutionary colleagues to overthrow him, otherwise I cannot guarantee to avert a bloody conflict.'

'I'll do my best,' said Quaver. 'You know where Winger lives?'

'I've already told you that I do. What I don't know is whether he is still there or has already joined his three females in Ferocity and Ripper's wood.'

'Not yet. He wants them to spend some time there eating uncontaminated food before he mates with them.'

'Then I'll fly to his headquarters now!' I said.

'Wait!' Quaver exclaimed as I prepared to take off from my branch in the willow. 'I'm glad you came tonight, for there is something I must ask you.'

'What's that?'

'What really happened to my brother, Hunter, in the city?'

'I can't tell you that,' I said after a long pause.

'Why not?'

'Because he did not want it.'

'My mother wishes me to go in search of him,' said Quaver. 'She clings to the belief that he might still be alive.'

'That is understandable,' I said. 'It is one of the reasons why Hunter did not wish that either you or she should know the truth.'

'But I don't want to go on a wild goose chase,' Quaver protested. 'You who have done it must know how dangerous it is to fly to the city and back. Also, it would mean losing my position as apprentice Bard Owl. Winger would never give me leave of absence. He wants our whole epic to be recomposed from scratch and finished as soon as possible. He wants to make sure that his own self-glorification shall be transmitted down through history, instead of the real truth about the war, which you and I know well because both of us were there!'

'And he wasn't!'

'Exactly! So, for the Great God Bird's sake, tell me the truth about my brother!'

So, in part, I did. I told him all about Holly, our trip to

397

the city, about the feral cats and about Hunter's collision with the machine. I did not tell him about the prison because Hunter had made me promise never to divulge this to a living soul.

'What shall I tell my mother?' asked Quaver, when I had come to the end of my unfinished story.

'Invent something!' I said. 'Tell her anything. Make up a story. You are a poet, aren't you? I thought that sort of thing was your business.'

'Give me something to go on! Any kind of detail on which I can elaborate to give my mother hope.'

I thought hard for a moment or two, and then told him about the time we spent with Holly. 'You could suggest that Hunter might have gone to live with her, in that fertile, distant valley. As a matter of detail, tell her that Hunter seemed enchanted by the way she spoke or sang. He said her voice had a lilting cadence which soothed one like the song of a nightingale in some quiet glade, but at the same time sparkled and bubbled with the clear laughter of a mountain stream. He said it sang of woodsmoke and wild flowers, so that he fell in love with it at once. And I remember, too, that Hunter said you would like her because she wanted to study singing and poetry, just as you are doing. She wanted a higher education, but in the place she lived there were no owls left to teach her anything, except, of course, for her ailing mother. Your brother said that if he survived his journey to the city he'd bring her back with him, so that she could study under you and Bardic. Naturally, he did not know that Winger would have taken power. He thought that one of the older war heroes would be in charge, and that therefore it would not be difficult for him to make an arrangement of that nature.'

'I wish I knew a female like the one you have described!' Quaver said.

'I could tell you how to get there if you like. She might still be there, waiting for your brother.'

'You know I can't because of Winger, Bardic and the ballad. But one day I might go, when the new despot has been overthrown.'

'Speaking of your despot, I'm going to see him now,' I said. 'If he confesses to the murder of my son, your troubles may very soon be over.'

'Day is breaking,' Quaver said. 'Don't go now. At least wait until after twilight when your flight and fight powers will no longer be impaired. Though I believe him to be a bully and a coward, Winger is a strong bird and still in full possession of his faculties.'

'Unlike me, you mean?'

'Everybody knows you were once the best and bravest Tawny warrior in the district. But now you have lost a talon, things might be different. You were a good friend to my brother and I wouldn't like to see you killed. Winger might be with Dirge or another of his acolytes who supports the New Apostasy. Wait at least until you can meet him on equal terms.'

'If we are to avert war, there is no time to lose,' I said. 'I'll fly there now and kill him by daylight if I have to!'

'Vengeance is mine, our Great God Bird said. Why not leave the question of your son's death to a higher and divine judgement. You are needed, like Olmo the Little Owl, if our three species are to keep the peace.'

'I may have lost a talon, but I have not been entirely emasculated yet. One still has something of one's pride and, at the beginning or the end of the night, or even in the daylight, an owl must do what an owl has to do.'

Quaver looked at me, half-nodded and half-shook his head. 'Fly quickly, safely, and come back soon,' he said.

So I said goodbye, took off under the rising sun, and flew by daylight deep into Winger's territory, in search of the murderer who had killed my son.

CHAPTER

 34

Few of these events are rendered in the Barn Owl account of recent history. There is no mention of my son – no mention either of his birth or of his death. It is almost as if he never existed. But he did exist. He was my main reason for living, or *raison d'être*, as I learned to say in the city.

Why, I wonder? Why did the white owls commit their own sins of omission? Was it because they were ashamed of the murder that one of their own kind had committed? Was it because they did not want the history of their species to be sullied by such a heinous crime?

Also, why did Quaver change the sequence of events, the order in which things happened? One of the first rules for an historian is to observe chronology, or so Sage taught me in the city. He also told me that man – though a recent, inferior and upstart species – had even after such a short time on earth achieved supremacy because he had invented a way of recording information, either by scratching marks on wood, stone or paper, or by preserving or conserving voices in small boxes, which also reproduced human music. Some of these boxes, or so Sage told me, were even able to give visual images of the person who was speaking, and therefore almost certainly of those who had sung or narrated in the near or distant past, whilst we had nothing but the oral tradition to rely on.

If only we owls could devise some fixed way of recording both major and minor events for posterity! If only we could invent symbols of some sort to represent the words we use, and then scratch them on the bark of ancient trees, so that future generations would know more truthfully and more accurately about what happened in the past. But I suppose even symbols could be used to transmit untruths down through the centuries. Perhaps this is what men partly did, and perhaps this is why they still have wars and drop fire on one another from the sky. Surely, if they had truthfully recorded their own history, they would have discovered how to co-exist with one another, in the way that one day I hope we creatures of the night shall learn to do.

My own memory is fallible, this I must admit, but I would no longer stoop to invention or omission to cover my own sins, or to present a better image of myself or of my species. I might have done. Indeed, in the past I did, as my silent listeners already know. But now it is too late. The end is near, and only the truth will suffice when one knows that very soon one will be called to judgement by the omniscient God Bird in the sky.

Now, in my last days and nights, I wonder again why the honest and sensitive Quaver gave a false account of some of the following events. In retrospect I believe that it may not have been a matter of his own choosing. As I have said before, what an artist may say or not say is sometimes dictated from above – not by the Great God Bird, of course, but by those who hold power in the owl society of that time.

Though these things concerned me on that long-distant dawn, I must confess that they have since become something of an obsession. But I had another fixation then, as I left Quaver whilst the sun began to rise above the willow in the copse. At that time my overriding purpose was to find the killer of my son. So, as the sun rose higher, I flew on towards Winger's territory, determined to surprise him by daylight, when he would presumably be asleep, alone, in the ideal Barn Owl domain he had taken over on being appointed leader of the council.

Limping through the sky with my stunted daytime wings, I flew on until I came to a wide expanse of ripening corn which rippled below me in the early sunlight. This was Barn Owl country at its best, and I knew that Winger's residence lay beyond, as the vast, gently sloping arable land finally came to an end at the junction with a wooded glade at the bottom of the valley. Before long I saw the abandoned barn in front of me, standing out just before the first line of trees, the old, mellowed stone of the dilapidated building bathed in the unaccustomed sunlight that dazzled me as it poured down from a sky that was blue and almost clear, except for a few torn wisps of white, high-floating cloud.

I dropped down, dived in through the broken roof and, as I had hoped, took him by surprise. No one would expect a visit from a Tawny at this time of day, and Winger was no exception. Perched on a massive beam in the roof of this enormous barn, he stared at me with startled, bulging eyes. I settled opposite him on a rafter and stared back at him, determined to get as close as possible to the truth.

'Nice place you've got here,' I said, with a touch of irony in my voice as I glanced up and around me at the great vaulted space and the abundance of beams and rafters. Though not of course to my own tree-loving taste, I knew that this was the kind of residence most favoured by discerning Barn Owls.

'Yoller?'

'Yes. And you are Winger. We both know each other's names. Let me come to the point at once. I am here to find out who killed my son.'

'I heard that he was dead and I'm sorry,' Winger said, his eyes still bulging as he looked up at me with more deference than I had expected. 'But why have you come to me? Why do you imagine that I could possibly know anything about it?'

'Firstly because you were there on the night it happened. And secondly because you are now leader of this Barn Owl community, and it is your duty to find out who did it. That is, of course, if you wish to avoid a war.'

'How do you know a Barn Owl did it?'

'Olmo told me.'

'Olmo is an alien. It would be unwise to believe everything he says.'

'He saw it happen and was sitting by my son's body when I arrived.'

'Ah! How do you know he hadn't done it himself, and then blamed a white owl to save himself from your revenge?'

'Because he couldn't have,' I said. 'To begin with he's not a killer, and secondly no Little Owl on its own would have been big or strong enough to kill my son. I know it was his first solo flight, but he was already mature enough to take any Little Owl, either on the wing or on the ground.'

'How do you know Olmo did not have an accomplice?' Winger asked. 'However strong, your son could not have survived an attack by two of them.'

'I don't believe the immigrants did it. It's too easy and convenient to blame everything on them. I believe it was one of the Barn Owl community for which you are now responsible, and I want you to help me find out which of them is the guilty party. As I have told May Blossom, I don't want war and I don't want the blood of innocent Barn Owls on my talons.'

'I still think Olmo and another aliens are probably responsible,' said the tall, gaunt Winger. He was a lean, mean bird, but even so he seemed scared of me, in spite of the fact that I had lost a talon. He would have known about this, of course. In small country communities, all news travels very fast.

'However,' he continued, 'there is an outside possibility. No, two possibilities.'

'What are they?' I asked.

'Well, first there is a Barn Owl who has just arrived in the district – an extraordinary bird who thinks he is part-human. Apparently he fell from the nest as a fledgling and was weaned by a human mother. At the moment he is living in the Lost Domain.'

'With the Little Owls?'

'Yes.'

'Why do they allow him to stay?' I asked.

'Because they want him to analyse the behaviour patterns of the new humans who have taken over the great house. Apparently the men with firesticks have left and the place is now occupied by a mass of human fledglings, with only a few adults to look after them. The immigrants want this semi-human Barn Owl to study these new incumbents and find out whether they represent a greater or a lesser threat than those who have gone away.'

'And you think this half-human creature could have killed my son?'

'I said that was one of the two possibilities.'

'And the second?'

'The second hypothesis is very sad,' Winger said.

Because of my time in the city I knew the meaning of the word hypothesis. In our language you would say a theory, though Sage taught me that that word too comes from an older root. Even idea, possibility or conjecture all come from other languages. In plain Tawny terms there was no way one could have said it.

'And what is your second hypothesis?'

'If I divulge this, you must promise to keep it in the strictest confidence!'

'Of course!'

'Then you must know that there is a conspiracy against me, both within the council and also among the Barn Owls in the district.'

'Are you sure?' I asked, knowing full well that what he said was true.

'I am sure,' Winger said, looking at me balefully with his bulging, manic eyes. 'Not everyone approves of our New Apostasy. All owls tend to be bogged down and enmeshed by tradition. It will take many springs of patient indoctrination before our revolutionary philosophy is believed and embraced by all. In the meantime, I suspect some conspire against me. And sad to say, among these there may be some of your ex-comrades and allies from the war!'

'I'm sure there's no such owl,' I lied. 'Especially not any one of those Barn Owl heroes who fought against the monster. But even if such a plot did exist, what could it possibly have to do with the death of my son?'

'It could have everything to do with it,' Winger said. 'By killing him the conspirators would have hoped to provoke a revenge invasion by you Tawnies. During the ensuing war and confusion, they would have hoped to bring me down. In other words, what they were hoping to do was to destabilize the New Apostasy and restore the ancient solitary reign, returning themselves to power after having made some sort of pact with you Tawnies.'

Personally, I thought this theory was preposterous, but at that time I said nothing. I was too interested in finding out more about Winger's devious train of thought. He was clearly scared of me, and I had the strong impression he would say anything or answer any question simply to get me to go away. This meant I could get more information, and I had learned that information meant power, so I stayed, staring back at his manic eyes with what I hoped was a sane and steady gaze of my own.

'You see, for some megalomaniacs, power means everything. They have no scruples left,' Winger continued. 'For them, the end justifies the means! They would do anything, however dreadful, to achieve the objectives they have set themselves.'

Listening to this gaunt, haunted bird, it struck me that he must be speaking about himself; as I have observed so often is the case, what one says about others so often unconsciously reflects oneself.

'If they did as you said and killed my son to provoke a conflict between our two species, then they were very much mistaken,' I said. 'One does not go to war because of a personal tragedy. War is about territory, about boundaries, about food and about the survival of the species.'

At the mention of territory, Winger twitched and flinched, and I guessed he was thinking about his annexation of Ferocity and Ripper's wood.

'For example,' I continued, having decided to repeat my ultimatum to him, though still respecting Quaver's request about not giving away any specific information, 'for example, if you Barn Owls usurped any traditional Tawny territory, that would lead to a war between our species. The murder of my son is a private matter, and when I find the killer I shall exact my own very private revenge!'

'But we need some virgin territory for a vital experiment,' said Winger, and for a moment he sounded almost sincere. 'We need land uncontaminated by man. We must know whether the decline in our birth rate is due to pollution, or whether our species is being struck down by some unknown disease.'

'Why don't you ask this owl called Humanoid? If he was brought up by a female human, in the city, he might be able to provide an answer to your questions.'

'That is precisely what I intend to do!' said Winger. 'But

in the meantime, I must proceed with my own research and my own experiments. The future of our species depends on my taking action now.'

'You are referring to Ferocity and Ripper's wood?'

Winger looked at me with his manic eyes, and if it were possible for a white owl to pale, one would say that is what he did. He paled and flinched.

'So you've heard about it?'

'Of course. You have usurped our territory by installing three females there. Three females with whom you intend to mate. If they conceive and breed successfully you will conclude that uncontaminated woodland is what your species requires for survival. You will therefore attempt to annex more and more Tawny territory, deserting your polluted farmland to keep yourselves alive and to guarantee the survival of your species.'

'Who told you this?'

'No one,' I lied. 'I worked it out for myself. You may not be aware of it, but I, too, have travelled and have studied briefly in the city. But I can tell you this,' I continued. 'Unless you vacate Ferocity and Ripper's wood, there will be war between us. I shall do all I can to prevent it, but my powers are limited. Tradition dies hard. In the case of Tawnies, very hard!'

'But it's only an experiment,' Winger protested. 'If it is successful, we shall move and resettle in the Lost Domain, driving the aliens out and leaving Ferocity and Ripper's wood to you!'

'But by right the Lost Domain also belongs to us!'

'Yes, but you cannot stand by and witness genocide!' Winger said. 'You don't need the Lost Domain. Your numbers are too depleted even to fully occupy the territories in which all of you now live.'

'And if you occupy the Lost Domain, what will happen to the Little Owls? Where will they go, supposing you succeed in conquering them?'

'Back to no man's land where they belong,' Winger said.

'So to prevent genocide, you are prepared to commit it?'

'Yes. Wouldn't you be?'

'Personally, no. But there are those of my species who would agree with you. And there's another question I want to ask you!' I added, as Winger cringed, shrank back on his beam beneath the crumbling roof, and stared at me with a paranoid fervour in those bulging eyes of his. 'Who are these three females with whom you intend to conduct this breeding experiment in Ferocity and Ripper's wood?'

'That does not concern you.'

'Since the territory is ours, it does! I already know two of them. One is Ivy Perch, the daughter of your henchman Dirge, the one you have appointed to your council as the Owl for Dogma and Dialectic – whatever Dogma and Dialectic are – and the other is Dawn Raptor, your disciple and the sister of my lost friend Hunter. Who is the third?'

'Very well, then, since you are already so well informed, I will tell you,' said Winger, flinching still further back on his rafter. 'The third is a young female to whom I was once betrothed, in the territory where I was born and grew up before moving north. Recently I went to see her in the district where both of us grew up. She agreed that when her mother died she would come here and mate with me. Not long ago, she arrived.'

'And what does she think about the other two?' I asked. 'About your also mating with Dawn Raptor and Ivy Perch?'

'She is a remarkably gracious owl,' Winger replied. 'She understands the need for sacrifice in a time of crisis such as this. When one's whole species is in peril, one does not dwell on the principles of traditional morality!'

'Indeed, one does not!' I said. 'That is why I shall now fly to the Lost Domain and seek out the Barn Owl called Humanoid. If I discover that he murdered my son, I shall kill him where he perches or where he flies.'

'Don't do that!' Winger said. 'We all need his skills. Having been brought up by a female human, and having spent much time among men in an animal prison in the city, he can teach us much about the ways of man and other creatures with whom we co-exist. We may gain knowledge from this Humanoid owl which will help all of us to survive.'

'Your real name is Westwood!' I said, challenging him as soon as I connected him with the story Holly had told us on our way to the city. 'You inherited a fertile valley in the south but came here before the invasion and the war because you wanted to spread your New Apostasy, and above all because you wanted power. I know the name of the third female you are planning to mate with. She's called Holly. She has a voice that bubbles with the clear sparkle of a mountain stream, a voice that sings of woodsmoke and of summer flowers!'

'How did you know?' asked Winger, who seemed too shocked by my challenge to find the courage to deny it. In fact, he was so agitated and distressed that he almost fell off his perch!

'I met her once,' I said. 'She told me a great deal about you!'

Winger stared at me, his mouth hanging open in shock and disbelief.

'Your father was one of the last Barn Owl aristocrats. He left his entire territory to you, but you abdicated and came here in order to spread your philosophy about equality.'

'Don't tell anyone!' pleaded Westwood, alias Winger. 'I have a hard enough time re-educating the Barn Owl population as it is. If they knew about my true origins, it would make the task of converting them still more difficult!'

'Yes, I can see that. It would be harder to indoctrinate them if they knew you were a landed aristocrat.'

'But that was an accident of birth. You yourself are a high-born owl. You can't help it any more than I can.'

'Being ashamed of one's origins is pointless!' I said. 'One is what one is, and however humble or high-born, of whatever species or whatever race, the only thing to do is to come to terms with it. What you are trying to do is create a new identity. I don't think it will work!'

'It is working!' Winger said. 'And it will go on working unless someone starts spreading these rumours about me.'

'Rumours? You've just admitted that it is the truth!'

'Yes, but how will anyone ever know, unless you tell them?'

'Sooner or later your past will find you out,' I said. 'One day or another it will catch up with you, probably when you least expect it.'

'Don't tell anyone!' Winger again implored me. 'In return for silence, I'm sure there must be something I can do for you!'

'There is!'

'What is it? You only have to ask.'

'Help me to find out who killed my son!'

On hearing my request, Winger seemed almost more frightened and distressed. It was almost as if this big, gaunt Barn Owl were disintegrating in front of my very eyes.

'I promise!' he blurted out. 'It shall be done, providing that you keep my secret.'

'Remember that you are still one of the prime suspects,' I said, without giving him my word or bond. 'It's in your own interests to find the guilty party. If you don't, I shall have to kill everyone who might have done it, including you!'

With this threat I spread my wings and left Westwood twitching on his beam in a state of fear and agitation. I flew out through a gap in the roof of the barn and set out across the open country, heading for the Lost Domain. By this time the sun was high. It was a time of day at which

I should long have been asleep. The bright light dazzled me, but I flew on and on above the golden, undulating corn fields, driven on through the mists of fatigue and pain by my obsession with justice, revenge and truth.

CHAPTER

 3 5

As I finally approached the confines of the Lost Domain the sun had risen to its noonday peak, and I was exhausted by the longest daytime flight I had ever undertaken. Having set out well after dawn, this expedition in the daylight had flogged me almost to the point of no return. I had been even longer under the sun than on that occasion when, flying to the city, Hunter and I had found no shelter and had been attacked by the two buzzards.

When I finally entered the mystery world of the forbidden territory I was so weary as to be past caring whether I lived or died. I flew low over the woods that protected the great house from the outside world, and then on across the lake and into the sloping parkland. Below me, I suddenly became aware of a commotion. Looking down on a flat piece of the parkland, I saw two dozen or so human fledglings, all armed with sticks, chasing and striking at something on the ground. Their shrieks wafted up to my flight path well above them, and so did some piercing whistles which emanated from the one adult who seemed to be in charge of them.

At first I thought that they must be attempting to kill some small animal – a mole, a vole, a field mouse or some other creature that scuttles across the ground by day and on which we owls feed at night. However, glancing down again, I saw that this could not be the case, for the object they were chasing and hitting with their sticks was round, man-made, in a shape and form which might be described as a small ball.

From the sky above, the behaviour of these fledgling humans appeared to be extremely vicious. Attempting to whack this small white ball, they frequently missed their target and hit each other on the legs or elsewhere on their spindly, unformed bodies. From time to time, as I flew above them, the adult human blew his or her piercing whistle, and for a moment the human fledglings would cease to batter the ball, or each other, with their sticks. As I flew on above them and approached the confines of the secret forest, I concluded that this must be some kind of training exercise. All species of owl are trained by their parents to hunt and catch the food necessary for survival, and I could only conclude that men taught their fledglings in the same way. In the city I had seen both young and older humans running after ball-shaped objects and either kicking them or hitting them with sticks.

I did not understand then, I do not understand now and, even if I lived to be a thousand, I should never be able to fathom the extraordinary behaviour patterns of the animal called man.

To my immense relief, the first line of trees in the secret forest soon loomed up ahead of me and, exhausted by the long daytime flight, I dropped down from the sky and crashed into the upper branches of a sycamore which lay within the forest borders, well out of sight of the human fledglings and their adult leader who made the sharp whistling noise.

For some time I slumped on my branch, torn between physical exhaustion and the racing mind that would not let me sleep. A mind in turmoil does not let you rest.

Neither does it lead to any sane conclusions. At such times images, memories and ideas flash through one's brain without any logical connection in a process which I believe is known as autistic thought.

Why had Winger concealed his background and his origins from the Barn Owl community of which he was now the leader? If he had lied to them, he could have lied to me. He could have been the one who killed my son. But why? He had himself said that young Hunter's death might lead to war with the Tawnies, which might in turn lead to Winger losing his position as leader. What this Winger needed above all was time – time to eliminate the conspirators within and time to conduct the sexual experiment in Ferocity and Ripper's wood.

In this respect I was disappointed to learn that Holly had abandoned her own territory and come here to seek him out, but then again one couldn't really blame her. Hunter was as good as dead and, even though she didn't know it, she could hardly have been expected to sit and wait for him until she grew old and died alone in her deserted territory.

As I perched in the safe sycamore just within the confines of the secret forest, Winger was still tormenting my tired mind, as were images of the three other main suspects: Bardic, Olmo and this strange creature called Humanoid.

At last I slept and did not wake till early twilight, when I sensed the presence of two other birds who had just landed above me on a higher branch of the sycamore. They were both aliens, and as they glowered down at me I saw that they were the most vicious-looking members of their species I had yet encountered. For a moment or two I thought they were about to attack me. It subsequently transpired that they were sentinels who had been ordered first to challenge and then kill any other type of owl that attempted to trespass in the secret forest which they had now colonized and called their promised land. Once upon a time I could have taken both of them, though not without suffering the odd scratch or two in the process. Now, with my missing talon, I wasn't quite so sure, so, wisely, I waited to see whether they would attack me first.

'You are Yoller?' the higher of the two enquired, as I gazed up at them in a way that I hoped showed that, if they did strike, at least one of them would die.

'How did you know?'

'Because by reputation you are probably the only Tawny brave enough to trespass in the secret forest,' replied the less ugly of the two.

'It is hardly possible to trespass on one's own property,' I replied. 'The Lost Domain has been ours by right not merely for hundreds or thousands, but millions of springs, summers, autumns and winters.'

'Things have changed!' the first alien said. 'The forest now belongs to us, and any trespassers will be first warned off and then killed if they do not go.'

'Does that apply to me as well?' I asked, whilst flexing my muscles and my talons for the fight.

'No.'

'And may I ask then why I am an exception to your rule?'

'Because in the war you were kind to little Alba. She is our first heroine – a martyr who fell in helping to found and form our new co-operative. You helped her and you were mainly responsible for bringing the monster down. Fortunately we do not forget these things, otherwise by now you would be dead!'

'I would like to speak to your poet, Olmo,' I said, unwilling to be drawn further into this exercise in brinkmanship.

'We guessed you might,' said the less fierce-looking of the two Little Owls. I later discovered that his name was Willow. Doubtless he was named not according to the tree, but after the poor plant known as rosebay willow-herb, a weed which is very common along the iron tracks and in no man's land where this now proud community land-owner had first seen the light of day and subsequently grown up.

What's in a name? they ask. I would answer, a great deal, if you will take the time and use your intelligence to look for it. Though not always reliable, etymology can be turned to as a source of intelligence and information, and parents would be best advised not to brand their children with a name that betrays any kind of origin that might stir up any further contribution to prejudice.

'You guessed I might want to see Olmo?'

'Yes. And so we have sent our third sentinel to fetch him. In the meantime, you may not leave. Is that clear?'

'I have no wish to leave,' I said. 'I have come here on a mission and I have no intention of going until I have accomplished it.'

As I finished speaking there was an almost silent rustling of wings in the sky above us, and moments later Olmo landed in the sycamore, accompanied by the sentinel the other two new guardians of the Lost Domain had sent to fetch him.

'How now, big brown owl,' Olmo said. 'May I ask to what we owe the pleasure of your visit?'

'I have come to see a Barn Owl called Humanoid, an unnatural creature whom I have heard you are harbouring here in the Lost Domain, or in what you now refer to as your promised land.'

'Why do you want to see him?' Olmo asked.

'Because I am searching for the killer of my son, and this hybrid monstrosity is one of my prime suspects.'

'I guessed as much, and I sent for him as soon as I heard you had arrived,' said Olmo, answering me with a sort of bland self-confidence that belied his small size and his rather unkempt feathers. But, then again, he was a poet – an artist – and such creatures do not always groom themselves as well as aristocrats or owls of the upper-middle classes.

'So you think this owl called Humanoid might have killed your son?' Olmo enquired.

'You were there on the night in question. You found his body and were perched beside it when I arrived in search of him. Let me tell you this, Olmo! If I discover that you killed him or, likewise, unless you help me track down the guilty party, I may kill you as well.'

'There are five birds perched here in this sycamore,' said Olmo, placidly. 'Four of us are Little Owls and you are the only Tawny. Be patient! The owl called Humanoid is on his way, and I think you may be in for a surprise!'

Sure enough, as Olmo finished speaking, I heard a rustling in the sky, and then saw a great white shadow descending on the sycamore through the semi-darkness of the twilight sky. He landed on the branch opposite the one on which I was perching, nodded politely to Olmo, and then turned his handsome head to me.

I saw at once that it was Hunter, though at first I could hardly believe my eyes.

'Hello, Yoller!' he said, smiling at me with eyes that looked older and even wiser than I remembered from the old days – from the times when we had fought together against the monster and later travelled to the city on a suicide mission which somehow both of us had survived.

Clearly I was overjoyed to see him, but I was so utterly astounded that I could not find the words of love and greeting that I desperately searched for in my mind. So instead of expressing my emotion, I gaped open-mouthed at him.

'What on earth are you doing here?' I asked eventually, much too overcome to express my real feelings, especially in front of the still-menacing contingent of Little Owls.

'Obviously, I escaped,' Hunter said. 'Just like you said I would!'

'But how?'

'We'll leave the two of you together now,' Olmo said. 'If you need us, call and we will come.'

'Thank you!' Hunter said, whilst I nodded briefly to the four little immigrants before they took off and flew away.

'How?' I asked again, as soon as Olmo and his sentinels had gone. 'How did you escape? And why are you masquerading as Humanoid?'

'It's a long story!' Hunter said.

'Tell me in any case!'

And so he did, as we perched close together on opposite branches of the sycamore just inside the secret forest. The story that Hunter told me then is already known to my silent listeners, since it forms an entire act, or movement, in Quaver's ballad, 'The Ancient Solitary Reign'. However, this was the first time I'd heard the story, straight from the owl's mouth, as it were, and so I will briefly recapitulate on the essential facts, since they have a close bearing on what happened next.

We already know that, having been brought up by one, this Barn Owl called Humanoid was obsessed with female humans. He wasn't interested in female owls, only in women – a fact that Hunter found most embarrassing while they were both obliged to share the same tiny cell in prison.

Though Hunter told me he had learned much – no, more, an enormous amount – about human behaviour from this owl, who had been fed and partly brought up by a female human, the whole idea of imprint or implant was alien to him. We know, of course, that if you take a duckling at birth and put it with some chickens, it will follow them about in the belief that it is one of them, and unless it is somehow persuaded otherwise, it will attempt to mate with a hen and not a duck when the urge first manifests itself. According to Hunter, this applies not only to ducks and chickens, but apparently to all species of animal, and human beings as well. Frightful though it may seem, Hunter's cellmate was incapable of loving a female Barn Owl, or even a male — which has of course been known to happen, though rarely, even among Tawnies.

Instead, Humanoid longed for a woman to mate with — a woman in the image of the one that had first fed and succoured him after he had fallen from the nest. Of course, in prison there was no opportunity for him to attempt the impossible by putting this sad perversion into practice. At least, not until the day a female warder came to their cell to feed Humanoid and Hunter their twice-daily ration of day-old chicks. Humanoid fell in love with her at once. Every time she came to the cell he ogled her. His eyes boggled with infatuation, and his whole body twitched with longing, love and lust.

For Hunter, having to witness such unnatural behaviour was bad enough. It made him physically sick, he said. But by a bizarre combination of circumstances, it was his cellmate's obsession with the female warder that led to Hunter's incredible escape.

Wishing to comply with both the owl and human behaviour patterns he had observed, Humanoid was desperate to begin his wooing of this female warder with a gift — a gift of human food. From his experience he knew that a present of traditional owl food would not be appropriate. In any case, he was in prison and could not hunt. Since he was behind bars there was no way he could catch a mouse, rat or vole to present her with, nor even a pigeon, starling or sparrow, the staple diet of town owls.

So instead he took to ingratiating himself with the human visitors who swarmed daily to the prison to observe the behaviour patterns of the sad birds and animals trapped inside. Of course, this was a useless practice, since none of the incarcerated creatures could behave behind bars as they would have done in the wild. However, much to Hunter's consternation, Humanoid took to dancing and putting on a show in the cell they shared, until one day two human fledglings pushed food to him through the bars. This food was wrapped in silver paper. Humanoid opened one of the two tiny packets and showed it to Hunter, who tasted a tiny morsel and found it horribly sweet and quite revolting. If humans lived on this sort of thing, he thought, no wonder they had wars and caused fire to fall on one another from the sky.

However, Humanoid expressed himself delighted with the silver-wrapped gift from the small humans, and decided to present it to the female warder at the first possible opportunity. Hunter was horrified, but there was nothing he could do. When the female warder came next day, Humanoid swooped down on her from his perch on a bar high up in the cage or cell. She shrieked in terror as he attempted to stuff the silver-wrapped human food into her mouth, and ran away, leaving the cell door wide open.

With one bound, as it were, Hunter freed himself. He flew through the open door of the cell and up into a cedar tree in the surrounding park. There he remained hidden until after sunset, when he took off again and headed north to find Holly in the fertile valley where they had met before he was imprisoned.

Sadly, she was not there. Holly's mother had died and she had left the valley, perhaps tired of waiting for Hunter, or perhaps to escape the constant expansion of the city, which spread like a spider's web to entrap and encompass all the natural life and land with endless new buildings, new roads, new smoke and lethal pesticides, which owls of all species have since discovered and from which they have suffered much.

'But why did you come to the Lost Domain?' I asked Hunter, when he had reached this point in his story. 'Why didn't you go home again?'

'Because of Winger and the New Apostasy. The counter-revolutionaries, led by the History Owl, the Geography and Language Owls, and others who fought beside us in the war, want me to remain hidden here until the time is ripe for their own counter-revolution.'

'Is that why you have assumed Humanoid's identity?'

'Of course. I cannot announce myself, otherwise Winger would have me assassinated.'

'Ah, but you have met him! He was the one who told me about an owl called Humanoid, whom he suspected of having killed my son.'

'I have heard about the death of your son,' Hunter said. 'And it makes me very sad.'

'Who told you?'

'Olmo. He arrived on the scene shortly after it had happened.'

'Has he told you anything else that might help to identify the culprit?'

'No. It was a Barn Owl, I'm sad to say. That's all he can be certain of.'

'Do you believe him?'

'Yes.'

'Then who was it?'

'In time and with patience, we shall find out,' Hunter said. 'In the meantime you must not become obsessed with the desire for revenge.'

'"Vengeance is mine, saith the Lord, and females are my favourite vessels of wrath!"'

'Who said that?' Hunter asked, looking at me as if my quotation had struck a raw nerve in his mind, his body or both.

'A Tawny poet who died not too long ago. You must remember that I have May Blossom to contend with. She would be prepared to slaughter any suspect, just to make sure that her son's killer would be among them. I have told her that I don't want the blood of innocent Barn Owls on my talons. But I do want revenge and justice for my son's death.'

'Tell me that again!' Hunter said.

'Tell you what?'

'What you just said, or quoted, about vengeance.'

'Vengeance is mine, saith the Lord, and females are my favourite vessels of wrath! How do you know?' I asked. 'You haven't mated, have you?'

'Sadly, I have!' Hunter said.

'You didn't waste much time!'

'Neither would you have if you'd been locked up in prison as long as I was!'

'So it was the urge that led you into it?'

'Again, sadly, yes!'

'Who is she?'

'She is called Ivy Perch. She's the daughter of Dirge, the owl Winger appointed to the council as the guru of Dogma and Dialectic. I met her in the confines of the Lost Domain, on the edge of the tree line, near to her father's Barn Owl territory, which belonged to Brook before he and his mate were killed by the monster owl during the invasion just before the war.'

'Do you love her?' I asked.

'No!' Hunter said. 'However, I must admit that, though mindless, she is physically attractive.'

'But if you don't love her, why have you decided to mate with her?' I asked.

'I didn't decide. She did! You see, she is expecting a fledgling of mine.'

'The urge!' I said.

'Indeed, the urge,' Hunter replied. 'Tell me, how are you getting on with May Blossom?'

'Not well,' I said, with a sad shake of my head. 'Since returning from the city and taking over the leadership with me, power seems to have gone to her head. But tell me, what will you do about Holly, now that she is here?'

'How did you know?' Hunter asked, his white eyebrows rising high in the handsome head.

'Winger told me. He says he's going to mate with her in Ferocity and Ripper's wood. Incidentally, he intends to conduct a breeding experiment with three females in our Tawny territory. You might be interested to know that one of them is your bride to be, Ivy Perch.'

'And the other two are my sister, Winger's acolyte, and Holly.'

'So you know?'

'Of course. I have met our new leader. He wants me to help him solve this infertility crisis.'

'But he thinks you are Humanoid?'

'Yes. On escaping from the prison I assumed his identity. I thought it wiser. Winger sees me as a threat. If he knew who I was, he would attempt to have me killed. Or so the Barn Owl resistance movement tells me.'

'But what about Holly?' I asked. 'Frankly, old boy, I'm disappointed in her. I know that she couldn't wait for ever, but why she chose to fly here in search of Winger I will never understand. He really is the most frightfully unbecoming sort of bird. You will realize that I don't intend this to be an insult to your species, but if all Barn Owls were like him I think I'd go along with May Blossom and declare war!'

'Is that what she intends to do?'

'She lost her son and is consequently obsessed with the idea of revenge.'

'Holly didn't come here to seek out Winger,' Hunter said. 'She came here in search of me.'

'Then for the Great God Bird's sake, why don't you fly to Ripper's wood and save her? Save her from this experimental mating with Winger. I don't know how female Barn Owls reason or function, but personally, if I were one of them, I would consider mating with Winger a fate worse than death!'

'Of course I would fly there at once and liberate her if I could!'

'Then why don't you? You may be thinner and older after your time in prison, but you could still take Winger out any time you chose. You are a brave and valiant warrior. He is a coward.'

'Then why didn't you kill him last night?' Hunter asked.

'A good question,' I said, nodding in reply. 'If you must know, I didn't kill him because I wasn't certain that he was guilty of my son's murder. As I've said countless times, I want the true culprit, not the blood of innocent owls, of whatever species.'

'I feel the same as you do,' Hunter said. 'Do you think I like living here in the Lost Domain under an assumed identity?'

'No, I don't suppose you do.'

'It's better than being in the human prison, this I must admit. But it is also highly frustrating to come home again and find that all we fought for, our old ideas and values, have been totally corrupted.'

'What I don't understand is why your so-called resistance movement doesn't act now,' I said. 'Why don't you, Rivers, the Geography Owl and the other war heroes simply fly into a council meeting and depose Winger and his plebeian gang of acolytes?'

'Because, unlike you Tawnies, we believe in democracy. After the war, and while I was in the human prison, Winger was properly elected as head of the Barn Owl council. Now that he is attempting to exploit that position and turn himself into a dictator, things are very different. I have been told by the resistance movement that I must wait until the time is ripe. When they are ready, they will act. In the meantime I must stay here in the Lost Domain and conceal my true identity.'

'And let Winger have his way with Holly?'

'With Ivy Perch pregnant, what can I do?'

'Ah!' I said, all other words having failed me.

'I can't offer anything to Holly now!' Hunter continued.

424

'It was the urge that did it. You must understand that after all that time in prison I was desperate! I made a great mistake and now I must suffer and pay for the rest of my natural life.'

'I know the feeling,' I said, thinking of Mallow and May Blossom. 'We all cripple ourselves with lust for one thing or another and must wait for death and the Great God Bird to exercise compassion. But the fact that you have misgivings after mating with this bird called Ivy Perch should not prevent you from helping Holly.'

'I have helped her!' Hunter said.

'How?'

'I have told Winger that one of the reasons for the Barn Owl crisis of infertility could be sexually transmitted diseases. I have warned him not to mate with any female outside this district. I told him that these maladies had been imported from the city and were part of the general human pollution that is now threatening all owl species!'

'And Winger believed you?'

'I think he did.'

'And does he know you've mated with Ivy Perch?'

'Not yet. Tonight she will meet him and tell him she is pregnant.'

'So that leaves your sister.'

'She is infatuated with him,' Hunter said. 'She is a disciple or acolyte of Winger's and would do anything she considered to be in the interests of the New Apostasy.'

'Do you think she might have killed my son?'

'No!' Hunter said, after a moment's hesitation. 'Dawn Raptor is an idealist, not a killer or a criminal. Misguided she may be. She might have tried to convert your son to some Tawny form of the New Apostasy, but she would not have murdered him. Of that you can be sure!'

'What is to become of us all?' I asked, as I sat in the sycamore close to my oldest friend in the secret confines of the Lost Domain, close to a friend with whom I'd fought and travelled far. As we looked into each other's eyes and I awaited his reply to my question, I thought how good it would be if Hunter and I could abandon our present separate predicaments and set off together once again as two free owls, of different species but together and lifelong friends, once comrades, under the same sky.

But, of course, this was not to be! What was to be was worse, infinitely worse. We should have slept side by side in the sycamore and then, as the moon rose high above the Lost Domain, we should have set off together in search of happier lands. Hunter was committed to the mindless Ivy Perch, who was about to bear his chick, and I had a duty to May Blossom and to the Tawny Owl community of which I was the leader. By this time it was becoming ever more apparent that I was the leader in name only, and that the real decisions were being taken behind my back by May Blossom and the traitor Birch, who came from a family which for centuries had disputed with mine the leadership of our community.

The future lay in my talons. It was a task that fate had unfairly thrust upon me. As I learned in the city, a foreign cousin of ours had said quite recently, 'What other satisfaction can be sought once one has confronted history!'

Well, I had confronted it, and now I must do the same again. It was quite clearly my destiny, and I knew that tied to my fate was the future of the Lost Domain. Was it to remain the Little Owls' so-called promised land, was it to be colonized by Winger for further sexual and ecological experiments, or would it one day revert to its rightful owners, the Tawny Owls, of whom – though, I repeat, in name only – I was now the leader.

'By the way,' I said. 'Since you are carrying out a study of this place on behalf of your unlikely hosts, the little squatters, perhaps you can tell me what conclusions you have come to. You understand that I shall have to report back on what I have observed.'

'And what did you observe?' Hunter asked, raising his eyebrows in an ironic smile. He was testing me, I knew, but I, too, had been to the city and studied man. Admittedly, I had not been in prison or observed these upstart creatures for as long as Hunter had been forced to do, but I was no longer entirely ignorant of their behavioural patterns and the mystery of their days and ways.

'I'll tell you what I observed,' I said to my oldest and best friend. 'Or, first of all, I will tell you what I did not observe. I did not see a firestick! Instead I saw a lot of human fledglings being cared for by only one adult, possibly a female. This adult made a strange whistling noise to control the young ones, all of whom seemed to be intent on hitting some kind of ball. They had sticks with which they attacked this small, round object. At first I thought it was an animal, but on second thoughts I would say that it was a man-made thing that humans use to encourage the young ones to hunt.'

'Congratulations!' Hunter said. 'You weren't long in the city, but in this case I believe you have come very close to the truth!'

'What is your theory, then?' I asked. 'And how are you advising the Little Owls? You know that if Winger's breeding experiment is successful he intends to take this place over. He believes that the Barn Owl farmlands have been contaminated by man, and that in order to survive they must move and settle in unpolluted woodland.'

'Like you, I am in a difficult and delicate situation,' Hunter said. 'I owe allegiance to my own kind, as you do, but I also have a moral duty to apply whatever I have learned to further the interests of science and of truth. Therefore I can tell you this. From what I can gather, the men with firesticks have gone away and the Lost Domain is now inhabited by a totally different sort of human.'

'So you think that there are different sorts of human, just as there are different sorts of owl?'

'Exactly! In my opinion, these new humans who have come to inhabit the Lost Domain are not interested in killing other creatures, or at least not in the same way their predecessors were. What I'm trying to say – and have already said to the Little Owls – is that these new humans probably do kill birds, fish, domestic animals and so on, but only to eat them, not for sport.'

'But why are there so many young ones and so few adults?' I asked.

'I don't know, but I have two separate, tentative hypotheses.'

'Which are?'

'First, it could be a gaol for small humans, rather like the animal prison in which I was incarcerated in the city.'

'But why would they put their own fledglings in a prison?' I asked.

'Perhaps because they had misbehaved. Or perhaps because their parents had been killed in the human war and there was no one left to look after them.'

'And what's your other theory?'

'My other thinking is that the Lost Domain might have been taken over by these new humans as a place in which to give their fledglings some form of education. As you rightly say, this apparently mindless pursuit of a small, man-made ball is clearly intended to train them in some way, either for hunting or for their human wars.'

'But what sex are they?' I asked. 'Though I spent but a short time in the city among men and women, I did get some slight idea of the difference. And from what I observed on my daytime flight above the great house and the park earlier today, I would have guessed that the human fledglings hitting wildly at that small ball were females.'

'In my opinion, you are right!' Hunter said. 'They are females.'

'How can you tell?' I asked.

'Well, to start with they usually have longer hair. Humanoid taught me that in the city. The second way you can tell the difference is that the adult males usually wear things called trousers on their legs.'

'What are trousers?'

'It's impossible to say in owl language,' Hunter replied. 'We don't need them because fortunately we have feathers. Human beings do not, and for this reason they are obliged to clothe themselves in man-made fibres, or in leather, wool from the sheep, or cotton, which mostly comes from a country across the salty waters.'

'And Humanoid taught you all this?'

'This and a great deal more,' Hunter said.

'So you don't think these new humans are a danger to the colony of Little Owls living in the Lost Domain?'

'No, I don't. As I said before, I think this type of human only kills animals in order to eat them. And as far as I know no human being has ever eaten any type of owl.'

'I wonder why? Surely we have flesh, like a pheasant, a partridge or a chicken?'

'Perhaps it is because we are a higher form of life,' Hunter said. 'Perhaps they don't eat us because they know that if they did the Great God Bird might punish them.'

'I sometimes wonder about this question of being a higher form of life, don't you? I remember Holly's song about the magpie, rook and crow. And even the worm! Remember, when we die we shall all be eaten by worms and maggots. Death makes no distinction between the so-called higher and lower forms of life.'

'I know that!' Hunter said. 'And in further answer to your previous question, I think humans know it too! That must be why they train their fledglings to run around on the grass and attempt to hack a small, man-made ball. It must be to encourage the survival instinct in them. What other purpose could it have?'

'Have you told the Little Owls that you think they will be safe here, in the Lost Domain?'

'Not yet, but I shall.'

'And Winger, what will you tell him?'

'What I have told you. I believe that such scientific knowledge as I acquired in the city and from poor Humanoid should be placed at the disposal of all owl species, not just my own.'

'But you know that Winger and his gang of henchmen will attempt to invade the Lost Domain and settle here once they know that the men with firesticks have gone away?'

'And what about you Tawnies?' Hunter asked. 'Wouldn't you attempt to do the same?'

'Not if I can help it, no!'

'But can you?'

'Can I what?'

'Avoid it. Avoid an attempt by May Blossom or Birch to resettle in what you consider to be your ancient homeland?'

'I shall try,' I said.

'But will you succeed?'

'I don't know.'

'I wish you the very best of luck,' Hunter said. 'We are old friends, old comrades, and I believe we should do everything in our power to avoid a war.'

As I sat and gazed at my resurrected friend, the evening sun sank below the secret forest in the west, and the mantle of descending darkness told me I must leave and fly home under the cover of our sacred, soothing elements – the stars, the moonlight and the ever-haunting mystery of the night.

As I prepared for take-off, I turned back to Hunter and asked him one more question.

'Why don't you fly to Winger's territory and either kill or depose him before he has a chance to mate with Holly?'

'The History Owl doesn't want me to,' Hunter said. 'He

is leader of the resistance movement and in his opinion Winger needs more time to discredit himself with the ever-thinning Barn Owl population. All leaders are always blamed for whatever disasters happen while they are in power, even though they may be unconnected with them and powerless to avoid whatever tragedy is taking place at the time. The History Owl is of the opinion that we should wait and allow the population to rise up against him.'

'What will they blame him for?' I asked.

'For this infertility crisis,' Hunter said. 'It has nothing to do with him, of course, but it all started to happen after he took over the leadership. The History Owl says that if we wait long enough he will get the blame for all the still-born chicks and the breaking eggs. By waiting, Rivers says, we can overthrow him without a civil war.'

'You've changed since your time in prison,' I said impulsively. 'When you were younger, you would not have waited. You would have acted now!'

'We all change!' Hunter said. 'An owl has not only different ages but also different stages. The instincts and impulses of youth should give way gracefully to the pondering and reasoning that come with the onset of early middle age. This is why I want you at all costs to avoid a war. An outside threat from you would only serve to unite our Barn Owl community behind Winger. It would take their minds off the crises of pollution and infertility. If you allow May Blossom to attack, it will make things more difficult for our resistance movement. It will make it harder for us to bring him down!'

'I promise I will do my best. But you must remember that May Blossom is a mother who has lost her son. She is presently filled with a lust for indiscriminate revenge. I shall prevent it if I can. War between us would be unthinkable. But stranger things have happened.'

'They have indeed!' Hunter said. 'Do you remember when we flew through this secret forest in our early youth, perched in a clearing not far from here and discussed the war between our species that took place more than four hundred springs ago?'

'I remember vaguely, yes.'

'Well, you said another war between Tawnies and Barn Owls might one day be possible. I did not believe it at the time, and at the time I said so. But look at us now! Even within our own communities we are bickering and flocking to the edge of violence. It is up to us to stop it if we can.'

'I shall go back now and try,' I said, as the half-moon bathed the tree tops of the secret forest in its incandescent, muted light. 'I shall go now and do my best. Just do me a favour, old boy.'

'What's that?'

'Just try to survive until all this is over. We've only just got you back again, and it would be a tragedy to lose you again quite so soon!'

Hunter smiled at me as I left, overcome with emotion, and flew out of the secret forest and across the parkland and the lake without once thinking of man and his firesticks.

When I finally got back to my ancestral domain, the sun had risen high in the east and banished the soft glow of the moon with that harsh, glaring light under which so many species move, live and have their being. From the moment of my return I tried to avoid war, as I had promised, but tragically I failed. The consequences of my failure are known to those of my silent listeners who are familiar with Quaver's epic ballad. However, he told the story from the Barn Owl point of view and could not have known the true reason for my being unable to prevent the forthcoming, bloody conflict.

After the wonderful surprise of meeting my old friend alive, I returned home to another kind of shock. Or two kinds of shock, of which the first and most devastating was to discover that, during my brief absence on my mission to the Lost Domain, my mother had given up the ghost and died. The second shock came later, as my silent listeners are for the first time about to discover.

CHAPTER

36

As I returned on that long-distant dawn, under the new threat and mystery of the rising sun, I had of course no idea of the events that were about to occur.

May Blossom greeted me courteously but gravely, and then told me at once that my mother had died whilst I had been away.

As soon as I had absorbed this blow, we flew to see her body, which lay on the woodland floor below the ancestral oak my father's family had inhabited for centuries and which now, through my mother's death, had become my own.

When we arrived there I looked down on my mother's corpse, soon to be eaten by worms and maggots, and for some time I could not bring myself to speak. Though I had never liked her, and although I had rebelled against the narrow-minded and traditional ideas she represented, there had always been an element of love between us. After all, she had laid the egg from which I had burst and grown. She had nurtured me as a fledgling, fed me and possibly adored me – though never showing it – as I had doted on my own son, young Hunter.

How hard it is to be a parent! But equally, how hard it

is to be a daughter or a son. As I looked down on my mother's body, with May Blossom perched beside me on a lower branch of our ancestral oak, I recalled my journey to the city and the knowledge I had acquired both there and along the way of how human beings bury their dead below the ground. Agreed, they too will soon be eaten up by worms and maggots. The wooden boxes in which they are buried cannot keep out these tiny, wingless predators for too long. None the less, looking down on the body of my dead mother, I envied them, and I realized that I would have liked to have seen her entombed in some kind of shrine – in a place where I could regularly revisit her, perch on the earth under which she lay, and under which owl, man or sparrow would ultimately go to rest in the place from which they came.

I must admit that May Blossom was kind to me as the dawn broke above my mother's corpse that day. Whilst the sun rose higher, we flew back to our own oak, and I slept until twilight came and began to bathe the earth in the darkness and the beauty of the night to which I and all natural owls cleave, and which has for millions of years been our heritage.

But then, as twilight fell and gave us back the vibrant gift of life, May Blossom presented me with an ultimatum.

'You must fly with Birch and his task force to liberate Ferocity and Ripper's wood,' she said.

'With Birch?'

'With Birch, yes.'

'With Birch and who else?'

'With Hook and Cleaver.'

'But they are thugs!' I said. 'Hook and Cleaver are worse than Ferocity and Ripper were. You can't ask me to lead troops like that into battle against semi-civilized creatures like the Barn Owls.'

'I'm not asking,' May Blossom said.

'What do you mean?'

'I'm not asking you, I'm telling you. Birch is now in charge of our military operations. He will lead this attack with the troops that he has chosen. Your role will be that of a guide, or scout. After all, you are the only Tawny with a knowledge of the terrain. And not only the terrain, but also the perfidious Barn Owl mentality.'

'You mean I shan't be in charge of this ill-fated expedition?'

'No! Birch will. In your absence, and since your mother's death, you have been deposed as leader of this community.'

'Oh, have I?'

'Yes!'

'By whom, if I may ask?'

'By public opinion. Your fawning and conciliatory attitude to the Barn Owls and to the aliens has placed you in an impossible position. You do not seem to understand that in order to survive we must defeat these upstart creatures and impose our will on them!'

'And not learn to live together with them, under the same sky?'

'No! Absolutely not!'

I perched there with May Blossom, listening to all this but also thinking of my mother's body rotting on the ground beneath the tree in which she had fed me when I was a fledgling.

'You no longer have any stomach for a fight,' May Blossom said, as I sat and pondered there in silence. 'If you were still the owl I left the city and came back to settle with, you would already have killed Bardic, Quaver, Winger, Olmo and any bird who might have been suspected of murdering our only son.'

'When does this expedition leave?' I asked, having now digested this new information and decided that I must accept the role for which I had been chosen, if only in order to limit the damage that Birch and his gang of thugs might wreak on the innocent Barn Owl community.

'You leave at twilight tomorrow,' May Blossom said. 'As guide and scout, you will choose the route and lead our task force to liberate Ferocity and Ripper's wood.'

'What if the incumbent Barn Owls won't leave?' I asked.

'Then Birch and his troops will kill them.'

'I see. On whose orders, may I ask?'

'Mine!' May Blossom said. 'I've already told you that in your absence you have been deposed as leader of this community. Even your mother wished it so. She told me before she died that you had become a liberal ditherer and as such unable and unsuited to act in the interests of Tawny Owl survival.'

'My mother said that?'

'She did. I must add that she didn't blame you for it. She merely said that although once very brave, you were too soft-hearted to lead us up the ever steeper path to survival.'

'And who is the leader now, you or Birch?'

'I am,' May Blossom said. 'And Birch is the new military commander. However, you still have a most important role to play. You know the enemy and you are familiar with the terrain. You will therefore act as chief adviser to the task force I am sending.'

'Very well,' I said, hearing the voice of my dead father as I spoke. 'Very well, then, I will lead this mission for you. You have told me that we leave at twilight. All I need to know now is the trysting place.'

'In Birch's sycamore, as soon as the sun has set,' May Blossom answered. 'You will find him ready and waiting there with Hook and Cleaver.'

'I shan't take them through the Lost Domain,' I said, thinking and playing for time as I spoke.

'Why not? Surely that is the quickest route to Ferocity and Ripper's wood?'

'It might be the quickest route to death!'

'Why?'

437

'Because the Little Owls in the Lost Domain have multiplied. They have also created a defence system that would take many more than four Tawnies to penetrate. I shall take your troops by the longer route, and at least one conflict will be avoided.'

'Negative thinking!' May Blossom said. 'As I've already told you, since losing your talon in the city you are no longer the bold young Tawny that I once mated with.'

'I think you, Birch and the others have made a disastrous decision,' I replied. 'I shall lead this expedition merely in an attempt to limit the damage to both sides. A show of force is one thing. With that much I can agree. But war itself is something else. With due respect, May Blossom, I have been in one, so I know!'

'Well, if you don't succeed in this expedition, you may find yourself in the middle of another one quite soon!'

'Another what?'

'Another conflict. This time a civil war!'

'But I thought I had already been deposed!'

'You are still leader, though in name only. Both your parents are now dead and our only son has been murdered. Unless you – or we – can prove that we can help our own community to survive, we shall lose the power-base from which we both operate.'

'And this is your considered opinion?'

'Yes!'

'Very well, then. At twilight I will do your bidding. Now let me sleep. The sun is high and I need peace and quiet in which to mourn the carcass of my mother, now rotting in the daylight under our once sacred oak.'

'Well, honour your mother and then sleep,' May Blossom said. 'Out of respect for her, I have not told you everything. When your grief has abated and you come back successful from this essential mission, you will be better able to absorb the blow!'

'Tell me now!'

'No! Rest and honour the memory of your mother. Now is not the time for bickering.'

So, as the sun rose higher in the sky, I dozed on my separate branch of the oak. I thought of my mother, my father, Hunter, Alba, Olmo and all the diverse owls whom I had ever known. Even Sage! But most of all I thought about my son, and realized that, had he still been alive, I might have had more stomach for the battle that lay ahead. I would have wanted to make the Tawny world around me a safer place for him. I would have wanted to pass on to him what my sometimes clumsy and overbearing parents had given me. But now it was too late. He was dead, and I no longer cared about our dynasty. I no longer cared about which owl species was superior or right.

I just wished that they would learn to live together, under the same sky.

CHAPTER

 37

We left as the moon rose on that fatal night. I say 'we' left, but that's not strictly true. When I arrived at the trysting place in Birch's sycamore, I found that he and his troops had already left. Only Rowan was waiting, and as I landed he glowered at me as if I were an enemy. 'You're late!' he said. 'My father, Hook and Cleaver have already left.'

'Where have they gone?' I asked. 'Which route have they taken?'

'I thought you might know,' Rowan said. 'I thought you were supposed to be their guide!'

'Tell me!' I said, looking at this aggressive young male and praying at the same time to the Great God Bird — praying that such a churlish thug was not my one surviving son.

'They are flying first to Bardic and Quaver's place,' he said. 'You must follow and meet them there.'

'Must I?'

'Yes. Those are your instructions.'

'Instructions?'

'Yes. Perhaps you don't know it, but you are no longer in charge of anything. From now on my father and May Blossom are the leaders of this community.'

'When did they leave?'

'Not long ago. At sunset, when you were supposed to be here to guide them into battle!'

'Battle means disaster, my son,' I said, the words escaping from me on some strange paternalistic impulse. 'You don't know,' I added quickly, attempting to cover my slip of the tongue. But I was too late.

'Don't you dare patronize me!' Rowan said. 'I am not your son. I am the son of Birch, who is now our leader. Later, when you and May Blossom are dead, or gone, I shall take over from my father. After centuries, my family will have reclaimed their rightful heritage as head of this much-misled community.'

'You may be taking over sooner than you think.'

'What do you mean?'

'I mean that this punitive expedition may well end in disaster, with your father, Hook and Cleaver all killed!'

'And you?'

'Me too!' I said. 'I've been down the road to war before, and I therefore know exactly where it leads.'

'Where does it lead?'

'To death and destruction,' I said.

'You think like that because you lost a talon in the city and are therefore no longer able to fight!'

'I am still able, but unwilling,' I said. 'Fighting gets you nowhere except an untimely grave.'

'So it's true what they say about you.'

'What's that?'

'They say you are weak. And they are right!'

'It's hard to distinguish weakness from strength,' I answered. 'It may be something you learn as you grow older!'

With that riposte I left him and flew fast in the wake of Birch, Hook and Cleaver, who had headed first for the Barn Owl domain once inhabited by Beak Poke, then by

Hunter and his alien sweetheart, and now by Quaver and the foppish Bardic.

I flew fast, sensing disaster in the darkness. As I crossed the copse and flew over the willow and the sluggish stream where Hunter and I had so often met, I sensed a presence flying through the darkness in my wake – a presence, not a threat. I paused in mid-flight and turned to see Quaver close behind me.

'What are you doing here?' I asked.

'I'm coming with you.'

'Why?'

'I saw your troops pass by.'

'Where were you?'

'In the hollow tree where little Alba used to squat, in Beak Poke's time, and later, when my brother took over this territory. That was before she moved in with him, of course.'

'But why?' I asked again.

'Because I can't stand Bardic, that's why.'

'Why can't you stand him?'

'Because he is a sycophant who will compose or invent anything that Winger wants. For his own self-advancement he is prepared to pervert the course of history. In fact I am currently composing a song, satire or lampoon about him. It begins:

> 'The fickle Bard Owl lies
> Or tells the truth invented
> His own success in such a wise
> Was by himself fomented.'

'So you have abandoned your studies – your apprenticeship?'

'Yes. You know I am now a member of the resistance movement?'

'You've all left it rather late,' I said. 'Birch, Hook and

Cleaver have been sent to liberate Ferocity and Ripper's wood.'

'And you?'

'I have been demoted from commander to the role of scout.'

'Then let's hurry!' Quaver said. 'When I saw your troops they were heading for Bardic's place. I can't bear him, but it doesn't mean I want him killed.'

I nodded in agreement, and we both accelerated our wing beats as we sped across the flatland between the willow in the copse, the hollow tree and the abandoned farmhouse, where Bardic was now composing his mendacious ballad.

We arrived too late. I had already been dreading what we might find, and as soon as we got there my worst fears were confirmed. Birch was perching on the roof of the abandoned farmhouse, and as we landed beside him a blood-curdling howl of pain emanated from within the building below us. The scream was followed by a choking, bleating kind of gibberish, and then there was a final cry, and afterwards there was silence. All this is very well related in Quaver's ballad, and his reaction as I sat by him on the roof proved that, although only a poet and not a warrior, he was braver than one might have expected. I suppose that since he was Hunter's brother, this should not have come as a surprise. But it did, and quite soon he was to prove his worth in a way that I, Birch or May Blossom could never have imagined. Though clearly frightened by the harrowing screams that both of us had heard, Quaver flexed his trembling limbs and prepared to fly down and save what was left of his tutor. But as he was poised for take-off, Birch turned to him and placed three vicious claws across the slender Barn Owl's chest.

'Stay here!' Birch said, in the cold tones of a practised killer. 'He has been executed. There is nothing you can do!'

As Quaver looked back at Birch, frightened but still defiant, there was a noise just below us from within the ruined building. I looked down over the brink of the roof and saw Hook and Cleaver dragging Bardic's torn and bleeding carcass out on to the window-sill. There they let the body lie, suspended high above the ground, with blood still welling from a great gash across the severed, lifeless throat.

'Shall we eat him?' Hook called up, not addressing his question to me, but to Birch.

'No!' Birch replied. 'I want his body left there hanging and dangling as a warning.'

'That's a shame,' said Hook, looking down at the mangled corpse of his victim. 'Oi've never tasted Barn Owl meat before.'

'We'll soon get the chance,' Cleaver said, ripping his talons across dead Bardic's bloody chest. Death upon death, I thought. For the Great God Bird's sake, where will it ever end?

After that, things rapidly got worse.

'May I introduce you to Quaver?' I said, attempting to preserve some element of form in the midst of all this mind-less slaughter. 'Quaver, this is Birch, the new leader of our Tawny troops. Birch, this is Quaver, the apprentice poet and the brother of my dead friend Hunter. On no account are you to harm him!'

'What a pity!' Hook said. ''E do look tender. Much younger and more appetizing than that old ponce we just killed.'

'You shouldn't have done it!' Quaver said. 'It wasn't necessary to kill him.'

'Quaver is a member of the Barn Owl resistance movement,' I said. 'Whatever happens he and his co-conspirators must not be touched. And remember, though you may be proud of just having murdered a cowardly, middle-aged Barn Owl, I repeat, remember that we

Tawnies do not jest over dead bodies and we don't eat our victims in a war.'

'Your Bard Owl could hardly be considered a great loss,' said Birch, addressing himself to Quaver. 'Your tutor, wasn't he? Well, in future, when you are over this slight shock, I hope you come to look upon it as a favour. I hear – we have all heard – that he was a lousy poet anyway.'

'That was murder!' Quaver said. 'He didn't stand a chance.'

'Neither did my son!' I said.

'No, but Bardic didn't kill him!'

'Then who did?'

'I don't know. For the Great God Bird's sake, just give me time. Give me and the resistance movement time to bring Winger down and liberate Ferocity and Ripper's wood. That way all this senseless bloodshed will be avoided.'

'Listen!' I said, torn between my preference for Quaver's Barn Owl logic and my own atavistic instincts as a Tawny, 'Listen, Quaver, the trouble with your so-called resistance movement is that you Barn Owls are far too democratic. You talk and talk and talk and nothing ever gets decided.'

'And you are much too impulsive,' Quaver said. 'You have a long way to fly across Barn Owl country, unless you risk a dangerous short cut through the Lost Domain. You and your task force could be wiped out long before you reach Ferocity and Ripper's wood!'

'I'm sorry about this, but it is a thing that must be done.'

'Why?' Quaver asked.

'Because it has been decreed.'

'By whom?'

'By destiny and fate!'

'And by May Blossom?'

'And by May Blossom, too. You must remember that one of your Barn Owl community murdered our only son.'

'Well, you are making a mistake,' Quaver said, and

though I profoundly disagreed with him, I wondered at how brave he was to face up to me and to Birch, Hook and Cleaver, who could have killed him as easily as they had slaughtered Bardic, and dragged his mangled body on to the window-sill for a public display.

'You are making a mistake,' Quaver repeated. 'You are falling for the old Tawny sin of arrogance. You think you are the best. You believe all Barn Owls are cowards. Well, let me tell you this! There are only four of you and, though you were once a brave warrior, you are now approaching middle age and you lack a vital talon.'

Birch turned on the slender Barn Owl then, and would have killed him had I not prevented it. The three of them would have torn him to pieces had I not intervened and slashed our new leader across the head with the talons that were still intact on my right claw.

This episode is one of the many facts that Quaver does not recount in his ballad. Why, I do not know, for had it not been for me he would have been butchered then and there, and his body displayed beside the torn corpse of Bardic as a warning to anyone who challenged the Tawnies' role as patriarchs – or matriarchs – of the night sky.

We left Quaver then, with Birch bleeding from the slash across his head. It was the first and last time that I clashed with Mallow's mate. I realize now that I should have killed him and taken Hook and Cleaver out as well, or else persuaded them to return in peace to the territory whence we came.

Instead we embarked at once on our long journey, with me as the guide, leading the task force across Barn Owl territory and circumnavigating the secret world of the Lost Domain.

It was a long, unhappy journey that we had, and when the sun rose we were still twelve or fifteen meadows' distance from Ferocity and Ripper's wood. When the daylight began to scar the night with stripes of red, we landed in a flatland copse, inhabited by a Barn Owl called Ratto. An odd name, I thought.

However, this spinney set in the midst of farmland was still relatively close to the place where young Hunter had been murdered. Therefore the incumbent was another suspect, like Bardic, Winger, Dirge and even Olmo. It must have been one of them who killed my son. One can neither love nor murder another creature unless one is in the immediate vicinity.

This Barn Owl called Ratto was a disciple of Winger's. Why Quaver never told this part of the story I shall never know. On arriving there, as the sun burst through the lowland mists, Birch, Hook and Cleaver slaughtered him before I had a chance to intervene. From his grey chest the red blood flowed down and down, staining the trunk of the great chestnut tree in which he had lived, and from where he had bred his family.

This is when I finally rebelled, and how we came to lose the conflict that lay ahead.

'Why did you do that?' I asked, as Ratto's blood dripped down from the broad branch on which they'd slaughtered him, and stained the great trunk of the chestnut tree with the deep crimson juice of what had moments before been a living Barn Owl.

As I watched the life ebb from his bleeding body, his mate returned from wherever she had been hunting. I have forgotten her name now, and I suppose that in the cosmic scheme of things it doesn't really matter. She was a rather lean, mean and ungenerous-looking creature – the kind of female one might have imagined would mate with an owl called Ratto. What's in a name, they ask, and in answer, from my long experience and as I enter my third age, I dare to say that there is a great deal. For example, there is an owl who has now befriended Rowan, son of Birch. His name is Savage. Does this not mean that his ancestors were atavistic killers who flew down from the midnight hills and slaughtered all those who dared to obstruct their path?

Another acolyte of May Blossom's is called Northorpe. That means, of course, that he was born in the north of a village, which was once upon a time called a thorpe. So in a name there is more than meets the eye or ear. I repeat, I do not remember what this lean, mean female was called. But had I been in charge of the baptism or whatever it is the Barn Owls call the absurd ceremony they perform on the naming of their young – had I been able to choose the name, I would have called her Misericordia, Pain or Puritan, for all these things she looked.

None the less, however lean, mean and haggard, I did not want her killed, but Hook and Cleaver tore her limb from limb whilst Birch placed one great claw on my chest so that I was prevented from intervening.

I should have killed him then, and saved the life of this female Barn Owl. But I didn't. None the less, this is when I finally rebelled, why we lost the forthcoming war, and also why I am now branded a heretic.

'You shouldn't have done that,' I said to the three of them, as the dismembered corpse of this plain, nameless and uncommemorated female fell, bathed in still-welling blood, down from the branch of the chestnut on to the earth on the floor of the spinney in which she and the dead male Ratto had for so long lived.

'So we shouldn't have done it?' Birch asked. 'Tell me, whose side are you on anyway? This is a task force of which I have been appointed leader. You have been demoted to the role of guide or scout.'

'I don't agree with mindless slaughter,' I said. 'And I must warn you that when we arrive in Ferocity and Ripper's wood I will not be a party to the killing of the three female Barn Owls that Winger intends to mate with!'

'Oh, won't you?' Birch said. 'Then just wait and see what happens! Your job is to lead us there. From then on, I take over!'

Of course, in retrospect I realize that I should never have taken them. I should have got them lost somewhere or other on the long journey, and let the Barn Owls pick them off, one by one. Even if they had killed me, it wouldn't much have mattered. But I made the fatal mistake. For the last time I was loyal to my own kind and to the task for which I had been commissioned.

It was undoubtedly the worst decision of my life, and led to consequences more disastrous than my silent listeners could possibly imagine.

CHAPTER

 38

When we finally arrived at Ferocity and Ripper's wood, we found that Hunter had got there before us. Warned by Quaver, he had flown the short distance from the Lost Domain to persuade his sister, Ivy Perch and Holly to evacuate the place before it was too late. But Dawn Raptor insisted on staying. She was Winger's acolyte or disciple, and totally committed to what he called his New Apostasy.

The tragic events that occurred next have been well told by Quaver, but his account still misses the essential truth.

To start with, at the beginning of the conflict he was not there. Hunter had persuaded him to leave with Holly and fly to the relative safety of the Lost Domain. He had also attempted to persuade his pregnant mate, Ivy Perch, to return to her father's territory, where she would be safe from our Tawny task force. It seems that he was still trying to persuade her when we descended on the clearing and found the three of them together – Hunter, his sister Dawn Raptor, and the pretty but mindless Ivy Perch.

My purpose was to persuade the female contingent to evacuate Ferocity and Ripper's wood, thus leaving it free for its ancestral Tawny owners. At all costs I wished to avoid unnecessary, senseless killing, but due to the blood lust of Birch, Hook and Cleaver, I failed. I failed in more ways than one. I failed to prevent this minor holocaust, but in the vain attempt I let my own side down and disgraced myself for ever with those of my own kind.

But let me tell it exactly as it happened. I have said that when we arrived we found Hunter, Dawn Raptor and Ivy Perch. But almost at once, as we hovered above them, I sensed the coming of another Barn Owl from the west. As the newcomer flew into the clearing, Dawn Raptor turned and called out his name.

'Dirge! Fly on by!' she said. 'Otherwise these savages will kill you!'

Birch, Hook and Cleaver turned on Dirge and prepared to rip him into shreds in the manner in which they had slaughtered Bardic.

'Wait, Yoller!' Hunter shouted. 'Don't attack. He's innocent. He hasn't occupied your territory. He doesn't live here. He knows nothing!'

In the meantime Dirge stopped, hovered in mid-air, and stared in amazement at the three Barn Owls in the beech tree and the four Tawnies who blocked his path across the clearing.

'Dirge is one of Winger's acolytes,' Birch shouted. 'Kill him, Hook! And this time do it cleanly.'

'Stop!' Hunter cried, as Hook's back arched and he hurled himself across the clearing towards the bewildered, hovering Owl for Dogma and Dialectic, otherwise known as Dirge.

'Stop!' Hunter shouted once again, but it was too late. Warned of the attack in time, Dirge flexed the muscles in his portly frame and prepared to sell his miserable, pompous life as dearly as he could. And he did! As Hook rose up against him, confident of an instant kill, Dirge climbed higher in the sky and braced himself for the coming onslaught. Hook climbed fast with his talons bared for the attack. I looked at Hunter across the clearing. The message in his eyes was the same as mine. Sit still and do nothing. He knew and I knew that if either of us intervened at this point, the killing would go on until the clearing in Ferocity and Ripper's wood was littered with the corpses of torn and mangled owls, as it had been on the famous day we brought the monster down.

Over-confident, Hook rose recklessly into the attack and, as he did so, Dirge plunged down upon him from above and struck at him with his powerful Barn Owl talons. No one would have guessed it. No one could have expected a brave reaction of this kind from a Barn Owl who was one of the least cultivated and intelligent of his species. But 'cometh the hour, cometh the owl', as Quaver is fond of quoting in his ballad. The fact remains that with one unco-ordinated blow from above, Dirge tore Hook's head wide open just above the right eye.

Hook screamed out in pain and faltered. Then he rose higher in the sky and launched himself head-on at Dirge, who struck at him again and wounded his head for the second time before Hook's vicious talons ripped into the Barn Owl's chest and tore clawfuls of flesh and feathers from the bone. Dirge reacted *in extremis* by digging both of his talons into the side of Hook's exposed body. Hook screamed out in rage and pain and tore into Dirge in a frenzy of furious destruction.

As the two of them murdered each other in mid-air, the brainless Ivy Perch moved, and by so doing brought the holocaust upon us. Dirge was her father, after all, and she was only attempting to save his life. For this she must be forgiven. But had she sat still and waited, as Hunter and I were doing, the rest of the mindless slaughter would never have taken place. But by moving instead of acting she involved all of us in violence the like of which I had only ever seen in the war against the invading monster.

Before Hunter could stop her, his pregnant mate took off from her branch in the beech tree and flew fast across the clearing, up towards the place in the sky where the two owls were locked in combat, and where her father was being progressively torn apart by the wounded, profusely bleeding Hook.

As she rose above the two battling males and prepared to sink her talons into the back of the Tawny, Cleaver threw himself forward to intercept Ivy Perch before she could reach her target. As soon as he saw this, Hunter took off and hurled himself across the clearing, ready to take us all on in defence of Ivy Perch and her unborn chicks. Wishing to avoid this senseless combat, he had hesitated too long, as I had done, and he arrived too late. Cleaver decapitated Ivy Perch with one stroke of his lethal talons, but even as the female Barn Owl died, she ripped once more at Hook's unprotected neck. Only a fraction of a second too late to save his mate, Hunter none the less tore Cleaver's left eye from its socket before he had a chance to disentangle himself from the dying Ivy Perch.

From then on things got worse. With Hook dying and Cleaver partially wounded, Birch entered the battle, and surged across the clearing to put Hunter down. At the same time, Dawn Raptor left her perch and flew in my direction, presumably to prevent me from joining in the killing of her brother.

In doing this she made a great mistake. I had no intention of killing anyone. Mine was merely the role of a guide and scout. If I could, I would have prevented the slaughter of my best friend, but with Birch now rampant and the conflict in full flow there was little or nothing I could do.

The outcome of the battle was inevitable, or so we all thought at the time. Ivy Perch fell lifeless to the floor of the clearing, her body landing beside that of her father, Dirge. Hook lay close beside them in mortal anguish, and the one-eyed Cleaver, howling in pain, rounded to help Birch dispose of Hunter, who stood no chance against the two of them.

But here my hesitation proved fatal to our Tawny cause. As Hunter fought with Birch and the mangled, one-eyed Cleaver, Quaver and Holly suddenly re-emerged into the clearing. This brilliant strategy totally changed the nature of the battle, for we Tawnies were now outnumbered and the Barn Owls had the advantage of surprise.

I could still have saved the situation had I killed Dawn Raptor at once, and then gone to the aid of the troops that I had guided into battle. But I didn't, partly because I was sick of bloodshed, and partly because the surprise factor of Holly and Quaver suddenly returning was the kind of master-stroke that turns certain victory into sudden, ignominious defeat.

After this I remember things as in a dream. Quaver's account is probably more accurate, since he was not hurt in this last phase of the battle. I was! First, Dawn Raptor tore at me with her talons and with a ferocity that one would scarcely have expected of a female Barn Owl. Reluctantly I killed her to save my own life. I did it clinically and made it as painless as I could, but while she clawed at me and before I reacted, Hunter called out to Holly and Quaver, ordering them to save her life. He did not like her, but she was his sister after all.

Holly and Quaver obeyed his instructions and flew at me across the clearing. As they came through the air, I could scarcely believe that such sometime friends and comrades could be locked in a battle to the death.

I dropped the dying Dawn Raptor from my talons and rose up to face the two of them. But instead of hitting me head-on, their flight paths divided, and one flew above me to the left and the other to the right. Then they wheeled and flew back to where Hunter was still engaged in a battle to the death with Birch. By this time he had already ripped Cleaver's other eye out, and my unloved comrade had fallen to the ground half-dead.

As Holly and Quaver homed in on Birch, he let go of

Hunter and rose upward to defend himself. This was his fatal mistake, for as he let the Barn Owl go, Hunter slashed at his neck and half-severed his head with one simple blow.

As Birch fell to the ground to join the accumulating pile of bodies, the three surviving Barn Owls turned again, and in unison made a direct attack on me. I do not blame them for it. Had I been as consistent and loyal to my cause as they were, I could have won the war. Now, suddenly, I was alone, with a choice between surrendering or fighting my three friends to the death.

I chose the latter path and suffered dearly for it. Holly and Hunter came first, and as I lunged upward to attack, they once more swerved to either side of me. As I hesitated in mid-air, Hunter dropped on me from above and struck me a blow to the head that should have killed me. To this day, I don't know why it didn't. Owls who believe in the Great God Bird speak often of miracles, and this was one of them. Though I fell to the floor of the clearing, bleeding and unconscious, after what seemed a century I came round again to see a white owl perched on the ground, gazing down on me. It was Hunter and he was soaked in blood. In fact, the blood had soaked into his feathers, making him look more red than white. Surfacing rather groggily from the blow he had inflicted on my head, I at once expressed concern for his condition.

'For the Great God Bird's sake!' I said. 'I've never seen an owl so drenched in blood in my entire life.'

'Don't worry!' Hunter replied. 'Not much of it is mine.'

Surfacing still further, I became aware of Holly and Quaver, also perching on the ground but at a slightly greater distance from me. They seemed quite unhurt but wary, as if I might suddenly arise like a Phoenix from its ashes and kill them with one single blow. And it was on the subject of killing that I spoke to Hunter next.

'Do it now, old boy!' I said. 'Finish me off now. Don't keep me in suspense. We've lost the battle and there's no future for me. There's nowhere for me to go.'

'Nonsense!' Hunter said. 'You're coming with me first, as a hostage, and then you're going home.'

'I don't want to be a hostage and I can't go home again. My task was to lead the troops here and then take them safely home again. How can I possibly go back alive when all of them are dead?'

'I need you,' Hunter said. 'I need you as a hostage in order to depose Winger. We are flying to the council meeting now to confront him. You will come with us and, after the job is done, you will be free to fly home or to any other place you wish. Back here, to this wood of Ferocity and Ripper's, for example. It is a traditional Tawny territory, and I shall convince the new council to lay no further claims to it. And as for the killing, you can forget it. There are too many dead already.'

With this, Hunter nodded to one side to indicate the mangled bodies that were strewn about the woodland floor. Ivy Perch, her father Dirge and Dawn Raptor – three Barn Owls dead; Hook, Cleaver and Birch, whom Hunter must have killed after stunning me – three Tawnies, too. Six owls dead for the sake of two extremists, May Blossom on the one side and Winger on the other.

'All right, dear boy. I'll come with you. But please don't exhibit me. If that is your intention, then I'd rather fight the three of you and die here and now.'

'Don't worry!' Hunter said. 'You won't be shown as a hostage, but you will be mentioned. If we are to co-operate in the future, and all this senseless killing is to end, then I must show the council that we succeeded in bringing your task force down. I must also speak to them of those who died in a futile manner in the name of Winger's New Apostasy.'

'If you think it will help to favour peace in the future, I

456

will come. Though you must understand that it will be the biggest humiliation of my life.'

'Sooner or later we all need to learn humility,' Hunter said. 'Get ready now, we're going!'

So I took off with them, struggling with my aching, bleeding head to keep up with the swift Barn Owl wings of Hunter, Quaver and young Holly. We flew south-east through the dormant trees of Ripper's wood, while behind us a strong breeze rippled through the tall, late-spring grass, and gently rumpled the blood-stained feathers of the dead.

CHAPTER

39

The next episode in the story is best told by Quaver. It is, after all, their Barn Owl saga, not mine. We flew to Winger's domain and to the council meeting, though I of course did not enter. I was made to wait outside on the branch of a great oak tree on the borders of the wooded glade that surrounded this luxury residence, which the leader of the new, egalitarian apostasy had allocated to himself.

Holly was delegated to stay and watch over me while Hunter and Quaver went in to carry out their counter-revolution. She told me then that Quaver was in love with her. They had in common a passion for poetry and singing, whereas Hunter was a natural born leader who would always put the first things first. But which are the first things and which are the last, I asked myself, sitting as a miserable hostage, guarded by a female Barn Owl on the edge of the clearing that surrounded Winger's farm.

There was a time not long before when I could never have imagined a humiliation of this kind. But, as I have said before, humiliation in some shape or form comes to all of us in time. Indeed, it came to Winger that same night. Drenched in blood, Hunter confronted him and the other ten members of the council. There should have been twelve present, but Dirge, the Owl for Dogma and Dialectic, lay dead alongside his daughter in Ferocity and Ripper's wood. Hunter confronted them, revealed his true identity and also that of Westwood, alias Winger. The founder of the New Apostasy was banished, and presumably returned to the fertile valley whence he once came. All this is well told in Quaver's version, and I shall not repeat the details. It is their story, not mine. Suffice it to say that Hunter emerged triumphant from this historic meeting of the Barn Owl council, and told me that he had refused the role of leader and that the History Owl had been appointed to this post instead. This did not sound a good idea to me, for as my silent listeners well know, history tends to repeat itself. However, that is the way it came to pass. Hunter told me that he had agreed to act as a consultant to the council, but that his two main aims from now on were to find a solution to the crisis of infertility that plagued the Barn Owls, and at the same time to search for a safe place where he could mate with Holly and produce healthy chicks of his own.

Then he told me to go home. I went, not of my own volition, but because I had nowhere else to go. In my wounded condition, the journey was long and slow, so that when I got there I found that news of the defeat in Ferocity and Ripper's wood had long preceded my arrival. Bad news travels fast, they say. Good news lies harboured in the mind or in the breast.

I arrived to discover that Winger was not the only leader to have been deposed that night. On receiving the news of our defeat and of his father's death in combat, Rowan and his acolytes had overthrown May Blossom.

Rowan, son of Birch, or Rowan, son of Yoller? This we shall never know, but the fact remains that, young as he was, Rowan acted without scruples, like Birch, and with the intelligence I like to think that I possessed.

Though I had long ceased to love her, I was sorry for May Blossom on that night when she had seen all her hopes and ambitions dashed and swept away by the perennial wind of change.

'What are you going to do now?' I asked, knowing that she would not be content to remain inactive and stay with me in the ancestral domain I had inherited.

'I'm going back to the city.'

'To live with Sage?'

'With or without him,' May Blossom said. 'What matters is to get more knowledge. Those owls who remain static are bound to die.'

'So are the active ones!' I said. 'None the less, I wish you well. But if you'd care to stay here with me, you know that you are very welcome.'

'You should get out yourself. As soon as possible!'

'Why?'

'Because Rowan hates you. He and his gang of thugs will kill you as soon as the time is ripe.'

'And when will that be?' I asked.

'As soon as more owls begin to return here to take refuge from the ravages of man. For the moment, you have been granted leave to stay in your ancestral territory. But your days and nights are numbered. They will turn on you in the end.'

If May Blossom was not kind to me that night, I was soon to discover why.

'I am leaving now,' she said. 'And I strongly recommend that you do the same.'

'Can you explain why Rowan hates me?' I asked. 'Is it because of the family feud that has lasted for so many centuries?'

'That as well. But mostly because you seduced his mother!'

For some moments I sat on the branch and thought. Was there any point in denying this? Now that May Blossom was leaving, and Birch and Mallow were both dead, it struck me as more honourable to confess.

'If that were the case,' I said, taking the confession slowly, 'if I had seduced Mallow, how does Rowan know that he is Birch's son not mine?'

'Because Birch has told him he is quite certain.'

'And how do you and Rowan know that I once mated with his mother?'

'Because Mallow told Birch just before she died.'

'Why would she do that, do you suppose?'

'To expiate her guilt. She knew she was going to the Great God Bird in the sky, and she wanted to die in peace with Him and with herself.'

'And Sage?' I asked. 'Did you mate with him in the city? Or did you mate with Birch, so that the two of you could take your revenge on me? According to your own theory, if you confess to me now, before you leave, you will be in a better state to meet your maker when you die.'

'I mated with neither Sage nor Birch,' May Blossom said, with a conviction that forced me to believe her. 'Young Hunter was your son, as you well know. But now, if Sage wants me, I will take him, since things between the two of us are permanently over.'

'Then, again, I must wish you well. If you must know, your leaving distresses me. Together we could have shared the memory of young Hunter. I shall find it harder to cherish that memory on my own. But your life belongs to you and you must live it in the manner of your choosing.'

'And will you leave as well?'

'No! I shall stay here in my feudal territory and wait for Rowan and his acolytes to depose or kill me. I will not be forced to run away. Much as I hate violence, running away is not my style.'

'You make your own choice, as I make mine,' May Blossom said. 'But I warn you that in the end you will be

461

either killed or evicted. Leave now, before it is too late!'

But I did not leave. She did, that same night, and so once again things came full circle. She left me as she had done so long ago, when we were first betrothed. Then she had promised to return. This time she did not. As she flew out of my ancestral domain and up into the night sky, I knew that we would never meet again, and that I had spoken with her for the last time.

May Blossom left, I stayed, and things have come to pass exactly as she predicted.

Since her departure, I have now spent twelve seasons here, telling my story to the wind, to the trees and the water that gushes from the rock, while men build new towns and enormously wide roads which cut great swathes through what was left of the countryside. Displaced Tawnies came here for refuge, to these ancient woods which must be some of the last to remain intact.

During all this time, none of my own kind came near me. I was ostracized but none the less allowed to stay in my own ancestral wood. Then two nights ago it happened. Rowan appeared at midnight, with two of the most repellent among his guards.

'We must retake the Lost Domain,' he said at once, without any kind of greeting or preamble. 'With all these refugees, we are becoming overcrowded.'

'I don't think that's a good idea.'

'Why not?'

'For two reasons. Firstly, the aliens, or immigrants, have a right to survive. As much right as we do. This also means that they must have a place or a territory in which to live. They have colonized the Lost Domain, proliferated but lived there in peace.'

'And the second reason?' Rowan asked, looking at me with hatred in his eyes.

'The second reason is that if you attempted an invasion, you would be defeated. It would be the same story as

Ferocity and Ripper's wood. I would not care to see you meet the same fate as your father!'

'If you had fought better he would not have died.'

'That may be true. But it means that others would have died instead.'

'Only Barn Owls! You have become a traitor and an outlaw. You are considered beneath contempt!'

'I had noticed. It has been self-evident for quite some time!'

'You have one chance to redeem yourself.'

'Oh yes?'

'Yes! One and one only.'

'Tell me!'

'You will fly to the Lost Domain in search of the poet Olmo. He is after all an old acquaintance of yours, and you will be granted a safe passage.'

'And?'

'And your excuse will be to get news of your Barn Owl friend.'

'You mean Hunter?'

'Yes. They say that he is dead. Killed by a firestick while attempting to defend his mate and her chicks.'

'Where?'

'On his mother's territory. They say she died and he went back to live there and to breed with this bird called Holly. Olmo will know if this is true. Enquiring about his death will be your excuse to visit the Lost Domain. You will then have the opportunity of assessing their defences and calculating the best time and place for our attack.'

'You mean you want me to act as a spy?'

'If you want to put it that way, yes. I would have thought that patriot was a more becoming word.'

'And Holly?' I asked, at this moment more concerned about Hunter than about myself.

'They say she has taken the chicks to live with Quaver, who is now the official Bard Owl on the Barn Owl council.'

'Where did you hear all this?'

'From a media bird,' Rowan replied. 'But as we all know, one cannot rely on them. So you should go and enquire for yourself!'

'So that I can spy on them and then betray the Little Owls?'

'You can't betray another race. Only your own.'

'I don't agree.'

'Don't you? Then you had best know what will happen if you refuse.'

'I'm longing to hear!' I said.

'You may be executed as a traitor. You will in any case be evicted. We need your territory for the refugees.'

'You mean you want it for yourself! Your family has coveted this domain for centuries.'

'It is ours by right! Think on it very carefully. I will give you two days and two nights in which to make up your mind. In the meantime, you may not leave your territory.'

'My mind is already made up. I shall not go.'

'Be reasonable!' Rowan said, suddenly becoming less aggressive. For a moment he turned on a spurious sort of charm that was almost worse than the cold-hearted confrontation which had gone before. 'Be reasonable!' he repeated. 'We need to recolonize the Lost Domain and we need your reconnaissance. You are still not old enough to die. Take this opportunity to redeem yourself!'

'I do not require that kind of redemption!'

'Don't you? Then we shall see how you feel when the time comes for you to die!'

With that Rowan took off from the branch of my ancestral oak and left, with his two silent, stupid guards following obediently in his wake.

Two days and two nights! I still had time to think, but I knew then that I should not change my mind. Though I was brought up on the two concepts of class and race, both have since become abhorrent to me. As the end for me draws near, and as I have told my silent listeners before, the only chance of true survival would seem to lie in trying to co-exist together, as in the little alien's song, under the same sky.

CHAPTER

 40

During the next two days and nights I thought as much about Hunter, Quaver and Holly as about myself. Could this news of his death be true, or was it mere myth and legend, or more likely a cruel trick to tempt me into a final mission that would lead to a blood-bath of the kind that I no longer wished to witness. If it is true, and if Quaver is still alive, he will sing of it some day. If Olmo survives the Tawny attempt to recolonize the Lost Domain, he too may recount history, not only from his point of view but with a certain objectivity. He may even discover which owl it was that killed my only son.

Or was young Hunter my only son? For many reasons I like to think he was. It would not please me to have fathered a ruthless monster like young Rowan, but we Tawnies have some notion of genetics and therefore we know that the old adage of the son being like the father is not necessarily true.

So this is the end of my story. For the first time in living memory we lost a war, and if we attack the Little Owls I believe we shall lose a second. I believe we should allow them the right to live in the territory and the nation they have created in the Lost Domain. We should be content to remain in our own ancestral woodlands – in what is left of our own ancient solitary reign.

Cutting through the trees, man climbs the hill to build ever closer to the sanctuary where we have lived, moved and had our being since time began.

But man is not our only enemy, and I shall long be dead before he fells my oak and pollutes the stream that gushes from the rock beneath me. Long before man can do so, my own kind will kill me. They have the perfect excuse, because I preached against the war – the war they lost. And now I rebel against the next.

I have done bad things in my life and suffered worse. Now, being close to death, I believe that the Great God Bird does exist, and I believe that He will forgive me. This is all I ask. Not vengeance, but forgiveness.

As I have known in my time, those who win are heroes and those who lose are branded criminals of war for the killing they committed, or permitted. Whether more innocent birds were slaughtered by the victor or the vanquished is no matter. It is always the loser who must pay. This is a rule of life and of survival which, sadly, one must accept. And by some strange irony, which only poets like Quaver or Olmo can understand, the greatest loser and the worst war criminal of all is he or she who has – from the first dawn of impending conflict – opposed the coming war. He is always blamed, while those who died in senseless battle are forever glorified and praised.

Now that we have lost, there is no space left for me. I can hear them coming, Rowan and his sycophantic friends, flying through the sleeping, still-virgin woods to kill me. Now there is no space left for me, and maybe they are right. Perhaps I should have accepted their sometime offer of eviction instead of death, and at the onset of my third age flown down from my ancestral hills to where men live, accepting the slower death of their chaos and pollution rather than dying by the cruel talons of my own kind. But though long branded a heretic, though crippled by war and the accidents of time, I am still a proud member of our ancient, solitary race.

But now it is too late. I hear them coming now. They are too close and would kill me in any case. Instead, I choose to fight my last battle with some dignity and to die here, rather than attempting to escape in my early dotage to a life of squalor in what is known as no man's land.

I have told my version of the truth to the wind and trees, and to the stream that gushes from the rock beneath me. Perhaps they will whisper my message on, not only to those of my own kind, but also to other creatures of the night. Perhaps the wind and water might even one day talk to man. Perhaps my story will not end as I am killed tonight. Perhaps, one day, creatures of the night and even man will listen.

Or perhaps they never will.

Frost Dancers
A Story of Hares
Garry Kilworth

Amongst the gorse and the heathers of his native highlands, Skelter the mountain hare enjoyed an idyllic life: browsing and gambolling; taking in the superb scenery and making female friends, including the beautiful Rushie. Then one day Skelter's life of ease came to an abrupt end. Netted and captured, he and several other hares are transported hundreds of miles, to the strange lands of the south, destined for the cruel sport of hare coursing. Amidst a hell of shouting men and howling greyhounds, Skelter witnesses a nightmare, before making a miraculous escape.

Alone, stranded in a landscape he does not understand Skelter must learn to survive, despite the hostility and distrust of the local hares and other natural hazards.

By far the most horrifying peril that faces Skelter is the *flogre*: a vast, flying monster which is terrorising the countryside, killing indiscriminately.

Raised in isolation by a man, thousands of miles from his native habitat, Bubba is a killer more terrifying than any natural creature: for he believes himself human. Can one small mountain hare survive against such a monster?

ISBN 0 586 21463 1

Born to Exile
Phyllis Eisenstein

Winner of the Balrog Award for best fantasy novel of the year

Alaric, a young minstrel with a talent for magic, roamed the lands in search of his fortune. And in Castle Royale, it seemed he'd found both his fortune and his true love, the beautiful Princess Solinde.

But could a penniless orphan hope to claim such a royal treasure? And in a land where witches were burned and the court magician looked on Alaric with suspicion, did he dare remain for long? For Alaric had a magical power which, in the blink of an eye, could transport him to any place that his mind could recall – a power that revealed itself at the first sign of danger. And for Alaric, Castle Royale held more danger than he could imagine . . .

'The best fantasy novel I've read this year.'   Jerry Pournelle

'One of the best fantasies I have read in a long time.'
Oxford Times

ISBN 0 586 20732 5

CLOVEN HOOVES
Megan Lindholm

A remarkable tale of the fantastic in everyday life.
One of the most original fantasies you will ever read.

Growing up unwanted and untamed in Alaska's wild
country, Evelyn found refuge in the depths of the forest.
She didn't fit in with the other girls – all they could talk
about was boys and clothes.

But out in the forest, an escape from isolation, she could
spend time with her only true friend: a young faun – half
boy, half satyr – called Pan.

Maturity brings unexpected happiness: a husband and a
son. But this short trip into normality comes to a
shattering end; and Evelyn's real journey begins – away
from the mundanities of shopping malls and frilled toilet-
rolls, away from appalling parents-in-law and the
claustrophobia of their pedantic lives – out into the
wilderness with the wildest creature in the world.

WINNER OF THE HUGO AND NEBULA AWARDS

ISBN 0 586 21518 2

Night Relics
James P. Blaylock

'Thoroughly satisfying, memorable, and the best thing that James Blaylock has ever written.'   Dean R. Koontz

In a blend of the supernatural, the magical, the fantastic, *Night Relics* continues Blaylock's progression towards a magical-realist literary style with thoroughly convincing elements of horror.

When Peter Travers moves into an old house in a remote canyon to try to separate himself from his old existence, his wish becomes reality . . . all too literally. For his wife and son vanish and the people of the idyllic rural town begin to relive the horrors of a nightmarish crime committed one windy autumn, sixty years earlier. Against a backdrop of murder and midnight terror, Peter must contend with the abandoned relics of his own past before he can overcome the dark forces that haunt the canyon and the people he loves.

'Blaylock is better than anyone else at showing us the magic that secretly animates our world'   *Tim Powers*

ISBN 0 586 21780 0

Midnight's Sun
Garry Kilworth

The transfixing tale of an all-too-brief truce between two species forever at war with each other – man and wolf . . .

Meshiska gave birth to five cubs on the night before the full moon. Outside the den a storm was lashing the spruce trees. The sky and the land had become a part of each other: a scatterwind night swirling with fragments of black and white. Snow became darkness and darkness snow, and any creature lost between the two found a rock or tree and lay down beside it to wait until the world had formed again.

Into this bleak landsape Athaba is born, a young wolf destined for great adventure. Exiled from the pack for breaking its rigid codes of behaviour and showing too much imagination, Athaba becomes a raven-wolf, a lonely scavenger living on scraps and his wits.

Survival in the icy wastes is precarious without the protection of the pack. But adversity breeds an alliance with a hunter who has lost his way and teeters at the brink of starvation. If they are both to survive, the man must learn the ways of the wolf.

ISBN 0 586 21495 X

☐	MAGICIAN Raymond E. Feist	0-586-21783-5	£6.99
☐	SILVERTHORN Raymond E. Feist	0-586-06417-6	£4.99
☐	A DARKNESS AT SETHANON Raymond E. Feist	0-586-06688-8	£5.99
☐	THE SILVER BRANCH Patricia Kennealy	0-586-21248-5	£4.99
☐	THE ELVENBANE A. Norton/M. Lackey	0-586-21687-1	£5.99
☐	MASTER OF WHITESTORM Janny Wurts	0-586-21068-7	£4.99
☐	THE DRAGON AND THE GEORGE Gordon R. Dickson	0-586-21326-0	£4.99
☐	BLACK TRILLIUM May/Bradley/Norton	0-586-21102-0	£4.99

All these books are available from your local bookseller or can be ordered direct from the publishers.

To order direct just tick the titles you want and fill in the form below:

Name: _____

Address: _____

_____

Postcode: _____

Send to: HarperCollins Mail Order, Dept 8, HarperCollins *Publishers*, Westerhill Road, Bishopbriggs, Glasgow G64 2QT.

Please enclose a cheque or postal order or your authority to debit your Visa/Access account –

Credit card no: _____

Expiry date: _____

Signature: _____

– to the value of the cover price plus:

UK & BFPO: Add £1.00 for the first and 25p for each additional book ordered.

Overseas orders including Eire, please add £2.95 service charge.

Books will be sent by surface mail but quotes for airmail despatches will be given on request.

24 HOUR TELEPHONE ORDERING SERVICE FOR ACCESS/VISA CARDHOLDERS –

TEL: GLASGOW 041-772 2281 or LONDON 081-307 4052